Beyond the Olive Grove

Volume Two of The Magdala Trilogy:
A Six-Part Epic Depicting a Plausible Life of
Mary Magdalene and Her Times

Peter Longley

iUniverse, Inc.
New York Bloomington

Beyond the Olive Grove
Volume Two of The Magdala Trilogy: A Six-Part Epic Depicting a Plausible Life of Mary Magdalene and Her Times

iUniverse books may be ordered through booksellers or by contacting:

iUniverse
1663 Liberty Drive
Bloomington, IN 47403
www.iuniverse.com
1-800-Authors (1-800-288-4677)

ISBN: 978-1-4401-7892-4 (pbk)
ISBN: 978-1-4401-7890-0 (cloth)
ISBN: 978-1-4401-7891-7 (ebook)

Printed in the United States of America

iUniverse rev. date: 11/18/2009

Dedicated to

Kazumi Masuda

Bettine Clemen

and

Nicole Glenn

INTRODUCTION

Beyond the Olive Grove is the second volume in a trilogy of novels that include *A Star's Legacy* and *The Mist of God,* all speculating on the plausible life and times of Mary Magdalene. The series traces the lives of a fictitious Roman named Linus Flavian and the quasi-historical persons of Joshua of Nazareth (Jesus Christ), Maria of Magdala (Mary Magdalene), and their fictitious son, Ben Joshua.

Star of Wonder, the first part of *A Star's Legacy,* the previous volume, is set in the turbulent Jewish state from 7 BC in the latter years of King Herod the Great, through to his death in 4 BC. The intrigues and hopes of the Jewish people are revealed at a time when global prosperity and trade is paramount in the region, fostered by the rapidly growing influence of the Roman Empire. For a few months in the winter of 5 BC, an unusual heavenly body in the form of an elongated star travels across the Middle East in a westerly direction. The characters all form their own opinions about what this heavenly sign could mean and adapt their interpretations to their goals and aims. Central to this is Miriam (The Virgin Mary), who sees the star and other mystical night experiences, as signs from God that a child she is carrying will have a special purpose for the Jews. Others foster her viewpoint, although their own beliefs about the star are different. In the innocence of her youth, Miriam is caught up in a political plot. After her child Joshua is born, the plot places her life and that of the child in danger. In order to protect her vision for this child, she is forced to flee Judea.

Children of Destiny, the second part of *A Star's Legacy*, deals with the childhood, adolescent years, and early adulthood of Linus, Joshua, and Maria, all of whom were born at the time of the mysterious star. These are the years which Christianity and history have generally termed the missing years in the life of Jesus. For this reason, the storyline of *A Star's Legacy* can be called true fiction within an historical context.

This second volume in *The Magdala Trilogy* starts the process of meshing early Christian sources and interpretations of the life of Jesus with a fictional story. *Beyond the Olive Grove*, comprising the two parts *Pickled Fish* and *The Judas Triangle*, deals with the biblical ministry of Jesus and its plausible interaction with the fictitious lives of Linus and Maria (Mary Magdalene) and growing tensions between Joshua (Jesus) and his disciples over the roll that Maria seems to play. We also see the development of an alternative view of Jesus' divinity that Maria grasps over the other disciples and that will become essential for her role in the final volume of *The Magdala Trilogy*.

Although the Christian story, as handed down through generations of believers, is recognizable throughout this trilogy, and particularly in this second volume, the interpretation and handling of history is decidely different, reflecting the forefront of a diligent search for a plausible historical Jesus at a time when world consciousness is in turmoil and change.

The third book in *The Magdala Trilogy* continues this challenging interpretation, taking the reader from Judea to Gaul, Rome, India, and Asia Minor. From India, this final volume gets its title, *The Mist of God*, and is comprised of two parts, *The Magdala* and *Apocalypse*. This volume will take a bold and different look at the birth of Christianity after Jesus' death, and the possibility that a part of the real teaching of Jesus might have been distorted or lost. *The Mist of God* also will introduce a fourth character, Ben Joshua, a child born of Joshua (Jesus) and Maria (Mary Magdalene).

The Magdala Trilogy is a rich blend of Jewish, Roman, and Greek traditions that mingle at times with Asiatic thought. It opens with a messianic plot that results in the birth of Joshua into a little known family with some biblical historicity. I have molded real historical persons with fictitious and semi-fictitious people. As much as possible, I've given those who are biblically historic, their true Aramaic names rather than the Greek and Latin translations with which we are more familiar. (See the Cast of Principal Characters). The result is a refreshingly different look at the biblical First Century AD and of the circumstances and people of this well-known story.

Likewise, for Aramaic authenticity, I have used the term 'rabbi' loosely in these novels. There was not an official rabbinate in Judaism until after the fall of Jerusalem in 70 AD, however, the Aramaic for teacher is 'rabbi' and many towns and villages in Judea and Galilee had learned men expounding the scriptures before the fall of Jerusalem. Synagogues were more like house gatherings at the time of Jesus and were not part of the official religious structure until after the fall of Jerusalem and the destruction of the Temple, but at the time of Jesus, unofficial Synagogue groups were forming.

The opening events happen against a backdrop of anti-Roman zealot rebellion and the various interpretations of the passage of that moving star, or comet, which was easily visible throughout the Middle East in the tumultuous latter years of King Herod the Great. Joshua of Nazareth, known to us as Jesus Christ, is generally considered by most scholars to have been born shortly before the death of King Herod the Great in 4 BC. I have followed this preference for dating events in these novels.

At the birth of Christ, the Roman Empire had only recently come to the area of Judea. Not all the known Western world was encompassed within its sphere, but Roman influence was as far-reaching as its Oriental counterpart in China. China and Rome had trade connections with India. Given that the Americas were unknown, it can be said that at no time in history had the world seemed more as one than two thousand years ago. This is a striking parallel to today's global reach.

It was at this time that the Roman calendar was created. The old calendar had been updated first by Julius Ceasar and then by Augustus. The two additional months that they conceived to correct the seasons, gave us our present twelve-month calendar. Julius and Augustus are immortalized in the summer months of July and August. With only minor adjustments, the Augustinian calendar has become the measure that unites our world today. Two thousand years ago was the start of the Pax Romana, an extraordinary concept of global peace based on the passage of goods in free trade, and again, a striking parallel with the hopes of our present era.

Two thousand years ago also saw a world afraid of change and fearful of the new Roman order, one that spawned aopocalyptic prophesies and resistance movements along with the fledgling religion that became Christianity. But the prophets of apocalypse were proved wrong. The world did not end. Christianity was not the swan song of an old belief system, but became the foundation of two thousand years of western civilization. So the world today unanimously dates its calendar from the legendary birth of Jesus Christ, but the wheel turns full cycle. At the start of the Third Millennium, we see a revival of those same apocalyptic fears and resistance movements as the world parallels its past. As we potentially approach unity and a new order, we find ourselves also afraid of change, listening once more to prophets of doom.

PETER LONGLEY
August 2009

ACKNOWLEDGEMENTS

I am indebted to many who have contributed to my thinking and enabled me to embark on this work. Scholastically, I stand in the tradition of the great Anglican twentieth-century theologian John A.T. Robinson and my contemporaries, Don Cupitt, John Dominic Crossan and A. N. Wilson. I have been drawn to the scholars of the Jesus Seminar with special mention of Robert W. Funk, Marcus Borg, Karen Armstrong and Elaine Pagels, and all those, who like me have seen importance in the *Nag Hammadi Texts.* I have admired the critical stance of Bishop John Shelby Spong, who treads new frontiers in Christo-centric thought. Philosophically, I have learned much from such contemporary writers as Deepak Chopra, Harry Palmer, author of the *Avatar* materials, and Neale Donald Walsch, author of *Conversations with God.* All of us owe a debt to Albert Einstein, Stephen Hawking, and others for the advance of quantum physics that has so dramatically changed our thought patterns and practices as we look to the future in this Third Millennium.

Specifically, in regard to the text of *The Magdala Trilogy*, I acknowledge the patient reading and encouragement I received from Waldemar Hansen, author of *The Peacock Throne,* who was my predecessor as World Cruise Port Lecturer on board the ocean liner *Queen Elizabeth 2.* I am also grateful to Rabbi Harry Roth and The Venerable Canon

Robert N. Willing, chaplains on board the *Queen Elizabeth 2*, for their support in the early stages of writing and their sound advice on some of the religious practices I have described. I am also indebted to The Reverend Lawrence H. Waddy for input on aspects of the Graeco-Roman world in the first century.

The non-fiction geneological tables are taken from Stewart Perowne's *The Life and Times of Herod the Great* (Grey Arrow 1960), for which he in turn relied largely on the *Cambridge Ancient History*.

I am grateful to Anthony J. W. Benson, and James A. Veitch, Associate Professor, Victoria University, Wellington, New Zealand, for their encouragement and promotional work on my introductory novel to this trilogy—*Two Thousand Years Later* (Hovenden Press 1996).

Finally, I sincerely thank Kazumi Masuda, Bettine Clemen and Nicole Glenn for their endless support and patience with me through half a lifetime of research in bringing this project to fruition, and most of all my late father, Charles William Hovenden Longley, for his eternal encouragement and belief in my goals. I also thank my godfather, Oliver Gyles Longley, C.B.E., for his unfailing faith in my spiritual vocation despite my breach with orthodoxy. I have tried to create a framework for the teaching and healing ministry of Jesus and a plausible life of Mary Magdalene that can be more popularly acceptable in the philosophical and spiritual thinking of the Third Millennium. Scholastically, I have advanced on my own background as a graduate in theology from Cambridge University in the 1960's much of the discussion and interest engendered from using the tools of textual criticism advanced by scholars of the Jesus Seminar.

PETER LONGLEY
August 2009

CAST OF PRINCIPAL CHARACTERS

First Century Names	Popular Name in History
Maria of Magdala	*Mary Magdalene*
Joshua (Yeshua)	*Jesus Christ*
Joanna	*Fictitious deceased wife of Jesus*
Linus Flavian	*Fictitious Roman centurion and later tribune*
Flavius Septimus	*Fictitious Roman father of Linus Flavian*
Copernia Tarquin	*Fictitious Roman mother of Linus Flavian*
Jon	*John the Baptist*
Elizabeth	*Mother of John the Baptist*
Joachim	*Father of the Virgin Mary*
Anna	*Sister of Elizabeth, mother of the Virgin Mary*
Joseph	*St. Joseph of the Holy Family*
Miriam	*The Virgin Mary*
James	*James, the Brother of our Lord*
Rachel	*Fictitious wife of James, the Brother of our Lord*
Little Joanna	*Fictitious daughter of James and Rachel*
Jonah	*Fictitious prodigal son of Joseph*
Amos	*Fictitious son of Joseph*
Ruth	*Fictitious daughter of Joseph*

David Levi	*Fictitious husband of Ruth and fictitious father of St. Matthew the Apostle*
Esther	*Fictitious mother of Mary Magdalene*
Delilah	*Fictitious friend and lover of Mary Magdalene*
Marcus	*Fictitious son of Linus Flavian and Mary Magdalene/St. Mark*
Antonias	*Fictitious Roman suitor of Mary Magdalene*
Zadok	*First century Jewish spiritual leader*
Brother Solomon of Anathoth Essenes	*Fictitious Jew*
Lazarus	*Lazarus whom Jesus raised from the dead*
Mary	*Sister of Lazarus*
Martha	*Sister of Lazarus*
Judas Iscariot	*Judas Iscariot*
Simon of Bethsaida/Cephas	*St. Peter, the Apostle*
Janus, son of Zebedee (Boanerges)	*St. James, the Apostle*
Jonas, son of Zebedee (Boanerges)	*St. John, the Apostle*
Susannah	*Susannah, wife of St. Peter*
Jezebel	*Fictitious camp follower of Jesus*
Matthew	*Fictitious son of Ruth and David Levi/St. Matthew the Apostle*
Thomas	*Fictitious fishing partner of Judas Iscariot/St. Thomas the Apostle*
Simon the Zealot/Simon	*St. Simon the Apostle*
Zebedee (Boanerges)	*Father of St. James and St. John*
Barabbas	*Barabbas, First century Jewish zealot rebel*
Saul	*St. Paul*
Questus	*Questus, First century Roman governor of Syria*
Tetrarch Herod Antipas of Galilee	*King Herod, tetrarch of Galilee*
Pontius Pilatus	*Pontius Pilate, prefect of Judea*
Joseph of Arimathea	*Joseph of Arimathea*
Caiaphas	*Caiaphas, High Priest at the time of Jesus' crucifixion*
Annas	*Annas, Assistant High Priest and brother-in-law of Caiaphas at the time of Jesus' trial*

Beyond The Olive Grove

Part One

Pickled Fish

Chapter One

New Beginnings

Joshua glanced over his shoulder to see that he was alone. The late afternoon sun filtered through the olive trees in shafts of gray and blue, complimenting the dusty leaves. He was still a young man—just twenty-four—but his settled life had been shattered by forces that seemed beyond his control. He had lost his young bride in the colic plague. Married to Joanna for only a year, he missed her laughter and love. They would have had a family. Possibly, Joanna was pregnant even as she died. He knelt down among the dead leaves that lay scattered over the floor of the grove. He buried his face in his hands and began to cry.

A voice called to him. He looked up from his cupped hands and thought he saw Joanna approach him through the olives. She seemed to glide effortlessly, almost as if her feet were not on the ground. He heard her laugh. He saw her smile.

"Elijah came," the apparition seemed to say joyfully, "Elijah came and all is well."

"Joanna!" Joshua cried out.

The apparition disappeared. Nobody was there.

He turned round and called again:

"Joanna!"

The olives stirred, but nobody came.

Joshua sat back on his haunches and stared at the shafts of steely light. Then, up above him, he was sure he could see Joanna's face—it was just her face, looking down from the gnarled old branches.

"Joanna!" he cried again, but as before there was no answer.

There was a strange contentment on the grinning face as it faded in and out among the moving leaves. It said nothing, but somehow Joshua drew comfort from its presence. He was not afraid, but felt only Joanna's strength, her love and support, as he contemplated on his future. He had allowed himself his moments of grief and disappointment, but somehow in this vision he saw the encouragement for his future.

"Elijah has come," he called up, as the face faded. "You are right, Joanna. Elijah has come and a new beginning has dawned. I will follow my destiny. I will go to Jerusalem. God will reveal his purpose for His 'Prince of Peace.'"

Joshua spread out his arms and prayed. He contemplated and prayed until the sunlight faded into dusk, and darkness descended. He knew that he was ready to follow a new path and he put his faith in Almighty God that his destiny would be revealed.

When he returned to Joachim's house, he sought out Jon. He found his dark-haired moody cousin in the courtyard, putting logs in the brazier.

"It's time, Jon," Joshua said deliberately. "It's time for us to start making that journey to Jerusalem."

In the orange glow of the beacon, Joshua could see excitement in Jon's deep mysterious eyes.

"In the morning?" Jon asked.

"Well, as soon as James can leave. We must tell the others, and collect up some provisions."

* * *

James, the scholarly rabbi, who had been Joshua's childhood mentor and was married to Joanna's sister, Rachel, was prepared for the move. He had appointed a young rabbi named Eliezer in his stead, and persuaded Rachel, who had been deeply effected by her sister's death, that the change would be good for them all. He looked forward to a renewal of rabbinical scholarship in Jerusalem.

When it was time for them to travel, Joachim, the old family patriarch, insisted that James and Joshua should ride from Nazareth to Jerusalem.

He remembered only too well the old days when he had walked the journey year after year.

"Why walk?" he questioned. "I have two spare mules and Joshua has his own and a cart."

Joshua's mother, Miriam, had thought it far safer for them all to travel by caravan, but she had been overruled. Her father might now be old and white-haired, but Joachim ben Judah was still a man of decisions. Besides, in Nazareth, they never knew when a caravan would be coming through, and both James and Joshua seemed to want to be independent on their journey.

Joachim made sure they had a good supply of food and wine that Joshua packed. Finally, Joshua carried out his old wooden box, which he carefully hid under the packing straw in the cart. He thought of its origins. *This is my legacy. It's the legacy of the star that blessed me at my birth. Mother and I have kept this all these years, knowing that one day my destiny would be revealed and I could use this gift that was given to me from God. May I use it wisely?* He had no idea of its real value, but there was something sentimental about the old box. Whatever the worth of the strange gold coins within, the box was a symbol of his destiny. It was a manifestation of his call to serve the Lord as a son of God and as the 'Prince of Peace'.

James's brother, Jonah, came over to Joachim's house to send them off, and gave them a few tools from the carpenter's shop.

"You never know when you may need these," he said. "You've proven to be a good wine maker, Joshua, but you weren't a bad joiner before that."

"Thanks," Joshua replied to Joseph's prodigal son. "That's really very generous of you and a pretty sensible suggestion. Whatever we do in Jerusalem, we will more than likely have to earn our keep."

He smiled, reflecting on his inadequacies.

"I'm sorry I didn't help you more here," he said.

At this point, Joshua looked at the man he called 'Father', blind old Joseph, and put his arms around him.

"Who knows, Joseph? I may be a carpenter yet. I keep trying to fight it, but thanks to your excellent training I still have a chance."

Jonah laughed.

Joshua hugged Joseph.

"You've been a wonderful father to me," he said, "and a great comfort all these years to my mother. Whoever was my real father could never have given us the inner love that you have shared with us. God bless you, Joseph. Blessed be God forever!"

When they were ready to leave, they all embraced each other again. Both Joshua and James knew in their hearts that this was the break up of their family. They did not expect to return to Nazareth any time soon, and possibly never.

Rachel said goodbye to her family, who had also gathered at the old patriarch's house, and along with them were Benjamin Levi, David, Ruth, and Matthew. Only Amos and Salome were missing. Since Amos' marriage in Cana, the family had rarely seen their brother and sister-in-law.

The sun was warm, but not unpleasantly hot as the cooling air of autumn gave the travelers a crystal clear day. They were ready to leave.

Joshua hugged his mother one last time. Jonah was standing beside Miriam. Joshua looked at Jonah.

"You are the only one left now," he said. "Take care of my mother and Joseph."

He kissed Miriam on her forehead.

"Mother, treat Jonah as your son. Jonah will take care of you as if you were his mother."

Joshua and Jon climbed into the cart, while Rachel and James mounted Joachim's two mules. Waving final farewells, they rode out of Joachim's gate, leaving Miriam holding on to old Joseph, and Joachim's wife, Anna, supported in the arms of her beloved. Jonah stood there with them, looking serious as if he realized the sincerity of Joshua's request. Someone would have to look after these helpless old folks and he was the only member of the younger generation left to do so. Only Matthew and Ruth ran out to see the travelers off down the hill. There, they stood until looking back, Joshua could see them no more.

* * *

The young Roman officer, Linus Flavian, was not without heart. Although he had swiftly adapted to the military lifestyle that had been his father's wish, he did not forget Maria of Magdala, or the knowledge that his probable child by this Hebrew girl was now almost certainly born.

Perhaps Maria has drowned it like the whores in Rome, he thought sadly, looking across the rooftops of Damascus from his barracks dormitory. *The product of our love may be lost forever.* Linus wiped away a tear and thoughtfully pulled at his chin. *Perhaps the child was never mine anyway. How can anyone ever prove who is the father of a whore's child?*

It was some consolation for him to think this way. After all, his father, Flavius Septimus, and his high born mother, Copernia Tarquin, would expect him to marry a Roman, and not to seek to live out his life with a foreigner—a Jewess of no position or background. He was a Tarquin and a Flavian and he felt a responsibility to his illustrious families. He was part of the establishment of Rome.

Linus' thoughts turned to the view. Damascus was an oasis of green in an otherwise barren landscape of sandy gray. The country around was flat, dull, and boring. Surprisingly, Linus missed the hills of Galilee and the rich vineyards and olive groves of his father's estate above Magdala. He also missed Maria.

The young officer turned from the window and strapped on his cuirass. He was on guard duty and needed to muster his men to man the gates.

* * *

The Roman youth now disrobing before her had fine features and smooth skin, reminding Maria of Linus. Maria had not seen this man before, but there were many like him who came to prove their manhood in the sensual atmosphere of the brothel. What they lacked in experience they made up for in zeal. The boy was rigid and ready. Eagerly, he climbed onto the bench, and straddling Maria, knelt there, gazing at the fullness of her breasts and the free flow of her hair. Like so many of his age, however, he didn't seem to know what to do.

Maria silently stroked him, as the boy arched his back in delight. He was instantly hot and panting as she cupped his male member between her breasts, teasing him and kneading her fleshly mounds around him, caressing them to her own satisfaction. She felt the familiar pulling sensation in her loins as she grew in her desire to have him. She knew it would be quick, over almost before it begun, but if he liked it he would come back for more and the more they came back the more secure her position in the brothel became. She had her baby to bring up—Linus' son Marcus. For his sake, she needed to satisfy these eager young Roman men.

Maria pulled the lad on top of her and felt the smooth skin of his chest massage her uncontrollably erect nipples as he wriggled into place and entered her. Maria moaned just slightly with the pleasure of his hardness. A few thrusts were all the youth needed. He gave out a cry as he pushed himself deep into the softness of her flesh, stayed there for a moment, and then collapsed in release. Maria felt the warmth of his seed and then the tingle of withdrawal. It was over, but she knew he would be back.

In the small room that had been appointed to Delilah and Maria for their professional duties, Maria watched as the youth hastily got dressed. She lay back comfortably on the bench, surrounded by soft cushions covered in silk. The linen drapes that hung from the bed were fresh and clean unlike those which hung in her mother's house in Magdala. Only the perfume from the scented oils and the acrid smell from the oil lamp were the same. Although Maria had always known that she had the power to satisfy her men, other than when she had shared her love with Linus she had never herself felt as satisfied in return as she did now. Sometimes, her eager satisfaction gave her a feeling of guilt, something she confided to her partner, Delilah; but Delilah dismissed her fears as she exchanged sensual details of her own satisfaction gained in performing her duties for their clientele. Delilah and Maria were the most popular ladies in the brothel and shared customers that numbered many of the young men of Tiberias.

* * *

After Joshua and Jon arrived in Jerusalem they reveled in their freedom. The city created a whole new experience, especially for Jon. Excitement abounded. The market places spilled over with rare foods, fresh fruits from the Jordan valley, and spices from the Orient. Everywhere seemed colorful, with a lively hustle and bustle. Linens and cloths of fine colors, even silks from Cathay, stacked the stalls. In one spot, perfumed sandalwood filled the air from woodcarvings. Merchants shouted their wares, and thieves ran off with their gains. Bright open spaces filled with busy people contrasted with dark twisting alleys where few ventured.

Jerusalem breathed variety—from the Temple to its humblest dwelling—from its busy streets to the peace of the Mount of Olives.

On their way to a market to purchase flat loaves and lentils for Rachel, Joshua and Jon noticed a considerable crowd. A man with the looks of a prophet, dressed only in a goat's skin and holding a long staff, his white beard unkempt and trailing to his waist, commanded their attention. Joshua and Jon joined the throng of listeners.

"You have seen the signs," the prophet said. "The time is now. Elijah will come and you will be caught. Those who are not prepared will be cast aside, but those who are ready will be led like lambs. The Kingdom of God is upon us. Are you ready to receive Elijah? Are you ready to seek the Messiah?"

Jon looked up at Joshua intently. There was something in this message that instantly attracted him.

"That man is giving my message," he said. "Be prepared because we do not know when our end will come. It will be like a thief in the night—Remember, Joshua?"

Joshua was also in deep thought as he listened to the mysterious old man. Thoughts of Joanna and her last words echoed in his ears.

"Well, that's partly what he's saying," he answered. "He believes Elijah is about to come, and that there will be a messiah to save those who are prepared. But the Scripture always warns us to 'beware of false prophets'. This man could just be another false prophet."

The old man started to list the Commandments of Moses, pointedly asking with vigor if they had been obeyed. His voice was powerful and his conviction frightening:

"Those who have not obeyed the Commandments will be cast into eternal fire. The forces of the Messiah, the good lambs, will rise up against the evil one that leads the forces of the damned, and there will be a great victory. The followers of the Messiah will win, and God will reign over the just forever. Time is running out for you. I tell you that Elijah is on his way. The first trumpet call has been made. Are you with the lambs, or will you be led to the slaughter?"

The voice of the old man was hypnotic.

"We are ready!" some in the crowd shouted.

Others, skeptics who were used to hearing false prophets and charlatans preach in the market places, began to chide him. Figs and soft fruits from the market stalls flew through the air splattering on the old man. A near riot ensued.

The prophet mesmerized Jon, but Joshua remained calm and philosophical. It was for him a matter that needed study and discussion, but the references to Elijah struck a chord as he thought of Joanna's death. Joanna had been so insistent in her deathbed delirium to tell him that Elijah had come.

Has Elijah come? Joshua wondered. *Are we living in the prophet's end time? If I were to fulfill my special role as a chosen one, and a son of God, would this not be the time and the place to begin?*

The old prophet did not really impress Joshua. There was no substance or backup to his comment and no pointer as to whom the Messiah might be. But, the message did spell out that this could be a time of destiny. That interested Joshua.

A rotting juicy pomegranate hit Joshua's shoulder scattering seeds.

Jon laughed, but the crowd began to disperse. Many had heard all this before. Sundry lunatics were continually peddling their thoughts on the streets of Jerusalem.

Joshua wiped off the debris of the pomegranate and tugged at Jon.

"Come on," he pleaded. "We need to get Rachel her bread and lentils or we won't have anything to eat tonight. Maybe James was lucky today and they have accepted him as a teacher in the rabbinical Temple schools. We could do with a little good news. There are so many people like ourselves, who have come here to seek a new life. We haven't found much yet, but maybe today will have been James' lucky day."

They purchased two flat loaves, and enough lentils to make their evening soup. Going up a ladder of steps back into the maze of narrow streets, they made their way back to the room that James had found for them. The place was dark and dank, but Rachel had done her best to make it home. The room was divided by a great yellow hanging so that the men had a separate sleeping area from her. She already had a fire going in the little oven they had built against the wall, and the pot was beginning to boil. Two jars of precious water leaned there, and a pile of dung cakes acted as future fuel for the fire. The smoke lingered with the acrid odor of the oil lamps and filtered out through the entrance to add to the street smells rising up from the open drain.

"That took you a long time," Rachel stated, more curious than angry.

"There was a strange prophet in the market place," Joshua explained. "People were heckling him. He maintained that we are living on the brink of judgment. He claimed that this is the time of Elijah's return and that we should be prepared for an instant judgment and only those saved will be led by a messiah to the Kingdom of God."

"The judgment will be sudden, coming like death as a thief in the night," Jon added.

Rachel was only mildly interested in what they were saying. For her, the trivial round of domestic chores was of far greater concern than the words of an eccentric prophet of no repute.

"I'm sure that there are many strange people around in Jerusalem," she said without looking up. "You say the crowd heckled this man?"

"Yes," Jon answered. "They threw rotten fruit and vegetables at him from the stalls and shouted and laughed at him."

He laughed.

"A pomegranate hit Joshua."

Rachel eyed the mess on Joshua's shoulder and sleeve.

"You'd better let me wash that out," she said.

"The man was a bit strange," Joshua agreed. "He had a beard right down to his waist, and rough skins for clothing."

Rachel cast her eyes upward at Joshua.

"I suppose all the prophets must have seemed a bit strange to their contemporaries," she said. "Anyway, James should be back soon. Hopefully, he's been accepted to teach at the rabbinical school in the Temple. We haven't much to live on these days, and you two aren't contributing much."

"I know," Joshua quickly replied.

It was somewhat on his conscience that they had spent these first few days drinking in the sights and exploring the city with little thought about finding work and creating viable living conditions.

"We will have to hire ourselves out as builders now that Jon and I have had a good look around," he suggested. "There are several projects under construction apart from the work at the Temple. However, perhaps the Temple is where we should start. They are rebuilding several of the gateways, and it might be easier than the Roman works."

Joshua thought of the box of gold coins. He really didn't want to open it up unless they were in dire distress. He felt convinced that if there was any truth in the mystery that surrounded its origins, he should keep it until his role was established and he had worked out his destiny. Joachim's mules had already been sold, and the cart that the Roman had given to him in Magdala had barely survived the journey down from Galilee. The profit the mules had made for them had gone into paying the merchant landlord for this dingy room that was their home. It was not easy.

As he thought on these things, James arrived.

"They've accepted me!" James shouted with great joy and animation for the normally cool methodical rabbi. "I'm going to teach in the rabbinical schools and I'll be allowed to attend the open Sanhedrin debates! They were pleased to know of my experiences in Alexandria, and they'll pay me Temple shekels."

James placed his hands on Joshua's shoulders.

"We're on our way!" he said. Then, removing his hand, now soiled by the pomegranate residue, he looked at Joshua. "What's all this?"

"Joshua was hit by a stray pomegranate in a sreet brawl at the market place. They were throwing all sorts of rotten fruits at an old prophet."

"Really!"

James embraced Rachel with more than his usual affection, before collecting one of their few precious skins of Galilean wine from the inner part of the room. He drank from the skin and passed it on to Joshua and Jon.

"These are exciting times, Joshua. It'll be good to be at the center of things again."

Before Joshua had a chance to speak, Jon gave James a glowing account of the bearded prophet and his message.

"Beware," James replied soberly. "There are many false prophets in Jerusalem. In the Court of the Gentiles at the Temple you hear all manner of things. Even today, I heard some charlatan claiming to be a messiah—one sent by God for our deliverance. The pilgrim public here is very gullible and easily impressed."

There was a slight stab in Joshua's stomach as James so calmly dismissed these prophets of messiahship. Although confused as to how his role would unfold, Joshua was instinctively aware that it could well link with the messianic movement. He thought again of Joanna's words when she spoke to him of her vision of Elijah in her dying moments and mulled on them as later that night he tried to sleep.

The next day Joshua and Jon went with James to the Temple to look for building work. James wished them success as he entered the rabbinical schools.

"They never seem to quite finish the work here," Joshua said as he looked around with Jon. "They were building here when we visited Jerusalem over ten years ago."

Joshua gazed at the long colonnade with its walkway that surrounded the great Court of the Gentiles.

"There is nothing to match the serene and simple splendor of this structure," he observed. "This has to be the most magnificent building in the world."

Beyond the main gateway, known as the Triple Gate, a new entrance was being opened in the wall.

"That looks like our best chance," Joshua said, pointing toward the work. "Let's see if we can locate the foreman at the construction over there."

They made their way across the court and along the south-facing colonnade. It was less busy in that area, away from the moneychangers and the animal cages, nonetheless, a few sundry beggars sat in the shade of the architrave.

The new gateway was for a single opening, leading out toward the narrow streets of Mount Zion. Joshua found the foreman.

"We are builders and craftsmen from Galilee," he informed the man. "Could you use some extra hands to help in this work? I have all the skills, and my companion here is a good worker."

The foreman looked at them both suspiciously.

"Can you dress stones?"

"Yes," Joshua replied.

"Can you carve?"

"Better in wood than stone."

The foreman looked Jon up and down.

"He looks strong enough to do heavy work, but I have my doubts about you," he said, still addressing Joshua.

"I'm better at carving than my companion. We need the work, sir. Are you prepared to take us on?"

"Try your hand today. I'll let you know if I will hire you tomorrow," the foreman advised.

He called over to one of his stonedressers.

"Samson! Here are two more for you. Put them to work right away and let me know if they're up to it."

Joshua feared for their chances. He was a good stonedresser, but he was aware of Jon's incompetence. Jon had helped him to build walls in the vineyard, but he was clumsy at the best of times. As the day wore on, Joshua did his best to cover Jon's inadequacies, but if there was heavy moving to do in placing the newly dressed stones, he made sure that such tasks went to Jon. Joshua busied himself with hammer and chisel and kept dressing the stones.

Joshua's fears were put at ease in the evening.

Samson, the foreman, returned to inspect the day's progress.

"The extra hands do help," he said, and without any further questioning, Joshua and Jon found themselves hired for the duration of the work.

"We start at dawn," Samson shouted to his laborers. "Make sure you're all here. I'll need to send four of you out to the Kidron quarry tomorrow, so be on time."

The men picked up their tools and departed their separate ways.

Joshua and Jon were anxious to give their news to James.

Chapter Two

The Patriarch's Passing

More than a year passed since Joshua left Galilee and Miriam anxiously wondered what her son's new life was like. She busied herself in her responsibilities of running Joachim's house, taking care of her mother Anna and of her old patriarchal father, as well as the daily care of blind Joseph. Her maidservant, Judith, was less and less help, as she, too, slowed down with the passing years. Anna's other maid, Hannah, only attended to her mistress' needs. These responsibilities helped Miriam not to pine over Joshua's absence. She took pleasure, too, in seeing what an excellent job Jonah was doing keeping the carpenter's shop. Ruth and David Levi incorporated Miriam into their lives as much as possible. Miriam took great delight in seeing their son, Matthew, grow into boyhood.

Nazareth had a new rabbi, Eliezer ben Hananiah, an older man who had moved to the village shortly after Ruth's wedding. He seemed quiet, but regularly attended the synagogue group. James, before he left Nazareth, admiring Eliezer's scholarship and sound principles, willingly handed the synagogue over to him. Joachim ben Judah no longer sat with the synagogue group, and his household had become rather isolated and independent of Rabbi Eliezer's ministry. It was quite a surprise, therefore, when the rabbi knocked at Joachim's gate and asked to visit.

"Shalom! Greetings!" Miriam said on seeing him. "Goodness, we haven't seen you for so long. Please come in. I think Joachim's sleeping, but Joseph's awake. Come and talk to him. It will do him good to hear another voice."

She brought the rabbi into the living area off the old porch. Joseph was sitting down holding his blind man's stick, looking very frail. His beard was now white and his head of hair thin. He had aged fast since his affliction.

"Joseph, someone to see you and talk with you," Miriam said as she beckoned to the rabbi to sit beside him.

"Is it David and Matthew? Is Ruth here?" Joseph asked excitedly.

"No. It's Rabbi Eliezer ben Hananah. We don't see the rabbi often, so make him feel at home while I see if Joachim's awake."

"Yes, please see if he's awake," the rabbi said pulling a scroll out from his billowing sleeve. "I have news for all of you. I've received this epistle about your family in Jerusalem."

"An epistle!" shrieked Miriam, before she ran off into the house to rouse the old patriarch and his beloved wife.

"Father! At last we have news from Jerusalem!" she cried. "Come quickly, and bring out Mother. Rabbi Eliezer is here. He can read it to us all."

Joachim and Anna joined them on the porch.

The rabbi stood to greet them and embrace them.

"Shalom! It's good to see you Ben Judah, and you Anna. How are you both doing?"

"Fine Rabbi," Joachim answered. "Now, I believe you have some news for us all. We are more than curious. I hope it's good news."

"Yes, Joachim ben Judah. I think you will all be pleased. I have this scroll that was delivered to me by an old friend of mine in Jerusalem. It was written by Rabbi James."

"An epistle from James?" Joseph repeated.

"Yes, my dearest," said Miriam. "Listen as Rabbi Eliezer reads it to us."

"My son James?" Joseph asked again.

"Yes."

The rabbi started to read from the scroll:

"'To Joachim ben Judah! Greetings! This comes from us here in Jerusalem and I am sending it by Abraham Hillel, a close friend of Rabbi Eliezer ben Hananah. We hope that you will be able to convey our greetings to Joseph, my father, and Miriam, and accept these greetings from Joshua, Jon, Rachel, and me. All of us have kept well and we have become established here in the city in our several ways. I was fortunate enough to gain a position as a rabbi in the Temple schools and I have found the work very stimulating over the past year. It gives me the opportunity for scholarship that I missed in Nazareth and I have access to the Sanhedrin chamber for debates. Possibly, since there are several vacancies on the council of seventy-one at this time, I may be asked to take a seat as a member of the Sanhedrin. This would be a great honor. It would be interesting to observe the Hillel and Shammai debates here, but I confess that neither of these Pharisaic schools really satisfy my own interests.'"

"What's he talking about?" Joseph whispered in Miriam's ear. "I don't understand what he's saying."

"It's all right, Joseph," Miriam replied. "Just listen. It's wonderful to know that we are still in touch and that James is thinking about us."

A breeze rustled through the olive trees in the courtyard.

"'These Pharisees,'" the rabbi continued reading, "'have become too concerned with refining the small matters of our Law's interpretation to the point where it has become retrogressive. I wish that we had a little more of the broader scholasticism I experienced in Alexandria. There, thoughts on revision were more practical, and encouraged by that more cosmopolitan environment. In my school, however, I have had some wonderful opportunities to teach and study with enthusiasts truly thirsting for scriptural knowledge. I still believe in the strong basis of our scriptural tradition, which is why I have become concerned with some of the excessive Pharisaic interpretations. At the same time, however, I do not see the Temple ritual and the role of sacrifice as essential as do the Sadducees. I have made sacrifices, but I do not value the laws of sacrifice, as they do.'"

Anna's head dropped as she fell back into slumber. Joachim nudged her to try to keep her awake. The rabbi's reading droned on:

"'I feel like the prophets Hosea and Micah when I look at the Temple excesses in sacrifice. It is tradition, but I do not believe it leads us any closer to God. There are many devout Pharisees who are not caught in the legalistic debates, including the Essenes, but it is hard to know what their true belief is. These Essenes seem to live very pure lives according to a rigid rule, but their rule is secret, and I have not sought them out.'"

A colorful finch darted from the olive branches and landed close to Anna on the marble flags of the porch. The sudden movement caught her sleepy eye.

"Look, Joachim," she called out loudly, interrupting the rabbi's reading and pointing at the little bird. "Isn't that beautiful?"

The rabbi looked up, gave a false smile, and then carried on where he had left off:

"'Jon has shown a great interest in them, however, and from time to time he has asked my advice as to whether he should try to join them in a community.'"

"Join whom?" Anna interrupted again.

"These Essenes," Joachim reminded her quietly.

With this mention of Jon, Anna leaned forward as if to listen more intently to the rabbi.

"'I think it is too soon for him to make such a commitment,'" the rabbi continued. "'Now, he is talking of possibly joining a simpler and less scholastic group—the Nazirites. I am sure this phase will pass, however. You know Jon. He is well, and working with Joshua who has taught him a great deal in the stonemason's craft.'"

They all perked up at this mention of Joshua.

"'Joshua has set up a small business, working as a craftsman. There is much demand for good workmanship in the city at present because there are many new buildings being built both by the Romans and the wealthy Jewish merchants. The markets here are unbelievable. There are riches from the Orient, from as far away as Cathay. Every day, Jerusalem is becoming more like Alexandria in excitement and fashion. Rachel is well and sends much love to you all. We have a house close to the Temple now, and Joshua and John live at their shop. We all think about you in Nazareth often and we pray for you. May God send you his many blessings and, hopefully, further prosperity. Greetings from us all. Blessed be God forever! James.'"

For a moment, they sat in silence, looking at the rabbi.

Joseph was the first to speak:

"Typical of James. The man has no heart. He tells us about things we do not understand, and we learn nothing about the things that count. What does Rachel think of living in the city? She's a village girl."

"Oh, Joseph!" Miriam interrupted a little angrily. "It's good to hear from them at all. I never thought that we would hear anymore than you ever heard of Jonah all those years. Joshua and Jon are using their skills as builders. We should be proud that Joshua has managed to do so well with Jon. None of us were able to make much progress with him. Remember, too, it was you who taught them their craft."

"Joshua was always good with Jon," Anna added, one step behind.

"I think it's wonderful," remarked Joachim. "Who would ever have thought we would hear from them? Rachel and Jon can't write, so it was only natural that if we heard anything it would be from James or Joshua. Joshua is scholarly, but he doesn't write much. It really had to be James. Joseph, you should be very proud of James. James might become a member of the Sanhedrin Council. You have a great son there."

The rabbi held out the scroll for Joachim to take.

"I would treasure this if I were you," he said. "I am glad that I could be the purveyor of this good news. Would you like me to read it to you again?"

"That might be a good idea, Rabbi," Joachim agreed. "I shall not be able to read it to them. My reading days are long over. I'm getting too old. Please read it again."

The rabbi opened the scroll and read it through to them a second time. They were all more responsive. Their selfish wishes for particular news of their family members merged in a general euphoria that they had received the epistle at all.

"James must be an important man if he can write and dispatch epistles," Miriam observed.

Joachim asked that he might lead them in prayer. He stretched out his arms.

"Blessed be God forever!" he said. "The Lord has taken care of our loved ones. Blessed are you, Lord God of Abraham, Isaac, Jacob, and our forefathers. Blessed be God forever!"

The rabbi handed Joachim the scroll and took his leave.

Miriam was curious about the news concerning Jon. Possibly, this gave some clue about Joshua's current thinking.

"Joachim, what do you know about these Essenes?" she asked quizzically.

"I thought you might ask that," the old patriarch said, twisting his fingers in the end of his beard. "I really don't know much about them. You don't come across them much up here in Galilee. They used to be found in communities near the Salt Sea at the end of the Jordan. Like James said, they are Pharisees who have separated themselves even from their own kind. I have heard that they are expecting the end of the world to be imminent and that they prepare themselves for this with special rules for piety and righteous living. Nobody really knows, because they've always been a secret sect of our faith."

"The secrecy would appeal to Jon," Miriam said, goading Joachim to continue with his explanation.

"I suppose it would. Poor Jon!" sighed Joachim. "I agree with James, though. I'd be a bit careful about these Essenes. I have heard that they hold strange ritualistic feasts where they drink blood together. They've always sounded pretty odd to me. Some have described them as the spiritual arm of the political zealots anxious to rid our land of the Romans and set up a Pharisaic state. There were lots of Jews who felt that way in my younger days. But after so many defeats, and with the realization that the Romans haven't tried to interfere with our faith, it all seems rather a waste of time now."

"Do you believe we are living in the end time?" Miriam asked Joachim. "Don't you remember all the strange things people said when that bright star from the east lit up our night skies? That was when Joshua was born. Some people said then that the world was going to come to an end."

"I don't know, Miriam. I've been a farmer up here in Galilee for so long now that I've forgotten about those things."

Joachim looked at Anna.

"Anna, my dear," he said, "if the world were to end tomorrow it would barely effect our old lives, would it? I shall go on counting my blessings until the day I die."

Miriam realized that Joachim was tired, and didn't want to discuss these matters any further. Privately, she sensed that Joshua and Jon were planning something to fulfill their purpose. *Perhaps these Essenes might be a route toward their goals?* she thought. Sleep came slowly that night as she speculated about them in Jerusalem as members of a secret sect that one day might establish them as leaders of the Jews. *Is this the road that will lead to Joshua becoming a 'Prince of Peace', a son of God, reuniting all our people into one strong nation of faithful Jews?* she questioned. *The faith of the Jews could then be seen in the divine love that would manifest itself all over the land—the light of God and his angels shining forth in this world of foreign influences and political oppression.* Miriam silently asked God to guide Joshua in all things and to bless Jon, before finally, deep in the night, she fell asleep.

* * *

The next six months brought tragedy into Miriam's life. She knew that her father and mother could not live much longer and it was not such a shock to her, therefore, when Anna died peacefully in her sleep. When her own Joseph passed away a few weeks later, his death brought a double sorrow. She had nursed him in his blindness for several years and she had watched as he became ever more frail. But in some ways, Joseph's death lessened her burden and gave her more time to spend with her father. Joachim and Miriam often sat together on the porch as they talked for hours. They talked about the past, Joachim rambling on about his days at the Temple and his exile in Bethlehem. He described the great joy that he and Anna felt when God redeemed them giving her to them. He expressed to Miriam how difficult their decision had been to dedicate her to God in thanks and have her taken away to the Temple to join the virgins. Many days, he repeated these same memories but Miriam always listened.

"I'm so glad," she said one evening, "that in the end we were all reunited. I'm so glad that we were able to become a family after all."

"So am I," the old patriarch replied. "We didn't have a large family as we would have liked, just you, my precious one. But, look what you have given us. All of Joseph's children we call as if our own, and then there's Joshua. Joshua will be a great man one-day, if he ever makes up his mind exactly what he wants to do. You should be very proud of him, Miriam. He's a scholar like Joseph's son, James, but he has more humanity with it. It seems that he makes a success of everything to which he turns. He's a good carpenter, an excellent stonemason, and he grows better grapes than I do."

Joachim laughed.

"He has a sense of humor, too," he continued. "He and Jon were always laughing together. With all these gifts he will play his part."

Joachim sat for a while, holding Miriam's hand. He felt a pain in his chest. These pains pierced him from time to time. He placed his hand on his chest and began a choking cough. He started to pant rapidly and leaning forward fell from the bench. Miriam struggled to prop him up as he gasped for breath. He tried to smile at her, but his face fell softly and his head felt heavy in her arms. Then, it felt cooler and clammy. Joachim, too, had passed away.

Somehow, Miriam was prepared for Anna and Joseph to die, but the loss of her father, the old patriarch, hit her much harder. In her grief, she remembered Joshua's poignant instruction to Jonah and her...'*Jonah, take care of Miriam as your mother, and Mother, see that Jonah is as your son.*'

David and Ruth ben Levi moved into Joachim's house. Miriam went back to the house in the village square with its carpenter's shop, where Jonah did do his best to comfort her and take care of her.

Chapter Three

The Prophets

Joshua observed how Jon's fascination with prophets of the end time continued to grow. It was a common sight in Jerusalem to see and hear these unkempt men of God preaching in the Nazirite tradition, preparing men for the end of the world. They preached abstinence from strong drink and sexual relations and they stressed personal sacrifice in fasting. Some spoke, just like that first old man Joshua and Jon had encountered, of preparation for a coming messiah who would lead them in a future reign of God after the judgment had passed. Others spoke longingly of political messiahs, leaders in the zealot tradition who would free God's chosen people from the bondage of Rome. Joshua was more wary than Jon of this rash of prophets challenging traditional Judaism and the Temple. So many of their high-minded schemes, he considered, would only bring further destruction to Israel.

"Remember what happened in Galilee?" he reminded Jon. "Those who rebelled against Rome were crucified. Remember how I was enslaved in the retribution that followed, and Jonah, too. The Romans are our masters, and we must accept that. They don't interfere with our faith—that's what really counts."

Joshua's words did not dissuade Jon. Frequently, Jon left him alone at the stonemason's shop as he went to listen to the prophets. Joshua observed that not all of these prophets were advocating political suicide. Many were merely calling for purity and preparation before the establishment of a better kingdom fit for God.

Eventually, Joshua became attached to such a group, himself. They were not Nazirites like Jon's mentors, but a small group of men inspired by a middle-aged prophet named Zadok. Zadok had taken the vows of an Essene, but became disillusioned by the isolationist nature of the movement and left it to attract his own followers. He did not believe that the world order was about to disappear. He laid the emphasis of his teaching on the existence of a holy spirit that would be the life force of a future kingdom. Zadok also possessed remarkable gifts of healing. Many came to him to feel his power. Joshua was used to seeing the charlatans in the Temple courts try their magic on the sick and afflicted, but there seemed something much greater in the powers of this man. He taught his followers to believe in this spirit within them and work with that force. Then, the power of God could be enacted within them and bring about wholeness. Joshua became drawn to the idea that a future kingdom governed by this indwelling spirit might be preferable to a political kingdom ruled by a Zionist triumphant messiah.

"An indwelling holy spirit, what do you feel about that?" Joshua asked James one evening.

"The ruah," James said. "The still small voice that called to Elijah?"

"No, this is different," Joshua continued. "Zadok's holy spirit is no less than the power of God, dwelling within us."

"But what of the end time?" Jon interjected.

"I'm not sure we would need a messianic end time, if we were all united in this holy spirit."

"No, there will be judgment," Jon insisted. "It will come like a thief in the night, remember?"

James remained his skeptical self, fearful of any movement that did not hold the Law as its basic covenant.

"Remember our scriptures and all I have taught you," James said clearly. "There are too many false prophets these days, and they're dangerous, especially if they seek to fight Rome. Jon's doing all right as a stonemason."

Joshua felt the pull of family in supporting Jon as much as he could. He kept further thoughts on Zadok to himself. He had watched Jon mature during their first two years in Jerusalem. It seemed it had done

Jon a power of good to leave that sheltered life in Nazareth and be thrust into a more active world. Jon was backward, but he was not stupid. He had never been given a chance, coddled as he had been by his mother, and hidden away in Joachim's staid house. With Joshua, however, who had trusted him and given him a measure of independence, he had blossomed. Not only was Jon now a reasonably competent craftsman, but he could hold a moderately intelligent conversation.

Jon's interest in both the Essenes and the Nazirites continued, however. The inevitable day came when he told Joshua that regardless of the opinion of James, he was going to join one of these separatist sects. After flirting with the Essenes, he became drawn to the more simple Nazirites. In time, he presented himself to take their vow. That day, he enthusiastically returned to the stonemason's shop.

"I took a vow today!" he informed Joshua.

Joshua looked at Jon skeptically, but without surprise.

"I vowed that I would never cut my hair again."

"Why?" Joshua asked, although he was pretty sure he knew the answer.

"It's our sign, Joshua. I have become a Nazirite."

Joshua put down his chisel and rubbed the stone dust from his cutting. He brushed off his hands on his old brown shift and looked at Jon.

"Do you mean this?" he asked.

"Yes. It's already done. I was with Elias today. He initiated me in the sect. I'll be leaving you soon, Joshua. God has called me to my task. Elias will take me to the Nazirites. I need to be prepared, Joshua. Remember, we are living in the end time."

Jon looked at Joshua with a penetrating gaze.

"You are a chosen one, too," he continued. "You need to think about your future as well. We are living in the days of Elijah. He may already be here. Just as we can not tell when the Lord will take us, so, too, we can not tell when He will choose to lead us to His kingdom and end this world of ours. We must be prepared. We are prepared when we know we can call to God that we are ready. Are you ready, Joshua? Remember, the Lord, like death, will come as a thief in the night. Only those who have forsaken the sins of this world and purified themselves, will be able to follow Him to His kingdom."

"But Jon," Joshua pleaded, "we have the Law. If you obey the commandments and the Law and if we show love to one another as we would expect from each other, we will be prepared."

"The Law is confused," Jon retorted. "Did the Law save us from being conquered by the Romans?"

"But, we can give to Caesar what is Caesar's, as long as we give to God all that is His."

"We are God's chosen," Jon continued vehemently. "We must give ourselves to God before it's too late."

Joshua was considerably troubled by Jon's remarks, not because he disagreed with them, but because he knew that he was personally fighting from agreeing. He couldn't quite detach himself from tradition, as Jon had done. Jon was all emotion and little scholarship, but Joshua was conscious that at this point in time he might, himself, adhere too much to scholarship and not enough to his emotions.

"If you leave me, Jon, I will have to look for something else myself. I will not be able to carry on our business alone. Either, I will have to become a laborer again with casual building work like we had when we first arrived here, or I'll have to change the direction of my life altogether."

As he said this, Joshua's mind was already wandering. He considered Jon to be a little hasty in his decision. He didn't see much could be achieved in the Nazirite movement. He was personally drawn to the more intellectual separatist camp of the Essenes. One thing Jon had said, however, particularly troubled him.

"We are living in the time of Elijah," Joshua repeated to himself.

Joanna saw Elijah on her deathbed, he recalled again. *These prophets also seem to frequently speak of Elijah and his time. Could this mean that Elijah has come in some spiritual form and that the messianic age truly is about to begin? Could this be my role as a chosen one, a son of God spreading His divine love? Could this be the task of the 'Prince of Peace'? I need to do a lot more thinking. The time has come that God is calling me to reveal His purpose for me.*

"You are right, Jon," Joshua said in slow agreement. "We were both born for a purpose. I hope you can be more than a Nazirite. Prepare the way for me, Jon, for when I have sorted myself out, we will be a team. We can lead our people into a messianic age, which God will reveal to us. You need time to think as I do. Maybe that is why God has led you to become a Nazirite. But, that's not the end of your work Jon, it's just the beginning. I don't think I could find my destiny as a Nazirite, and I doubt that is yours either. Just use the time wisely to think. I need to get away to think as well. We could both be stonemasons for many years to come, but that's not really what we came to Jerusalem to be. We came to fulfill our destinies. We were led here by God to fulfill the great purpose that I feel sure He has for us both."

"That's right!" Jon agreed excitedly. "Now you are beginning to understand. We were chosen to place ourselves in the special service of God."

"Do you really think that the Nazirite sect is the answer for this?" Joshua asked, obviously still unhappy with the particular path that Jon had chosen.

"If we can not cleanse ourselves first, how can we purify others for the end time?" Jon replied.

Joshua made no comment as he stared blankly at Jon. He had never heard his backward cousin speak with such authority.

"If the Lord has led you in this path then you must go," he said at length. "How soon will this Elias take you to his Nazirite community?"

"I'll be on probation here in Jerusalem for a while. At this stage, I will still be able to work with you. Elias will tell me when he thinks I am ready to go. They will send me out to the desert wilderness. We live roughly, like the prophets of old. I will be like Elijah in his cave at Horeb."

"Do you believe Elijah has already come, Jon?" Joshua asked. "Or do you think Elijah might manifest himself as one of the prophets, preparing the way for a coming messiah?"

"Don't ask me, Joshua," Jon replied simplistically.

He looked up, and turning very serious he spoke with the same surprising authority as before:

"Elijah alone knows when he comes, as this is his age. After he comes, the righteous will survive led by the Messiah. Those who are not prepared will be taken as they are and cast into darkness."

Then, he gave a satisfied grin.

"It will happen like a thief in the night!" he repeated.

Joshua was afraid that the Nazirites, who had obviously successfully converted Jon to their way of thinking, might take advantage of his seeming simplicity. Jon might lose his destiny to the message of Nazirite false prophets. Over the next few days, Joshua discussed the matter at length with James. Joshua still liked to share most things theological with the rabbi who had taught him so much. Jon's present obsession with Elijah's second coming and the dawn of the messianic age, coupled with Joshua's own feelings of destiny and purpose, caused them to examine the word of Jeremiah. They also discussed the other prophets who had predicted the end of the world at the time when the Babylonians and Persians had overcome the Judean kingdom. Jeremiah had fled to Egypt at that time and become a prophet in exile. James remembered how much the Alexandrine Jews revered the word of Jeremiah, even to this very day.

"Jeremiah always inspired our people in Egypt," James acknowledged. "He and those in his school of prophecy likened us to the clay of a potter. The Davidic pot had been broken, but the clay could be remodeled, and in the word of Jeremiah we have been remodeling this clay ever since."

"Ezekiel went further when he likened our people to a valley of dead bones that God was able to resurrect by blowing life back into them," Joshua added, and for a moment he became very thoughtful. *Could Ezekiel have been predicting that this holy spirit that Zadok and his followers believe to be the force within, is to build the kingdom of the end time?* He hadn't thought much about the followers of Zadok in recent weeks.

He looked at James and returned to their subject:

"James, the crisis that Jeremiah and his school faced passed when this Temple was rebuilt and our people returned to our land. But, how stable is the Temple? What will happen to this Temple in the end time?"

James nodded in agreement but offered no answer.

"Many, like Jon," Joshua continued, "believe that we are now living in that end time. Possibly we are. I have been uncomfortable about this ever since Joanna died. She was so sure that Elijah had visited her on her deathbed. Do you believe the age of Elijah has come? Do you believe that a messianic age is about to begin?"

"We've discussed this many times," James said. "It's academic. I don't need to believe it. It's not essential to our faith. Jeremiah and Ezekiel believed in it, but the end didn't come. The Temple was restored and our people returned from exile."

"Yes," Joshua acknoweldged, "but were Jeremiah and Ezekiel

referring to that restoration or a resurrection at the end time? That's what these prophets of the end time preach, and they are the ones who have influenced Jon."

"I'm not very taken by messianic dreams," James answered. "They are too nationalistic and militant for me. There are Jews visiting the Temple here from all over the world. Our faith has never been to me one that is geographically restricted to the land that we conquered at Moses' command. There were so many good Jews in Alexandria, remember? But Jews come here to Jerusalem from Antioch, Asia Minor, and the cities of Greece just the same way. Our Law is our faith and the Temple here is a focus for all Jews and not just Judean Jews. We became a scattered people in the time of Jeremiah and not everyone returned. In fact, few did. There are almost more Jews in Alexandria than there are here in Jerusalem. You remember how big the synagogue was there with its library and schools? How stimulating the debates were? To be honest with you, Joshua, I found Alexandria theologically more stimulating than Jerusalem and the Sanhedrin."

Joshua slowly stroked his light-brown beard. He liked James' argument.

"Then, you would see a more universal Jewish leader in a messiah, James?" he rhetorically suggested. "A leader whom all Jews could follow whether in Judea or not? Perhaps a moral leader, who might base his leadership on our Law rather than on our land or birthright?"

"Such a messiah makes more sense to me," James agreed. "We don't need to fight the Romans. They don't interfere with us. They even allow us to use our own Temple shekels. I'm not sure about this end time. Maybe we can have a messiah or spiritual leader who will be the herald of an era of universal peace based on devotion to our traditions and the Law."

"A 'Prince of Peace,'" Joshua said knowingly. "Yes, we've talked on these lines before, but somehow it's now beginning to make more sense. Maybe through a messianic interpretation of our Law we can create a rule of peace where God's will is supreme. The message of such a messiah might eventually replace this Temple as the focus of our faith."

James looked a little taken aback.

"Now, Joshua! You are talking like an Essene. The Temple has always been a focus for Jews. It is the outward symbol of our Law and faith."

Joshua, still curious about the Essenes, sought an opportunity here to glean information from James.

"Aren't the Essenes only extreme Pharisees," he said, "Pharisees who have isolated themselves to create purity in the Law and for purposes of scholarship?"

"I don't know," James replied skeptically. "I don't know much about them. They never come to the Temple, although for such a small sect they are quite often discussed in the Sanhedrin. It seems that they believe that only descendents of Zadok, the Davidic priest of Solomon's Temple, have the right to the priesthood, and I've also heard that they don't follow our sacrificial calendar. They're shrouded in secrecy."

Joshua listened intently. *The Essenes have a reputation for scholarship even if they do veer away from Temple traditionalism,* he thought. *The Nazirites appear to be separatists with little purpose other than personal abstinence and a renouncing of most of the pleasurable things in life. There seems to be more substance to these Essenes. Perhaps I should investigate this Pharisaic sect. They have communes. Such communities may be just right for me at present. Places where I can think and pray in spiritual peace to work out my destiny.*

In the days ahead, Joshua discussed the Essenes frequently with James as they tried to get a broader picture of what the secret movement really believed.

Two months later, Jon left Joshua when Elias sent him off to join his band of desert Nazirites. Joshua was sorry to see him go, but knowing his own thoughts, he had no argument to stop him. Jon was now so full of zeal and enthusiasm for his mission that he was truly a different man. James continued to dislike Jon's decision, and blamed Joshua for letting him go. He was not too happy with Joshua's interest in the Essenes either, although he sympathized with their pacifism. Even as a universal theologian, James was a conservative when it came to tradition. He liked the Temple and what it stood for as a focus for universal Judaism. However, he also agreed with Joshua's thoughts on a non-political messiah. James had never supported the Galilean revolt and had advised against it as Nazareth's rabbi. He was attracted by the words of the prophet Micah where universalism was acknowledged, but the inspiration still came from Jerusalem.

'Come, let us go up to the mountain of the Lord, to the house of the

God of Jacob that he may teach us his ways and we may walk in his paths. For out of Zion shall go forth the Law and the word of the Lord from Jerusalem. He shall judge between many peoples, and shall decide for strong nations afar. They shall beat their swords into ploughshares and their spears into pruning hooks. Nation shall not lift up sword against nation; neither shall they learn war anymore. They shall sit every man under his vine and under his fig tree, and none shall make them afraid, for the mouth of the Lord of hosts has spoken.'

As Joshua became more drawn into the Essenic idea, James used this passage to dissuade him from rejecting the role of the Temple in his concept of the pacifist messiah. Joshua, who had by this time made contact with an Inspector of the secret society, reiterated by also quoting from the prophet Micah.

'With what shall I come before the Lord, and bow myself before God on high? Shall I come before him with burnt offerings, with calves a year old? Will the Lord be pleased with thousands of rams, with ten thousands of rivers of oil? He has showed you, O man, what is good; and what does the Lord require of you but to do justice, and to love kindness and to walk humbly with your God.'

Their arguments were scholastic. Joshua was less protective of the Temple institution, but still fulfilled his obligations. Before he finally left to join a small community of Essenes just to the northwest of Jerusalem, he made a sacrifice at the Temple, asking for a greater understanding of his destiny.

"Father," he prayed, "in this sacrifice cleanse me. Make me at one with You that I might understand better the destiny that You have set for me."

He watched the fatty smoke rise from the well-worn altar.

"Show me my destiny, Lord!" he cried. "I have dedicated myself to You that Your strength and wisdom may flow through me."

The smoke rose higher in the stillness of the clear sky, hanging like a silken cord from the heavens.

"Help me as I enter this new phase of my life," he continued in prayer. "May I become a worthy member of the Essenic movement and share my life fully with those others who have chosen to dedicate themselves solely to You. May I learn from their wisdom and find there the message that will reveal my destiny."

An elderly priest raked the fire and placed a disemboweled turtle dove in the glowing embers. Joshua's half-burned fowl fell to one side, and the still cord of smoke wafted and dispersed as the fresh fat of the new sacrifice took its place. Joshua turned, his prayer disturbed, but his thoughts fulfilled. He felt confident that he was set on the road that would lead to his destiny.

Chapter Four

Essenic Interlude

Joshua pulled on his old mule, as they passed through the northern gate of Jerusalem. The beast dragged a cart Joshua had built for himself. They now reached the open road leaving the dense streets behind. Following the Essene Inspector's instructions, he was to turn off the Roman road and follow a path to the left of the Mount of Olives. This path would lead him to a hillside of caves looking out from a plateau above the Jordan valley. Here, Joshua would find the Jerusalem Essenic community. In the cart, he carried his carpenter's tools and stonedressing chisels, along with the old wooden box of gold coins, which he would have to declare to the community. Thrown in with them, he had put an extra pair of thong sandals and some linen garments. These would be his total worldly goods.

The track was rough on the cart. Stones and boulders strewed the way. At length, Joshua sighted the settlement. He could make out several loose-stone buildings. Closer, he could also see the caves in the limestone cliffs. The settlement was larger than he had imagined. The stony bed of a dried up brook, a little shallower than that winding through the Kidron valley between Jerusalem and the Mount of Olives, ran through the community property. It then passed on down the rugged hillside into the hazy blue of the Judean wilderness, heading toward the distant mirage of the Salt Sea. To the left, far below, Joshua could see the lushness of the

Jordan valley, and the silver snake of the river that marked the boundary of the 'Promised Land'.

* * *

A preliminary interview back in Jerusalem between Joshua and the Overseer, who was visiting the Inspector of the Jerusalem Community, had been satisfactory. The Overseer and the Inspector had been astounded at the candidate's scriptural and legal Pharisaic knowledge. The Overseer admired Joshua's ability as a craftsman, and showed interest in the fact that Joshua claimed he was a competent vinedresser. They were a little disappointed that Joshua couldn't bring obvious wealth to their community, however, which made them all the more surprised when Joshua, almost as an afterthought, informed them of the box of treasure. The Overseer hadn't yet seen the gold coins, but he took Joshua's word that they were substantial in quantity and value. However, Joshua's nature had bothered him a little. The man seemed fit enough, but he hoped that Joshua's obvious gentleness was not going to hold him back when it came to the rather strict disciplinary rule and physical hardship that their life entailed.

* * *

On arrival at the community, Joshua was escorted to the Overseer's building. He stooped to enter and descended two steps into the cool darkness within. An oil lamp lit the room, otherwise brightened only by the doorway entrance. The room was sparsely furnished with a table and stool. The Overseer was bent over, writing on leather parchment. He looked up when the escort brought Joshua inside.

"This is Joshua, Brother Solomon."

"Ah! Yes! The stonemason and carpenter from Jerusalem," the Overseer replied as he waved the escort away. "You may leave us, Brother."

Then, adjusting his phylactery, Solomon spoke to Joshua:

"So you really did decide to join us. I thought you'd come sooner or later."

"I brought my things as you asked," Joshua said, feeling a little sick in his stomach.

He was nervous about the box of treasure, but he was gambling on the possibility that this might prove to be the key to unlocking his destiny.

"Good," the Overseer responded. "We must record your possessions. Should you eventually take our vows, your possessions, including the box of gold coins, will become common to us all. You must serve two years with us first, however. We'll keep your treasure in trust until you reach that stage. Should you decide not to take the full vows of the community, your treasure will be returned to you. You can use your mule and cart during your work here while you are on probation, but again, once you attain full membership, these, too, will become common property."

The Overseer sounded very matter-of-fact and rather boring, but he seemed shrewd as if he was looking out for Joshua's reactions.

"Are you still sure that you want to join our community?" he asked.

There was a fearful feeling in Joshua as he saw a curtailment to his natural freedom coming with his answer, but other needs tugged his senses.

"Yes, Brother," he said rather unconvincingly.

Joshua wanted to work out his destiny. Yet he was not without doubt as to whether he was making the right decision, but he didn't have time to dwell on doubt. The Overseer was anxious to initiate Joshua as a novice.

"You will be appointed to a brother," the Overseer continued. "Your brother will instruct you in the Manual of Discipline. You will live by the rule of the manual, but you will not be able to share food at the same table as the members, or bathe with them. First, you must enter into our covenant."

The Overseer walked over to Joshua and placed his hands on his shoulders. He looked intently into Joshua's eyes. The light of the oil lamp reflected in the gold that decorated his wide phylacteries that held the Shemah, the Commandments and the prayers of the Essenes, close to his chest.

"By this laying on of hands I admit you, Brother Joshua," the Overseer declared, "as a novice into the Community of the Essenes. You have solemnly stated your intent to follow the rule of the Manual of Discipline. I have inspected you, and deem you worthy to join the Community of the Essenes, but not to have full fellowship in our sect.

Brother Joshua, you are admitted on probation, and at my will and discretion only. Should I feel for any reason that your probation should end, then my decision will be final. Remember, you are sworn at this time into secrecy before me and before God."

Brother Solomon took his hands off Joshua's shoulders and picked a small cruse of oil from the table. He poured a few drops on Joshua's forehead and smeared the oil with his thumb to stop it running. Then, after returning the cruse, he again placed his hands on Joshua's shoulders.

"With this oil I have anointed you as a chosen one who has made a commitment to the rule of the Essenes," the Overseer solemnly stated. "Anything that you learn about us during your period of probation you are sworn not to divulge to anyone, and by this laying on of hands, and through this anointing, you have been sworn into this covenant. Should all of our community eventually approve your full commitment, you will again be initiated, this time in public baptism, from which time you will have the privilege of sharing ablutions in the waters with the 'Many'. This privilege is a sign of the purity that full fellowship brings, which will be in your third year."

The Overseer then took his hands from Joshua's shoulders and stood back.

"Welcome, Brother Joshua!" he proclaimed.

Joshua smiled nervously.

Brother Solomon took Joshua outside and led him to another simple stone structure similar to that where he had admitted him to the covenant.

"This will be your residence," he said. "There are four of you on probation at this time. You cook for yourselves, although you will be given the community's vegetables and grain as you need. Brother Daniel will join you here in a short while and show you around. Our community is a little rugged as the soil here is poor, but we have a good supply of water in the caves. Our vines are probably thinner than those you tended in Galilee, but our olives are excellent. You will notice that we have also developed a hardy grain crop in spelt and millet."

The Overseer left, and in a short while a young man joined Joshua.

"Welcome to our commune," the man said in greeting. "My name is

Daniel and I will be your brother and show you around. Joshua's your name, isn't it?"

"Yes."

Brother Daniel embraced him.

"Let's start," he said, "by showing you your water supply. There are very strict rules here for using water. You can not bathe in the water used by those in the full fellowship. We have two different pools."

Brother Daniel led Joshua to the caves. In one cave there was an underground lake fed by dripping limestone springs deep in the hillside.

"This is the purification pool of the 'Many,'" Daniel announced. "This is the one you must not use. Now, follow me."

Daniel led Joshua through a rocky passage to a much smaller cave. Here was another pool of cold clear water, but it was barely more than three cubits long and two cubits wide. This cave was cold and uninviting.

"This is your pool," Daniel informed Joshua. "Only here may you bathe and collect your water for cooking. Now, let me take you to the storehouse so you can see where to draw your millet, raisins, and other necessary food supplies."

Joshua was led to the store, and then on to the stony vineyard with its straggling vines.

"All our grapes are harvested for drying," Daniel explained. "They make good raisins."

Among the vines in the appalling soil, vegetables struggled to grow.

"As you can see," Daniel continued, "we also grow our vegetables here among the vines. You can see we have lentils and peas, and over there some beans and onions along with garlic and herbs."

Beyond the vineyard were the olive terraces, and then, the pathetic patches of millet and spelt. If Joshua had not lived in the prosperous agricultural area of Nazareth all those years, he might have been more impressed, but he felt disappointed. Brother Daniel, however, was obviously quite proud of the commune's achievement.

"As you can see, Brother Joshua, we are pretty self-sufficient," he maintained. "Our main problem is the water. It all has to come from the caves. In the dry season we have to constantly carry water out to these ledges."

Joshua was familiar with the problems of drought and water. This exposure to agricultural needs momentarily made Joshua homesick, and he thought of his family. Neither he nor James had ever received any news of them since leaving to move to Jerusalem, despite their attempt to get an epistle to Galilee.

Joshua was not able to reminisce for long. Daniel called him back along the path on which they had come.

"We will get you your robes next," he said.

When they were back at the settlement, Daniel collected two simple white robes for Joshua to wear. He also issued him with a white rope to hold them in place.

"You must wash one of these every three days," Brother Daniel instructed. "It is one of the rules of purity—'Not more than three days must pass without the garment being washed and pummeled so that the community member may always be reminded of the purity of the sect. Members of the sect are devoted to the purity of life that can only come from absolute compliance with the Law, which is symbolized in the purity of the white robe that must be worn at all times.'"

Joshua took the robes. The sun was beginning to set, causing long shadows to fall over the settlement, and the filmy haze of late afternoon light had begun to fill in the depth of the Jordan valley below.

"We meet for evening prayers at sunset outside the caves," Brother Daniel said as he embraced Joshua in a clinical and perfunctory way.

Joshua was now alone, his old mule tethered beside the hut, still harnessed to his cart. Joshua rubbed the beast's ears and patted his back.

"Thank God for you," he said. "I feel so depressed."

He unhitched the cart to give the mule his freedom, leaving the old beast on the long, tether rope.

"We'll survive this together," he said, before he entered the low hut that was to be his shelter.

It's too late now. I'm committed, he thought. *I can't turn back.*

* * *

From a cave entrance in the rocky terrain below Herodium, Jon watched the sunrise. He could see the wilderness stretching way out below him, leading down to the craggy area of salt-weathered rocks that surrounded the deep crevice of the inland sea. Rising majestically, in the clear light of the early day, guarding the Salt Sea, was Masada, the mountain fortress that was the last outpost of the 'Promised Land'. Beyond, lay the desert wastes of Arabia. The goats that were Jon's charge bleated outside the cave, as the Nazirite offered up his morning prayers.

It had been several months now since the novitiates from the Jerusalem Nazirites had moved south into the wilderness. Elias had explained that this was part of their initial trial—a period of severe fasting and discomfort to prepare them for their coming campaign. Later, they would preach the imminent arrival of the Kingdom of God, and call on all Jews to repent from their sins in preparation for the Day of Judgment when the Messiah would count his lambs. The novitiates slept rough, clothed themselves in smelly goatskins, and foraged for honey and locusts to make the dull cakes of bread that were now their staple diet. Many days, Jon had nothing but goats' milk, as he moved his small herd from cave to cave in this barren wilderness. He had lost weight, and his longer hair only emphasized the thinner appearance of his once robust round face.

From time to time, Jon met up with his fellow novices. They would exchange locust cakes, goats' milk, and cheese, and guide each other to forage grounds in the barren hills. They were forbidden to camp together, having to fend for themselves, each man dwelling in his own shelter. They lived as hermits, ascetics cut off from the world, to pray and contemplate on the coming end time. Their companions were their goats, and their comfort was in the rising and setting sun—God's eternal reminder that ultimately He is in charge. Occasionally, as the sun rose over the barren landscape, they could find the white substance that had sustained Moses and the Israelites in their desert wanderings centuries before. It appeared with the dew, especially in the spring and fall, the life-giving manna, or 'bread of heaven'. These small crystalline drops melted as the sun rose. They were a welcome addition to the novitiate's meager diet and when the miraculous food appeared, Jon thanked God for his desert blessing. The manna from heaven required certain desert climatic conditions to make it manifest, however, and most of the time Jon felt undernourished. The Nazirite preparation was proving tougher than he had anticipated.

As the sun rose, so the lower rocks changed from gray to white, and the tussocks of sage, from black to dusty green. Eventually, the white light filled the wilderness. The chill of the night air rapidly gave way to the heat of the day.

* * *

Joshua's first year with the Essenes dragged by slowly. He was disappointed. He had chosen to join the commune because of the reputation of Essenic scholarship, but at this rustic site to the north of Jerusalem, Joshua found the community more devoid of scholarship than at anywhere he had lived. Brother Solomon obviously had a very sound scriptural knowledge, but he chose for some reason, not to share his scholarship. So Joshua's duties became purely agrarian. He hauled water, and hoed weeds in the primitive fields of spelt and also around the vegetables that grew between the struggling vines. They dried the harvest of grapes for raisins, because the grapes, even as they came off the vines, were barely edible in their sourness. This was a far cry from the rich agriculture of Nazareth where the grapes had been sweet and succulent and had been the cause of much merriment at harvest time.

Nearly eleven months passed. Joshua was seriously thinking of giving up his preliminary vow and returning to James in Jerusalem, but events overtook him unexpectedly. When he returned to his stone hut after a day of separating darnel seeds from the spelt in the community storeroom, he found Brother Daniel waiting for him.

"Brother Joshua, come with me to the Overseer's building," Daniel said. "We have a visitor here from Qumran, and he has expressed an interest in you changing communities."

"Qumran? Isn't that where the library is, and where all the brothers are engaged in scholarship?"

"Yes. It's the great monastery of our movement down by the Salt Sea."

"They want to see me now?"

"Yes, Brother Joshua. Please come with me and stop asking questions. They are waiting and need to see you before our evening prayers."

Joshua brushed the dirt particles off his white robe that now looked positively gray. The Granary was always such a dusty place to work. His eyes were smarting, and his hands filthy from the dirt of the spelt grains.

"All right, Brother Daniel. Let's go to the Overseer's building."

They walked over to the dark stone dwelling where they had both at different times been initiated into the first stages of the covenant by Brother Solomon. They stooped to enter, and the smell of the dirty oil lamp greeted them from the gloom.

"Brother Joshua!" Daniel announced.

"Ah, good! Thank you Brother Daniel," the Overseer replied.

Daniel left.

"Brother Joshua," the Overseer continued in a rather patronizing way. "Meet Brother Nathan from Qumran."

Brother Nathan stepped from the gloom. Joshua began to see him as his eyes became accustomed to the dim light. The visitor from Qumran embraced him. In the yellow glow, Joshua could make out the gilt of a phylactery against the pure white linen garment that the visitor wore. He seemed to be altogether far more worldly than Brother Solomon.

"I have observed you over the past year," Solomon said to Joshua. "You have worked hard and efficiently, but I feel you are wasted in our community here. It is obvious to me that you need to be in a more scholastic atmosphere where your linguistic skills and vast scriptural knowledge can be of advantage to the community. Brother Nathan has informed us that he has vacancies for scholars in the library at Qumran."

Joshua looked up with more than mere interest. His heart leapt with joy.

The Overseer continued to address him:

"Brother Nathan has asked me if I can have you transferred to the monastery by the Salt Sea. Have you any objections to making such a move?"

My prayers had been answered, Joshua thought.

"No, Brother Solomon," he said, trying to control his obvious delight, a playful smile running across his face. "I will go wherever my superiors think fit for me. If it is their wish that I should go to Qumran, I will go."

"Good, Brother Joshua," Solomon said without looking up. "I knew you would agree. You will finish the year here and then transfer to Qumran in the early spring."

The playful smile disappeared as Joshua's immediate excitement was dampened. *Next spring...why not now?* he thought, but the news was unquestionably good. He was dismissed as quickly as he had been summoned. During the prayers at the caves that evening, he thanked God quietly for showing him a way out from the dead end that he seemed to have encountered as a community worker in the Anathoth monastery.

When spring came, the Overseer called Joshua to his hut again.

"Brother Joshua," he said, greeting him in his usual impersonal way, "I have been in discussion with our brothers in Qumran about your dowry. We are holding your treasure in trust for you until such time as your probation period is approved by the 'Many' at the end of your second year. It will be necessary, however, to transfer half of this to Qumran, as it will be their decision to approve you after your second year. We have agreed to split the dowry. I am arranging, therefore, to return half for you to take with you to Qumran. Take care that you hand this over to the Inspector at the monastery on your arrival. It will be safeguarded until you become a full member of the brotherhood. Likewise, we will keep your other portion here until your probation is ended, at which time it will become communal funds. You may keep your cart and mule for your journey, but they must be handed over to the Inspector on arrival at Qumran."

"I doubt my poor old mule will stand the journey," Joshua commented.

The mule was in pretty poor shape when he had first arrived at Anathoth and had not improved during the intervening year.

"I think we could give you another for your journey," the Overseer suggested with a wry smile. "It can be our way of sending a fresh mule down to Qumran. Meanwhile, you may need to work on the cart. It could use a carpenter's skills."

Joshua was glad that half of the gold coins were going to be returned to him, even if it was only for the journey. He felt a strange possessiveness about the treasure. They were his one link with his past, and to him the key to his destiny. He felt that they should really be in his trust rather than that of the Essenes. At least the coins would be close to him.

"When am I to leave?"

"You are free to make the journey at any time from now," the Overseer announced. "Be careful, though, the road from Jerusalem to Jericho is noted in the spring for its thieves and robbers."

"I will, Brother Solomon. I'll leave as soon as I've restored the cart.

I'm anxious to get to Qumran to study again. Can everything be ready for my journey this week?"

"We could have everything ready for you by tomorrow."

"Good. It will take me a couple of days to restore the cart".

The Overseer stepped forward and embraced Joshua.

"Good luck. I am sure that this move will be good for you," he said. "You have been obedient to our ways and a perfect novice in the movement of the Essenes, but deep down I've known that you were not content here. I believe you will find a far greater fulfillment in the monastery at Qumran."

Joshua was quite surprised, and felt for the first time that somebody at the commune actually cared about him. He left the Overseer's building and returned to the novices' hut. At last, he saw a constructive turn in his destiny. He excitedly tossed on his pallet as he prepared his mind for the journey to Qumran and a new future.

The morning Joshua set out on his journey dawned a crisp clear spring day. As he left the commune, Joshua was full of optimism. He could see clear across the Jordan valley and down to the Salt Sea. Somewhere, way down there, was his destination—the Essenes' monastery at Qumran. He knew that he would have to take the road from Jerusalem to Jericho, so he decided to stop off first in Jerusalem and visit James. Although only two or three hours journey from Jerusalem, Joshua had not visited the Holy City since he had joined the Essenic commune.

As he approached the Mount of Olives, the sight of the city brought tears to his eyes. Joshua had become so conditioned to the tough agrarian life of the commune that the splendor before him quite took his breath away. From his vantagepoint to the northeast, he could look down on the city. In the bright spring light, the buildings sparkled and the great colonnade surrounding the Temple on Mount Moriah seemed more magnificent than ever. Beyond Mount Moriah, Joshua could make out the huddled buildings of Mount Zion, and to the west, the gleaming aqueducts that brought water to the Roman buildings. Spring flowers in blue and yellow, white and orange, covered the Kidron valley and surrounding hills in a carpet of beauty that Joshua realized he had always taken for granted.

He stopped the mule and surveyed the scene in wonder. It was uplifting, and he thought on the words of the psalmist.

'The Lord builds up Jerusalem; He gathers the outcasts of Israel. Praise the Lord, O Jerusalem! Praise your God, O Zion! For He strengthens the bars of your gates; He blesses your sons within you. He makes peace in your borders; He fills you with the finest of wheat. He sends forth His command to the earth; His word runs swiftly. He declares His word to Jacob, His statutes and ordinances to Israel. He has not dealt thus with any other nation; they do not know His ordinances. Praise the Lord!'

The familiar haze of smoke rose upward from the Temple's sacrificial altars. Joshua felt homesick for the Temple, for the learned leaders, and for James. He pulled the mule's tether and made his way down to the city.

Joshua found Rachel at their house on Mount Zion, near the Temple. She was more than surprised when the mule cart pulled up and she saw Joshua.

"Joshua! Is it really you?" she said, mesmerized as Joshua stood in front of her in his clean white robe. "Have you come back?"

"No. I'm just passing through."

He walked forward, taking Rachel into his arms. He had not embraced a woman since he had left to join the Essenes. Holding Joanna's sister gave him a mixed feeling of physical release and gnawing pain. To a great extent he had been able to forget his personal tragic loss in the hard life at the commune, but Rachel's warm embrace only reminded him of the love he had shared with Joanna.

"James will be so pleased to see you," Rachel commented, as she brushed her dark hair from her face. "He often talks about you and wonders how you are doing. Are you still with the Essenes?"

"Yes, I am, but I'm not sure that I've found what I need. It was a very simple life at the commune, but it wasn't very stimulating. It was better as a builder here in Jerusalem. They've transferred me. I'm going to be at their monastery in Qumran. I'll have the opportunity to study with learned men again, and I think I'll like it a lot more. This last year has been good for my discipline and patience, but I don't think it's given me a chance to grow. Qumran should be better."

"James will be back soon and you can tell him all about it then," Rachel continued. "Can I get you some fresh bread from the oven? I've just baked for the evening."

"You know how I would love that," Joshua said enthusiastically, as he was reminded of their breadmaking feasts with Joanna in Nazareth. "In the commune all our bread was hard, being made from spelt. It tasted more like locust cake than the bread that we always made."

As Rachel busied herself with the bread, Joshua asked about her:

"How are you enjoying it here in Jerusalem now? Do you ever regret our move south?"

"Sometimes," Rachel admitted. "I miss my father. He was always such a comfort. It's good for James here, however. He's on the Sanhedrin council now, and very busy most of the time."

She turned to face Joshua carrying the freshly baked bread, hot from the oven. She eased it off the clay tray, dropping it onto a wooden plate. Little bits pulled away where the dough had not fully formed, but the aroma that the bread produced filled the small room, causing Joshua to feel a hunger he had not before realized. He had become conditioned to the meager meals at the novices' hut, and the rich smell of Rachel's fresh new bread excited his taste buds. As soon as it was cool enough, they broke the loaf, pulling warm doughy chunks off.

"We'd better save some for James," Rachel said laughingly. "He won't be too pleased if he comes home and he finds no bread."

Joshua chuckled.

"Just like Jon in the old days," he said.

They settled down reminiscing about their earlier days in Jerusalem and wondered what may have become of Jon since he had joined the Nazirites.

"His life can't have been more rigorous than mine," Joshua observed.

"But, don't they have to find their own food in the desert?" Rachel asked. "At least you were fed in your commune."

Joshua laughed.

"True. I expect Jon has had a harder time than I have. I wonder how he is surviving his vows of abstinence. Jon used to like to imbibe in good wine. I used to rely on his reaction to the new wine in the vineyard in Nazareth. He was a better taster than I was."

Rachel started to giggle.

"It used to go a bit to his head, if I remember rightly," she said shaking hers. "Poor Jon. What do you really think will become of him now?"

"I don't know. He's on his own. But I'll tell you one thing; Jon changed a lot before he left to join the Nazirites. He spoke with such authority, Rachel. He never displayed such authority in Nazareth. He believes in his destiny. He was very determined before he left Jerusalem. He believes he has a role to play and that God has chosen him for a special purpose. Jon's been an inspiration to me. He's made me believe in my own destiny."

Rachel looked surprised.

"Hasn't James always been your inspiration, Joshua?" she said.

"James has taught me more than anyone else, that's true. He taught me Greek and Hebrew and guided me through every facet of the sacred writings. What knowledge I have I owe to James. But there's something that moves our lives that's above scholarship. It's an instinct, a knowledge that God is calling you to be His servant, to be used whatever way He so devises. Jon has that call. I've seen how it changed him. I could sense the new authority in him. It was as if God Himself was speaking through him. It was that inspiration that has spurred me on, Rachel. I believe that God will use me as well as Jon and speak through me also. I've always believed that God has a purpose for me, but I've never understood it. Seeing Jon change the way he did has inspired me to finally discover my own purpose."

"And do you think you've found that purpose?" Rachel asked a little skeptically.

"No, not yet. But, at least with the Essenes I have time to be disciplined and to think, and now I can combine that with further scholarship in the library at Qumran. One day, God will reveal His purpose for me. One day, I will understand what it is that God wants me to do."

Rachel took Joshua's hands into her own and sat looking at him. She didn't quite fully understand what Joshua meant, but she felt that she was in the presence of a great man.

"Joanna was lucky to know you," she said softly, after a long pause. "You've always been an inspiration to us in the calm way that you have gone about your daily life. You always speak with such authority and yet with so much love and kindness. It is almost as if God is speaking through you. You are a symbol of His Divine presence. God bless you, Joshua. God bless you and blessed be God forever."

Joshua looked down and they sat in silence. He remained in deep thought. He had never really talked much to Rachel. She had always seemed rather drawn into herself, unlike her vivacious sister. What she had just said deeply moved him. Now, he felt even more determined than ever to find his destiny. As they sat thinking, oblivious of the street sounds outside, James returned home.

"Joshua!" he shouted, seeing them sitting together in the darkening room. "When did you get here?"

Joshua rose and embraced James. The two men held each other in more than formal greeting. Tears of joy welled in both their pairs of eyes.

"I've missed you all," Joshua said. "James, it's been a very lonely year."

"We've missed you, too. How have you been?" James asked, as he turned to Rachel not giving Joshua a chance to answer.

"How can we celebrate tonight? Have we some good wine, and what can you prepare for my dear brother?"

"You can start by having your share of today's fresh bake before Joshua has it all," she said, offering him what was left of the loaf.

James took the fresh bread, but it had already lost the doughy warmth that Joshua and Rachel had enjoyed when she had first taken it from the clay oven.

"I'll prepare the best meal that I can for tonight," she suggested. "Now, while I get on with that why don't you and Joshua go out for a while to tell each other all your news?"

"Good idea," James agreed, and the two of them left the house to take a walk through the city.

By the time that James and Joshua returned, they had talked about almost every aspect of their separate lives over the past eighteen months. Joshua learned that James had been elected to the Sanhedrin Council and that the Hillel and Shammai debates were as fervent as they had always been. Joshua noted with interest the references that James made to the end time. It seemed that the question of resurrection was now a serious theological topic. The Pharisees apparently openly debated their belief in the resurrection of the body to an after-life as they embraced the current ideas on the end time. The Sadducees, however, refused to acknowledge any kind of resurrection and constantly reminded all in the Sanhedrin that only in the written word of the Law could truth be found and that the Law did not allow for resurrection.

"What do you think, James?" Joshua asked.

"I have to agree with the Sadducees that I would rather see the evidence in Scripture," he replied. "I am not as certain as many of the Jerusalem Jews that we are living in the end time. The Roman world is not all bad, as you and I have discussed many times. Why should God end this world at a time when it is possibly becoming more civilized than ever before? Look at the majesty of these Roman buildings that we now have in Jerusalem."

"The buildings are fine," Joshua quickly retorted, "but what about the vices? What about the gladiators trained to fight to the death for the amusement of the people? How can that be reconciled with: 'You shall not kill or set brother against brother?' Before I left, I heard that here in Jerusalem the Romans sometimes sell slave boys for sexual favors and that adultery is commonplace in their homes. How does that stand beside our Law?"

"We are Jews, Joshua. We do not have to try to live as the Romans do. We have our Law and they have their laws. Which law is Divine?"

"The Law of Moses," Joshua replied.

"Exactly. If we live by the Law of Moses, the Romans do not interfere with us. We gain the benefits of Roman peace and protection, but we do not have to change one thing about the way we live. In civil matters, we honor the Romans, but in religious matters, we honor our God."

"Render to Caesar the things that are Caesar's, and render to God the things that are God's," Joshua interjected.

"Precisely, Joshua. Aptly put."

"So you don't see the Roman occupation of our land as a symbol of the end time?"

"I'm really not much concerned with the end time," James replied. "This is why I can not get too excited over this resurrection issue. Unless the end time is imminent, is there any need for resurrection? Surely an afterlife can only exist when this world has passed away. So long as we live in this world we can only prepare ourselves by following the Law as best we can."

Joshua did not want to drop the subject. Something instinctively told him that the prophets of the end time might be right. *God is somehow going to intervene. I wonder if my role as a son of God and 'Prince of Peace' might not be part of that intervention.* He looked very thoughtfully at James, almost fearfully.

"What if God Himself came into our world as our messiah?" he suggested. "If God lived as one of us He would have to die, but James, it would be impossible for God to die. If God comes into our world He will have to be resurrected before the end time."

"That would put man on an equality with God," James replied nervously. "That's dangerous thinking. Actually, some would call that blasphemy. Why would God want to come into the world as one of us? Besides, who would believe such a thing? God will speak to us through our own prophets and our own messiah. We are His chosen people!"

Joshua remained silent. He could hear his own heartbeat as the world around him dissolved. Sweat formed on the nape of his neck and on the top of his hands. An inner voice cried out from within him. *Who was my father? Is this my role… to speak to my people as a son of God and to be the mouthpiece of God Himself as my father? Could the end time actually begin with my time?*

James's voice broke Joshua's trance:

"Are you all right? I hope I haven't upset you. I just cannot get very excited about resurrection and the end time. You can not believe how much senseless discussion there is about this subject from Pharisees in the Sanhedrin council chamber. They get so concerned over status in resurrection. They have come up with arguments such as this—'If a man has been married to several different wives all of whom die, which wife will he claim in the afterlife at the time of resurrection?' Better just to stick to the written Law, Joshua, that's what I think."

"I'm fine, James," Joshua responded pensively. "It's dark now and we've been walking a long time. Perhaps we had better get back to Rachel. She will be wondering where we are."

James put his arm around Joshua.

"It's good to have you back with us. How long are you going to be able to stay?" he said.

"Oh, only a day, or maybe two. I would like to come to the Temple tomorrow and offer up a sacrifice before I move on to Qumran. I think I had better start my journey the day after tomorrow."

They were passing one of the new gates into the Temple's Court of the Gentiles.

"Let's go on in and say our evening prayers before returning home," James suggested.

Together, they stood in the great court along with many other devout Jews, and they stretched out their arms to recite the well-known Shema.

Afterward, they returned to James' house and enjoyed the evening meal that Rachel had prepared. They feasted well and drank good wine. Their conversation turned to lighter topics. Joshua felt more relaxed. He reveled in the temporary freedom he was experiencing after the strict discipline of the Essenes. Finally, he received news of his family in Nazareth as James read from scrolls sent from Rabbi Eliezor.

Chapter Five

On the Road to Jericho

Joshua set out for Qumran early. He was anxious to complete his journey before the Sabbath. James and Rachel made sure that he had fresh bread and fruit to take with him. Rachel packed these in a box, which Joshua covered with a damp cloth and placed in the cart along with the two sacks of gold coins, still firmly tied with leather thongs, and a bundle containing some fresh linen and two white robes. Joshua took leave of James and Rachel, unhitched the mule and was on his way. Jerusalem seemed quiet other than the rumbling of the cart's wheels. A crescent moon hung over the city at this early hour, and as Joshua left the North Gate, the dawn began to spread out to the east.

Joshua felt that his life was about to take on a cataclysmic change. He was not sure of his instincts, but if they were correct he was fearful of their potential meaning. He had a new sense of his own importance and responsibility that had been encouraged by his talks with Rachel and James. The ideas that he had begun to form about his destiny were indeed frightening and dangerous, but they were also stimulating and exciting. He had begun to believe that he himself could be the Messiah, and that as a son of God he might possess Divine powers that had been given to him mysteriously through the circumstances of his birth. In deep thought, he set out on the road from Jerusalem to Jericho.

As the sun rose, he traveled down the familiar route from the north gate toward the Mount of Olives and the lush area known as Gethsemane. He passed the rough track that lead northeast to the rugged Essenic commune that he had now left. It gave him comfort to know that he was not returning there. The road then dipped as it skirted the Mount of Olives and followed the Kidron valley, rising up the far side to reach the small village of Bethpage. From here, there was a fine view. Joshua looked back. The bright colors of myrias of spring flowers merged from their dawn grayness, as the shadows cast by the Mount of Olives and the eastern ridge receded before the climbing sun. A lump formed in his throat.

"O Jerusalem! City of God!" Joshua cried out in the silence of the spring morning. "Jerusalem, you are blessed forever!"

He turned and pulled on the mule's tether.

"Up, old fellow," he instructed the beast. "We have a long way to go."

The mule plodded on and they left Bethpage behind. The road dropped through rocky terrain between the ridges until it reached the village of Bethany, where the reek of tanning leather polluted the fresh spring air.

At Bethany, Joshua stopped by the busy well. He refreshed himself and chewed slowly on a piece of Rachel's fresh bread. When his turn came, he fetched up water for the mule. By now, the sun had gained strength and the coolness of early morning had passed. The villagers were busy starting their day, and the young maidens gracefully carried their water pots high on their heads. Joshua didn't rest long for fear of not completing his journey before the Sabbath dusk. Besides this place smelled—a tanning village. He pulled on the mule, and began the slow and difficult descent down the rocky road from Bethany to Jericho.

It was easy for the mule to stumble on the loose stones and difficult at times to hold back the cart from rushing the beast as the cartwheels slithered over the uneven ground, gaining momentum on the downhill run. This was wild territory, a spur of the Judean wilderness running up between the Jordan valley and the Judean high country. Although, on this clear day, the Jordan valley was always visible below, the going was slow and it would take most of the day to cover the distance. The sun beat down on Joshua while its glare reflected off the stony ground. By late morning, it seemed that the most rugged part was past. The roadway leveled off, leaving the more dramatic craggy outcrops behind. Joshua pulled on the mule, and they made better progress approaching an area of large boulders.

Suddenly a group of brigands appeared as if from nowhere. They hurled stones at Joshua and the beast, forcing them to stop. A heavy missile hit Joshua on his right temple. He fell to the ground. The mule brayed. The men rushed at Joshua, beating him with heavy sticks. Joshua was too stunned and surprised to fight back, pain throbbing from his head wound. The brigands ripped off his simple leather tephillin, and rolled his now limp body into a hollow beside the roadway. Only half-conscious, and through blurry, blood-smeared eyes, Joshua painfully watched them help themselves to the contents of his cart and heard them shout for joy when they found the two sackcloth bags containing the golden coins. The sounds of their voices drifted in and out as Joshua's head continued to throb. More missiles flew. Several heavy stones landed on Joshua's back and legs and finally again hit his head. He blacked out.

When Joshua came around, the cart and mule were gone. He was abandoned, scarred, half-naked, and covered in blood. He tried to move, but his legs were lacerated and pinned down by heavy stones. When he turned his head, his wounds began to bleed afresh. He feared for his life as the afternoon sun beat down on his back, and ants crawled into the congealed blood of his cuts and abrasions. There was a deathly silence in the wilderness landscape.

At length, the sense of futility broke. Two men approached. Joshua made muffled cries to attract their attention. The younger man heard him and stepped over to where he lay.

"Leave him!" his companion shouted. "Don't touch him for he's unclean."

"But he's wounded and half-dead," the younger man protested.

"Come back here. Leave him, I say. Do you want to make yourself unclean for the Sabbath?"

The more compassionate man looked at Joshua one more time, and then walked on with his friend. As they left, Joshua could hear the younger man say that he thought Joshua would be dead by nightfall to which the other man replied:

"That is no concern of ours."

About an hour later, a lone traveler approached on his way from Jericho toward Jerusalem. Joshua weakly cried out again. The man heard him and came over, stooping to take a closer look. He saw Joshua's wounded head, and started to pick the rocks and stones off Joshua's lacerated back and legs.

"How long have you been here?" the stranger asked.

Joshua groaned with the pain as he tried to move.

The stranger took off his own outer robe, tearing it into strips. He took water from his traveling skin and soaking the strips began to bathe Joshua's wounds, clearing away the congealed blood, insects, and dirt.

"Where were you going?" the man asked.

"Qumran," Joshua feebly replied.

"You had better come home with me," the stranger continued. "It will take us some time in your condition. You've been badly beaten up. Can you move at all?"

Joshua turned on his side, but his whole body was racked in pain. The stranger tried to lift him up, but each time he did so, Joshua collapsed back into the hollow beside the roadway, wincing in agony.

"It will be difficult to get any kind of help here," the man said, thoughtfully. "Obviously, we're not going to be able to move far today. See if you can put your weight on my shoulder and I'll try to lift you up. We can't stay on the road all night, but there are caves in the rocks a little farther on. I'll stay with you there, and we'll see if we can get help from other travelers."

Joshua put his arms around the man's neck and shoulders, and made a massive effort to raise himself. Although in great pain, he found that it was a little easier when he was standing.

"That's better," the stranger noted. "Now, hold on as we try to take a step or two."

Very slowly, they made advances and moved away from the scene of the brutal attack toward the caves.

"Where are you from?" Joshua's rescuer asked him.

"Galilee."

"What's your name, then?"

"Joshua."

Well, Joshua, my name's Lazarus and I live in Bethany. I was on my way home after conducting business in Jericho. I'd hoped to be home tonight, but we'll get you there sometime tomorrow."

"Tomorrow's the Sabbath," Joshua cautioned. "You'll carry me on the Sabbath?"

"Of course. You are my wounded brother. It's the least that I can do for you. These bandits are always thieving and robbing. If I find someone unfortunate like you, I believe it's my obligation to take care of you. If we can't help each other, we certainly can't help ourselves."

"But, the Law would tell you that I am unclean and fit only to be left to die," Joshua insisted. "You've been contaminated by the blood of my wounds and now you're risking the wrath of the authorities by breaking Sabbath observance. Leave me at these caves, Lazarus. Don't contaminate yourself on the Lord's day. I'll survive. After the Sabbath, I will be able to journey on."

"With these wounds!"

Lazarus laughed.

"No, Joshua. You are coming with me to Bethany where my sisters and I can take care of you. The Law also tells us to love our neighbor as ourselves. What better way to love our neighbor than on the Lord's day?"

"May God bless you!" Joshua exclaimed, as he realized the deep sincerity of this man. "Many would have abandoned me, but you have saved me."

"Well, not yet, my friend," Lazarus cautioned. "I need to get you as comfortable as possible up in these caves and see how you are in the morning."

They hobbled a little farther and at length reached the place that Lazarus had in mind. As the long shadows of evening began to point to the valley, and the late afternoon sun hid behind the crags above, Lazarus made Joshua as comfortable as he could. He hadn't much water left, but what he had he shared and used to bathe the worst of Joshua's wounds. It was hard to sleep, and the spring night came in cold, but Joshua was alive, and Lazarus was aware that he had done all he could.

At dawn, Lazarus gave the last of his flat matzoth to Joshua before leaving him to get help.

"You will be safe here, and I'll be back with help as soon as I can," he said.

Then, after taking a drink, he left his cool goatskin of fresh water with Joshua.

* * *

Lazarus set off up the stony road, knowing that at the worst he would at least be able to get to Bethany by early afternoon and bring back a donkey for Joshua. He knew that it being the Sabbath he would have difficulty in persuading others to assist him. He had only gone a little way, when he heard horses behind him. It was a small detachment of Roman soldiers, the type that frequently patrolled the road from Jericho to Jerusalem. Knowing that the soldiers would not be Jews and Sabbath observers, he waved frantically to try to get them to stop. Somewhat to Lazarus' surprise, the little cohort of soldiers shuffled to a halt and their leader brought his horse alongside.

"A man needs help!" Lazarus shouted, pointing back down the road and gesticulating wildly.

He realized that the Roman probably didn't speak Aramaic, but he knew no other way to communicate. The leader of the cohort understood enough to see that this roadside stranger was seeking help. Being in charge of the Jericho patrol, he felt a moral duty to try to assist. He was also aware of the scheming plots of Jewish fanatics and wasn't going to fall into the trap of allowing this nobody to lead his men into an ambush. He shouted to the members of his cohort in Latin, and they separately rode out, forming a wide circle around their leader and Lazarus.

Lazarus continued to point back down the road, waving with his arm. The leader turned his horse, and signaled for Lazarus to show him the way.

It was less than an hour back to the cave where Joshua lay. Once there, again the Roman horsemen circled the area cautiously. Lazarus went into the cave and found Joshua where he had left him.

Although he was no longer bleeding, he was by now very stiff.

"I have help," Lazarus informed him. "They have horses, and I'm sure we can get you back to my village."

Joshua groaned rather feebly in acknowledgment.

Lazarus put his arm around Joshua's sore back and pulled him up.

"Try to hold on to me as I take your weight," he instructed as he stooped, taking Joshua's body on his back and pulling his arm around his neck.

They staggered out of the cave. Joshua screwed up his eyes, almost blinded by the bright light of day. He winced as the action intensified the pain from his head wounds.

The Roman gave a crisp, clear order, and the horsemen of the cohort closed in on Joshua, Lazarus, and their leader.

"Romans?" Joshua whispered to Lazarus.

"Whom else would you expect me to find out here on this road on a Sabbath?" Lazarus whispered back.

The leader gave additional orders.

Two of the men dismounted. They lifted Joshua up on one of their horses. Joshua groaned with pain, despite the genuine care that the men took. While one held Joshua in place, the other mounted behind him. The first soldier then roped Joshua's beaten body to his companion so that he would remain in the saddle.

The Roman commander continued to give orders, and the other mounted men spread out before and after Lazarus and the Roman carrying Joshua on his mount. The commander helped Lazarus up onto his own horse, and barely at a walking pace, they moved up the road toward Jerusalem.

Joshua groaned with the movement of the horse.

It was well into the afternoon before they arrived in Bethany. The soldiers dismounted to take refreshment at the well and water their horses. Lazarus attempted to explain that this was as far as they needed to go. Joshua, more bruised than ever after the hardship of the journey, which had opened many of the sores of his wounds again, heard Lazarus's remarks and, seeing the miscommunication, uttered a few feeble words of explanation in Greek. The Romans were surprised when they heard Joshua speak to them in the language of the empire, and respectfully helped him down so that Lazarus could take care of him.

Lazarus carried Joshua to a simple stone house in the village. Two Hebrew women greeted them and assisted Lazarus in helping Joshua into the house. The Roman members of the Jericho patrol, satisfied that they had done their duty, watched, and after freshening up, remounted and rode from Bethany toward Bethpage on the road to Jerusalem.

"Where did you find him?" one of the Hebrew women asked.

"He was badly beaten up and stoned, Martha. He was practically dead when I found him by the roadside down where the land begins to level off from the upper slopes."

They laid Joshua on a pallet.

"Fetch some clean water and cloths, Mary," Lazarus ordered the other woman. "We should try to clean his wounds."

Mary left, returning with a pitcher of clean water and several linen cloths. Together, she and Martha began to wash Joshua's body and clean the wounds.

"These are my sisters, Mary and Martha," Lazarus explained, as he watched them.

Joshua attempted a smile in acknowledgment, but the pain from his wounds caused him to grimace instead as Mary and Martha lovingly tried to clean them of dried blood and dirt. The painful procedure continued for some time, but as Joshua became more used to the stabs of pain, he began to relax in the comfort of knowing that these good people really cared. Martha fetched a jar of soothing balm, and dressed the wounds as best she could, wrapping the worst in cooling linens. Finally, they placed a clean robe around Joshua and left him to rest. Darkness descended. In relative comfort, Joshua drifted into sleep.

* * *

It was some time before Joshua's body and head wounds healed. Lazarus and his sisters continued throughout to take care of him. The two women helped him to gain strength as they propped him up to feed him, and later to help him shuffle a few steps at a time as he began to walk. Lazarus, one of Bethany's tanners, made Joshua two crutches, and for a couple of days Joshua was able to hobble around the village, gaining strength with every step he took. Then, he tried without the crutches, and to his great joy found that he could walk normally.

Joshua had never really had a close personal friend. He had always been with his family, especially James and his cousin Jon, and outside his marriage to Joanna, he had not developed any strong relationships. Even Joanna was James' sister-in-law. In those days at Bethany, however, as Joshua recuperated in the tanner's house, Lazarus and his two sisters became his firm friends. He had been so totally dependent on Mary and Martha. Mary was the quieter of the two, being the less industrious. Martha was always busying herself with something and even liked to assist her brother in the foul-smelling tannery. Mary, however, spent much of her time with Joshua, having more patience in nursing him back to health. Lazarus cut Joshua a new pair of sandals, and a leather girdle for his girth, using pieces from the smelly hides he cured. In a matter of days, Joshua was ready to continue his journey down to Qumran, but not before Lazarus invited many friends from the village to join them for a feast. Martha cooked all day, while Mary gathered vessels and pots from their friends. The villagers brought all manner of things with them to the feast, for Joshua had become a familiar sight to them hobbling around on his crutches. Besides, having Joshua convalesce with them, and knowing that one of them had saved Joshua's life, was one of the most exciting things that had happened to Bethany in years. In essence, the village was a rather unattractive place that had developed around its good supply of water and resultant tanning industry. It had taken Joshua some time to get used to the dreadful smell of the washed and cured hides, but it was easy to succumb to the sincerity and the warmth of the people.

They gave Joshua homespun garments, a water skin and flat matzoth for his journey. They even contributed a donkey for him to ride. At dusk, fires were lit in the street, and the feasting and dancing to send Joshua on his way, commenced. Joshua sat with Mary and Lazarus, enjoying the happy scene. It reminded him of weddings and the High Holy Days in Nazareth, but somehow, it was more spontaneous and less contrived. There was no rich man like Joachim ben Judah or Benjamin Levi to provide for this village. Here, everyone was poor, but they all seemed so generous.

Martha, along with many of the village girls, served the menfolk. Afterward, she joined them all in songs and circle dances, where they held hands and clapped with joy.

"I'm going to come with you tomorrow," Lazarus said, as he sat with Joshua watching the fun. "I'm not going to let you travel the road alone again and have to bring you back here half-dead."

"No, Lazarus. I'll be all right," Joshua replied. "Besides, if you come with me you will have to return alone."

"True, but I'm used to this road. Besides, I have nothing for them to steal."

Joshua reflected on the loss of his gold coins. *It hurts to think that I've lost this legacy that was entrusted to me*, he thought. *What would my mother think of me now?*

"You had a cart before, and some valuable contents," Lazarus continued. "You were easy prey for the brigands. I know how those people work. I'll be all right, believe you me, but I want to make sure of your safe passage down to Jericho."

"If you insist, Lazarus. What can I say? Of course I will be delighted if we can travel together. Will you have a donkey?"

"I can get a donkey. Gideon will lend me his. With two donkeys we are much less likely to be attacked than if traveling on foot."

The two friends picked up goblets of wine.

"My grateful thanks to you," Joshua declared.

They both drank.

"You know something, my friend," Joshua confided, "in the Essenic community I'm forbidden to drink, even at the covenant feast, although, if I join the sect I will have wine with the others on those occasions. The discipline is good for me I suppose, but I've missed the joy of wine. When I had my vineyard in Galilee, we grew good grapes and had excellent wine."

Joshua sipped on his wine like a connoisseur. He could tell it was rather rough, but Joshua enjoyed the richness of the drink.

"Excellent," he commented in gratitude, as he looked at his friend.

They drank together in contentment.

* * *

Mary stayed with her brother and Joshua most of the evening. This stranger who suddenly brought purpose back into their house captivated her. Neither she nor her sister had married, and both their parents had died in sickness just a year ago. After Lazarus took over their father's tanning business, life had gone on, but she had become withdrawn into herself after the grief of their loss. Joshua put a new ray of hope into her existence. She felt as if she had breathed new life into the wounded stranger, and she longed for his response. She was not unattractive, just reserved, unlike her sister Martha, who had overcome her grief by burying herself in the simple chores of daily living. Martha was more vivacious, and some of the village bachelors had started to court her after suitable mourning. Mary felt left out. Neither as much help to her brother in those struggling days after their loss, nor as admired as her sister by the menfolk around her, she was strangely drawn to this rough-looking stranger with penetrating eyes and light-brown hair, who somehow had dropped into their lives.

* * *

Joshua was obviously aware of Mary's constant attention, but expressed no feelings toward her other than gratitude for her tender care. Her glances in his direction seemed only to build up a wall between them. He still missed Joanna and his own loss in life. The wine, and his conversation with Lazarus, only seemed to bring this memory closer. Besides, he knew that if he was to follow through with his intentions to become fully initiated into the Essenes, chastity and total abstinence from all sexual impulses was a disciplinary requirement of the community. Family ties would hold members back from total love of the brotherhood, as their natural instinct to place family first would overrule the law of community love. Joshua dismissed Mary's glances, and with a certain feeling of frustrated guilt ignored her presence as they watched the festivities in the street.

At length, Lazarus and Joshua retired for the night, leaving the revellers. They needed to sleep and rest for their journey on the morrow. They slept until the crow of a rooster awakened Bethany to another day.

Joshua noted with pained embarassment Mary's warm embrace as they took their leave of the two sisters and set out on their journey.

"Thank you!" was all he could say to her as he turned to mount his donkey and wipe a tear from his eye.

The donkey carried a couple of water skins along with a small bundle of linen garments. There was barely room for Joshua to straddle the beast. Lazarus traveled light. As they set off, the refuse of the previous night's feasting lay littering the street. Although early, those who were up and about stood to cheer Joshua on his way, and the village that had held no attraction to Joshua when he had first traveled through, left its mark. Joshua felt a lump in his throat as they passed down the hill and the pungent odor of the tanneries faded in the clear air of the Judean wilderness. The donkeys started their steady clip-clop and gave out their occasional brays as they followed the tortuous track that led through this wilderness to Jericho.

"Your village seems so content and happy," Joshua commented to his friend. "Your people are so generous, and yet you have no synagogue and no guidance in observance of the Law. Has that ever bothered you?"

"We are not troubled by what we don't know," Lazarus answered. "Sometimes, our poverty can be our best protection. If I had observed the Law, my friend, I could not have rescued you from almost certain death because it was the Sabbath."

Joshua felt humbled by his friend's reply.

"Nature doesn't observe the Sabbath," Lazarus continued. "She rests when she can. One day is good for one thing and another for something else. It's like that with us in Bethany. We work when the conditions are right and we rest when we can. If we do not know the Law, Joshua, how can we break the Law?"

Joshua laughed.

"You make a lot of sense, and I can see that for the people of your village this works, but what will happen in the end time? Will God accept ignorance of the Law as an excuse when he separates the sheep from the goats? Are the ignorant poor ready to enter the Kingdom of God?"

Lazarus looked puzzled.

"Why must we believe that we are approaching the end time? Who says that there will be such a judgment?"

"That is my quest," Joshua replied. "We have lost our entity as Jews. Our land is occupied by foreigners."

"You mean the Romans?"

"Yes, of course, who else?"

"But it was Romans whom I was able to get to help rescue you," Lazarus insisted.

"I know. That's what makes it all the more strange. The Romans are not necessarily bad. They're just a symbol that the time is near. We don't know when, Lazarus, but it will happen when we least expect it, like a thief who comes in the night. We must be ready for the final judgment and the coming Kingdom of God. Like death we can not tell when it will be, but it will come to us all."

"What advice would you give to us then, who have no rabbi, no leader to show us the way?" Lazarus asked. "Are we doomed? Will there be no place for us in the kingdom of which you speak?"

"Oh yes! There will be a place for people like you, Lazarus. I have learned so much from staying with you, and your friends, and the people of your village. It will be harder for a rich man to enter the kingdom of heaven than for you who are poor. You may not have worldly goods, but you have the spirit of God... the greatest treasure of all. When a man shows compassion and there is love and mercy, the kingdom is already established. Remember the words of Micah: 'What does the Lord require of us, but to do justice, to love kindness and to walk humbly with our God.' You have the Law in your hearts, for it is written: 'You shall love the Lord your God with all your heart, and love your neighbor as yourself.' The Law leads to such love, but such love does not need the Law."

Lazarus looked intently at Joshua.

"You speak like a prophet or a soothsayer, Joshua. Who are you? Whom did I rescue from the jaws of death?"

"A man on his way from Jerusalem to Jericho," Joshua replied. "A man seeking out his destiny, unsure of where he is going. I live with the Essenes, but I am not sure that I am really one with them, although I do believe I will find Qumran more rewarding than my experiences in that commune at Anathoth. I need time, Lazarus. We all need time, but time is precisely what we may not have. I pray that God will reveal His destiny for me. As I said, I learned much from being with you and your sisters in Bethany. I have learned a little more about humility. We are always learning. God is always reaching out to us, showing us the way, and we must accept His challenge and walk with Him in our daily life. Blessed be God forever, Lazarus, and blessed be you for rescuing me, and teaching me so much."

Lazarus looked mystified. Joshua spoke with such authority and yet with such humility.

They rode on in silence for a while until they passed the spot where Lazarus had found Joshua beside the road.

"That's where you were!" Lazarus exclaimed, pointing at the hollow still filled with the stones that the brigands had hurled at Joshua's wounded body.

Joshua looked down, stopped his donkey, and stared ahead at the parched terrain of the lower slopes. The wild flowers had stopped blooming now. The landscape looked more remote, barren, and desolate.

"It was your luck that I should have been traveling this country that day," Lazarus said, a little impatient that Joshua seemed to be so distant.

"Maybe it was God's will," Joshua replied.

Joshua turned around, smiled at Lazarus, and then kicked his donkey. Swiftly, the two friends traveled the easier ground of the lower slopes. By early afternoon, they reached the fertile plains of the Jordan valley.

They made a camp for themselves in an olive grove just outside Jericho. The air was stifling after the purer atmosphere of the high country. There was no breeze, and the presence of scattered date palms among the olives, with their long feathering fronds, reminded Joshua of his Egyptian childhood. As the stars appeared in the night sky above, he lay in the grove with thoughts of those days. He remembered how he had lain then, looking up at the stars, wondering what his destiny would be. Silently, he prayed: *Lord God Almighty, help me to understand Your will for me. Reveal to me the fullness of my destiny as I submit myself once more to the disciplined life of the Essenes. Guide me, Lord, and help me to know who I am and what Your purpose really is for me.*

Lazarus was already snoring as he lay on his back, his head resting on his donkey's saddlecloths. In the humid heat of the night valley he smelled of the tannery, but the goodness of Lazarus' heart had lifted Joshua to new heights of hope.

Blessed are the poor for theirs is the Kingdom of God and blessed are the meek for they shall inherit the earth, Joshua thought, looking at his friend. He was reminded of a story that he had heard with James long ago in the great synagogue in Alexandria. As he himself drifted into sleep, the story unfurled again like a dream…

There was a rich man clothed in purple and fine linen that feasted sumptuously every day, and at the entrance gate to his house lay a poor man covered in sores whose name was Lazarus. Lazarus ate the slops of food that were thrown out at the gate of the rich man's palace, and dogs came by and licked at the poor man's sores. Lazarus soon died, and angels swooped down and lifted him up into the arms of Abraham where his sores vanished and he lived in radiant light. The rich man also died. He was buried in a magnificent tomb with his treasures, but his body was taken from there and thrown down into a flaming pit. From the pit the rich man could look up and see Abraham far away. He could see that Lazarus, who had always lain at his gate, was now seated in Abraham's arms. He called out to Abraham:

"Father Abraham, have mercy on me, now. Rescue me from this pit of fire, or at the very least send the poor man down here with water to cool my tongue."

Abraham answered him from afar:

"Son, remember that you in your lifetime received your good things whereas Lazarus had nothing. Now, he is comforted here, and you are in anguish down there. Between us there is a great gulf through which no man can travel."

The rich man in his frustration called out to Abraham again:

"Then, I beg you Father, send Lazarus back to my father's house as I have five brothers. Let him warn them of their shortcomings so that they, too, will not end up here where I am."

Abraham answered:

"They have Moses and the prophets; let them hear them..."

Half memory, half dream, the story ended.

Joshua slept soundly beside Lazarus in the peace of the olive grove.

* * *

At dawn, Lazarus and Joshua parted company. Joshua traveled on down the Jordan valley toward the Salt Sea in search of the monastery at Qumran, while Lazarus journeyed back to Bethany on the craggy road from Jericho. In the separate silences of their journeys, each contemplated on the tremendous impression that their presumed chance meeting had made on the other.

Chapter Six

Palmyra

Linus proudly wore the uniform of a centurion. He had now been stationed with Governor Questus' Syrian Legion for just over three years, but he did not find Damascus all that stimulating. He would rather have been in Antioch, the most prosperous center of Syrian politics. The governor did not show him any particular favors, excepting on the three occasions that Linus' father had journeyed north to visit him. It was obvious then that Flavius Septimus was more anxious to meet with the governor than to see his son. Damascus duty was boring. The Parthian threat had diminished to nothing, and army life had become a drudgery of discipline and training. It was with considerable relief, therefore, that Linus found himself called by the governor to head an unusual expedition.

The governor greeted Linus as the centurion was led into the audience room at Questus' Damascus headquarters:

"Centurion Flavian, welcome. Come on in."

Linus removed his helmet and advanced toward the governor who beckoned him to be seated. Questus pulled his chair closer to that of Linus with an air of confidentiality.

"Young Flavian, I have a task for you that might prove interesting and could certainly be profitable to us all."

At last, Linus felt important. Perhaps his time in Damascus had been politically worth it after all.

"Now that a lasting peace seems to have settled in our province, new opportunities have arisen for trade," Questus continued. "We are not getting the maximum reward from trade that we could. The Syrian Semites to the northeast and the Nabataeans in Arabia are growing rich on the profits of oriental trade, filling their coffers at the expense of our seaports on the coast of the Levant, notably Tyre and Caesarea. They are even cutting into the profits of Antioch on the Orontes. Palmyra, which was a battered outpost during the Parthian wars, is now flourishing. This Semitic city stands in a well-watered oasis right on the borders of our province and Parthia. The rich trade routes from India and Cathay converge there, bringing enormous wealth to this once battered region."

The governor looked at Linus intently.

"I need to know more about Palmyra, Centurion Flavian. I need to pave the way for a trade treaty with these crafty Semites that will be beneficial both to them, on the outskirts of our Empire, and to us. Palmyra controls this important Syria-Euphrates trade route, just as Petra controls the routes through the southern deserts to Judea and Egypt. We can't let these independent centers become all-powerful. Better that we be their partners rather than their strong neighbors to the west."

Linus listened intently. *At last a challenge,* he thought, *an opportunity to win back my father's respect.*

Governor Questus raised his eyebrows confidentially.

"This must not seem like a military expedition, Centurion Flavian," he said. "I will send you out with twenty men of whom only five will be soldiers. You will also have a support team of ten additional men as bearers for your supplies. You and the soldiers will ride horses, but the men will ride camels. A mule train will carry your supplies. I've chosen you to lead this expedition because of your expertise in Aramaic."

Momentarily, Linus thought of Maria. He knew his relationship with the 'Hebrew whore' as his parents refered to her, had greatly helped his fluency in Aramaic.

"The Palmyrians are very independent." Questus continued. "They have never been officially recognized as a part of Syria. Although they use Greek, their first language is Aramaic."

A friendly smile then crossed the governor's face as he could see he had caught Linus' attention and imagination.

"Your father's decision to raise you in Galilee may yet have its purpose. You are good for Syria, Linus Flavian, because you understand our province."

"Thank you, sir."

The governor suggested that Linus leave in about a month.

"This could be important to us all, Linus Flavian," he intimated. "Can I rely on your help?"

"Certainly, sir!" Linus answered enthusiastically. "Would you prefer I select the soldiers from those under my charge?"

"Yes, centurion. You have freedom to pick your own men. Good luck to you, and we will be in touch with you again very soon."

Linus stood and saluted the governor, placing his right hand across his chest. He picked up his helmet, and moved toward the door. The governor's escort then showed him out, and Linus, elated, returned to his barracks.

In a few days, Linus got his expedition together. With the governor's blessing, they left for the desert road north.

* * *

Dawn brought its rose and then amber light to the stony desert after the first night of their mission. Linus ordered his men to strike camp and load the mule train. Pockets of thorns and sage, and occasional gray-leafed palms marked the indentures in the flat plain that held what little moisture there was in this hostile region. This was no man's land, the desert fringe of the Roman world, pocked only by this string of small oases that curved from Damascus across the barren landscape to the riches of the Euphrates valley and the bounty beyond. The amber light gave way to a yellow and white light as the sun rose, and the chill of the cold desert night air warmed to the early rays of this new day.

Their camel train had not traveled far when a larger one approached from the east. At first, it was a moving blur on the horizon, but as the camels came closer, Linus could see that this was a sizeable group of traders. Linus called his men to a halt.

The camel train came alongside. There must have been forty camels altogether, and with them there were also heavy carts pulled by mules that carried wild beasts and exotic dancing girls. Some of the merchants shouted greetings of which the traditional 'Salaam' of the desert was all that could be universally understood. Linus returned greetings in Aramaic. Several of the drovers smiled and touched their foreheads in salutation. One of the caged wagons that passed was filled with sad-faced women, young and lithe, who had been sold into slavery. They were dark-skinned, with wide flashing eyes and long waves of hair. For a moment, Linus was reminded of Maria. It was something about long waves of black hair.

"Persians, or even from the far reaches of India," he suggested nonchalantly to his aide, Jairus, as his horse pawed at the ground and whinnied with boredom.

The wagon rolled on, followed by camels laden with silks from Cathay and sweet balms from the East. Jairus protected his face as the dust swirled upward. Linus waved his arm up and forward. Their party began to move onward as the last of the camel train passed them by. With ease, they followed the recent track made by the passing merchants in the desert road. Within about two hours, they reached the large oasis where the travelers had obviously passed the previous night, but it was too early to stop and Linus only let them stay long enough to water their animals and fill their skins before he pressed them on toward Palmyra.

It was a full two-day journey before they came to the oasis city. At first, Palmyra appeared as a dark green island in the flat, rocky desert, but when they entered the city the buildings emerged from the lush foliage of this huge oasis. They were not Greek structures nor were they obviously Parthian. Here and there a portico, or columned architrave showed evidence of past Hellenism, but for the most part they were Semitic, being large, flat-topped buildings with outside steps, or enlarged versions of those found throughout the Levant. Even the palm fronds seemed bigger, fanning out from the ground and sheltering stems laden with dates. Only in the Jordan valley could such palms be found in Judea. The massive fronds made each building seem like it was set in a garden. There was a lushness and obvious appearance of wealth and prosperity in the setting, making such a contrast to the arid acres of desert all around.

Linus and Jairus led their caravan into the inner part of the city. The lush greenery gave way to more concentrated buildings. The street leading to the center was wide, but to either side, narrow passages echoing with the sound of merchant cries ran between the buildings, exuding the customary smells of dung and freshly baked loaves. Streams of urine mingled with the discarded rinds of watermelons, to be soaked up in the dust and dirt. Owners and aimless wanderers in search for a deal, shouted at their mules and camels. They bargained with the merchants, whose wares were laid out under colorful awnings that now lined the way. The street opened into a square surrounded on three sides by busy merchant stalls and camel lots. Ahead of them on the fourth side, and still under construction, stood a Temple. It was built more like the sanctuary of the Holy of Holies in Jerusalem than any Greek or Roman structure. This was truly a Semitic temple around which men, presumably priests, sold doves and goats for sacrifice. A pall of smoke rose up from a fatty altar that stood before the entrance, reminiscent of the great bronze altar in front of the Jerusalem sanctuary. There was no statue of the emperor here as in the Roman temples that showed the patronage of the empire. The priests, however, were swift to gain their reward from strangers. No sooner had Linus stopped his caravan than these temple servants surrounded them, calling out in Aramaic for their temple denarii.

"Pay them, Jairus," Linus instructed, as he listened to their demands.

"How many camels in your train?" the Semitic priest demanded.

"Fifteen," Linus answered.

"And mules?" the priest added.

"Ten, sir," Linus assured him.

"There's a fee of five denarii for each camel or mule," the man replied. "After you have paid these temple dues you must register with the Tariff Master. Are you traveling on to Parthia and the Euphrates valley?"

"No, sir. We want to buy here in Palmyra direct, and transfer goods to Damascus."

"Ah, well, that will be different. You will need to register before you depart. Meanwhile, welcome to our city."

The wily priest started to count the camels and mules.

"Let me see, you say you have twenty-five camels or mules here."

"Yes, sir," Linus replied.

"That's one hundred and twenty-five denarii for them. Now, what about your horses? Do I see six horses?"

"That's correct," Linus confirmed.

"The horses will cost you two denarii each. That's twelve denarii for the horses and one hundred and twenty-five denarii for the camels and mules, my friend. I think that totals one hundred and thirty-seven denarii altogether."

Jairus unsaddled the treasury bag and paid out these temple dues.

The priest poured the coins into a sack that he tied with a cord.

"Would you like us to make a sacrifice on your behalf?" he asked, looking up with a superior swarm. "We would be pleased to sacrifice seven doves on your behalf."

"You have our money, my friend," Linus answered. "Do with it what you will. It is no matter to us if you make sacrifices on our behalf. Put the money toward your building. I see that you have not yet finished the structure."

Linus touched his forehead in salutation.

"Salaam," he said, before motioning his caravan onward.

He suggested to Jairus that they return the way they had come, and make camp on the city outskirts among the lush date palms near the main entrance. Once they were on their way and out of the square, Linus opened up his feelings on their treatment thus far, and how to set about making the deal that was their commission.

"I can see these people are spoiled, growing fat on the extortion of easy passage money. No wonder we've been commanded to strike a deal with them for Rome. There's easy money in trade tariffs."

"Surely, the Parthians can see how Palmyra is benefiting from this trade," Linus' aide commented.

"Exactly, Jairus. That's why the governor wants us to seal a treaty with these independent Semites first. Remember that the Parthians are already making money off the caravans coming up the Euphrates valley. Merchants pay nearly one hundred times more in Antioch and Caesarea than the traders do at the source. It's all passage money, and on the excuse that Palmyra could still be the envy of the Parthian hoards, we need to strike a deal here to gain a portion of this easy money for Rome in exchange for guaranteed protection."

"Why don't we just annex Palmyra?" Jairus suggested.

"It's just too far for easy supply lines. We'd have to keep a large permanent garrison here," Linus answered. "Such a garrison might actually provoke Parthian attack rather than deter it. This is a buffer area. Governor Questus is right. We need these people as independent allies. A garrison would cost us, but a trade deal will simply enrich us. We must make them feel that they need our ultimate protection while guaranteeing them their freedom. That's why we won't argue over their high tariffs and dues, Jairus. I saw the way you eyed that Semitic priest."

"Well, it was a bit steep, sir. After all, we aren't even carrying any goods."

"It was steep, Jairus, but the higher the tariffs are here, the bigger the commission that Rome can take. We should not discourage them. This is business, my friend, but it's also diplomacy. This is why we're here."

The bustle of the inner city gave way to the lush groves of date palms once again, and the two adventurous soldiers led their men to a suitable place to set up camp.

During the course of the next three months, Linus and his men watched the business practice of the Semitic priests and Tariff Master's office as they lined their pockets on the easy passage money of passing caravans. About once every five days, a large train would approach Palmyra from the east, and almost daily, groups of travelers would seek rest at the inviting oasis in the desert. Each time, fees were extracted. It was time now for Linus to make his move and seek a deal with the Tariff Master.

The offices of the Tariff Master were above a large hall where several Palmyrian agents measured the quantities of spices and precious salt and counted the wares of the worried merchants. If a merchant could pay his way at all the stops along the long trade route to the seaports of the Roman world, he knew that he would do well, for the Romans paid a heavy price for these luxury goods. Many, however, could not pay the demands in passage money, and fell victims to the system along the way. Other merchants would then buy up their goods and even their camels, and carry the goods onward to rich rewards on the Syrian coast. Palmyra was often the scene of such exchanges, being the last, and one of the most expensive, of all the tariff stops. There was always, therefore, much wheeling and dealing outside the Tariff Master's Hall. Rich merchants in Palmyra brought up stocks of goods discarded cheaply by less fortunate kinsmen, and traded them to others at even higher prices. It was such a merchant that Linus had befriended, and who was able to gain him an audience with the Tariff Master.

Linus took Jairus with him, and they made their way through the melee of traders to climb up the wooden steps that led up from the Tariff Hall to chambers above. There, they were presented to the Tariff Master. The city was governed by an oligarchy of the most powerful merchants, but the Tariff Master was the most influential of the few. He greeted the Roman strangers cautiously.

"Please be seated, my friends," he said, pointing at two wooden chairs with leather seats in an otherwise sparsely furnished room.

Sitting back in his own chair, he stroked his long, dark and curling beard. His eyebrows were bushy, bristling, and quizzically raised as he posed his first question:

"What have you come to discuss? I understand that you are from Damascus. We send many merchants to Damascus on their way to the ports of Tyre, Ptolemais, and Caesarea."

"In the Roman peace, Master, we have all gained much from trade with the Orient," Linus acknowledged.

The Tariff Master smiled smugly, as he looked at the rings on his slender fingers.

"Yes, my friend," he agreed. "This is a prosperous time for us all."

"Rome has never interfered with your operation here in Palmyra, Master," Linus continued. "We have always felt that you knew best how to marshal the great benefits that come from this oriental trade."

"Quite so, my friend," the Tariff Master agreed.

"The Syrian governor, however, the noble Questus, has expressed some concern that the excellence of your endeavors could stand in danger from Parthian greed," Linus indicated.

At this, the Tariff Master again raised his black bushy eyebrows.

"Have you evidence of fresh Parthian attacks, my friend?" he asked with concern.

"No, Master. It seems that the Roman peace holds well," Linus intimated. "However, should the Parthians realize the enormous profits being made here in Palmyra, they might in their greed, want to absorb your city and make it one of theirs."

"And Rome! Has Rome no designs to do the same?" the Tariff Master asked sarcastically.

"No, Master. It is not in the government's mind that Imperial Legions should take control of your city. Rather, Master, we would like to offer you a partnership. We would like to guarantee the independence and safety of your Semitic city in exchange for a share of the passage money to be made here."

The Tariff Master shook his head and momentarily looked away.

"You expect me to pay tribute to Rome!" he said angrily.

"Not exactly, Master. We are offering you the protection of Syria against the possibility of Parthian greed. The Parthians have seemingly settled their differences with Rome, but Palmyra is in no man's land. You do not belong to the Syrian province of the empire nor are you within the lands of the Parthians. Your oasis is rich and a crossroads for trade. The Parthians will surely consider this, and in time will seek to annex your city to their chain of outposts. I repeat, Master, Rome has no designs on your territory, merely on our alliance. If you have the security of knowing that the legions in Damascus and Antioch will support you, your position as the most influential trading post in the desert trail will be assured. That protection will be guaranteed if we can make a deal on the percentage of the profits."

"You don't call that tribute!" the Tariff Master hastily interjected with continued dismay.

"No, Master, I call it a business deal. For every sum that you can make from the passing merchants you will share a part with the Syrian Province. You will not be subject to any regulations from Antioch or Damascus, nor will we interfere with any of your practices in trade and mart. Your temple taxes will remain your personal prerogative. We would not dream of interfering with your religious practices or the flow of income that comes from your temple here. Our deal is purely a business proposition, Master. We ask for only one seventh part of the tariffs raised, which can be banked with an agent whom we will appoint right here in Palmyra."

"One seventh, my friend! A seventh part of all that we gain!" the Tariff Master derided.

"Yes, Master. One seventh part," Linus insisted.

The Tariff Master stroked his beard nervously.

"Let me think on it," he said slowly. "You drive a hard bargain, but you do assure us that our independence will be guaranteed?"

"Guaranteed, Master. In the name of Tiberius Caesar and the noble Questus, Governor of Syria, I give you my word," Linus proclaimed.

The Tariff Master rose from his chair.

"Return here tomorrow," he said.

Linus and Jairus stood up and touched their foreheads pronouncing their good wishes for a happy conclusion to this deal.

"Salaam!" they said.

The Tariff Master replied in kind. Linus and Jairus left his presence to return to the crowd of bargaining merchants in the melee below.

"Do you think he will agree?" Jairus asked.

"I think so," Linus replied. "Independence is very important to all Semites. He wants to protect the independence of Palmyra more than a seventh of their income. Besides, I know the Semitic mind, Jairus. They will soon make up the seventh part by raising the tariffs even higher. Then, more merchants will be forced to sell off their goods before they reach the coast."

"Yes, Jairus, and we can send in Roman caravans just like ours to pick them up. Goods bought here in Palmyra will be cheaper than those bought in Antioch, Tyre, or Caesarea, and even though the Palmyrians will tax them on leaving, remember that one seventh of that tax will be coming back to Rome."

Jairus laughed. He slapped Linus on the back.

"You're cunning, Linus. You're as wily as the Jews in the land that you love."

Linus smiled, but his voice remained serious:

"You can't trade with a Semite unless you think like a Semite. Now, let's see how our merchants have been doing. I want our camels to be loaded with the best silks and balms that we can carry. We have to prove the worth of our deal to the governor on our return."

The Tariff Master refused to see Linus the next day. He kept him waiting for three whole days. Then, he granted him another audience.

"I have discussed your proposition at length," the Tariff Master begun. "My friend, the Palmyrian leaders have agreed to your scheme for one tenth of our profits."

"One seventh!" Linus replied thumping his chair.

The Tariff Master looked uncomfortably serious.

"One tenth!" he repeated.

"No, Master," Linus replied. "We proposed one seventh."

"Would you not compromise on one eighth?" the Tariff Master countered.

"No, Master! I gave you Caesar's word. One seventh it is or I shall leave and there will be no deal."

Jairus could feel the sweat beads forming on the nape of his neck. They were so close, and yet Linus might destroy all that they had achieved in driving his bargain.

"One eighth!" the Tariff Master repeated sternly.

Linus rose to leave. Jairus, cold with the thought of their failure, joined him, but without taking his eyes off the Tariff Master, who stood stroking his beard contemplatively.

"One seventh, as you say," the Tariff Master said gravely.

"One seventh!" Linus repeated as he turned to face the Semite once again.

The Tariff Master's face relaxed.

"Let us drink a cup of wine and draw up documents giving authority to our deal," he proclaimed.

Linus also relaxed, knowing he had not let the Tariff Master get the better of him. Jairus felt a load fall from his back as a hot flush swept across his face. A servant brought them cups of cool wine, and a scribe began to draw up the necessary documents. Linus had a deal. He could take it back to Questus holding his head up high. The provisional documents would be signed and sealed in his name—'Linus Flavian, Centurion.'

"You speak good Aramaic for a Roman," the Tariff Master noted.

"I was brought up in Galilee, my friend," Linus replied.

Jairus remained speechless, but he had learned the art of the deal.

Chapter Seven

Antonias

As the new town of Tiberias grew on the hillside overlooking the Galilean lake, so it attracted more and more Romans from all over the Syrian Province. Tiberias was a town with a free spirit. Unlike most Roman cities, Tiberias did not grow up on a trade route or house a garrison, but developed because of the beauty of its location as a retreat for wealthy Romans—a place for rest and recreation for those serving in the province. It was no wonder that the town's brothel thrived.

Maria and Delilah both proved themselves to be the most popular girls of the Roman matron's troupe. Men, snared by Delilah's classic beauty and Maria's sensuality, came back again and again. But Maria's baby was now nearly three and it was hard to leave the child, especially now that Marcus could freely move around. Delilah had been very good about sharing time with the boy, but the novelty was wearing off. There were days when Maria felt obligated to her son, and missed her turn at the brothel. On such occasions, Delilah did her best to cover Maria's time, but Maria's special clients felt cheated and began to complain. This problem was resolved in the strangest way.

Maria met Antonias, a wistful Roman, whose father, Syllus, had been stationed in Damascus and Caesarea Philippi, and had built himself a vacation villa in Tiberias. His father was rarely at the villa, and Antonias lived there alone with dreams of becoming a poet.

Antonias first came to the brothel more out of boredom than anything else. He had expressed no preferences, and was appointed to Maria's booth because he was next in turn. Their first meeting was perfunctory to say the least. It was almost as if Antonias felt some guilt or shame in being in the brothel as he hastily disrobed and pumped himself into Maria. There was no gentle playfulness or physical enjoyment. He barely looked at her as he withdrew, hastily dressed himself, and left. It was a week before he returned, and again he sat and waited his turn.

Maria was not used to men passing through her booth without some sense of special fulfillment. She oozed sexuality, and her breasts caused the shiest of men to at least stare in appreciation, if not to touch. Antonias had been a cold customer. For that reason, if no other, she recognized him when he parted the drape and peered into her booth.

Maria smiled dutifully, although a slight sense of disappointment could not be denied. Maria always felt that if she had to make her living this way she might as well enjoy it, but she remembered only too well what little pleasure this man had given her. She beckoned Antonias to enter.

Antonias wore a toga, which he removed with the same cold precision as on the previous week. Maria observed him closely. He was actually surprisingly good-looking, with dark, curly hair and a fine body, but he was shy and nervous, showing no joy and emotion. She was quite surprised when he spoke to her, and doubly so that he spoke in Aramaic.

"You're a Hebrew woman, aren't you?" he asked.

Maria was not used to hearing her clientele address her in her own language, and she never understood the men who babbled on their shouts of ecstasy in Greek and Latin. She looked up at him.

"Yes, I'm a Jew. Am I the first Hebrew woman you've had?" she asked.

Antonias blushed.

"Yes..." he stammered.

"You are not used to coming to places like this, are you?" Maria asked directly.

"No..." he stammered again.

"Why did you come back?"

"I don't know, curiosity I suppose."

Maria smiled at him, this time with sincere compassion.

"Come here, you poor curious Roman," she said invitingly. "When I've finished with you today you'll want to come back every day. What is your name?"

"Antonias," he replied.

Maria took Antonias' hands and placed them on her breasts. She sensed his growing excitement as he felt her nipples harden. She educated him slowly, using every trick she knew, and the Roman did, indeed, appear to feel a satisfaction that he had not shown on his previous visits.

After his fulfillment, Antonias lay beside Maria for some time. He was no longer nervous, but enveloped in a great calm. He could have slept there, but Maria would not let him.

"You must leave," she said, shaking him as he dozed. "You can't stay. There are others waiting."

"When can I see you again?" Antonias asked pathetically.

"You can come here anytime. Ask for Maria, but on alternate days."

"That's your name, then…Maria?"

"Yes. Now, you must hurry. Get dressed."

Antonias put on his tunic and toga.

"Will you be here all day the day after tomorrow?" he asked.

"From midday until sundown and possibly later," Maria answered impatiently. "You must go!"

Antonias left.

Maria swiftly straightened the linens, then, took up her customary seductive pose. The curtain opened and a middle-aged man with a wicked leer looked in.

On her next working day, Maria wondered each time the curtain opened, if Antonias would be there. She had developed certain sympathies for him, and at least he shared her language. He was sexually a challenge, but her profession was full of challenges. But… Antonias never came. Maria faked her way through a series of sexual exploits with a succession of over-excited men until the sun set and there was nobody seated in the marble courtyard. The night girls were now ready to receive their regular patrons. The Roman matron dismissed Maria for the day.

Dressed in her simple shift and thong sandals, Maria left the brothel. As she turned into the narrow street with its steps going down to the market place, the light of the burning wall torches illuminated the luster in her free flowing hair. The street was usually empty after dark. Maria was always a little afraid until she reached the open light of the market's square. Sometimes, strange men would hover in the shadows and chide the girls as they left the brothel. They were more an irritation than a danger, but once in a while the perverted would pounce. She hurried on down the steps.

"Maria!" came a voice from the shadows.

Maria faltered instinctively, turning toward the voice. From a niche in the wall, Antonias came forth. As he came toward her, Maria moved away, until she had trapped herself against the far wall.

"No! Antonias, leave me alone!" she yelled, her arms stretched out, gripping the stones behind her in fear as she stood there helplessly.

"Maria," Antonias replied, "I haven't come to harm you. I just wanted to see you."

He reached out toward her, showing his hands held no weapon, and he beseeched her to join him.

Maria eased up in her fear. Putting her arms down, she stepped toward him.

"Antonias, you scared me so. What are you doing here?" she asked.

"Like I said, Maria. I just wanted to see you. Where are you going? Can I walk with you?"

"If it will please you," Maria answered rather coolly, but relieved. "I'm going home. I've finished for today. You can find me in the brothel in two days time if you like, but right now I must go home to my child."

"You have a child?" Antonias asked with surprise.

"Yes! A Roman boy! Is that such a surprise?"

"I suppose that's a risk you take in your profession," Antonias said calmly. "Why didn't you drown the infant? That's what I understand most of you do."

In the darkness of the narrow street, Maria slapped Antonias across the face.

"Who do you think you are?" she shouted. "My life is none of your business!"

Fearfully, she immediately regretted her action. The Roman could make serious trouble for her. At the very least, he could have her removed from the brothel—her livelihood. But, to her surprise, Antonias didn't retaliate. He apologized.

"I'm sorry, Maria. I don't understand. You wanted to keep your baby?"

"My baby was not born out of the brothel," Maria answered proudly. "He was a child conceived in real love. I owe it to his father to give our son all that I can. Now, if you don't mind, let me go home."

"Can I come with you?" Antonias begged again.

"Why are you trailing me?" Maria cried.

"Because you intrigue me. You Jews intrigue me. I want to learn more about you. Let me walk with you to where you live."

Maria had her own curiosity about the Roman.

"I suppose you're harmless enough," she said. "I'm sorry, I should not have hit you. You really are a very strange young man. Walk with me if you wish, but please, don't scare me like that again."

The young man was obviously painfully shy, and yet he had been bold enough to wait for her in the dark. He had a tacit determination to get his way, but at the same time a graciousness that she rarely experienced in the men that used her and abused her. He seemed well educated and yet he didn't appear to have any purpose in life. He was probably lonely. *Who is this Antonias?* Maria thought. *Why has he put himself upon me?*

They reached the brighter area of the market place where the aroma of spices greeted them. The Forum was closed on three sides, but the fourth was open to the shore of the lake. An exaggerated orange moon had begun to rise, making broken reflections on the water's surface. Antonias stared at the moon seemingly lost in its wonderment. The peace on the lake contrasted with the bustle in the market place, where lamps and braziers illuminated the marble columns and frieze of the architrave that covered the merchants' stalls.

"The lake is so beautiful," Antonias remarked at length.

Then, he turned and tried to kiss Maria.

She pulled away, still wary of the Roman.

"Don't! We are not in the brothel!"

Antonias respected her reticence.

"It is not surprising that so many of us Romans have chosen to settle here," he continued in a matter of fact way that covered up his emotions. "Tiberias has grown up overnight. When my father came here just four years ago, they had barely begun. This market place was just a shingle beach."

"I know," Maria said a little impatiently. "I've been here for over three years myself."

"Where did you come from?" Antonias inquired "There wasn't a Hebrew village here before we Romans started to build Tiberias."

"Magdala" she answered.

"Is that Taricheae?"

Wistfully, she looked up at the moon. Her voice softened:

"Yes…according to you Romans, but it's Magdala to us. The people there turned on me because I was carrying a Roman child in my womb. My own mother rebuked me, and I decided to leave. I walked along the lakeshore until I reached this place. Here, I met Delilah, one of the girls from the brothel, and we've made our home together ever since. Delilah helped with the birth of my baby and she has been wonderful in caring for both of us."

Maria looked at Antonias again. She realized that she was becoming emotional.

Antonias held her momentarily, lightly kissing her hair.

At first, Maria did not resist, but then frustrated by her own weakness she broke loose.

"Why am I telling you all this?" she said. "I need to get home to Delilah and my boy."

She crossed the square and set off toward her home; but he followed her. She couldn't shake him.

"Have you no home to go to?" Maria asked.

"Yes. I'm living in my father's villa. My father and mother are in Antioch and they won't be back for a long time."

Thoughts of Linus and the Roman villa above Magdala ran through Maria's mind.

When they reached the vaulted dwelling beside the street where she and Delilah had made their home, Maria turned and faced Antonias. She knew that she must either tell him to leave her alone, or she would have to accept his childish persistence, and warm toward him. He was an irritation, but if she did tell him to leave her alone he would only have to come back to the brothel to find her. Deep down, she felt he was a good man. Despite his persistence, he had a gentleness that she had not encountered in most Romans. He, Linus, and Linus' father, were also the only Romans that she could recall who also made the effort to speak her language.

Antonias interrupted her train of thought.

"If you're not going to be at the brothel tomorrow, would you like to spend the day with me?"

Maria smiled. She knew which choice she was going to take, although she knew it was against her better judgment. Antonias was so vulnerable.

"Perhaps," she said. "If you insist, meet me here in the early afternoon. Now, if you don't mind, I must go in and see if my child has had enough to eat."

Maria called Delilah and heard her answer from within. She pushed aside the hanging drape and entered, leaving Antonias standing in the street. She knew the lonely Roman would be back.

* * *

After Marcus had gone to sleep, Delilah's love felt particularly comforting for Maria as they lay in each other's arms. Delilah's customary light caresses relaxed her as she pondered on the strange young man who had walked into her life. She kissed Delilah lightly in response to her touch, although it was her mind that needed relaxing. Maria had a slow longing to share the inward thoughts that were flooding into her head.

"Something's on your mind, Maria. I can tell," Delilah said, as she stroked her lover's hair.

"Delilah, I have met a most unusual man," Maria whispered, without looking Delilah in the eye. "He's not a good lover, he's shy and very inexperienced, but he's moved me. There's something about him that is...well, different."

"Maria, you know the rules. You can't fall in love with the clients," Delilah answered.

Delilah held Maria in silence for a moment, and lightly caressed her lover's back. Maria said nothing, but Delilah could sense her wants and needs as she felt her warm body close to hers.

"All right, Maria, who is he?" she asked.

"He came to the booth, Delilah, but he had no idea what to do. The first time he behaved like one of those excited youths sent down to us by their families for education. It was over before he begun. He was so shy,

Delilah, he never spoke; he almost ran from the booth. I think I scared him. I was too much for him."

Delilah kissed Maria and held her close. She nibbled on her ear and whispered:

"So, you were too much for him… but not too much for him not to return. He came back, didn't he?"

"He came back two days ago. I felt sorry for him. He was so shy, but obviously he wanted me. I tried to help him. I really gave him a good time. I enjoyed it. He was so appreciative and so gentle. The poor young man, he was in heaven. He wanted to sleep with me, and he lay there on the bench so relaxed. It was hard to tell him he had to leave."

"Maria, you've got it bad," Delilah said, giving a little excited laugh, and laying her cheek against the warmth of Maria's breasts. "So what's next?"

"He waited for me outside today. He scared me Delilah. He jumped out at me in the dark. He was too shy to come into the brothel this time. I don't think that's what he wants. I think he thinks he loves me. He wanted to walk home with me. He just said he wanted to see me. In the light of the rising moon, he tried to kiss me down by the beach."

Maria looked up into Delilah's eyes.

"All I wanted to do was to get home and share time with you," she continued. "It was boring at the brothel today. Hardly anybody came by that we know. They were all young impetuous boring youths."

"I love you," Delilah whispered, as she blew lightly into Maria's other ear.

"I know," Maria replied.

They stayed in a warm embrace for what seemed a long time until Maria revealed the whole truth.

"He's coming tomorrow, Delilah. He wants to spend the afternoon with me. I've invited him here. I know he's going to come. Actually, I'm secretly looking forward to it."

Delilah smiled.

"Will I get to see him?" she asked. "Will he be here when I come back?"

"Maybe," Maria answered, with a look full of unknown anticipated affection.

They quietly touched each other in shared joy, and fell asleep in each other's arms.

* * *

It was easy for Antonias to recognize the house again the following afternoon because Maria was sitting outside the entrance talking to her son. The opening in the wall looked smaller in daylight, but Maria looked more beautiful than ever. This was the first time Antonias had seen her in the open light of day, and could really appreciate her face and the luster of her thick dark hair.

"You came," Maria said nonchalantly, pretending to be surprised.

The Roman stood in front of her, drooling over the beauty of her face and form.

"This is my boy," Maria said, as she looked down at her son's face. "This is Marcus."

Antonias grinned rather awkwardly, and held out his hand to Marcus. The child slapped his hand in Antonias' and laughed.

"He must like you," Maria said. "Marcus, this is Antonias. He's come to spend the afternoon with us."

Maria beckoned to Antonias to sit beside them on the stone slab that served as a bench in front of the vaulted cavern that was Maria and Delilah's simple home. Antonias meekly obeyed, and sat with his hands clasped in the skirt of his tunic. Maria sat Marcus on her knee, and for what seemed like an eternity, neither she nor Antonias spoke. Finally, it was Antonias who plucked up his courage. There was an aching pit in the shy man's stomach as he sat so close to the Hebrew beauty that had become his obsession.

"You didn't think I would come, did you?" he said.

Maria turned and looked at him.

"Oh, I wouldn't say that, Antonias. I'm a pretty good judge of men. I think I knew you would come. I was sitting here waiting for you, wasn't I?"

Antonias raised a hand to her face, and lightly caressed her cheek and the side of her neck. Maria made no effort to pull away, but she encouraged him no further.

"You men are all the same," she said. "You lust after us women until you're satisfied, and when your passion is cooled, you leave us to fend for ourselves."

"No, Maria," Antonias pleaded. "It's not like that. I came back, didn't I? I came back today, not for sexual gratification, but to share time with you."

He removed his hand from her face and neck and looked her straight in the eyes.

"It's a beautiful day, Maria. Why don't we walk along the shore of the lake?"

He turned to Marcus.

"You'd like to come walking with us, wouldn't you Marcus?"

The boy laughed again.

"Marcus won't be able to walk far," Maria said, slightly blushing over the courtesy that the Roman had shown. She warmed to him, and put an arm around his waist. The sparkle returned to her eyes, and Antonias felt his stomach twinge with excitement.

"Let's go down to the lake," she agreed.

As she stood up, Antonias could not help but notice that her nipples were erect as the loose folds of her shift clung to her body.

"Marcus, you walk between us," Maria said. "Hold on to Antonias' hand."

Antonias reached for the small boy's hand and the three of them walked down the narrow street to the open square and the fishermen's beach. There were about five boats pulled up on the shingle and the fishermen were selling some of their fresh catch to Roman matrons and culinary slaves.

"Do you like to eat fresh fish?" Antonias asked.

Maria had eaten the dried fish at Magdala, but it was not a common Hebrew custom to eat fresh fish from the lake. Most of the lake fish were still dried, or pickled, and sold direct to the Romans.

"I rarely eat fish," she replied.

"Why don't I buy us a couple?" Antonias suggested. "We can build a small fire along the beach and cook them. Fresh fish are so different from dried fish, Maria. You'll love them."

Antonias went to the nearest boat as Maria and Marcus stood back on the beach. He selected two fat-looking fish with clear eyes that looked as if they were still alive. The vendor put them in a small reed basket.

"Thank you, sir," Antonias said, as he exchanged two small coins that he handed over to the burly fisherman.

He proudly returned to Maria.

"Look, Maria. Two beautiful fish," he said peeling back the basket cover.

Maria blushed.

"You want to see the fish?" Antonias asked Marcus, lowering the basket to the boy's height. "Look, see their great eyes and smooth skin."

Marcus stroked the fish.

"They're cold," he said.

"Yes. That's because they've just come out of the cold water in the lake. Just a short while ago they were swimming out there. That's what makes them so good to eat. They're so fresh."

He took hold of the boy's hand again.

"Come on, Marcus," he said, "we're going to take another walk along the beach to a place where the groves come down to the water. There, we'll build a fire and we'll cook these fish for your mother."

* * *

Maria hated herself for feeling emotional, but she loved the way this Roman openly used her name. No men ever called her by name with such natural affection. Her men merely used her and abused her. No man had called her Maria since Linus. She liked Antonias' gentle ways. This man was a client, a bored shy Roman who had come into her booth for carnal gratification. He was so kind, however, and so good with Marcus that she couldn't help but feel a real affection for him. There was a lump in her throat as she followed close behind them, a glistening tear forming in her right eye.

They made their way along the stony beach, leaving behind the buildings of Tiberias. Olives and date palms fringed the shore, and Maria was reminded of those carefree days four years earlier when she had spent the summer in the arms of Linus. She had also walked the shore with Delilah many times, but this was different. She was with a man who really seemed to care about her and her small son. She felt young again, vulnerable in her desire to be loved, and carelessly content.

"This looks like a good place," Antonias said, as they stopped on a little promontory that jutted out into the clear waters of the lake.

Beyond a clump of feathering palms, stood a grove of olives that ran along the shoreline. Their twisted trunks and flaking bark caught the afternoon sun. Rocks and stones, holding grass and wildflowers, formed a hillside backdrop.

Strewn around were dead palm fronds, twigs of olive, and sundry timbers swept in by the waters of the lake. Antonias began to gather kindling. He set it down on the stony beach and took out a flat piece of bevelled glass from his tunic. Carefully, he guided the rays of the afternoon sun through the glass until a small coil of fresh blue smoke rose from the fronds. He blew on the dried material. It burst into flame.

"Look, Marcus," Antonias said excitedly. "We have a fire."

Carefully, Antonias nursed the small fire, building up a blaze of fronds and adding to them small olive twigs, until there was enough heat to ignite the driftwood. In no time, he had a fierce fire that he then surrounded with a ring of stones.

Mesmerized by the blaze, Marcus squeezed his mother's hand with excitement. Antonias stood back and joined them.

"That should do," he said. "We will be able to cook these fish in no time."

He stood looking at the fire. Maria reached out and held his hand. He turned and instinctively their lips met in a gentle, but far from passionate kiss. Marcus pulled at Antonias' tunic and started to laugh. The Roman looked down, breaking away from Maria. He picked the boy up and took him on his shoulders. Carrying him thus, he ran along the beach a short distance and then back again to where Maria stood. He let Marcus down again, and went back to tend his fire.

Maria held onto her son without taking her eyes off Antonias. The Roman had cut through all her barriers. The hopeless and dull lover, who had spent his silver aimlessly in the brothel and scared her like a perverted creep in the alleyway outside, had turned out to be a man with a warmth and kindness that touched her heart. She watched him as he rearranged the fire, and then turning to Marcus, smiled at her son.

"You like Antonias, don't you?" Maria said.

"Yes," the boy replied with a giggle. "Will he come and see us again?"

"I hope so," Maria answered. "Let's sit down."

They sat together on the beach.

Antonias finished smoothing off the fire so that the red glowing driftwood was evenly spaced within the ring of stones. He turned around.

"It's time to cook the fish now," he said. "Bring over the basket."

Maria picked up the basket.

"Stay where you are, Marcus," she instructed her boy. "I don't want you to come near the fire."

Marcus sat and watched as his mother took the fish over to Antonias, who had prepared four sharp sticks. He speared the fish in the gills and tail flesh, then, propped them over the fire.

"It's a bit makeshift, but I think this should do it," he suggested. "Watch them, Maria. In a moment the skin will begin to peel, and the fish will cook."

They watched the fish sizzle in the heat.

"Thank you for letting me visit with you today," Antonias whispered. "You have made me very happy."

Maria weakened, giving her hand to the shy Roman. He squeezed it, and putting his other arm around her, lightly kissed the side of her cheek.

"Mother!" Marcus called out.

"He needs you," Antonias intimated, pulling away. "Let him sit with us?"

Picking up Marcus, Maria returned, sitting the boy safely in her lap. Marcus continued to appear mesmerised by the fire.

* * *

Antonias could see the flesh of the fish was softening as it responded to the heat and the broken areas of skin peeled back.

"They're nearly ready," he said gleefully.

He turned them over above the hot ashes. The tails that had looked so fresh were now dry and charred, and the glassy eyes had lost their life. In a short while, the fish were sufficiently cooked, and Antonias took them off the fire, laying them down on the stones of the beach.

"We must leave them awhile," he said. "They are too hot to pick up yet."

After the fish had cooled a little, Antonias picked one up, peeled back the rest of the brittle skin so that the succulent flesh was revealed, and handed it to Maria.

"Try this," he said.

Maria chewed on the fish skeptically.

"It is good," she admitted and broke off a piece for Marcus to try.

Marcus devoured it as if it were his normal diet.

Antonias, seeing that Marcus was happy to eat the fish, then gave him part of his. In no time, the two fish were reduced to skeletons supporting just the burned out heads and tails. Nonchalantly, Antonias tossed the skeletons into the embers of the fire. He washed his hands in the waters of the lake, while Maria wiped hers on the folds of her shift.

"Will Marcus manage the walk back?" he called from the water's edge.

Maria, smiling with perceived inner joy, looked down at her son.

"Do you think that you are big enough for that long walk?" she asked.

"No," came the boy's reply. "I'm tired."

"You will have to walk part of the way," Maria said. "I can't carry you all the way home. You're getting too heavy to carry now."

"Carry me!" Marcus pleaded.

"I'll carry him," Antonias said. "Come on Marcus, up on my shoulders again."

Marcus grinned.

With Marcus straddling Antonias' shoulders, they walked back. They didn't talk much, but Antonias occasionally made noises like a donkey, pretending to give Marcus a ride. Maria ran on ahead of them, laughing. Eventually, Antonias gave up. He put Marcus down to walk, and they returned to Maria's home.

"Can we do this again?" Antonias asked.

Maria held the Roman in her arms and hugged him.

"Marcus will be disappointed if you don't come again," she said.

Antonias stood back.

"I'll be on my way home now. Thank you for a very special day," he said.

Maria and Marcus watched as the Roman skipped down the street until he was out of their sight.

* * *

It was several days before Antonias saw Maria again. Two or three times he made a point of passing by the house in the narrow street leading up from the square, but Maria was never there. One time, he saw a lady leave the house—a slim, lithe Hebrew woman, whom he assumed must have been Maria's friend Delilah. He was afraid to speak to the woman and kept on walking past the house. He considered waiting for Maria outside the brothel as he had before, but he was not sure which days she would be there or whether she would want to meet him that way. Eventually, he plucked up courage and took the easiest course. He would visit her in the brothel. He would visit her as if he was one of her regular patrons, and hopefully, they could make plans from there.

* * *

Maria was caught unawares when Antonias opened the drapes to step down into her booth. An unusual sense of modesty came over her as she quickly pulled the linens around her.

"No! Not you! Not here!" she whispered.

"Maria, if this is the only way I can get to see you, then it must be here."

Antonias advanced toward her as she lay back totally out of charge for the first time in her life. He sat on the bench, and held his hand out to touch her face. Maria backed away.

"I've missed you," he said looking soulfully into her eyes.

He brushed his hand against her waves of hair.

Maria responded, taking hold of his hand, but she stared blankly ahead. Eventually, she spoke:

"I've missed you, too. I thought you would come to the house, but you never did."

"I did, but you were never there, at least not outside the house as before. I think I saw your friend once, but I never saw you or Marcus."

"Oh, Antonias. I would have been so pleased to see you there, but here in the brothel…it isn't right. You're not a client any more. You're one of the kindest men that I've ever met. I'll never forget the day that we spent together. Marcus often asks when you're coming back. He loves you, Antonias."

"What did you tell him?"

"What could I tell him? I said I hoped we would see you again. Delilah didn't believe you'd return, though. She kept telling me to forget about you."

Maria looked up at him.

"Antonias, I haven't forgotten you," she said softly. She took his hand and laid it across her breasts. Then, sitting up, she kissed him lightly on the lips.

Antonias didn't need much encouragement as he fondled her breasts. He leaned against her and their tongues met in their first passionate kiss. When released, however, Maria pushed him away. She was not scared now, but was smiling warmly. She was in charge again.

"I'd like to make you very happy, Antonias, but not here," she insisted. "I never want to see you here again. I suppose you paid silver to come in, but I'm not going to give myself to you. You are too good for this place. Meet me outside my home tomorrow, shortly before sundown. If I have Delilah stay with Marcus tomorrow night, I'd like you to take me to your house? I'll show you something that no silver here in the brothel can buy."

Antonias was trembling. He knelt down beside the bench and buried his face in Maria's breasts. Then, looking up at her beautiful face, he grinned.

"I'll be there tomorrow," he said, before rising to leave her booth, "in the late afternoon."

* * *

As Antonias came out into the marble court, two young blades, waiting their turn, sniggered and mocked him.

"That was quick! Are you sure you got what you paid for?" one of them asked.

"Isn't that the notorious Maria's booth?" the other inquired. "Maybe she was too much for you. Did she cause you to spill your seed on sight?"

The two men then broke into stupid laughter.

Antonias passed on. *Maria's right,* he thought. *This is no place for us to meet.* Slightly embarrassed, he made his way out of the brothel, but once in the street he felt a great relief and joy. Happily, he made his way back to his father's villa.

* * *

The following day, Maria was waiting for him as she had promised. It was shortly before sundown, and Delilah returned from the brothel in time to take care of Marcus. She teased Maria, knowing that her friend was going to spend the night with Antonias.

"Be careful," she advised laughingly. "You know what they say about the shy ones. When you go to the mouse hole you may well find a lion inside."

"Sometimes, we just have to follow our instincts," Maria answered, as she lightly kissed and hugged Delilah. "This man may not be the greatest lover, but I like him. Anyway, it makes him more of a challenge. I'm fed up with the routine of the brothel. I could use a break from the monotony of overexcited Roman brats, rough soldiers, and passing merchants. Antonias needs to be loved, because he has so much gentleness to give."

"Oh, Maria, you do have it bad! Do you think I'd like him, too!" Delilah said, flashing her dark eyes seductively.

Maria glared at her.

Delilah realized that Maria was in no mood to be teased.

"I'm sorry," she said apologetically, "I hope you find the night as rewarding as you anticipate, and remember that you, too, have so much gentleness to give. Don't forget me, though. We will be here waiting for you in the morning."

Maria looked at her son.

"Be good, Marcus. Don't cause Delilah any problems."

She kissed them both, but she felt Delilah's reticence. *I think she's jealous,* she thought, before going out into the street to sit on the bench and wait.

* * *

Antonias was watching for her from across the street. As soon as she came out, he moved up and greeted her. He looked unmistakably Roman, wearing a toga over his tunic. He was freshly shaved and recently bathed.

"You really are going to come with me?" he asked with a look of almost disbelief.

"Of course, Antonias. Now...you have to show me the way."

She looked back and saw Delilah peering through the door drape.

Antonias then led Maria back down the narrow street and on to a road that led out from the town. Tall cypresses clung to the hillside and little vineyards surrounded palatial Roman villas. Farther on, the villas became more scattered, and the grass track into which the paved road had merged, led to a square looking one set apart on its own. The sun was setting. Long golden streaks intermingled with the shadows of the cypress trees. On the far side of the lake, the distant Gadarene cliffs began to pick up their pink evening glow.

"Isn't it beautiful up here?" Antonias said. "Often I sit out here at this time of the day and try to compose appropriate verses. I have not yet, however, been satisfied with anything that I've written. Nothing can do justice to the great beauty seen from here as the sun sets."

Maria smiled.

"Well, nothing other than the beauty that I see in you," the poet continued.

Maria stood looking out over the lakeside view, seemingly nervous. An evening breeze caught her shift and moved the folds of her garment. Antonias felt a lump in his throat and slipped his hand around her waist as he joined her in placid silence. There, they stood, while the gold turned to a grayish green and then to the pink light of dusk.

"It's time to welcome you to my home, Maria," Antonias whispered in her ear. "Publius will have dinner for us, and then the night will be ours."

Maria turned and allowed him to kiss her on the lips. She took hold of his hand, and he led her to the gate in the villa walls.

* * *

Maria awoke to the unfamiliar sound of birds singing in the atrium. Comfortable cushions and fine linens surrounded her. It took a moment for reality to set in. *Was she back in Linus' house?* Then, she realized where she was. Now, there was no turning back. Antonias lay asleep beside her, naked as on the day he was born. The first rays of the dawn light had begun to obliterate the darkness of the night. The oil lamp that had made such a warm and pleasing glow for their lovemaking had burned out. It all seemed like a dream that had begun with Publius serving them sweet delicacies and dishes that she had never seen before. She wondered, momentarily, if the Roman food had been clean, although it really did not bother her. Religious rules of food preparation had never played a part in her life. It had all seemed very good at the time, and she remembered the wine had tasted so smooth. The servant had poured them several goblets. It had been a wonderful and relaxing feast. Then, had come the night. This had been no quick coupling to honor silver, but a long, slow night of gentleness. She had roused Antonias to heavenly ecstasy, and then cooled his ardor in order to build his hopes again. She had teased every inch of his body, massaging him gently and kissing him passionately. She had been totally in control, and loved every minute of her role. His helpless gropes and premature lust had not bothered her, for she had controlled his every move. Slowly, but surely, through the night she had educated him, using all the stages of love, so that when the time came, and she had allowed him to enter her, it was with true tenderness and not the lust of unbridled passion. Their final coupling had been like a soft dream in itself as they had slowly moved together in ultimate fulfillment.

Maria looked at him, sleeping beside her, and kissed his upper arm softly. Antonias awoke. He turned over and nuzzled up to her. She could feel the sleepy warmth of his body, and put her arms around him. They dozed together but not for long. The birds stopped their dawn chorus, and sun started to fill the atrium, streaming across the portico and into their chamber. They kissed each other.

"Thank you for coming," Antonias whispered.

Maria raked her fingers through his hair.

"Thank you for bringing me here," she replied softly.

"Maria!" Antonias continued. "I was thinking. Could you not stay here with me? I really don't want you to go back to the brothel. Marcus would like it here. I'll be his tutor; I'll teach him Greek."

Maria didn't answer. She remembered how Linus had asked her to stay in his rich Roman villa. *It took only three days for that to end tragically,* she reflected. *How can I take another chance, and what will Delilah think?*

"Maybe I can start a school," Antonias suggested. "There are several young Roman boys in the villas. They are in need of a good tutor. It is difficult for Romans living in Galilee to give a good education to their children. The boys are taught Greek at home, but rarely learn to write it. Some write Aramaic better than Greek. Marcus seems a very bright boy for his age. He's only three years old, you say?"

"That's right," Maria answered.

"He speaks Aramaic quite well already," Antonias observed. "It wasn't difficult to talk to him that day on the beach."

"Delilah has taught him a lot," Maria explained. "I think she's a better teacher than I am."

"But you say his father was a Roman?"

"Yes."

"If he is a Roman boy, Maria, he really should be able to speak some Greek as well as Aramaic. Will you let me teach him?"

"You mean here…if we stay with you?"

"Yes. Why not? I'll take care of you both, and then, when we have made a little progress, I can see if some of the other boys can join him. It will be good for him to meet other children. Besides, if you bring Marcus here to study, you will be here all the time, too. That's the best part!"

Maria looked at him nervously. *What of Delilah?* she thought.

"Won't you stay?" he pleaded.

"If I do, will Delilah be able to come here with me?" Maria asked. "She's so good with Marcus, and apart from Marcus' father, she's the only friend I have ever had."

"Of course! I'm really rather bored here," Antonias confessed. "My father and mother had to leave Tiberias suddenly to take up an appointment in Antioch. My father had just completed building this villa. He asked me to stay here and keep the villa for the three years that they anticipated being away. I wanted to write poetry, and this is such a beautiful place, so I said I would stay, although originally it had been planned that I would return to Athens and continue studies there that I had started four years ago."

Maria was becoming lost in his geographic wanderings. Her world was limited to the shore of the lake. The only places she even knew about, outside Magdala and Tiberias, were Capernaum and Damascus.

"Linus went to Damascus," she said interrupting Antonias, trying to keep up with him.

"Linus!" Antonias repeated knowingly. "Is that Marcus' father?"

"Yes."

"Was Linus from Tiberias?"

"No. He came from just above my village. We were both from Magdala."

"Taricheae, that little Hebrew village just along the shore?" Antonias repeated, using Magdala's Roman name.

"Well, it can't be too far away," Maria agreed. "As I told you, I walked here from the village when I was pregnant. Marcus was born here in Tiberias. My friend Delilah delivered him. She managed to persuade the Roman matron at the brothel to keep my position open as her partner. When I worked, Delilah took care of the baby. We named him Marcus, for no better reason than that a young Roman of that name was one of our most regular clients."

* * *

Antonias suddenly realized how little Maria knew about the world in which they lived. A brief moment of disappointment preceded a sudden sense of responsibility. Antonias could see that the brothel was really the only world that Maria knew. It was, therefore, his responsibility to rescue her from this plight, and to educate her son.

"Maria," he said gently. "Someone needs to look after you outside that brothel. Please let me be that someone. Can we bring Marcus up here?"

Maria remained thoughtful. "Would you really teach Marcus?" she asked.

Antonias kissed her.

"It will be wonderful, Maria. We will be able to live here like a family."

"And Delilah, too?" Maria appealed.

Antonias smiled. He slapped her backside.

"It's time to get up Maria. If it's a clear day out there you'll be able to see Taricheae, or at least the area of the lakeshore close to your village. I'll point the area out to you. Then, after that, we need to go back into town to pick up Marcus and Delilah so they can come back here with us."

Chapter Eight

Qumran and The Wilderness

The temperature soared to most uncomfortable heights in the Judean wilderness during the summer months. It was punishing on Jon with his now long, unkempt hair. Like an animal drawn to a watering hole, he was inevitably drawn toward the great lake in the deep wilderness cleft where the river Jordan becomes soaked up in mineral rocks. He clambered over the lunar-like landscape searching for a ravine that would take him down to the waters way below. To reach such a ravine, he had to climb down a chimney in the rocks, groping for a hold. His rough-cut, goatskin garment kept catching on sharp ledges, but the cooling shade of the narrow funnel brought temporary relief from the heat. Jon's face was burned from the constant sun, and his hands had become as rough as any animal hide. For three years now, he had lived as a desert Nazirite, but the end time still had not come, and each season seemed to burn on in equal intensity. The summers had been unbearable; but especially hard, without suitable shelter, was the bitter cold of winter nights. The sight of the blue water on the lake below drove Jon on, and he jumped down the last five feet of the rock passage landing on the scree of the ravine below. Despite the hard calluses on his feet, the impact grazed him, deeply scratching the skin. He sat and rested his bone-weary body, carefully rubbing his wound.

His thoughts wandered back over the last three years. He had traveled many miles in the southern desert.

My wanderings have taken me farther than Moses led our people, he mused. *I must have covered much of the same territory. I've eaten the manna that God sends from heaven and caught the low-flying desert birds for sustenance just as our forefathers did in their wanderings. I've been burned by the heat of the summer sun, and frozen in the pale moonlight by the winter cold. I've learned to live without water and have known the pangs of hunger. I've chastised myself in every way. Surely now, God has cleansed me. Surely now, I am ready for the kingdom to come!*

The water still beckoned. Jon staggered on. Any water would be a joy after so many days of drought. It was a long climb down the trail of scree and rocks streaked in green, rust, and white. The minerals from them stung his grazed foot. Although he was now partially shaded from the direct rays of the sun, in the depths of the valley, the air became more dense and heavy in a soporific heat. He could not wait to reach the lake, so casting aside his goatskin, he ran the final distance into the water.

Jon screamed with agony. The salt bit deep into his wound. He froze with pain. After a while, however, the pain passed as the graze adjusted to the minerals in the warm lake. Jon stepped out deeper. He lost his balance and fell, finding himself sitting at a crazy angle suspended in the water. In the relative comfort of this position he allowed himself to drift. When he tried to stand, he realized he had gone beyond his depth and instead of reaching the bottom he found himself walking on the water as he sank in an ungainly manner to his knees. Jon took several steps in this fashion before he fell again and struggled to return to the shallows. During the process, he had swallowed a mouthful of the water and realized that it was full of salt. His eyes stung, and his long beard and heavy head of hair felt twice their normal weight. He continued struggling until he reached the shore. Inviting though the water had seemed, it had neither refreshed him nor relaxed him.

The sun quickly dried Jon off, but it left an uncomfortable crust of salt on his body that aggravated his already rough skin. Disappointed, and somewhat frustrated, he wandered north along the shore. He stopped for a while in one of the caves. It was cool, and there he slept.

Early the next day, Jon continued to follow the shore of the lake. He rested several times in the cool of other caves, coming to the Jordan valley as the day drew to its close. He was hungry, having found nothing to eat along the shore, but here in the valley, greenery returned encouraged by the fresh waters of the river Jordan, promising berries and fruits. As the shafts of golden evening light fell on the valley, he felt as if he had found the kingdom. He went to sleep in one of several groves of feathery date palms in a grassy verge up from the pebbles of the shores. As he lay under the night sky, thoughts came to him encouraged by the sight of the valley ahead that had now become his inspiration. In his sleep he dreamed…

Clouds hung high over the valley and as they turned gold at the edges heralding the passing of day, a shaft of perpendicular light rained down from their gilded opening. At the place where the rays hit the valley floor, there arose a golden city like none that Jon had ever seen. Trumpets blared, and the voice of God came down from the clouds…

It was not really clear in Jon's dream exactly what the voice was saying, but the resulting action was visually clear…

From all sides of the valley, men came running like ants drawn to the golden city. They were answering the call from the heavens…

Before Jon could discern the call, he awoke.

It was still dark and very quiet. Jon returned to sleep. Next time he awoke, it was light with the break of dawn. He heard voices along the shore, and peering out from the date grove, he saw three men in white robes walk out into the waters of the river. Two others joined them, submerging themselves in the water in front of the three in white. The men appeared to be naked. The leaders cupped water in their hands and emptied it over the naked men's heads.

"On behalf of the 'Many' we baptize you into the Covenant of the Essenes," they said, their voices drifting over to the shore. "As the water washes your bodies so your sins are washed away. You now enter into the full brotherhood. Prepare yourselves for the coming kingdom, living in the purity of the Teacher's ways."

The naked men stood up in the water, and stretched out their arms in prayer. Jon thought he could make out the words of the Shema:

"Hear, O Israel: the Lord our God, the Lord is One! And we shall love the Lord our God with all our heart, and with all our soul, and with all our might. And these words, which have been commended to us, shall be upon our heart, and we shall teach them diligently to our children, and shall talk of them when we sit in our houses, and when we walk by the way, and when we lie down, and when we rise up."

The three leaders in white embraced the baptized, and they all returned from the water to the shore, disappearing from Jon's view. Jon lay still for a while as the sun rose, streaking its light through the fronds of the palms. The shafts of light reminded him of his dream. He saw the golden city again. Scarabs that ran through the palm fronds reminded him of the men, running like ants drawn to the golden city. *I must baptize those who repent before it's too late,* he thought. *Nobody will be able to enter the golden city unless they have been washed of their sins.* Then, he jumped up, and looked north toward the widening valley.

The white light of the new day almost blinded him after the shade of the fronds. He swore he could see the golden city once more in the light of the valley.

"The kingdom is here!" he shouted. "My God! I am ready! I have prepared myself, and now I must prepare others for the coming of the Lord."

* * *

A shaft of light from the same morning sun passed through the doorway of the cool storage room where the Qumran scrolls were kept. Joshua made his selection. He loved this place. There was such a keen sense of scholarship among the members. Not only were the Scriptures presented here in dozens of scrolls, beautifully written on leather and papyrus, but also there were so many other interesting Jewish works. Joshua had become fascinated by the messianic themes in the works of the Essenes. He had read the writings of the Teacher of Righteousness, and noted the sense of urgency that the community's authors had placed on the coming of God's kingdom. It was believed that the Teacher of Righteousness would come again at the end time and reign over his people as the Messiah—the anointed one of God. Some of the writings also alluded to a priestly messiah, uniting all the people together in that golden age. Joshua liked the messianic hope. The Jerusalem priesthood was to him, however, an historic vestige in his faith. He believed in priestly power as a means to cleanse the soul, and he recognized the priestly power to heal, but his thoughts were far more excited by the Teacher of Righteousness concept of the Messiah. This was closer to the religious teachings of the Pharisaic rabbis who lived closer to the people, guiding them with kindness and love. In contrast, Joshua also read the text of the scroll described as 'The War of the sons of light against the sons of darkness'. There was urgency in this work. The establishment of God's kingdom would not be easy. Before the reign of the Teacher of Righteousness and the Priest of God, described in the Qumran scroll as the anointed one of Israel, could begin, there would be terrible suffering and conflict, the sons of light needing to overcome the sons of darkness. This conflict bothered Joshua. Some of his contemporaries at Qumran, notably Brother Macabee, a rather zealous young man, suggested that in part this conflict was already taking place. First, there had been the onslaught of Antiochus Epiphanes that their forebears had so nobly destroyed, and later, the march of the Romans under Pompeius. The Romans were yet to be defeated, but if they were ever defeated, the world would be God's as surely as the world now belonged to Rome.

"It will not be long," Brother Macabee said. "The time for the establishment of the kingdom is at hand. The Teacher of Righteousness will return and bring in his kingdom with power."

"You speak like a zealot," Joshua replied with a smile. "What have the zealots achieved in their struggle with Rome?"

"The zealots do not believe in the return of the Teacher of Righteousness, Brother Joshua. The zealots fight only for their freedom and a return to the Davidic State."

"But, there are Pharisees, Brother Macabee," Joshua insisted, "who believe in the establishment of a righteous kingdom after the tribulation. They follow the tradition of the prophets that state God's remnant will survive. We are God's chosen people. God will not abandon His people."

"I agree, Brother Joshua," Macabee said. "But it will be the Teacher of Righteousness and the Aaronic Messiah, the anointed priest of God, who will make that judgment."

Joshua shrugged his shoulders. He never felt very comfortable around Brother Macabee. The attitude of most of his contemporaries in both the novitiate and the monastic order of the Essenes was peace loving. Rarely, was the struggle against Roman authority brought up for discussion.

Joshua pulled one of the scrolls of the prophet Isaiah from the stone enclave, and took it out into the light of the courtyard, while Brother

Macabee went about his own studies. Joshua unrolled the scroll until he came to the section that interested him. He wanted to see if he could make any connection between The Teacher of Righteousness and Isaiah's 'Prince of Peace'. Quickly, he found the passage he had so often pondered and discussed with his mother. He read it again...

'To us a child is born and a son given upon whose shoulders will be the government of our people. And he will be called Wonderful Counselor, Mighty God, Everlasting Father and Prince of Peace. His peaceful rule will last forever.'

Doves from the monastic cote cooed overhead as Joshua bent over the scroll that he had flattened out on a wooden trestle in the open. Other brothers in the courtyard were also studying, some in the shade of a lean-to porch, thatched simply with palm fronds, and adjacent to the library walls. Many of them were copyists, who painfully reproduced the Sacred Hebrew writings on scroll after scroll. Carefully and precisely, they painted the Hebrew characters onto the newly stretched leather, while others stitched the pieces together to make up these scrolls. Joshua continued to unroll the document. He looked for a passage to link with that about the 'Prince of Peace'. He found what he was looking for, and again flattened the relevant part of the scroll, pondering over it as it lay on the trestle table...

'Behold my servant, whom I uphold, my chosen in whom my soul delights. I have put my spirit upon him, and he will bring forth justice in the world. He will not cry or lift up his voice or shout in the street; a bruised reed he will not brake, and a dimly burning wick he will not quench; but he will faithfully bring forth justice. He will not fail or be discouraged until that justice has been established on the earth and all await his law. For thus says God, the Lord who created all things—"I am the Lord and I have called you in righteousness and have led you by the hand because I have given you as a covenant to the people to be a light for all nations."'

A dropping fell from a passing pigeon, and splattered the leather scroll. Joshua looked up as the bird flew away. He brushed the gray excrement from the parchment and wiped it off his hand on the side of his white shift. He thought of that day long ago when he had made mud doves in the brick kiln ponds at Alexandria. He remembered his idle dream of flying like a bird, out of reach from all who could do him harm, and looking down on the whole world in peace. *Only God can be beyond the reach of destructive men,* he thought, *and in the same way, only God can look down and see all mankind. Just as a bird can fly beyond our reach, so at times he can come down to us and eat out of our hand. That same bird can carry the seeds of our food, dropping them wherever it chooses. Could God have such properties? Could God live among us? Could the 'Prince of Peace' or the Teacher of Righteousness actually be the same God who chose Israel to be his own?*

Joshua looked up again. He felt the warm sun on his face.

The 'Prince of Peace' must be like a servant, he concluded. *The Teacher of Righteousness is a servant. If God cannot reach the humblest of us, there cannot be a fair judgment of all. The 'Prince of Peace' or the Teacher of Righteousness, if they are to establish the Kingdom of God, must be no greater than the simplest of us in order to give to us all the opportunity of life in His future kingdom. Didn't Isaiah tell us that we should not be looking for a king, or even a prince? Rather, we should be looking for a teacher of harmony and peace to which kings will come.*

Joshua began to roll the scroll on again. He looked at it, scanning for the section he wanted. *Let me see,* he recalled. *Isaiah described the Messiah as a servant…a simple servant—the servant of the Lord.* He found the relevant quotation, and spread the leather out once more on the trestle table in the sun…

'Behold, my servant shall prosper, he shall be exalted and lifted up and be admired by many, even by those who will not try to understand him because his appearance will seem so ordinary and plain and yet his mind so ethereal, even they will be startled by him. Kings will do as he commands because of his magnetism and mystique. They will obey him even though they may not understand him.'

Joshua's eyes raced on further down the scroll…

'Although so ordinary and plain, he will be rejected and despised by many. He will experience sorrow and grief and many will avoid him and fail to recognize him. Yet he will bear all our grief and carry our sorrows so that right when we think that he has been rejected by God he will be wounded for our sins and bruised for our sorrows, being chastised for us that we might recognize our foolish ways.'

Joshua closed the scroll and returned it to the library niche. He felt afraid. The back of his neck was cold. His hands were sweating.

Looking up from his work, Brother Macabee saw that Joshua was troubled.

"You look pale, Brother Joshua. Are you all right?"

"I'm all right, Brother Macabee. I just need some time alone with myself and God."

Joshua left the library storeroom and crossed the courtyard. Some of the scribes working on their manuscripts called out to him, but he barely heard them. Leaving the complex, he walked through the groves that surrounded Qumran. Ahead, lay the rugged north shoreline of the Salt Sea and the great jagged cliffs of mineral rocks that somehow dwarfed the importance of man. Here, he could think and be alone with God. The haunting fear that had found him before descended again. *Could I be the 'Prince of Peace'? Could I be the Teacher of Righteousness? Could the 'Prince of Peace' and the Teacher of Righteousness be the same person as Isaiah's suffering servant? Could I, Joshua, the son of Miriam, be the incarnate power of God commanded to establish this kingdom on earth?* The great cliffs humbled him, and in the mouth and shelter of one of the numerous caves, he knelt down and prayed.

* * *

By the time of the High Holy Days, word had spread about the new firebrand baptist in the Jordan valley. The pilgrims who had gathered around Jerusalem for Rosh Hashanah, Yom Kippur, and Succoth poured to Bethany beyond the Jordan. They were curious to be baptized by Jon, to see him, hear him, and be touched by him. It was believed that the baptizer had magical powers, and that in his message of redemption through repentance, he could wash away ailments and disease. The Essenes at Qumran were mixed in their reactions to the cry of their near neighbor. Many of them believed, like Jon, that the kingdom was imminent, and that the end time had begun. They were skeptical of the baptist's scholarship, however. They were Pharisees who believed in Pharisaic discipline, but this Jon of the desert preached an instant repentance, appealing to the emotions of the moment. Some considered him a downright charlatan, a wandering Nazirite who had lost his mind. Joshua, who was positive that the desert firebrand must be his cousin, and knowing how they had discussed their future roles in preparing men for the end time, knew that Jon's message came from the heart. Jon had always seen things simply, but he had never been insincere. As Joshua himself began to ponder his own role with more and more confidence, he thought it an excellent idea that he should cross the valley, meet Jon, and reaffirm his own opinion about the baptist's message. Leaving his studies, he set out for Bethany of Perea.

Joshua didn't go up to Jericho to take the road across the Jordan into Perea and Herod's kingdom. Instead, he walked along the shores of the Salt Sea from Qumran to where the Jordan flowed. He then continued along the river on the Judean side, being close to Bethany on the other side by the afternoon. A crowd had gathered at the river. People were on both banks, many crippled and lame carried by friends and relatives. Joshua watched for a while.

Jon was in the river, stripped naked except for a loincloth. It was hard for Joshua to be sure that this was the same man whom he had known for so many years in Galilee. He looked taller, broader, and altogether more masculine. The long locks of matted hair, and the gargantuan beard that he had grown, hid his round face. Each person, who came to Jon, he submerged into the water, so that only his or her head was free. With one hand on their shoulders, he scooped more water with his free hand, and poured it over them.

After a while, Jon had exhausted the true repentants. Most of those left standing on the two river banks were now just curious onlookers, or suspicious men of religious principles—Pharisees and Sadducees more concerned about the competition he gave them than his message. Jon looked up and down this crowd.

"You snakes!" he shouted at the top of his voice. "Who warned you to flee from the wrath to come? I know your sort. Don't stay there and say to yourselves that you have Abraham as your father, for Abraham is no protection. If God chose, He could raise children up from the stones of this river as worthy of Him as you sons of Abraham. To repent, you need to bear the fruits of repentance and change your lives. The time has come. Our God wields His axe as He may, and it will fell all of you who are like trees that don't bear the fruit of repentance. You will be as worthless as timber cut down and fed to the fire."

Some of the fearful shouted back to the baptist.

"What should we do?"

"You want to know? You really want to repent?" he asked.

A silence fell over the crowd.

"Whatever man here has two coats," Jon continued, "let him share one of them with someone who has none. Whoever has brought food with him, share it now with this crowd. We must always share whatever we may have in abundance with those who have nothing, not just now, but always. In the coming kingdom, there will be no division between those who have and those who have not. All will be judged according to the cleanliness of their souls."

He looked around again with piercing eyes.

"Who now will repent?" he shouted. "In the words of the prophet Isaiah, who will prepare for the coming of the Lord?...'Prepare the way of the Lord and make his paths straight. Every valley will be filled in, and every mountain and hill leveled off. Things crooked will be made straight, and rough ways made smooth.' When all is prepared and the judgment has taken place, 'all those left shall see the salvation of God.'"

There was a deathly silence as the crowd hung on Jon's words. Joshua, remembering the days when Jon had meekly worked with him in the Nazareth vineyard, and comparing the man he knew then with the man he heard now, fell equally under his spell.

I saw Jon's personality change in Jerusalem, but the change is now unmistakable, Joshua thought. *Jon speaks with real authority, as if the Lord Himself has taken him over. It is as if God is now in control of both our lives. First Jon and now me. He has called us to our destinies.*

"Who will come forward?" Jon invited them. "I am not your judge, I can only prepare you for the judgment. Believe me, one will come after me who is mightier than I, the thongs of whose sandals I am not worthy to loosen. I baptize you with water, but he will baptize you with fire—the very spirit of God. He will treat you as threshed wheat using his winnowing fork to separate the chaff from the grain. The chaff he will burn, but the grain he will gather into his barn. Prepare for that day. Come forward and be baptized. Cleanse yourselves of your sins. Be ready for the kingdom to come."

A man cried out and waded into the river. Soon others followed, and Jon ceremonially baptized them each in turn. Joshua stepped forward, partly because he wanted to see Jon face to face, and to let him know that he was there. He also wanted to put a seal on his own destiny, and feel cleansed so he could take on the role of God's servant—the 'Prince of Peace'. He made his way through the crowd and down to the water's edge.

Jon methodically baptized each person who came before him. In front of Joshua were a tax collector from Judea and a soldier of the Herodian guard from Perea, men generally hated by their fellow Jews because of their collaboration with the Roman authorities. The tax collector looked up at Jon.

"I'm a tax gatherer, Teacher" he said. "We are despised by many of our people. What should we do to repent? I can not afford to give up my profession, hated though I am."

"As long as you collect only that which is appointed by the authorities, you will have done no harm. Repent only of your sins. Treat others as you would have others treat you. Honesty is of utmost importance in your profession where the temptation to cheat is too easy," the baptist advised.

Jon baptized the tax collector and turned to the soldier, who was still in the tunic of the Herodian guard even though he was standing half-submerged in the water.

"Are you Elijah, the forerunner of our Messiah?" the soldier asked.

"I am as one of the prophets," Jon answered. "And you, sir... you are a soldier?"

"Yes."

"Make sure you do not use your position to rob the innocent, or cause violence unnecessarily. It will be difficult for men of your training in the coming kingdom."

He baptized the soldier in the cooling water, and looked up to see who was next.

* * *

Jon and Joshua's eyes met.

They stood in the water staring at each other. Joshua was wearing the white robe of the Essenes, whereas Jon was naked except for his loincloth. Jon remembered the scene that he had witnessed at the entrance of the Jordan valley. It was the Essenic elders dressed in white who had baptized the naked novices. For a moment Jon seemed afraid. He had always held Joshua in such awe. Joshua had taught him everything worthwhile that he knew. He looked up as if to ask God for advice. The sun shimmered as he squinted at its orb. When he looked at Joshua again it was almost as in his dream. A shaft of light continued to dance before his eyes like the shimmering sun.

"You want me to baptize you?" Jon asked, almost in a whisper.

"Yes, Jon," Joshua said. "My work cannot begin until I feel cleansed of my past transgressions. Your work cannot be fulfilled until I have been prepared for mine. You are the herald of the coming kingdom, just as we discussed. I have thought a great deal since those days. I am ready, Jon. If you will cleanse me, I will bring the people into the Kingdom of God."

"Get down in the water," Jon said slowly.

He put his left hand on Joshua's shoulder, holding him firmly so that the cool water of the Jordan flowed over all of Joshua's body except his head. With his right hand, Jon scooped up water from the river and poured it over Joshua's light-brown hair. The water ran over Joshua's forehead into his closed eyes, then out like tears to join the river again. As it left, he opened his eyes and smiled up at Jon. A cooing dove circled above them, then, swooping down, alighted momentarily on Joshua's head. Jon leaned back.

"It's a sign!" he exclaimed.

As Joshua began to raise his body from the water, the dove flew away to become lost above the crowd on the riverbank. Jon trembled as Joshua turned to walk out of the river. *My God!* Jon confirmed to himself. *Joshua was right. He is a son of God. He's the anointed one chosen to be our Messiah!*

It was a few moments before Jon could regain his composure. By that time, Joshua had disappeared into the crowd. A man stumbled out into the river, carrying a child who had been crippled from birth.

"Baptize us, Master!" the man called out. "Touch my son so that he will be healed."

When they were in front of him, Jon looked at them with a sorrowful expression.

"I cannot heal him now so that he will walk," he said. "Believe in the kingdom that is coming and then your son will walk."

The man, holding his son, submerged himself in the water. Jon took up water from the river and baptized them both, and then, as he took his left hand from the man's shoulder, he placed it upon the child's head.

"O Lord God Almighty!" Jon prayed. "Give strength to this boy that life may come to his feet and that he will walk in your kingdom."

The father carried his son from the river, and Jon looked around to see if there was anyone else wishing to be baptized. Nobody else came forward. He waded back to the farthest bank, and the crowd made passage for him as he set foot on the track that led back to Bethany in Herodian Perea.

* * *

Joshua left the shelter of the monastery at Qumran to retreat into the wilderness for a few days. He needed to work out his destiny and to be alone and pray. He needed to test the bond between himself and God. He followed the familiar track south from Qumran that led to the caves overlooking the Salt Sea. From time to time, the brothers used the nearer caves for storage purposes, but farther along the shore they were always empty and awesome. The caves provided a basic shelter, especially now that winter had come. Although Qumran itself enjoyed the mild climate of the Jordan valley, it was amazing how quickly this disappeared to the south where the mineral cliffs came down to the desert lake. Joshua only had his white shift to wear, but he had borrowed a woolen shawl to help keep himself warm. The wind at this time of the year funneled down the lake, sweeping in the cold night air from the Arabic wastes farther south. As the wind howled outside, Joshua prayed in the shelter of one of these caves. Having said his evening prayers, he took out the last of the flat matzoth that he had carried with him. It was dry and tasteless, but at least it was sustenance. He was thirsty too; the more so because he knew he could not drink the water from the lake, and his plight and the scene around him reminded him of Elijah in his desert wanderings. *If God provided for Elijah,* Joshua thought, *how much more will God provide for His chosen one—the 'Prince of Peace'?*

He listened to the sound of the wind as it rushed by the mouth of his cave.

"Guide me Lord," he prayed. "Bring Your message to me in the wind. Tell me what I must do to lead Your chosen people to salvation."

He listened for the wind to reply, but like Elijah, he could not discern any answer in the rush of air. All he could feel was the bitter cold, and he wrapped himself tighter in his shawl and tried to sleep. It was difficult, because of the hardness of the cave floor, and he was bothered by a monotonous drip from the cave's interior where water seeped from the ceiling to fall to the floor. Eventually, in frustration, he sought out the source of the drip, and caught the water on his parched tongue. The drips tasted salty, and like the lake were not fit to drink. *In these rocks, even God's rain turns sour,* he thought. But, he concluded that if there was water seeping through the rocks from above he must climb higher to find its source and quench his growing thirst. The more he thought about water to drink, the thirstier he became. When the gray light of dawn revealed the outline of the cave's entrance, Joshua emerged into the cold morning air and began to climb.

Climbing up the scree and clambering over the rocks he found no visible source of the water. He looked down at his cold and sore feet. The more his feet hurt, however, the less cold they became, for his mind was diverted from the cold to the pain. As the sun rose higher, so the cold diminished. In time, it became quite pleasant, and Joshua rested, allowing the rays to warm his face. His stomach now growled with the need to eat. He knew from past experience on the road that if he could only drink he could stave off his desire to eat, but the source of water remained elusive. His hunger increased and he felt his energy sapping.

When Joshua was about two thirds of the way up the path, he rested again. By now, the sun was high overhead. The thought of food became more imminent than his physical discomfort. *If I am the Lord's chosen one, the 'Prince of Peace',* he thought, *and if the spirit of God is within me because He has sent me to bring in His kingdom with power, then surely I can use that power to help myself.*

Joshua observed the stones around his swollen feet. They looked like little puffs of risen dough that might have been freshly taken from an oven.

"Almighty God!" Joshua cried as he stared at the stones. "If I am a son of God, the 'Prince of Peace', by the power that You have placed within me turn these stones into bread."

He stared at the stones, but there seemed no difference.

Joshua cried out again:

"Lord God Almighty! I command that these stones be turned into bread."

Again, nothing happened. Joshua picked up one of the hard smooth stones, and threw it down the hillside with all his might. He heard it bounce on the scree as it rolled down through the rocks causing an echo off the sidewalls of the narrow ravine. In that moment of frustration, Joshua thought he could hear the echo cry out to him. He remembered how he had fooled so many of his acquaintances and even his family members, when he had put his good wine into Nathaniel ben Judah's water jars at his brother Amos' wedding in Cana. Many then had thought he was a miracle worker, and he had let them think so. When he had wrestled with this problem, he had justified it because his action had made the wedding feast a resounding success. He had even attributed that decision and its results to God's intervention, and thanked God for helping him. As the echo faded and disappeared, Joshua wrestled now with his failure to turn the stones into bread.

I must be a servant, he thought. *God will work through me, but it must always be His divine will that will be done and not mine. The power of God can perform any miracle, but I am not the power of God, not even as the 'Prince of Peace'. I am His servant and it is only if I allow His Divine love to show forth through me that He can use me to perform His miracles. God is in my Divine love and not in me. How stupid of me to think that I could perform a miracle for my own sake. What does the Law say? When our people were wandering in this similar wilderness what did God say to them through Moses His servant? "You will always remember the way God has led you these years in the wilderness, and how He humbled you, testing you to know what was in your heart and whether you would keep His commandments or not. He humbled you and let you go hungry so that He could feed you with manna…a food substance that you had never seen or known before, neither you nor your fathers. He did this so that you would realize that man does not live just by bread alone, but that man lives only through what comes from the mouth of the Lord. You must realize that deep down you are like children… disciplined by God as a father disciplines his son."*

Joshua looked up for a moment.

That's right, he thought. *A father disciplines his son because he loves his son, not because he hates him and is going to cast him out.*

"You're testing me, God! Aren't you?" he cried out, his words reverberating down through the rocks.

The echo sounded almost like a response.

"Yes, you're testing me!" he repeated in a quieter voice. "I will not let Satan come between us, Lord. Through Your Divine love, and only through Your love within me, will I perform Your miracles."

Joshua felt a new strength. The hunger left him, and he continued to climb up toward the plateau.

It was well into the afternoon when he finally reached the top of the ravine. The last part had been the hardest. The path had disappeared in a mass of fallen rock. Joshua literally had to climb up through the rocks to reach the ledge from which they had come. Once there, he found an area of relatively flat land, sloping away to the west before dropping down again to a more tortured surface beyond. To the north, he could see in the clear winter air the mountain where the Herodians had built their gateway fortress—Herodium. Way to the south, another high peak marked the outlying fortress of Masada. He could look over the Salt Lake, deep down in its valley, to the hills of Moab, and up to the Jordan valley from whence he had come. Desert spread out to the south and east interminably as far as the eye could see. Up on this plateau, there was a breeze that blew the sage bushes so that they all bent to the north, pointing to Judea, Samaria and Galilee. Joshua looked north and northwest. The kingdom lay there before him. The land that God had given to the Jews. Then, he turned and looked south again toward Masada and the Nabatean lands. From here, it seemed he could survey the whole world. *Somewhere, way beyond the horizon must be Egypt,* he thought. *Our people journeyed through this wilderness when they came up from Egypt. Mother used to describe our journey from Bethlehem to Egypt. We must have also passed through this endless wilderness.*

Joshua pivoted as he admired this whole vast panorama. The winter light was so clear that the rocks of the farthest horizon looked almost as sharp as those close by.

When the kingdom is established, Joshua thought, *there won't be any separate lands. The whole world will be one, united under me as the 'Prince of Peace'. I'll be the guardian of that perfect world, and every nation will know my name.*

A gust of wind stirred the sage bushes. It ate into Joshua, as he stood exposed on this high plateau. The sudden cold distracted him, and the pain from his sore foot throbbed. The majestic kingdom suddenly seemed unimportant. Joshua lay on the ground and protected his face from the blowing dust.

Joanna, he thought, *if only the plague had not taken you. We'd have had a family by now. We would be warm and cozy in our vineyard home. I would not have to endure this suffering…this pain. We were so happy, Joanna. Why did the Lord take you from me?*

The wind died down. As it slackened, the warmth of the now fading sun returned. Joshua looked up. The horizon on the ground level where he lay was only a few yards. The vast panorama had gone. He laughed.

"Go away, Satan!" he cried. "Remember what the Scriptures say: 'You shall worship the Lord your God and Him only shall you serve.'"

He propped himself on his side, still laughing at himself.

'Prince of Peace', ruler of the whole world, he thought, *you cannot rule except through God's will as His servant, and remember, as His servant you will suffer many things in order for Him to use you as His mouthpiece. There will already be earthly kings within your kingdom—leaders and rulers by profession. Your kingdom is not of this earth, O 'Prince of Peace'. Your kingdom is God's kingdom…a world where all men can listen to their own Divine love, knowing that they are hearing the still small voice that Elijah heard. Our kingdom will be from within ourselves…a harmony between every man and his Lord.*

Joshua roamed the plateau until he found a small spring that trickled fresh water into a gully running east. It tasted clean and free of salt. He cupped his hands and gathered the water as the sun began to set. Joshua drank quite a lot of this water, knowing that the Lord had provided it for him. As the sunset heralded the birth of a new day, he stood in that desolate place and held out his hands.

"Hear, O Israel: the Lord our God, the Lord is one," he cried out. "And you shall love the Lord your God with all your heart and with all your soul and with all your might."

Joshua paused for a moment as he thought on the words that he daily prayed—the Shema of Israel. He thought of the beautiful passage from the prophet Micah and the kingly role of servitude.

"You should love your neighbor as yourself," he said to himself, "for on these two laws, love of God and love of neighbor, really hang all the others. What does the Lord require of us—to do justice and to love kindness and to walk humbly with our God?"

Joshua found a hollow place as the light faded. Protected from the gusts of wind, and able to bury his legs and lower body in the dusty sand particles that had swept into the hole, he wrapped himself up in his shawl. Much of the night he prayed, earnestly asking God that he might better understand his role and humbly lead his people into the spirit of the kingdom God would want him to establish. The night air was colder here than in the shelter of the caves, but the sand protected his legs and torso and it was only his face and ears that suffered through the bitter night.

Up at dawn, Joshua journeyed northward, following the ridge until it narrowed and came to a point that looked out over the lesser escarpments that folded down to the Salt Lake and the Jordan valley. He began his descent, traveling very slowly. Little by little, he felt that he was coming more to terms with his commission. He believed that he was the anointed one, and that, in the short life that he might have as a son of God on earth, he must prepare as many of his people as possible for the new era that was about to begin. He knew that he would have to humble the rich and elevate the poor, so that all could accept a kingdom where only the Divine love of God would rule. He wanted to be able to prove that where Divine love takes over the heart of a man, pain and suffering will be no more. If he had learned anything on this desert retreat he believed that it was humility. He also now believed he could only effectively change both the lax and fervent expressions of the Jewish relationship with God, through his simple and humble example...by allowing the Divine love within him to become his most dominant emotion. It occurred to him that maybe the prophet Zadok and his followers in Jerusalem had been closer to the truth than he had thought, when he chose to leave their way and follow the path of the Essenes. Deep in thought, he descended down the escarpments and ravines until in the afternoon he reached the lake again. It was dark by the time he arrived back at Qumran.

* * *

Joshua's decision to leave the Essenes came as a surprise to the Inspector at Qumran.

"But you seemed to settle in so well here, Brother Joshua," Brother Nathan said as he tried to dissuade him. "You have proved to be one of our most diligent scholars and you will be much missed in the library and in the didactic classes."

"I have enjoyed my studies at Qumran," Joshua admitted. "I feel, however, that I must fulfill my own destiny in other ways. I just ask that I might be allowed to leave and that you will give me a notification for the Overseer at Anathoth so that I can reclaim my possessions there."

"Are you sure?" the Inspector pleaded again.

"Yes, Brother Nathan. I'm quite sure. It is God's will that I should leave the community at this time."

"We will not stand in your way, Brother Joshua," the Inspector assured him. "If you have doubts about going on to become a full member of the covenant it is better you should express them now than later."

The Inspector stood up and walked over to Joshua. He embraced him.

"Good luck, Joshua. May God's blessing go with you. You are free to leave at any time. Come by to see me before you go, and I will give you the release document that you will need at the Anathoth community."

The next day Joshua collected the document, and set out on the road to Jericho. Outside the city, he cut himself a sturdy staff for the morrow's long climb up to Jerusalem. He remembered only too well the danger of the Jerusalem road, and did not wish to be the victim of another brutal attack. Besides, the staff would be of help in pulling him up the steeper part of the arduous journey.

Starting out at dawn, Joshua walked toward Jerusalem. He felt a strange sense of freedom. He had appreciated and enjoyed his work at Qumran. It was those very studies, however, that had confirmed in his mind the need to leave and reach his destiny on his own. Jon's firebrand baptism had also influenced his decision. He felt a deeper commitment to Jon than to the Essenes. Jon had become both teacher and prophet. He, himself, needed to become teacher, healer, and the 'Prince of Peace'. He needed to take up where Jon left off, and bring in the Kingdom of God by making men see the Divine love at work within them.

Jericho and the green valley lay behind Joshua now. All morning he walked, climbing ever upward toward the high ground leading to the spinal ridge. He met no travelers on the road, but early in the afternoon Joshua passed a large flock of sheep being moved by two dark-skinned shepherds. He had already passed the place where he had been stoned and robbed. The rest of the afternoon he plodded on, climbing up the steeper track that took the road to the summit and within sight of the village of Bethany. The light was just beginning to turn the golden color of a winter's dusk when he reached the tanneries with their foul odor. After the purity of Qumran, Bethany stank. Mary and Martha were pleased to see him when he knocked wearily on their door, looking for food and a place to rest for the night.

"Martha, come quickly!" Mary shouted. "It's Joshua!"

"All in good time, Mary," her sister called back to her. "Bring him in. I've fresh bread in the oven."

Mary brought Joshua back into the little house where he had recuperated from the brutal attack the year before.

"Lazarus will be in soon," Mary said. "He'll be so surprised and pleased to see you. He's not been very well recently. I think he works too hard. I'm a little worried about him. He's been experiencing dizziness."

"I'm not surprised," Joshua remarked, wrinkling up his nose. "That odor all day would be enough to cause anyone to feel faint."

Mary laughed.

"You soon get used to it, just as you did before," she said.

"Well, that was last year. I need to get used to it all over again. It stinks, Mary."

She looked up into Joshua's eyes lovingly, refusing to answer his complaint.

"Tell us, now," she continued. "What brings you back here? Have you business with the Essenes in Jerusalem?"

"Mary, I've left the Essenes," Joshua answered confidentially.

"What!"

"Yes, Mary. I've decided that it is time for me to follow my own destiny."

Mary shouted back to Martha to come on out.

"I'm coming," Martha yelled, as she gathered up the hot bread.

She broke it so that it would cool more quickly, and carried it in to them.

"Joshua, what a wonderful surprise! I know Lazarus will be so pleased to see you," she said greeting him.

"Joshua's left the Essenes," Mary interrupted. "He says he's going to follow his own destiny."

"And what might that be?" Martha asked, offering him bread from her tray.

Joshua picked up the bread.

"I need to preach my message for the end time, Martha. You're always so busy performing your chores that you don't have time to listen to your heart and to hear the small still voice from within, but there is coming a time when the small voice will rule us all. When that time comes, we will all be sons of God, radiating His Divine love."

His language was too much for Martha, and in truth, although Mary hung on every word he said, she, too, really did not understand what he was talking about.

Joshua embraced Martha.

"I did not mean to chastise you," he said. "You are a good person and you work very hard."

He turned back to Mary.

"You should help your sister more," he said before continuing. "But my message can only be heard if you are receptive to it. Divine love comes from the heart. It is not the mechanical love that comes from doing the good things that others expect of us. The Pharisees do that, but I'm telling you that they are no closer to God than any of us. I was no closer to God as an Essene than I am here talking to you both. The members of the Essenic brotherhood lead good lives, but their goodness is to each other, and their Divine love is stifled by their good practices."

Both Mary and Martha sat staring at Joshua. Their friend spoke with such authority. They had loved him as they nursed him back to strength after he had been beaten up and robbed, but now they sat in awe of him.

Lazarus came in from the tannery. He stank. Joshua also thought he looked a little pale. When Lazarus saw his friend, he grinned from ear to ear and embraced him.

"Joshua! It's really you!" he shouted. "Welcome back to our house. Martha! What have we to honor our guest with tonight?"

Lazarus' body odor almost forced Joshua to step back.

"All I have prepared is fresh bread and lentil soup," Martha answered.

"And there's not too much of that bread left," Mary added.

"I didn't know Joshua was coming," Martha said apologetically.

Lazarus turned to Joshua again.

"It's a bad time of the year. There's so little we can gather right now—no fruit, no berries, it's right in between the seasons."

"I know, my friend," Joshua said. "I did not come here to feast. I'm used to fasting. I don't expect anything from you other than the joy to see you again, and the hope that you might allow me a corner of your room whereby to lay myself down for the night. I must return to the Essenic community near Anathoth and redeem my possessions, and then I'm going to Jerusalem to visit my brother James and his wife. I will probably stay with them for the Passover."

"Won't you come back here after that?" Lazarus asked. "Everyone in the village will be so pleased to see you again."

"Is that an invitation?"

"Of course, my friend. We feel as if you are a part of our family."

Mary's eyes lit up at the thought.

"Do come back to us, Joshua," she said. "Why don't you stay with us as our rabbi?"

"What a great idea, Sister," Lazarus agreed. "We have never had a rabbi here in Bethany."

He looked at Joshua.

"You can live with us until we build you a house. Summer will be coming and the conditions will be better."

"Let me think about it, Lazarus. It would be a wonderful start to my work," Joshua answered, as Martha got up to attend to their evening meal.

"Let's give thanks to God that he has sent us a rabbi," Lazarus suggested.

He embraced Joshua again, who by now had become a little more accustomed to the tanning odors reeking from his friend's clothing.

"Why don't we start by saying our evening prayers? The sun has now set," Joshua replied.

They stood and recited the Shema, giving their thanks to God.

* * *

The barren Anathoth commune, still in winter clothing, looked hostile to Joshua after the relative comfort and mild conditions of Qumran. The dormant vines and empty beanpoles showed only sandy stones and the poorest of soil. A rugged-looking brother guided a simple plow between the rows pulled through the ground by a flea-bitten donkey. The man barely looked up as Joshua passed by.

In the primitive stone shelter that Joshua remembered to be the overseer's hut, Joshua found Brother Solomon. The Overseer rose as Joshua entered. He was surprised to see a visitor at this time of the year, and at first he didn't recognize Joshua.

"Shalom!" Solomon said in greeting.

"Shalom, Brother Solomon. I'm Joshua, the brother you sent to Qumran."

"Of course, Brother Joshua!" the Overseer replied. "My eyes, you know, they have really deteriorated. I can hardly see now."

Brother Solomon walked over to Joshua. He embraced him.

"Brother Joshua," he repeated. "What brings you back? What news do you bring us from Qumran?"

"Everything is fine in Qumran, Solomon, but I've left the Essenes."

"What!"

"Yes, Solomon. I must follow my own destiny. I studied extensively in the Qumran library. I admire all that the Essenes achieve in their purity of life, but God has called me to something different. I have declined to join the 'Many' and take up the covenant, Solomon. Instead, I took the baptism of Jon."

"Jon?" Solomon queried.

"Yes, Solomon…Jon the Baptist. He was teaching his message of repentance close to Qumran. I need to work out my destiny closer to the life of the ordinary people…not withdrawn from the world, but fully within the world. I'm grateful for the discipline and the experience that my two years as a novice has given me, but I can't go on to the covenant. I've made up my mind."

* * *

Brother Solomon looked grave. *Simpletons fall by the wayside,* he thought to himself. *They are usually petty thieves and beggars that have sought refuge with us in the relative comfort and security of our disciplined commune. But, men like Joshua have usually become the pillars of our movement.*

"You are quite sure about your decision, Brother Joshua?" Solomon asked.

"Yes, Solomon," Joshua reiterated. "I've already left the Essenes. The Inspector at Qumran, Brother Nathan, has released me. I have the document here that he prepared for me. I have come to claim my possessions."

"I see," the overseer said gravely.

He remembered only too well the box of gold coins. It was still in the treasury building and not yet released to the community. He read the document. He looked back up at Joshua.

"Very well, I'll send someone over to the treasury for your box. Now let me see, you also brought to us a cart and mule."

"That's right, Solomon, but if you remember you returned them to me in kind when I went down to Qumran."

"I remember now. You also had half the gold coins. Were they given back to you in Qumran?"

"Unfortunately, they were lost—the cart, the mule and the gold coins. I fell among thieves on the road from Jerusalem to Jericho. I lost everything."

The overseer raised his eyebrows.

"Were you hurt?"

"Pretty badly, but a kind man from Bethany rescued me, and his sisters nursed me back to strength so I could travel on to Qumran."

"Well, I can't do much about the cart and mule," the overseer said. "However, we'll get your box as soon as we can."

He shook his head slowly.

"You lost the gold, too?"

"Yes, all of it."

"How are you going to carry this box? It will be too heavy unless you have a donkey."

"You raise a good point, Solomon," Joshua agreed. "I will need a donkey. Can I buy a donkey from the community here? I can sell off some of the remaining gold."

Solomon's eyes lit up.

"Let's strike a deal, then," he suggested. "We'll provide you with a good donkey. We have several at present. I'll let you pick the one you want. But you will have to pay us in gold coins from your treasure. Shall we settle for the weight of one hundred shekels in gold?"

Joshua did not know how to answer; he really had no idea as to how much gold there still was in the mysterious box. He could tell that there was an element of greed in Solomon's approach, which led him to believe that Solomon had a fairly good idea what the box was worth.

"I think that may be a little steep, my friend," Joshua said. "Shall we agree on the weight of seventy-five shekels of gold?"

Solomon's face fell, but he put up his hands in a gesture of acceptance.

"Who am I to argue with a free merchant? Seventy-five shekels worth of your gold for the donkey."

"As you say," Joshua agreed.

The deal concluded, they left the overseer's hut and went to the treasury building. There, another brother found the box and presented it to them. Seventy-five shekels worth of gold coins were weighed out.

The box was depleted by almost one half, but Joshua had bought himself a donkey. He selected a good-looking animal, and when the box was securely strapped to the beast, he led the donkey away, turning his back forever on the primitive commune that had been his home for a year.

Chapter Nine

Resurrection

James was surprised when Joshua found him at the Sanhedrin chamber. He waited patiently until the council session closed, and called to him as he came out.

"I don't believe it!" he cried, as he embraced his younger 'brother'. "When did you come to Jerusalem?"

"I've only just arrived," Joshua replied. "I went to the house that I thought I remembered, but neither you nor Rachel were there."

"No, we moved. We have three rooms now on an upper level. The house is south of the Temple on Mount Zion. It's really much nicer than where we were. You see, Joshua, we have a family now, a baby girl. Rachel was purified just a few days ago."

"A baby! Rachel has a little girl! James, this is wonderful news!" Joshua exclaimed. "You have been blessed at last. I'm so happy for you both. How delighted Joanna would have been with this news."

"It's funny you should mention, Joanna," James continued. "We decided to name our little girl after Joanna. We have a Joanna in the family again. Come on home with me. Rachel will be thrilled to know you're here, and then you'll see the baby Joanna for yourself."

James was truly surprised to see Joshua, knowing that few who joined the Essenes, other than those who might be escaping the authorities, ever left the sect. He had thought that Joshua was lost forever to the movement, and since he had expressed his doubts as to the merit of such involvement, he was doubly pleased to hear that Joshua had left.

"What are your plans?" he asked excitedly, as Joshua led his donkey while they walked over to the Triple Gate. "How long can you stay with us?"

"I would certainly like to stay until Passover," Joshua replied. "Will that be all right for you with Rachel and the baby?"

"Of course, Joshua," James agreed. "The longer you can stay the better. There have been some interesting debates in the Sanhedrin these days. There's a lot of discussion about life after death. The Pharisaic viewpoint seems to weigh quite heavily over that of the Sadducees."

"You are still happy here in Jerusalem, then?" Joshua asked, brushing aside James' attempt to start a didactic discussion.

"Very happy. Apart from my role in the Sanhedrin, I have a small school. I teach about six children now. I teach them both Hebrew and Greek, as well as instructing them in our ways. Greek is still very important, Joshua. Whether we like it or not, it's really the language of our country. I'm still amazed that some of our leaders are so blind to its importance. There are many Sanhedrin members who still have not mastered Greek."

"It may be the language of the rich and educated," Joshua interjected, "but it's not the language of the poor."

James was a little taken aback. He wasn't quite sure how to answer Joshua. The simple statement had been made with a great sense of purpose and a commanding authority. The intellectual James suddenly felt dwarfed by Joshua's presence.

"True," he said in a rather non-committal way.

They made their way down a narrow street, and then turned to the left up some shallow steps that led to a detached two-story building on one of the highest points of Mount Zion.

"Our new home," James pointed out proudly. "We have to take the steps up, but you can tether the donkey down here."

They tied up the beast and unstrapped the box. James helped Joshua carry it up the steps.

"What have you in here?" he asked. "It's pretty heavy."

In reality, Joshua knew that the old box was much lighter than it used to be. He remembered what a real effort it had been to bury it in the floor of the house he had built for Joanna in Nazareth. It had been even harder to bring it up from the ground when he had retrieved it.

"The box goes wherever I go," Joshua explained. "My mother kept it for me for years. Now it's all I own. It's full of gold coins, or what's left of them. It paid our passage from Egypt, if you remember. My destiny has been linked to this box. I'm the steward of its contents, and now that they're dwindling I must use them wisely."

"You mean this was part of Miriam's dowry when she married Father?" James questioned.

"No, not exactly. The box was given to us by strangers when I was born."

He remembered Miriam's story. *What sort of strangers would have left a box of gold coins?* James thought. But it was too late to pursue this conversation further as they had reached the top of the steps and Rachel was there to greet them.

"Joshua!" Rachel exclaimed. "James, you never said Joshua was coming!"

"No, Rachel. I didn't know. It's as much of a surprise to me as to you."

They put the old box down, and after James had embraced his wife, Joshua and Rachel fell into each other's arms.

"You have a baby!" Joshua cried joyfully.

"Yes," Rachel answered proudly. "We named our baby after Joanna."

Joshua looked faraway as if the memories of his own Joanna were haunting him.

"Where is she?" he said almost vacantly. "Let me see her."

"Asleep. Come and look at her."

They came into a large chamber furnished sparsely in Roman style with couches and leather thong seats. There were two tall oil lamps in the room, and light filtered in from square window openings that looked out southward over flat-topped roofs and across the valley of Hinnom. Nestled in swaddling cloths on one of the couches was the sleeping baby. As they approached, she awoke and smiled. Rachel picked her up and wiped the baby's mouth.

"Meet Joanna," she said proudly to Joshua.

Joshua held out his little finger to the child that took hold of it with her small hand as a tear ran down his cheek.

"What the Lord took from me he has given to you, Rachel," he said softly. "Joanna lives in your child."

Joshua lightly kissed the baby.

James poured out two goblets of wine.

"Can you drink with us?" James asked, remembering the Essenic rules of abstinence.

A broad smile cossed Joshua's face.

"Didn't God give us the best grapes in Nazareth, James? I have not had strong drink for a long time now, but I'm no longer one of 'the brothers'. Pour me a small goblet so that I can share your joy."

"I already have," James answered.

They drank together.

"It's good to have you back."

"It's good to see you all again, too," Joshua agreed.

* * *

When Joshua revisited the Temple, the bustle of the Outer Court fascinated him after the quiet of Qumran. At the approach to Passover, the whole world seemed to descend on Jerusalem. The court was full of many different people, busily changing their money for Temple shekels, and buying from the numerous stalls. Animals were everywhere, lambs and goats, along with cages of doves and pigeons. Some were being led or carried to the sacrificial altar. The merchants thrived as they sold elaborate phylacteries to the tourist pilgrims, along with gold, silver and beaded jewelry, brass and copper trays, kosher cooking utensils, and carvings in olive wood, depicting donkeys, camels, oxen, and birds. He walked past the gate that he and Jon had helped to build. The builders had long since finished here, but they were still working on the corner towers of the great court. The last decorative motifs of the turrets were being positioned. Two men were in the process of mounting a great stone. The stone slipped and fell. It missed Joshua by about four cubits, crashing to the paving where it shattered a marble slab. The men shouted. Joshua looked up at the corner turret. The two men managed to hold on, one suspended by a rope that had saved him from almost certain death. A near tragedy had somehow been averted.

But for the grace of God that man would be dead, Joshua thought.

He studied the height of the tower, as a crowd of onlookers began to gather.

I wonder if I had been up there if God would have saved me, he mused. *If I deliberately fell from that tower, and survived the fall, landing in the Great Court here on my feet, people would regard my survival as a miracle. It would make it so easy for me to preach about the coming kingdom if the people believed that I was Divine. If I could perform miracles, people would think I was God. How easy it would be then for me to believe that I am a son of God, the 'Prince of Peace' and the Lord's anointed one. After all, the psalmist said—"He will give his angels charge of you, and on their hands they will bear you up before your feet have time to be dashed against the stones."*

Rescuers began to climb up the tower to help the man who was dangling from the rope. Others were busy now, shouting instructions. Joshua realized that as the first on the scene he really should have been the first to help. It was these men, however, who had taken over, while he had stood there contemplating whether God would have rescued him, and whether he could have used such drama to back his claims that he was special—God's chosen one and the messiah of his people. He felt ashamed, as if he had forgotten all the lessons of humility that he had learned on his desert retreat.

"Get behind me, Satan!" he cried out.

A surprised young man, waving his arms in gestures as he shouted up to the rescuers in front of Joshua, looked around.

Embarrassed, Joshua smiled at him.

"I'm sorry," Joshua said. "I don't mean you."

The man swinging on the rope was pulled in. He regained his footing. There was a cheer from the gathering crowd.

Joshua, still feeling a little ashamed of his thoughts, retraced his steps, returning to the melee of Temple bargaining. Somehow, it all looked a little less colorful now.

The servant must suffer in order to be a son of God, he thought. *I must learn to be more humble. This return to Jerusalem is exhilarating, but these people are established...they know what they are doing. My message is for those who are lost like sheep gone astray. It is better that I should be a shepherd to those to whom I minister. Here in Jerusalem, you have to be a man of power like the High Priest. God has not given me that kind of power.*

The power He has given me must come from my heart. The Divine love of God that is within me must be the light to which my people will come.

Joshua remained very thoughtful during his days in Jerusalem. He prayed a great deal, and took himself away from the city, seeking God in the peace of the Mount of Olives where he could concentrate without the hustle and bustle that marred the Temple precinct. He stayed with James and Rachel through the festival of the Passover that they celebrated together. It was the first family Passover that Joshua had attended since leaving Nazareth. He knew, however, that much though James and Rachel might like him to stay, he had a duty to follow his calling and serve the village of Bethany as their rabbi.

Joshua explained to James that he would be leaving to go to Bethany. James tried to persuade him not to go.

"Bethany's a terrible place," he said with surprise. "It's a tannery and stinks! Why do you want to go there when you could stay here and teach at my school? There's no future for you in Bethany."

"James, your ministry is to established rich Jews, but the Lord has called me to serve the poor seekers," Joshua proclaimed. "He has led me to these people. They're my friends. They need a rabbi and I look forward to serving them."

"Joshua, you have become very strange. I am not sure that I understand you anymore," James said disappointingly. "You could have such a bright future here in Jerusalem."

"James, nobody has ever done more for me than you have, but you have never understood me. I believe in my destiny. God is in control. He controls my life as He controls yours, and He has a different purpose for me than He does for you. We must go our separate ways."

James fell silent.

"Well, remember that we will always be here in Jerusalem," he finally said. "At least at Bethany you won't be far away. You can always come back to us."

"Of course you will be back," Rachel added. "Remember that our baby is named after Joanna."

Joshua smiled. Momentarily, he was drawn back to thoughts of Joanna, his family, and those earlier years. Despite times of hardship, it had all really been too comfortable. The Essenic brotherhood had hardened him. *Grapes have to be grown in poor soil as well as good earth,* he thought. *I can't go back to the old life, but I must move on to my new destiny.*

"No," he said. "Much though you may want to persuade me, you have your work to do and I have mine. God has called us both to our destinies. It is time for me to use the talents He has given to me the way that He has planned for me."

He kissed Rachel, and held Joanna's tiny hand.

"I must leave you both," he said, as a lump formed in his throat.

Tears caught the corners of his eyes.

"I'll go to the Temple, James. There I will make my sacrifices. Pray for me as I will for you."

Joshua stooped to pick up his old box.

"I'll help you carry it," James offered.

Together, they took it down the steps and strapped it on the donkey's back.

"Shalom, James!" Joshua said as he embraced him.

He looked up and saw Rachel standing at the top of the steps with Joanna in her arms.

"Shalom!" he called up.

Then, taking the donkey's lead rope, he began to walk toward the narrow street of steps that led from Mount Zion toward the Temple area and Mount Moriah.

* * *

Lazarus could hear muffled voices. They faded in and out and he couldn't understand them. It was dark and he felt very cold. He remembered being in the tannery and everything going blank. Silence returned. Lazarus slept. He awoke and thought he could hear a dripping sound. It faded away. He felt even colder. He blanked out. Lazarus slept. He awoke again. His nose felt damp like that of a dog. He was too cold to move. He slept. His sleep was deep. He heard nothing and he dreamed nothing.

"Lazarus... Lazarus... Lazarus!" The sound of his name boomed around him as he awoke.

"Lazarus... Lazarus... Lazarus!"

It was his name. He was sure it was his name. *Have I reached Gehinnom?* he thought. *Am I being called to my torment?* But, he couldn't smell sulfur or sense the heat of the unquenchable fires.

"Lazarus... Lazarus... Lazarus!"

His name boomed around him yet again, and he felt sure he was being called. He attempted to move his arms, but they were stuck as if they were bound. He tried to shake them violently. They loosened just a bit. He felt warmer after the exertion. *I must be getting nearer to the fire,* he concluded. Afraid, but with a spirit to fight off the eternal punishment, he struggled to move his legs, but they seemed more solid than his arms. He was getting hotter and hotter. He panicked. *The flames of Gehinnom! They are getting closer,* he believed. He kicked out, but his legs wouldn't move. He twisted his neck, shaking his head. It hardly moved, but little by little it freed. He breathed deeply in the struggle, and choked on a wall of cloth.

"Lazarus! Come forth!" the voice boomed on.

Where am I? Lazarus asked himself. *Do I deserve this?*

He struggled with his arms. The binding loosened somewhat. He fought with his elbow. His right arm was almost free. As he struggled, however, he only felt the heat of the flames of Gehinnom coming closer... closer...closer. His left leg and left arm wouldn't move. He wrestled with his knee, loosening his right leg. The relative freedom now in the binding that held his right side caused him to be able to rock his whole body.

The voice boomed again:

"Lazarus! Come out!"

He rocked harder and faster until he fell, rolling onto a hard surface. The blow as he landed further loosened the bindings. His left leg still wouldn't move, but his left arm began to feel alive and in a final effort he freed his right arm. His head began to ache, but the alternate body chills and heat of the fire had gone. With his right hand he tore at the cloths around his face, freeing his mouth and nose, making it easier to breathe. He had escaped Gehinnom.

He heard a familiar voice:

"Lazarus! Is that you?"

Lazarus tried to answer, but no clear words came out. He just made a sound more like a groan than speech.

"Lazarus! I can hear you. Where are you?" the voice asked.

Lazarus blinked as he pulled the binding from his eyes. It was dark. He couldn't see.

He pulled himself along in the direction of the voice as best he could, the unraveled cloths trailing behind him. He began to see grays and browns in an abstract swirl. It was dark, but there was some source of light. He managed to free his right leg from the binding. His leg hurt. His whole body hurt. He advanced a little farther, pulling himself along the rock floor. He could see fuzzy light ahead, and then he felt a hand on his shoulder.

Lazarus thought the voice he could hear was that of Joshua:

"Lazarus! You're alive!"

He groaned again, and thought that he could see a shadowy face.

"It's Joshua!" the face said. "Let me lead you out of here. God has answered our prayers. You've come back from the dead!"

Joshua dragged Lazarus along the cave floor.

The light became more pronounced, and he could see that Lazarus was still partly bound. He pulled at the cloths, unraveling them. Lazarus' naked body felt clammy and cold. Joshua rubbed his friend's arms and legs to try to warm them up. The right one responded quite well, but the left wouldn't move. The pain in Lazarus' head increased. Blood ran down one side of his face. Joshua wiped it with part of the binding. It hurt. Lazarus cried with the pain. The cry seemed to free his blurred vision. He was able to see that he was lying on the floor of a cave. Joshua was kneeling over him massaging his body. The bright light of the outside world was a little way ahead of them at the cave entrance.

Joshua pulled Lazarus farther into the light. Lazarus groaned, and tried to say Joshua's name. It was garbled, but it was speech.

"You must stay where you are," Joshua said. "I need to get help to carry you out."

Lazarus watched as Joshua stood up and walked out of the cave. He could hear him shouting:

"Lazarus is alive! Lazarus lives!"

The pain from his head throbbed. Lazarus' mind went blank as he passed out on the floor of the cave.

* * *

Joshua was concerned when he returned with two heavy set laborers from Bethany and found Lazarus unconscious again. The men, named Samson and Gideon, had been afraid to enter the cave of the dead, but

Joshua had assured them that no harm would come to them. The place stank.

Seeing Lazarus unconscious, Samson and Gideon took him for dead and screamed. The sound echoed through the cave and brought Lazarus around. He opened his eyes. Joshua knelt beside him.

"I told you," Joshua said to the others. "God has raised Lazarus from the dead. Do you now believe?"

"Who are you?" Samson asked, looking at Joshua with skepticism and fear.

"You know me, Samson. I'm the same Joshua to whom you all showed such kindness when I was almost taken for dead a year ago. Lazarus saved my life then. It's only right that God has resurrected him from the dead."

"But, I helped carry him here. Lazarus was dead." he repeated, still totally confused. "Gideon was with me, weren't you?"

Gideon nodded in agreement.

"We laid him on the shelf. He's been in here for three days and died a day before we laid him here. See how this place stinks. Lazarus was dead."

"Well none of that matters now," Joshua said, taking command. "He's alive and he's injured. Help me lift him up. We're going to have to carry him."

They carried Lazarus out of the cave. Almost everyone from Bethany had now gathered outside the burial place. Mary and Martha, who had brought Joshua to the cave at his suggestion, after he had told them he might have the power to raise their brother from the dead, were in the forefront. They were stunned because they knew Lazarus had died. In their grief, they had, nonetheless, lovingly washed Lazarus' body, and bound it for entombment. Skeptical to the last, they stood close to the entrance as the men carried Lazarus out. He looked a ghastly white in the bright sunlight, and the blood had disfigured the side of his face. They propped him up against a rock.

"Has anyone a shawl or a water skin?" Joshua cried out to the incredulous crowd.

Martha turned to see if there was any response. A woman came forward offering her mantle. Joshua took it and wrapped it around Lazarus' naked body.

"I still need water!" Joshua shouted.

Struggling through the astonished crowd, an elderly man came forward with a skin. The crowd moved in, and Mary and Martha knelt on the ground beside Lazarus. Joshua fed Lazarus with water from the skin. Most of it spilled, but almost without being perceived, Lazarus swallowed a few sips. He blinked his eyes and raised his right hand to touch Martha. Martha screamed and pulled away, not able to believe that Lazarus was alive. Mary, on the other hand, took Lazarus' left hand into her own and caressed his fingers.

Joshua wiped away some of the blood from Lazarus' head wound with the spilled water.

"Speak to us, Lazarus," he said softly.

Lazarus groaned, and then looking up at Joshua slowly pronounced his name:

"Joshhhhuuuaaa."

"He spoke!" Martha screamed, still terrified.

"Martha, it's our brother!" Mary said, as tears began to run down her cheeks. "It's Lazarus! Joshua has raised Lazarus from the dead!"

"Maarrry," Lazarus said, and turning his head just slightly he called out Martha's name, too.

The astounded crowd began to shuffle and murmur as they crept forward for a better view of the miracle. A dead man had been raised from his tomb; not on the day he died, but after he had lain there bound in his death rags for three days. He really was alive, he was speaking, and with his right arm he was making feeble gestures.

"Samson, go and fetch my donkey," Joshua instructed.

"Mary...Martha..." he called to the two sisters softly. "It's up to us now to make sure he continues to live. We need to get him home and keep him warm. He's still very cold, but it must be God's will that he should live. This is nothing less than a miracle. I went into the cave knowing, as you said, that your brother was dead. Your brother saved my life, as did you all. I was stricken with grief just the same as you. It was a terrible shock to me when I arrived here, full of hope, only to learn from you this terrible news."

Joshua took Lazarus' wounded head on his shoulder.

"I prayed," he continued. "I called on the Lord that this miracle should happen. The power of God came to me."

Joshua stroked Lazarus' hair, and looked into his eyes.

"Lazarus, you answered my call and came back from the dead," he said.

Smiling, he then looked up at the two incredulous sisters.

"I can't believe it either, Mary! I asked God for this miracle that Lazarus might hear me. Martha! I asked God right there in the depth of the cave. I couldn't even see where your brother was laid out. I just prayed with faith that God would answer my call. I called several times and nothing happened. I prayed all the more, and then I heard a faint response. It was frightening, but in the gloom I heard Lazarus come to life."

The crowd opened up a pathway as Samson returned with Joshua's donkey. Carefully, Samson and Gideon lifted Lazarus up, straddling him on the beast. They held him in position, as Joshua led the donkey back to the village. Mary and Martha were right beside them weeping for joy.

Once at the house, the two sisters set about bathing their brother and cleansing his wound. Lazarus was able to fairly freely move his right arm, and there was life in his right leg. His left side, however, remained motionless. Each time he took a few sips of water more strength seemed to come to him. He was able to give them a slightly lopsided, tortured smile, and from time to time he repeated their names. They kept him warm and his color began to return. Little by little his speech improved, and as the days went by life returned to his paralyzed limbs. The head wound healed, and Lazarus was able to join them in praising God for his return from the dead.

Chapter Ten

An important guest

Linus knew Questus, the Syrian governor, was pleased with his achievement in Palmyra. The trade treaty that resulted from the preliminary agreement he set up was already proving more than worthwhile to the Roman province. The Parthians made no move to win Palmyra over with counter offers, and it looked like a perfect arrangement whereby at minimum expense the Syrian Legion would offer protection to Palmyra in exchange for a seventh part of their transit tariffs.

It did not come as a surprise to him, therefore, when he found he was called before the governor again.

Questus greeted him informally when he was shown into the Damascus office:

"Ah! Linus Flavian. Come on in."

Linus saw that the governor had a visitor.

"Linus Flavian, I would like you to meet Pontius Pilatus," Questus stated.

The stranger rose to greet Linus. He was not dressed in military fashion, but wore a toga. His hair was balding and curled around the edges. His appearance reminded Linus of the head of Tiberius Caesar as depicted on the Roman coins, and seen in the cheap-looking busts that adorned most military offices.

"Greetings!" Pilatus said. "I've heard about your achievement in

Palmyra, and I've heard good things about you from your illustrious uncle, Senator Tarquinius."

"Linus Flavian," the governor interjected, "Pontius Pilatus has been appointed our prefect in Judea. He will shortly take up his post in Caesarea Maritima. I have selected you to be his aide. Your fluency in Aramaic will be of enormous help to Pilatus just as it was for me in Palmyra. The Judean prefecture is always difficult. Pilatus will need skilled men around him who can understand the Semitic and Jewish mind. You will be promoted to the rank of tribune and you will be a go-between for the prefect and the people."

Linus could not conceal his pleasure. A grin spread across his face. He was longing to move out of Damascus, important though it had been for him to serve in the Syrian Legion there. Damascus was boring. He felt sure that Caesarea and Jerusalem would be more exciting. They were certainly more volatile.

"When do I take up this appointment?" Linus asked.

The governor looked at Pontius Pilatus.

"Pilatus, Flavian will be your aide," he said. "I now leave that for the two of you to work out. Good luck to you both."

Linus studied Pilatus. He looked more like a senator than a soldier. He wondered if he would be able to understand the independent mind of the Jew even with his help.

"I am planning on traveling south in about five days," Pilatus announced. "Naturally, Linus Flavian, I will wish you to travel with me. A cohort of the Legion will also be traveling with us. Meanwhile, I would like to have a meeting with you. Meet me in my quarters here tomorrow at noon."

Linus saluted, placing his fist to his chest.

"Yes sir!" he replied, and then added, knowing he was now a tribune: "Hail, Ceasar!"

He turned and left the governor's quarters content in the knowledge that the authorities for a future career had selected him.

I must tell my father, he thought as he left the governor's office. *I wonder if he already knows. Perhaps on the way to Judea we can stop off at Magdala and I can introduce the prefect to my father.*

Contentedly, Linus looked forward to starting work in his new appointment.

* * *

In his retirement, Flavius Septimus quite often came down to the village of Magdala to buy fresh fish. He couldn't pass the square house at the end of the village without at least giving a cursory glance in its direction. He hadn't spoken a word to Esther for years and he felt remorse and guilt of conscience that it had been necessary for him to destroy Linus' relationship with her daughter. But, he was almost sure that Maria was also his child. He could never prove it, and Copernia had never suspected his misdemeanor, but the possibility still haunted him. He noticed on one of his customary trips to buy the fish that there were quite a few people gathered at Esther's house and there was a fair amount of shouting. He stood for a moment watching, and hearing familiar Hebrew wails, he realized that a death had taken place.

Could Esther have died, or even Maria? Flavius wondered, moving closer to the scene. Four men were carrying a body out of the house. It was wrapped in a coarse sack that sagged in the middle.

Flavius followed them along the shore at a distance. Gravediggers had already dug a hole in the ground. With very little ceremony, the men rolled the sacked body into the hole and covered it up. Neither Esther nor Maria appeared to be present. Flavius could only conclude that the dead person had to have been either one or the other of them. His natural inclination, because of her greater age, was for him to believe that it was Esther who had died. Besides, he could not remember having seen Maria in the village since the day he had expelled her from his villa. She seemed to have vanished, no doubt rejected by both her fellow villagers as well as him. The recollection gnawed at his stomach as he remembered the little girl the first time he had seen her. *My daughter...* he thought, *I was sure even then that she was my daughter. I wonder if she ever bore me a grandchild. Maybe she drowned the baby.*

When the mourners left, Flavius walked over to the grave—a heap of earth and stones set on the edge of a natural grove close to the shore of the lake. He stood silently for a moment, staring at the loose stones and soil. He was tempted to dig it all up again just so he could be sure and know that it was Esther who lay there. Pomegranates and myrtle grew close by. He plucked a sprig of white myrtle and mixed it with some scarlet flowers from the pomegranates. He dropped them on the crude grave.

"For you, Esther," he whispered. "Although our worlds are far apart, I did not forget you."

Somewhat disturbed, Flavius returned to the village just in time to buy the fish. The pickling merchants were already on the beach. Most of the fresh fish already lay packed in the wagons.

A day or two later, back at his villa, Flavius plucked up the courage to confront his Hebrew maidservant concerning Esther.

"I noticed a death in the village the other evening," he said. "It looked like the mother of the unfortunate young girl Linus brought here might have passed away. Did you hear anything?"

"Esther!" Leah replied. "Yes, sir, you're right. Esther's gone. A good thing, too, I would say. She was never really part of the village. She was a bad woman. She took money from all those strangers that came in off the boats. She was a whore, sir. They wouldn't bury her in the burial ground, as they were afraid of her spirit. They buried her along the beach in a hollow in the ground which they covered with stones and loose earth."

Flavius didn't need to hear anymore. He knew it all anyway.

"All right Leah! That's enough. I don't need all the details," he said with irritation. "I just noticed there had been a death in the village the other day. As long as it wasn't one of your people, that's fine."

There was a heavy knock at the gate.

"Leah. Go and see who that is," Flavius said with surprise. "We're not expecting anyone."

* * *

Leah laughed to herself as she left to cross the courtyard and open the latch on the entrance gate. *Does he really think that we don't know? These Romans sometimes underestimate us Jews.* She was surprised when she opened the gate to find a detachment of Roman soldiers outside. Leading them, in his new tribune's uniform, was Linus, and riding beside him on an equally fine horse was a Roman stranger.

"Leah!" Linus called down. "Please fetch my father. We have an important guest."

Leah returned to Flavius Septimus, who was now out on the terrace, looking down on the scene below.

"Master!" she cried out. "It's Linus and a stranger. He says we have an important guest."

"I can see that," her Master answered. "Where is Demetrius?"

"He hasn't come in yet, sir. He's overseeing the olive press."

"Then you'll have to show them in, Leah. Bring them to me in the Atrium."

"As you say, sir," Leah answered, and she returned to the courtyard to invite Linus and the stranger in.

Linus instructed his men.

"You can make camp up behind the villa. There's water up there from the outside well. Be careful of my father's chickens. I expect to see the same number of hens in the morning as there are this afternoon."

Leah explained that Flavius Septimus was waiting to receive them in the Atrium. As Linus led Pontius Pilatus into the house, Leah tied up their horses in the outer courtyard.

* * *

"Greetings, Father!" Linus said as he brought the Judean prefect through to the large peristyle in the center of the house.

"Linus, my son!" Flavius replied, as he stood eyeing Pontius Pilatus.

Flavius walked forward.

"Who is your guest?"

"Father, let me introduce you to the new prefect of Judea, Pontius Pilatus."

"Prefect...Welcome, Pilatus. Welcome to the house of Flavius Septimus. Have you just come down from Caesarea Philippi, or did you come direct from Damascus making camp along the way?"

"We stopped over at Caesarea Philippi, sir," Pilatus replied. "Questus sends you his fondest greetings from Damascus, and I have a wonderful aide here in your son."

"Linus! You didn't say. So you are the prefect's aide?"

"Yes, Father! Tribune Linus Flavian at your service, sir!" Linus proudly announced.

Leah returned.

"Please call Demetrius to the house!" Flavius shouted. "We need wine to celebrate. Make sure he serves last year's. It's the best."

Leah ran out to find the Flavian steward. Meanwhile, Copernia, roused by the noise, joined them.

It was a warm sultry afternoon, but the fountain playing in the pool helped to cool the atmosphere.

"Copernia, my dearest. May I introduce Pontius Pilatus, Prefect of Judea and your son Tribune Linus Flavian, aide to the prefect."

"No. Really. Linus a tribune and aide to the prefect?"

"Yes, my dear."

Copernia nodded at Pilatus and walked over to embrace her son.

"You look splendid!" she said, admiring her son in his uniform.

The helmet that he wore was more elaborate than that of a centurion, but still lacked the plumage of a commander.

"Welcome home!"

Once they were all seated in the Atrium porch, Demetrius served them goblets of wine. Linus gave news of Damascus and the Palmyra expedition, while Pilatus brought news from Rome, and greetings from the Tarquins and the Flavians.

Chapter Eleven

The Miracle Worker of Bethany

Joshua's fame as the miracle worker of Bethany spread rapidly. The sick and lame of Jerusalem began to pour into the village, seeking a cure from the man who could raise someone from the dead. Among those who came was a woman suffering from internal bleeding, whom no physician had successfully healed. She was afraid to approach the miracle worker directly, somewhat embarrassed by the delicacy of her condition. She watched from a distance as Joshua laid his hands on the suffering pilgrims and gave obvious relief to many. She was moved by the response of those around her, and saw for herself that the miracle worker's ability to cure diverse diseases by his compassionate touch was true.

If I can just be touched physically by this man, she thought, *then maybe I will be healed.*

She edged a little closer.

Joshua was holding his hand to the forehead of a young boy whose father had brought him to be healed. The boy suffered from an impediment of speech, but as Joshua talked gently to him he relaxed, and the boy's tongue became more controlled. Joshua placed his hand on the child's mouth, and appeared to pray. When he removed his hand the boy smiled.

"What is your name?" Joshua asked.

"Jerem-em-em-em-iah," the boy stammered.

"Jeremiah?" Joshua repeated. "Jeremiah was one of our great prophets. He preached his message to our people in their time of need. Repeat your name to me again, Jeremiah."

"Jerem-em-iah," the boy said.

His father stared at Joshua in amazement.

"The boy had not spoken that clearly before. It's usually impossible to understand what he is saying," he stated fearfully.

Joshua placed his hands on the boy's shoulders.

"That's right," he said calmly. "Your name is Jeremiah, and you will use your voice just as your great namesake did in the days when our people were taken away to Babylon. Now, repeat it one more time."

"Jeremiah," the boy said perfectly, "Jeremiah!"

Jeremiah started to laugh. He looked up at his father.

"My fer-father," he said. "My father!"

"Yes", Joshua confirmed.

The boy turned and shouted to the crowd in a strong voice:

"I am Jeremiah! I am Jeremiah! This is my father!"

Jeremiah's father was still dumbstruck. Tears were welling in the corners of his eyes. But obviously the journey from Jerusalem to Bethany had been worth it. The miracle man had cured his son. The crowd gathered around Joshua and Jeremiah, marveling as the boy shouted his name. Occasionally, he faltered just slightly, especially when he tried to answer questions posed by others, but for the most part his speech remained remarkably clear.

The woman suffering from internal bleeding edged closer to Joshua through the throng. She knelt behind him and pulled on the hem of his garment as she tried to reach the flesh of his ankles above his open sandals. Others were reaching out to Joshua as he faced the crowd. Only those immediately behind him saw the woman approach. He appeared to ignore her touch, but there was such a pressing crowd at this point that it seemed nothing strange. By the time he finally turned to see who was pressing him from behind, the woman lost her courage and slithered away as quietly as she had come.

"Someone touched me," he said gently.

One of the men standing close to him agreed:

"It was a woman, a poor demented creature who felt a passion for you."

Joshua did not respond to the man's suggestion.

"Who touched me?" he repeated with authority.

The crowd stood back in surprise.

"How can you ask who touched you, sir?" one of those close by answered. "We are all jostled in the crowd."

The man, who had suggested the woman to be an awestruck admirer, trembled.

"Who touched me?" Joshua repeated.

The woman, who had tried to lose herself in the crowd, felt trapped. Everyone was now watching. She could not escape. She came forward and knelt before Joshua, refusing to look up at him.

"It was me," she said softly.

"What can I do for you?" Joshua asked gently.

"I am afraid to tell you, sir. I am suffering from an unclean condition for which no physician has found a cure."

Joshua did not push her for further information.

"Woman," he said, "your faith in my ability to heal you has made you well. Remember, however, that it is not by touching me that you have been cured, but by my faith that the power of God can make you well through me. You may go with peace in your heart, and you will be healed of your disease."

The woman said nothing. She stood up and turned away from Joshua. She knew that the bleeding had stopped, and when she was able to detach herself from the crowd and retreat to a private place, she proved to herself that her intuition was right.

* * *

Along with those who were genuinely anxious to receive miraculous healing came those who were curious and wanted to see the 'Wonder Worker' in action. The word also spread down to the Jordan valley, causing many of Jon's disciples from beyond the Jordan to make the one-day journey up the difficult road from Jericho to Bethany. The little village was not able to handle the people. Fights broke out for food and water, and worst of all, Joshua himself, the famed miracle worker, could not always perform a cure.

Joshua did his best to cope with the crowds. He believed that he now had the power of God within him. How else could he have raised Lazarus from the dead? Many of those who came to him he did successfully heal, but those with serious physical handicaps did not seem to respond as well as those with disturbances of the mind. He used the same techniques, encouraging the afflicted to pray with him and put their whole trust in God. There were those simple cases presented to him where he merely had to touch to cure. As time went on, however, Joshua observed that the cure seemed to be more and more related to the patient's response. If the patient really believed that Joshua could cure him, very often a miracle occurred. He had success with partial cases of blindness, and remembered how James, even though he had been unsuccessful, had applied mudpacks to Joseph's eyes. Joshua did the same in conjunction with his power of prayer. The dumb and those with speech impediments he often was able to heal. But, never was he able to perform a miracle that compared with the raising of Lazarus from the dead.

Some from Bethpage and Bethany even brought their recently deceased loved ones to the 'Miracle Man' in the hope of another resurrection. As hard as Joshua tried to breathe life back into these decrepit bodies, he met with no success. Joshua also failed to heal many that came with broken bones and permanent paralysis; but Lazarus remained living proof of his miraculous powers, and a sufficient number of successes kept the crowds coming, so that the villages of Bethany and Bethpage became totally overrun.

It was not long before Pharisees from Jerusalem came to investigate the wild claims that the people made. Some of these 'holy men' tried to talk to the crowds, discouraging them.

"This man is a fraud," one of them cried out, as Joshua tried desperately to revive the life of a young girl. "How can he bring life to the dead? All of you should have more sense. It is a sin to touch the unclean. Those who have died are not among the living. They've already taken their place in Gehinnom to stay until the Messiah comes. Don't touch the dead. Only harm can come to those of you who touch the dead!"

Some shrunk away, afraid of the words of the well-dressed Pharisee.

Others shouted back at them:

"Lazarus lives! Do you take all hope from us?"

A group of the Pharisees confronted Joshua directly:

"On whose authority have you set yourself up as a miracle worker for these undeserving poor? Don't you understand that the very same God in whose name you perform these miracles places their afflictions upon them? Most of these men are the scum of the earth, the dregs that beg falsely at the Temple gates and steal liberally from the market stalls. Why do you try to cure the ills of these lost people? It would be better for you to teach them the Law so that they can then teach their children as we have been taught. These are the lost sheep of Israel. You are wasting your time on them."

The crowd started to shout down these Pharisees. Some threw mud pats at them and more than one stone was hurled in their direction. Joshua knew that the people, who had come to seek his aid, even though they witnessed many of his failures, still lived in the hope that he could give them a cure.

"Woe to you Pharisees!" Joshua shouted, venting his feelings. "You pay your tithes in mint and rue, but you fail to do justice or show the Divine love of God. Shame on you because you should know better. You are in a privileged position whereby you can pay your tithes unlike these poor folk. You should not feel satisfied just because you have met your priestly obligations. It is just as important that you show love and justice toward your fellow men. Do you think, just because you have reserved seats in your synagogues, and everyone greets you in the Temple courts, that you are any better than these poor people who have come here in hope and faith?"

The crowd began to cheer, and pelted the Pharisees all the more.

Ducking and protecting their faces, their fine robes now splattered in mud, the rich 'holy men' began to retreat as Joshua continued to remind them of their own inadequacies:

"You hypocrites! You load less fortunate men with burdens that are hard to bear. You give tasks to the poor that you would never dream of doing yourselves. It will be hard for you when the kingdom comes."

Joshua's tirade had its effect. The Pharisees left. However, from that day on he had enemies in influential circles and he became branded in Jerusalem as a dangerous rabble-rouser who could well be troublesome if he gained too much popular support from the uneducated poor.

His popularity as the miracle worker of Bethany did not diminish, however. The crowds continued to grow daily and among those who made the journey to Bethany was an elderly man whose curiosity had been aroused. He sought Joshua out during a quiet moment after the sun had set and the crowds had settled down to their domestic routines around the numerous campfires.

The man found Joshua outside Lazarus' house where he was seated with Mary, discussing the success of the day's cures.

"Joshua!" he called out.

Joshua looked up and saw the older man. There was something about him that was familiar, but he had seen so many people during the summer months that it had become hard for him to put names to faces.

"It's good to see you again," the man continued. "We were all so sorry when you decided to leave us in Jerusalem to choose another path."

It's Zadok... Joshua realized, *Zadok, the prophet of the spirit.*

"Zadok!" Joshua exclaimed happily. "It's so good to see you, too! You can't imagine how often I have thought about you and the discussions that we all had in Jerusalem."

He turned to Mary.

"This is Zadok, the prophet of the Holy Spirit. He's a very spiritual man. Can we welcome him?"

Mary greeted Zadok and went back into the house to tell Lazarus and Martha that they had a visitor.

"Who is he?" Lazarus asked.

"A prophet named Zadok. Joshua says we should welcome him."

"Where is he from?"

"Jerusalem," Mary answered. "He knew Joshua when he lived in Jerusalem before he met us."

"We must welcome him, then," concluded Lazarus. "Have we extra food?"

"Enough," Martha replied.

Mary and Martha began to prepare the dishes. Lazarus looked for some more of the rough wine of which he was so proud, but which Joshua found almost unpalatable.

On the bench outside, Joshua and Zadok had become engrossed in deep conversation.

"I knew that you were filled with the spirit," Zadok said to Joshua. "It was always obvious to me that the Holy Spirit shone from you. When I first initiated you, I could feel the power from within. It's this power that you are now using so effectively in your healing ministry—the power of Divine love."

"Yes, Zadok. You taught me much about the power of Divine love, as did my mother," Joshua continued. "But why can I not always succeed if that Divinity of spirit is within me? Why is it that some who seek my powers are disappointed because I am unable to relieve their pain and restore them to health?"

"But, Joshua, you do restore them," Zadok continued. "We should not always be so concerned about our physical ailments, but should be more concerned about our spiritual growth. I've watched you today. The light of God shone from you as you touched those people. You are a manifestation of the light and sound of God. When a cripple sees the light shine forth from you he may not be physically cured, but he is spiritually refreshed. The work that you are doing is of great importance, Joshua, for the light of God is upon you, and the sound of the spirit vibrates from your heart."

"Do you still believe that the Kingdom of God will soon be established?" Joshua asked, not wishing to fully commit himself to Zadok's flattery.

"The kingdom has already begun," Zadok continued. "The kingdom is at work in you, and in all those who let the sound and light of God manifest through them. The power of light will be the power of the Holy Spirit, Joshua, that will govern the new kingdom. Our Law is good, but it is not enough. It enables us to have a dialogue with God, but it has not made us co-workers with the Almighty. We all have the potential to be sons of God. You are a son of God."

A son of God and the 'Prince of Peace', Joshua thought, still clinging to his mother's revelations.

"Do you think of yourself as the Messiah, the prophet of the kingdom?" Joshua asked, curious to see how close Zadok was to his own thinking about himself.

"No, Joshua. There is no need for a messiah to herald the kingdom," Zadok answered emphatically. "The spirit will establish the kingdom. There are too many who are searching for a messiah because they cannot open their own hearts to the light and sound of God. If they could be a vehicle for the Holy Spirit they would not seek for a messiah. The kingdom will already be established in their hearts."

"But, Zadok, somebody must show the way. Somebody must lead our people to the Holy Spirit," Joshua countered. "We have such strong traditions. It is hard for our people to kick the traces from the cart. Our tradition and our study of the Law of Moses and the prophets must be our duty. It is all part of the covenant that was established between God and our people."

"Perhaps that is why some will equate this with the end time," Zadok said, smiling mystically. "Many things will pass away, including, in time, the might of Rome. The kingdom, which the spirit will establish will never die, but will become a threshold into the light and sound of God."

"Sometimes, you talk in riddles," Joshua gently chided Zadok.

"I don't need to explain myself to you, Joshua. You already have reached the inner light. You must teach your way and I mine. Between us, we will establish the kingdom of the Holy Spirit."

He clasped Joshua's hand reassuringly.

Mary came out and announced their meal was ready. Joshua and Zadok went in with her and joined Lazarus and Martha in the simple and happy fellowship that was always their way. The following day, the old man left Bethany and returned to Jerusalem.

There were as many now who rallied around Joshua as a champion against their rich overlords as those who came to be cured of their various ailments and diseases. Bethany had become swamped. There had been no time to build the promised house. The village had become one giant campground of the sick and maimed, lying on pallets waiting their turn with the 'Miracle Man'.

The tanning industry had come to a near halt as all the water from the wells was necessary to take care of the mass of migrants seeking Joshua's aid. Mary and Martha had a team of the village womenfolk helping them care for the maimed and wounded. Lazarus was a pillar of strength as he testified daily to the miracle that had brought him back from the dead. He had made an almost perfect recovery except that he dragged his left leg. Others profited by cutting sticks from the few scrubby trees to provide staffs for those who could barely walk. The village was stripped of its identity. As the summer drew to a close, disenchantment followed the mass euphoria.

The land laborers had paid little attention to their crops. The spelt harvest was abysmal, and the straggling vines had lost most of their best grapes to the thieving crowds. Timber was running out, and much of the clean water needed for tanning had been fouled. Joshua realized that his simple call to be Bethany's rabbi was turning into Bethany's disaster. What at first seemed an exciting manifestation of the power of God was turning into a nightmare for the very people that he most wanted to help—the people of Bethany. He realized he couldn't stay. He wrestled with his conscience, knowing that many were depending on him, but his mind was made up. For Bethany's sake he must move elsewhere.

Mary and Martha had enjoyed the excitement. Lazarus owed his new life to Joshua. They tried to talk him out of his decision.

"Winter will be coming, Joshua," Lazarus suggested. "The crowds will diminish. Life will return to normal."

"No, Lazarus, you've forgotten that the High Holy Days come first. There will be more people here after Rosh Hashanah, Yom Kippur, and Succoth than now. You know how the crowds gather around Jerusalem at that time of the year."

"True," Lazarus said, as he massaged his paralytic foot.

Mary looked longingly at Joshua.

"If you leave us where will you go?" she asked.

"I think I have to get away from the environs of Jerusalem," Joshua answered. "Pilgrims come to Jerusalem and hear about our work in Bethany. Many of those who have come to us this summer are from far away. Some are Galileans and Samaritans, and others are Jews from beyond the Jordan. Then, there is the baptist in the Jordan valley. He has sent many to us giving them a message of hope. I don't think I have any choice Mary, much though I would like to stay and settle down as your rabbi here. My destiny is going to have to take me elsewhere."

"Where?" Mary repeated forlornly.

"I suppose, at first, I should go back to Nazareth in Galilee. I presume my mother and other members of my family are still there. Maybe I can stay with them and teach for a while. My old father-in-law might still want me to manage his vineyards. I just need to give you all a chance here in Bethany. I'll come back."

He kissed Mary lightly on the forehead.

"I think I understand," Lazarus said, keeping his head down and knowing that several villagers had complained to him about their agricultural losses. "You know you'll always have a home with us. It'll be good for you to see your mother again. She must have missed you these past years."

"Actually, its well over four years now since I left Galilee," Joshua added as Lazarus looked up, "It would be good for me to return, just for a little while."

He hugged Mary and Martha.

"You two are like angels," he said. "I don't know what I would have done without you."

As he held them, he looked at their brother.

"You are the closest friends I've ever had," he said, as he affectionately squeezed Mary and Martha again. "We'll all be together in the future."

Joshua didn't waste much time. He needed to get away before the new onslaught of pilgrims from Jerusalem heard about his miracles. He strapped the old box onto his donkey and began the long journey from Bethany back to Nazareth in Galilee.

Chapter Twelve

On the Gadarene Shore

After Joshua moved back to Jerusalem, Jon the Baptist and his followers moved up the Jordan valley. As they traveled, they increased in numbers, taking every opportunity to preach repentance and preparation for the end time. Jon had become a formidable speaker. His message appealed to the lost and the homeless as they sought a new life in the expected kingdom. His method was easy. All Jon's disciples had to do was to accept his baptismal ritual and acknowledge that they had been cleansed of their sins. There were no degrees of initiation and there was no hierarchy. At each small settlement along the Jordan's banks, the people flocked to see the baptist. The villagers often shared their food supplies to feed the growing crowd of Jon's hungry disciples. This, in itself, became an added attraction for those who had no place to go. A veritable peasant army, unaware of its potential power, was building up around the heroic character of Jon the Baptist.

When Jon and his disciples reached the place where the Jordan emptied out from the Galilean lake, they turned to the eastern shore. Here, they settled at Gergesa for the winter. The numbers of converts to the repentance movement diminished in this rugged terrain. There was no highway that followed the shore. Most traffic was by boat.

* * *

On a winter's day when dark clouds hung over the lake, a group of fishermen from Capernaum beached their boats on Gergesa's stony shore. They were soaked from the heavy rain and spray that had befallen them when a sudden squall had hit this far side of the lake.

There were three men in the first boat, two brothers Janus and Jonas, who jumped out and attempted to pull their boat in, and their older companion, who struggled with the steering board as the boat swung in the shore-side waves. Just two fishermen manned a second boat—a youth named Thomas and a strong-looking man with a black beard.

The older man in the first boat seemed to be in charge.

"Pull your boat up farther, Judas," he shouted at the man with the dark beard. "We'll be stuck here for a day or two. I think we've sprung a leak. How's yours?"

"It's hard to tell, Simon," Judas replied, cupping his hands to carry his voice. "We've shipped so much water."

Janus and Jonas secured Simon's boat, planting the anchor firmly into the beach.

"Once the wind turns to the north this time of the year you haven't got a hope out there," Janus commented.

"We're lucky to have come through," his brother agreed.

Judas' boat didn't beach as well as Simon's. The heavy shipment of water weighed it down. The young man, Thomas, was pulling on the anchor line as hard as he could, but the boat made no progress and was swinging dangerously in the waves.

"Give Thomas a hand there," Judas shouted down to the two brothers.

Janus and Jonas assisted Thomas, pulling with all their might, but they couldn't move the boat any farther. A large wave crashed into the stern and turned the boat sideways to the beach. Judas fell and let go of the steering board. The boat lurched over and drifted sideways on the wave. Judas clambered out as it hit the beach. More wood splintered. The boat swung out again to await further punishment from the wind driven waves. Judas joined the others, heaving on the anchor line for all they were worth. On the next wave, they pulled the boat in so it was partially beached and secured the anchor in the stones. It was enough to stop the side movement.

"That was close," Judas said.

Simon joined them.

"We'll have to wait until it dies down. I imagine there's some damage there."

Panting, Judas nodded in agreement.

"Hopefully, we can find the right timbers here for repairs," he suggested.

The disheveled fishermen walked along the shore to the seemingly deserted village. Soon, the squall passed and the lake subsided to its normal self.

"We'd have floundered if we'd stayed out there," Simon said. "You did well to get your boat in at all, Judas."

The following day, they set about their repairs. In much calmer conditions, and with the aid of some of the Gergesa villagers, they upturned both the boats on the beach. Simon's was easy to repair. One simple piece of planking was all that was required. Judas' boat needed a lot more work. There were two badly damaged sections and the steering board was gone.

While they were working on the boats, a large and ragged crowd appeared, heading toward them along the beach. The multitude stopped, and a massive looking man with an unkempt black beard, gestured with his arms and hands, addressing them with powerful words:

"Repent now!" he shouted. "Who among you will be the first to be washed of his sins? Who will come before me to be baptized and prepare his body and soul for the coming kingdom of the Lord?"

There were two or three shouts of agreement.

"Unless you come to me now it will be too late," the man continued. "We do not know when the kingdom will come. We are living in the end time, my friends. The Lord will decide when the judgment shall be. When that time comes, you will want to be on the Lord's side, won't you?"

He looked around at his motley crowd of followers with a hypnotic gaze.

"Yes!" some responded.

Most, however, said nothing, but listened intently to their leader's tone of voice as he repeated his plea:

"Repent, therefore, and be cleansed of your sins. Be prepared for the coming of the Lord!"

"It's Jon, the baptizer," one of the Geresa villagers explained to the Galilean fishermen. "I hope he doesn't make trouble for us."

Jon the baptiser, dressed only in his loincloth, strode out into the placid waters of the lake.

"I am ready to baptize you and cleanse you!" he shouted at the crowd now hovering on the beach. "Who will be the first?"

The fishermen from Capernaum watched as one in the crowd followed Jon. Jon, his beard trailing in the water, held the man, and scooping up water in his hand poured it over the candidate's head.

"Go in peace," the baptist said. "Your body has been cleansed. Rejoice, for you will have a place with the Lord when our messiah comes."

The candidate rose to get out of the water and another fell before Jon to be baptized.

"This man claims he can wash away sins!" Simon exclaimed. "Who is he? Who does he think he is?"

"He's some sort of a holy man," Jonas offered as an explanation.

"A prophet?" suggested Janus.

"More likely a lunatic," Judas replied.

"They call him Jon the Baptist," the Geresa villager repeated. "He has been here most this winter, gathering crowds along the shores of the lake. People come from miles around to hear this man."

Others then came forward to be baptized.

"Remember that the Kingdom of God will come like a thief in the night when you least expect it," Jon called to the crowd. "Be prepared, brethren! Be prepared!"

"What is he talking about?" the young man, Thomas, asked.

"Some mystical nonsense, if you ask me," Judas suggested.

"Don't be so skeptical," Simon, the older fisherman, said. "Many people have suggested that the Messiah will soon come. Some, whom we have thought to be the Messiah, have failed us when they thought their time was right. This man's different, though. He's claiming he can forgive us our sins and cleanse us in preparation for the Lord's anointed. Instead of throwing a thousand rules and regulations at us like the rabbis, or promising us freedom from our oppressors only to have our hopes dashed, he's simply asking us to be prepared by cleansing ourselves of our sins and following him."

"Why don't you try his magic, then?" Judas suggested sarcastically.

"Why don't we listen to what he has to say? What harm can be done by joining the curious?" Simon answered with authority.

Among those who came before the baptist were three lepers from the Gadarene caves, an area where these unfortunates were forced to live their last days as outcasts. Simon watched as they came forward, their bodies blemished and covered in sores. Some in the crowd drew back, fearful of the lepers. Jon, however, treated them just the same as all the others. He made them get down in the waters of the lake so their bodies were washed, and he held his hand to their unclean skin.

"Heal us, Master!" the lepers cried. "Wash away our leprosy so that we can be clean again!" they shouted, as Jon poured water over their heads and spoke kindly to them.

"I can only baptize you with water. I can only cleanse you from your sins in order to prepare you for the wonders that are to come. There is a man mightier than I who can baptize you with the power of the spirit of God. He is the true anointed one, and will reign over his kingdom in the days to come. If you are cleansed inwardly now, you will be cleansed outwardly when the Messiah comes. He will come with the power of God. You have my word. His kingdom is already being established. The day of the Lord could come at any time now."

Simon was impressed.

The lepers came up out of the water believing in Jon's message of hope.

"Do you believe what this holy man is saying?" Jonas asked Simon.

"Anyone who can give hope to these poor lepers and show kindness to these outcasts deserves a hearing," Simon replied.

Judas looked skeptical.

"What proof have we of this man's promises?" he asked. "The kingdom he speaks of may be close, but it is one thing to prepare us by cleansing us of our sins, but another to cleanse us of our Roman oppressors."

"I used to think like you, Judas," Simon answered. "I had hope in our freedom fighters. I was once one myself. They didn't call me 'the Zealot' for nothing. But, I've learned how to co-exist with the Romans. Too many good people died for the cause you suggest. Isn't a settled life better than the turmoil we knew in our youth? We sell our fish to the Romans, don't we?"

Judas remained silent. He knew he had been rebuked in front of the others.

Thomas, his constant companion, spoke up in veiled support.

"How do we know that this man isn't a lunatic…one of those crazed people banned to the rocks of the Gadarene shore like the lepers?"

Judas nodded his head in agreement. He turned to Simon.

"That's right, Simon. Whoever heard of a man forgiving other men's sins?"

"What harm is there in being prepared just in case?" interjected Janus, who had been listening quietly. "Why don't we offer ourselves to the baptist?"

Simon looked at Janus and Jonas.

"All right, why not?" Simon agreed. "The three of us will go forward. If the baptist cleanses our sins, God should be with us. When the boats are mended and we sail from here, our nets should pull the most fish."

He looked at Judas and Thomas as he challenged them:

"If your nets pull in more than ours, we will know that there is no truth in this holy man's magic."

Judas laughed.

"Fair deal," he agreed.

Simon, Jonas and Janus joined the crowd, while the villagers, who had been helping them with their boat repairs, slipped away to guard their few possessions from the intruders. Eventually, Simon and his two fisherman friends came face to face with Jon. Each in turn was baptized and fell under the hypnotic gaze of the baptist.

A few days later, after all the boat repairs were finished, they set off on the water again, making their way to their favorite fishing grounds. Jon the Baptist and his followers had moved on down the coast, south of Geresa. Once the boats were positioned, the fishing was good, as it usually was in the aftermath of a storm. The disturbance of the shallow waters in the lake somehow caused a change in the food chain. Great shoals of fish that normally hugged the bed of the lake swam up into the fishermen's nets.

At dusk, they beached the boats back in Capernaum. It looked like it might be a pretty even contest, but in the final countdown Simon's boat had taken in considerably more fish than that of Judas.

"The cleansed win out over the unclean," Simon taunted his partner.

Judas muttered under his breath, but couldn't help breaking into a happy smile, rubbing his hands at the plethora of fish they both had caught.

"You probably had more sins to wash away than Thomas and I," he noted, determined to have the last word.

"We'll see when the kingdom comes," answered Simon.

As the best of friends, the partners loaded the drovers' fish wagons.

"Today has made up for the few days we lost," Judas stated.

Simon embraced his black-bearded friend.

"You and Thomas join us," he said. "Old Zebedee was worried about us and so he's prepared a welcome feast. There's a chicken in the pot tonight!"

Chapter Thirteen

Return to Nazareth

With Nazareth in sight after the long journey up from Jerusalem, Joshua quickened his pace, leading his donkey up the hill past the familiar vineyards and olive groves of old Joachim ben Judah's property. They didn't look as well kept as he remembered them. Weeds grew between the vines, and broken limbs hung untended from the olive trees. He wondered if the old patriarch was still alive, and how Jonah and Miriam were coping.

I suppose the work is all being done by tenant farmers, he thought. *They never have the same care for the land. Their only interest is in what profit they can make.*

The sight of the unkempt vineyards made Joshua intuitively think the worst. He was quite prepared to hear that old Joachim had passed away.

Grandfather Joachim loved this land so much, he thought. *How quickly things can change.*

Despite this sad reflection, Joshua felt a great excitement. He was coming home! He considered his time in Judea to have been of enormous importance for his personal and spiritual growth, but it was time now to return to his roots and visit his family and friends. Joachim's courtyard wall was now on his right. He looked to the left and could see the house he had built for Joanna. It was still there, catching the sun nestled in his old vineyards. That familiar lump returned to his throat. Ahead, the scattered buildings of Nazareth caught the sun. They would lead to the old carpenter's shop on the square. He stopped and paused for a moment.

"Old son," he said affectionately to his tired donkey, "we're here! We've walked all the way from Jerusalem."

He stroked the beast's ears and patted his neck. The donkey brayed.

"Just a few more steps."

They stopped at the gate in Joachim's wall. Joshua picked up a stone and tapped the gate with it several times. There was no immediate response. For a moment Joshua feared that his family might no longer be in Nazareth at all. He shouted loudly as he knocked again:

"Shalom! Is anyone there? Shalom! This is Joshua! Let me in!"

At length, he heard footsteps on the other side and the latch board being removed. The gate opened. He saw Ruth standing there.

"Ruth!" Joshua shouted with joy. "O Ruth! How good to see you! Shalom! Shalom!"

"Joshua! I don't believe it! You've come back!" she cried.

They embraced each other and hugged, then, Ruth opened the gate wide so Joshua could lead the donkey into the familiar old courtyard..

"You look wonderful!" Joshua said. "Is the family all here? Are Joseph and Joachim all right?"

Ruth stepped back, looking quizzical and serious for a moment.

"Oh! You don't know! Father died about a year after you left."

"Joseph's dead?"

"Yes."

Joshua fell silent. He looked at the ground. Somehow, he had expected Joseph even in his blindness to live forever. Childhood memories flooded his mind, but there was no time to analyze them. He looked up.

"And Joachim?" he asked.

"I knew that would be your next question. I'm sorry Joshua... Joachim, Anna and Joseph...they're all gone."

"How's my mother and Jonah? Are they here?"

"They're fine, Joshua. They'll be so pleased to see you. No, they're not here; they're down at the old house on the square. Jonah has really done well with the carpenter's shop. It's hard to believe that he was my runaway brother, the one we thought we would never see again."

"The prodigal came home, Ruth. Remember!"

"David and I moved in here shortly after Joachim died. We are doing the best we can to keep the place up, but vineyards are not really David's specialty. He grows a lot of flax. His fields are on the flat land to the west. He took over some of his father's land adjoining Joachim's place. It's really pretty when it's in bloom."

"Is David here now?" Joshua asked.

"No. He's out in the flax fields. He'll be back before sundown. Matthew's here, though. You won't believe my boy when you see him. He's quite grown up."

Ruth called Matthew.

The boy came out from inside the house. He was tall for his years and rather skinny.

"Matthew, do you remember Joshua?"

The boy looked blankly at Joshua. A smile of recognition then spread across his face.

"Shalom!" he said. "I remember you."

They chatted for a while about the old house and Nazareth in general, but Joshua was anxious to find his mother.

"I think I'll go on to find Mother and Jonah," he said. "Let David know I was here. I'll come to see him soon."

Joshua led the donkey out into the street again. Entering the village he noted the square had not changed. Doves still flew overhead from old Benjamin Levi's cote. He looked in at the carpenter's shop. Jonah was busy planing wood.

Joshua coughed.

Jonah looked up.

"Joshua!" he shouted. "Is this really you!"

"Shalom! Jonah! It's me. Is Mother here?"

"Of course!" Jonah said, wiping his hands on his tunic to embrace his brother.

"Come on in. She's in the back."

Joshua tethered the donkey, and followed Jonah into the back of the house. Miriam was at her loom.

"Miriam! It's Joshua!" Jonah shouted.

"Blessed be God forever!" Miriam cried, dropping her wool before getting up to greet her son.

* * *

Joshua enjoyed time with his family. He helped David ben Levi with his vineyards and saw that good tenants were engaged at his father-in-law's. He liked working with the land again and it seemed more rewarding in Galilee than it had at the poor communities of the Essenes. He didn't have much time to help Jonah out at the carpenter's shop, but Jonah seemed to be doing well. Joshua tried to teach Matthew a little Hebrew and encouraged Miriam with her weaving. He reported on James and Rachel in Jerusalem and was the purveyor of the good news that Rachel had been blessed with a little girl, whom she had named after Joanna. But, Joshua found it harder to answer the pressing questions that came to him about Jon.

When Joshua spoke of Jon as a prophet baptizing his disciples, it reminded him of his own commitment to the coming kingdom. Jon was preparing men for the Messiah—the 'Prince of Peace' who would establish the Kingdom of God. Joshua felt that he was this chosen one. He had proven it to himself when he had brought Lazarus back from the dead. He had seen his Divine power work miracles on the blind, the deaf, and the lame. He had calmed madmen with his message of hope in the kingdom to come, and now, here he was in Nazareth, returning to his old ways. With these thoughts, he sought his mother out at her loom.

"Soon, I'm going to have to fulfill God's command, Mother," he said, as he sat beside her, looking at the floor.

Miriam pulled the shuttle through the ropes.

"I know," she said.

"What do you know, Mother?"

"I see that you still have the box."

Joshua looked puzzled.

"The box with the treasure that those men entrusted to me when you were born."

Joshua felt a little uneasy. How would he explain to his mother that he had lost nearly half the gold coins to robbers on the Jericho road?

"I always carry it with me, Mother. It's all I have," he answered.

"That box is a manifestation of God's purpose for you, Josh. It has always been the symbol that has made me believe that you have a special role. Remember how we used to talk about the 'Prince of Peace'?"

"Yes, Mother."

"You know who you are now, don't you?"

Joshua was still a little puzzled. He wasn't sure whether she still wanted to tell him something that she had held back all these years, or whether she was just astute and had noticed some change in his thinking about himself.

"I've learned that I have certain gifts of healing," Joshua admitted, still not looking his mother in the eye. "I believe God works through me. In Bethany, I performed many miraculous cures. People really believed in me. The crowds were amazed."

Miriam's eyes then met his.

"If you have this gift, don't you think you should use it here in Galilee?" she suggested.

"I'm not sure," Joshua answered pensively. "I came back here because it was causing too many problems for the villagers in Bethany. The pilgrims from Jerusalem, especially during festival times, swamped us there. Bethany was too close to Jerusalem."

"Don't you think you can use this power that God has given you here in Nazareth?" Miriam persisted.

Joshua felt a little frustrated that his mother was controlling him in this way:

"Mother, you are holding something back. What is it?" he asked.

"I believe that you are Divine, Josh," she finally said. "I believe that God used me as the means whereby to bring Himself into our world. You are the Messiah."

"Mother! Be careful what you say," Joshua appealed, as he took hold of his mother's hands. "I believe I am the Lord's anointed. I believe that God has called me to bring in His kingdom, and that the power that He has given to me is indeed His power. What you are saying, however, is blasphemy. You speak like a Roman or Greek, who believes that his gods can father humans. It is not in our faith, Mother. Remember the Shema: 'Hear, O Israel: the Lord our God, the Lord is One!' The oneness of God is the very heart of our faith."

"I know, Joshua. Didn't I teach you the Shema when you first learned to pray? But, Joshua, I am still convinced that you had no father."

Joshua looked at Miriam very seriously.

"You still persist in believing that my birth was a miracle, don't you?"

"It was."

"It's easier for you to say that now that Joseph is dead, isn't it?"

"Yes, I suppose it is," Miriam replied. "Joseph never really believed my story. I think he died believing that the High Priest's man, Gabriel, really was your father." She stared at Joshua indignantly before continuing. "I've told you the truth before. I can remember the night in the House of the Virgins as if it were last night. The power of God that you believe is in you Joshua, entered into me that night. It is impossible to describe what I felt. I know that God was one with me, then! He came to me in the light of the moonbeams and I heard him in the sounds of the rustling olive leaves. You were conceived that night."

"Mother! I know that's what you believe, but you must keep it secret," Joshua pleaded. "I sometimes describe myself as a son of God, believing as you do that the power of God came to dwell within me. Without that power, I could not have raised Lazarus from the dead or healed the sick and afflicted. I dare not call myself the Son of God, however, nor must others believe such a thing. That must remain your secret even if it might be true. I only need God's power within me to bring His kingdom to our people! The people must not think of me as God, but as one of His prophets who has been chosen—the Messiah, the anointed one for whom they are waiting."

Miriam stared at the ground.

"You must believe what you believe," she said at length. "God bless you!"

Then, she embraced her son, and picked up the shuttle to return to her weaving.

* * *

Rabbi Eliezer ben Hananah was not too happy to see Joshua in Nazareth. He knew the man's reputation as a scholar was well known in the village. Joshua had been Rabbi James' prodigy and much respected in the past, as well as a relative of the powerful Joachim ben Judah, with whom Rabbi Eliezer had never felt at ease. Now, however, the days of Ben Judah's influence had passed. There was a new generation growing up in the Galilean village that was not as liberal, and less Hellenistic in its ways.

Rabbi Eliezer ben Hananah was of this more conservative school and believed in obedience to every part of the Law. He was a true Pharisee. He was as skeptical of isolationists like the Essenes, with their obsession over the end time, as he was of the Temple party. Rabbi Eliezer was strictly a synagogue Pharisee, who believed in enforcing the absolutes of the Law on his village congregation. However, there were many in Nazareth, who through the poverty of their circumstances, accepted the reign of Rabbi Eliezer ben Hananah. Through fear, they had no choice, and they did not look favorably on the rich landlords who farmed the best land and whose family connections were with Benjamin Levi and the heirs of Joachim ben Judah. When Joshua set himself up as a miracle worker, telling the poor peasants that he could cure them from certain ailments and diseases, Rabbi Eliezer felt threatened.

Joshua successfully cured impediments of speech and minor paralytic conditions. As in Bethany, he did not always meet with success. He could not restore broken bones much though he tried, and those who asked for the ultimate, that he would resurrect a loved one from the dead, became equally disappointed. Joshua found it hard to believe that he could never regenerate the power that had raised Lazarus from the dead. This had been his greatest miracle and had established his fame in Judea, but he never seemed to be able to repeat the phenomenon. He prayed earnestly that God might give him the strength to do this again, but his prayers seemed to go unanswered. This combination of failures and successes caused mixed reaction to Joshua in Nazareth. There were some that would willingly have liked to have him replace Rabbi Eliezer as their spiritual guide. But, there were many more that questioned Joshua's authority as a holy man who could heal the sick and injured, especially among those for whom he could give no relief. Joshua continued to try to please them all, combining his healing ministry with teachings that he felt would inspire those that came to hear him, so that they might believe in a better world to come when God's rule would be established.

Ruth's son, young Matthew, often accompanied him, fascinated by Joshua's magical powers. Close to Joshua, too, were Bartholomew and Thaddeus, men who had both benefited from Joshua's healing ministry. Bartholomew had stuttered badly in his speech, but through Joshua's counseling he had gained far greater clarity. Thaddeus had overcome a serious limp and at length had thrown away the stick he had carried for years. Regularly following Joshua, also, was Jacob. He was the son of Alphaeus, who had been an old friend of Joachim ben Judah. They had been in the synagogue group together for years. Jacob hadn't received any cure from Joshua, but hung on to his teaching, believing, as did his aging father, that the Messiah would soon come and that the reign of God would begin. Alphaeus was too old to come out and listen to Joshua in person, but he sent Jacob to follow him and report back on his healing miracles and his teaching on the 'End' time.

* * *

In the warmth of late spring, Joshua had gathered his crowd of regular followers into the wild country northwest of Nazareth. This was still uncultivated land, too hilly for flax, and too stony for the growth of corn. Rugged outcrops of rocks dotted the treeless landscape. The warm days, however, had performed their annual magic. All around them, this harsh landscape had softened, the hillsides breaking out in a myriad of beautiful blooms. Blue and yellow heads of delicate wild crocuses shimmered in the breeze among the larger clumps of anemones, poppies, narcissus and spring chrysanthemums.

"Don't be too concerned about what will happen to you in the future," Joshua instructed. "When the kingdom comes, things like food, health and clothing, will no longer be as important. Life will be much more than food or clothing."

Two, large winged ravens crowed and circled above them before swooping to the ground below the slope.

Joshua pointed at the birds.

"Consider those ravens," he said. "They don't have to work. They don't sow crops to provide themselves with food or have to work in order to gather in their harvest. They don't even have any place to store their food, but God still feeds them. Look at yourselves! Aren't you worth more to God than these scavengers?"

Joshua looked at Matthew.

"The young are always anxious to grow up," he continued, pointing at the boy. "But, who can speed up the process? We physically grow as God dictates. If we can not control our own growth, why should we be concerned about how others grow? In the coming kingdom we shall all be one, the tall, the short, the young, the old, the handsome, and the ugly."

He dramatically swept his arm in a gesture over the landscape.

"Consider these flowers, they are magnificent. They appear miraculously every year. Our hills come alive with their beauty. They grow of their own accord. We don't plant them and they do nothing to make themselves the colors they are. King Solomon in all his glory was never clothed as finely as these. If God so clothes these flowers that are with us only for a few short weeks each year, how much more do you think He's going to take care of you? Have faith in the future. Don't think about what you will eat and drink. Don't worry about what is to come. Those are problems of this world, but in the end time, when the kingdom comes, God will take care of you because He knows your needs. Prepare yourselves for His kingdom by loving one another as you expect others to love you, and all these things will be taken care of by the Lord."

"How soon can we expect the end to come and this kingdom to be established?" one of them asked.

"Be ready! You should be like servants waiting for your Master to come home from some marriage feast and be ready to open his door for him the moment he returns. The servants that stay up and are awake to welcome him will be rewarded."

A heckler jeered at Joshua:

"You come from a rich man's family. What do you know about the hardships of service?"

Joshua thought momentarily about slaving in the Egyptian mud-brick kilns, sweating with Joseph in the carpenter's shop, and the day he was put into forced labor to rebuild Sepphoris. He recalled how hard he had worked, tending his vines in the Nazareth vineyard and later in the harsh conditions of the Essenic commune. He reflected on the endless hours comforting the sick and the lame amidst the stench of the Bethany tanneries, and he felt the bitter cold of the Judean wilderness on his retreat. Finally, he remembered the closeness of death when he had lain by the roadside beaten and stoned. He looked at his heckler with piercing eyes that showed just a little anger.

"The Master will sit those servants down at his own table and serve them himself because they waited up for him," Joshua continued emphatically. "In the kingdom, servants will become masters and masters their servants. The Master in that story was dependent on good servants. If they had not been diligent, a thief might have come in and stolen their master's goods. It could equally be said, however, that if that master had taken care of himself and not been dependent on his servants, he would not have gone out, so that he could be sure to protect his home. It makes no difference whether we are master or servant. We must equally be prepared for the Kingdom of God. None of us know when the judgment day will come. It may well be when we least expect it."

Joshua taught in the open air throughout the spring. From time to time he encountered spies in the crowd, probably sent by Rabbi Eliezer, hoping that someday they would be able to find fault with Joshua. Joshua knew it was difficult for Rabbi Eliezer to confront him personally, as there was living proof of his success in performing cures, despite an occasional failure. Joshua's success rate compared very favorably with the rabbi's own healing efforts. Shortly before the barley harvest, however, the rabbi got his opportunity.

* * *

Joshua had taken his crowd out of Nazareth to the more fertile uplands to the east. It was the Sabbath day and the crowd was larger than usual because the men were forbidden to work on the holy day. They made their way through the patches of barley where the ears were full and waving in the breeze. Several of the men plucked the enticing ears and chewed on the kernels, sucking out the raw flour. One of Rabbi Eliezer's spies noted the action and saw this as an infringement of the strict rules of Sabbath observance. He challenged Joshua:

"Some of the men are plucking ears from the barley and eating the kernels. Don't you think you should stop them? It's not legal to harvest on the Sabbath."

"I would hardly call that harvesting," Joshua replied. "They don't mean any harm. The birds pick up the fallen grain on the Sabbath. Will those few losses affect the harvest? I hardly think so."

"Those are the rules," the man persisted. "Do you teach your followers to break the Sabbath laws?"

Joshua stopped, turning on the man:

"Have you never read what King David did when he and his men were hungry one Sabbath?"

The man looked at Joshua, not quite sure what he was going to say.

"He entered the sacred place and ate the bread of the Presence, which only the priests are normally allowed to eat. He ate it and passed it around to his friends. Did that make King David a sinner?"

"So you think you are as great as King David?" the man asked, glaring at Joshua.

"Don't twist my words. There will come a time when everyone will be equal to David, and David no greater that the least of us. The Sabbath was made for man so that man could rest from his labors. The Sabbath was given to us so that we can reflect every seventh day on the many wonderful things that God does for us. God grew this grain, and so what better day for us to appreciate this gift to us than on God's holy day? My friend, it's right that we should not harvest and labor on the Sabbath, but there is no harm in appreciating this great gift that God has given to us. The Sabbath was made for man and not man for the Sabbath."

The man shook his head and backed away. Returning to Nazareth, he reported on Joshua's remarks to Rabbi Eliezer and his inner group of conservative Pharisaic friends.

"This man has divided our village," the rabbi said. "He has no respect for the Law, and he encourages the ignorant in wicked ways. So, he's able to cure a few ills, but generally he is creating more problems than he heals."

The others agreed. They decided to watch him more closely, hoping to find a concrete reason to expel him from the village.

* * *

The following Sabbath, Joshua went to the synagogue as was his custom. Many of those who had been following him came in with him. He took up the scroll of the Prophets and searched for the message of Isaiah. He wound the sacred scroll until he found the words he wanted to share. He wanted to use the synagogue as a platform to announce his ministry. In a clear voice he read to the people:

"The spirit of God has fallen upon me. He has chosen me to preach good news to the poor. He has sent me to free those in chains, and recover the sight of those who have gone blind. I am to set free all who are oppressed, and proclaim the coming Kingdom of God!"

There was silence in the synagogue as he finished and rolled back the scroll. Apart from those who had come in with him, there were others seated along the sidewalls that were strong supporters of Rabbi Eliezer ben Hananah. They listened, amazed at Joshua's brazen declaration. In the synagogue, there was also a man whose hand had been damaged in a stone quarry accident. His broken fingers had set in a curve and rendered his hand useless for normal work. He broke the silence crying out to Joshua in a loud voice:

"Joshua! If you possess the spirit of the Lord, can you heal my withered hand?"

Joshua stepped down from the reading desk.

"Let me see your hand," he said in a kindly way to the unfortunate man.

Some of those watching from the seats on the sidewalls whispered to each other. Word had spread amongst the rabbinical group about Joshua's disregard for Sabbath observance. They were curious to see how he would handle the injured man's request.

Joshua took hold of the man's hand and began to massage his fingers. He pulled on the man's index finger until he felt a bone click. The man uttered a muffled cry with the pain.

One of the Pharisaic onlookers stood up from his seat and called out to Joshua angrily:

"Aren't you breaking the Sabbath Law? You can't heal this man on the Sabbath. Let your miracle working wait until after the Lord's day is done."

Joshua turned to the man, astounded at his lack of human feeling.

"Is it lawful on the Sabbath to do good or harm, to save life or to kill?" he challenged.

The man did not reply, but watched in amazement as Joshua continued to pull on the injured man's fingers.

Joshua prayed earnestly that the man's hand would straighten out. He had to pull on all fingers several times, and every time he did so the man cried out with pain. So great was the pain that when Joshua had finished, the man's whole hand seemed to be throbbing, causing the man to look extremely skeptical, screwing up his eyes in the agony, even though his fingers appeared straighter.

Joshua embraced the man.

"Your hand is now very weak. Keep praying to the Lord that your strength will return. Your fingers are now straight. If you have faith in the power of God your strength will return."

The man looked down at his hand. He tried to move his fingers. There was just the slightest movement, and despite the pain he held open his arms and gave praise to God.

There were additional shouts from some of the Pharisees, disclaiming the miraculous healing on the grounds that no such cure could take place on the Sabbath.

"Do not believe this man!" a pious, white-faced leather worker called out. "He's a charlatan who does not respect the Jewish Law. Your hand isn't cured. Doesn't the pain you are experiencing tell you that, you foolish man?"

The man who had come to Joshua to be healed saw that his crooked hand was now straight, however, and knelt before Joshua holding on to the miracle worker's robe. Joshua placed a hand on his head.

"Go in peace," he said. "Your faith will complete your healing."

The man looked up and stood back.

Joshua returned to the reading desk and addressed his followers:

"Today the Scripture from Isaiah that I shared with you has come to be. But, it is a sad truth that their own people reject most prophets. I say to you, there were many widows in Israel in the days of Elijah, but when famine came and Elijah followed the call of God, he was not led to any of them except to a widow in Zarepath in the land of Sidon. There were also many lepers in Israel in the time of Elisha, but he chose not to cleanse them, but to cleanse Naaman the Syrian. I must proclaim the good news of the coming kingdom to the poor."

Several of Rabbi Eliezer's supporters shook their heads as if in disapproval.

"I will be leaving Nazareth," Joshua announced. "My presence here has caused a division in this village. Any of you who want to follow me please feel free to do so. It will be a sad thing for me to leave this place that has been my home most of my life, and particularly sad to leave my family, but you people have chosen to reject me, so I will travel elsewhere to teach my message and heal those who possibly need me more."

There was a near riot as Joshua left the synagogue. Some threw stones, and many yelled abuses at him. Fortunately, Joshua was not hurt and made his way down the street to his mother's house in the square.

* * *

Jonah and Miriam were standing outside wondering what all the commotion was about.

"Mother! Jonah! Come inside quickly!" he said breathlessly. "I'm leaving you. I can't continue my work here. There is too much dissension and division in the village between my way and that of Rabbi Eliezer and his Pharisaic friends."

A crowd gathered outside the carpenter's shop. Matthew ben Levi was among them. He pushed his way through into the house and joined Jonah, Miriam, and Joshua.

"Joshua! I want to go with you," the youth pleaded. "Please take me with you!"

"Matthew, if you want to stay with me, I'll take care of you, but I think we had better make sure that it's all right with your mother and father first. You're a little young to be traveling the country. One thing, however, if you come with me, we can continue with our studies in Hebrew."

What is all this? Miriam thought as she felt a stab of pain. *Is this the final breakup of our family?* She knew, however, that she could not stop Joshua from taking the course he chose. She had been the one who had planted the seed within him of this rebellion. She had encouraged him all the way with her discussions as to whom he might become. The Son of God must go on about his business.

"Jonah," Joshua said, "you must take care of Mother. I will try to get word to you from time to time."

"I did last time you left, didn't I?" Jonah reminded him with a grin.

"I will always be grateful to you for the way you've treated Miriam," Joshua replied.

He beckoned Matthew and went to the back room. They emerged carrying his old box.

"Jonah, you and Matthew wouldn't mind taking this round to the back and strapping it on my poor old donkey, would you? I need a moment or two with Mother."

Left alone, he took Miriam into his arms and held her close.

"I've not been much of a son to you, Mother," he said. "Somehow, I've always caused you worry and trouble, but I want you to know how much I love you and how much you mean to me. Wherever I go, I shall always think of you and I will always pray for you. Remember to keep our secret. I believe in my destiny now. I know that what you believe to be the truth is the truth. It's a truth, however, that cannot be said. It can only be revealed. When the kingdom comes, our people will recognize who I am, but until then, that will have to remain our secret. The Son of God will suffer many things at the hands of misunderstanding men, but through it all, Mother, you will be my inspiration."

He kissed her.

"We have got to go. Come with us to Ruth's house. I can not take Matthew with me unless she and David agree."

Jonah and Matthew led Joshua's donkey around to the front of the house. Bartholomew, Thaddeus and Alphaeus' son, along with some of those whom Joshua had healed, were waiting to join their leader. Joshua smiled when he saw them as he came out of the house with Miriam. The rest of the curious crowd that had followed Joshua down from the synagogue stood back.

Joshua took the donkey's lead rope.

"Come on, son," he said. "We've got a lot of traveling to do."

At Joachim's old house, Alphaeus' son, Jacob, made a passionate plea for Matthew to be allowed to travel with them. David ben Levi was not pleased with the idea, but knowing how much Matthew had come to look up to Joshua, and seeing how Miriam persuaded Ruth to agree, he gave in to his son's request, at least for a while.

"If he's any trouble to you, Joshua, you bring him back to us here in Nazareth." he said. "And Jacob, I'm trusting you to take care of Matthew along the way. He appears to be older than he is. My boy's still very young."

"We will," Jacob agreed.

Before the Sabbath was over, Joshua, with his small band of dedicated followers, left Nazareth, taking the road back down into the Plain of Esdraelon where the summer wheat awaited harvest.

Chapter Fourteen

Fishers of Men

Andrew, a fisherman from Bethsaida, a village north of the Gadarene country on the northwest shore of the Galilean Lake, knew about Jon's disciples at Gergesa. He heard stories about them living freely with the lepers, sharing their caves and showing no fear of their dreaded disease, convinced that they were immune from such suffering. When, he heard that the holy man was heading toward Bethsaida with his crowd of ruffians he was fearful.

The word came to Andrew from a passing shepherd who saw the mob moving in Bethsaida's direction.

"If they are coming this way, Simon," he said to his older brother, "they'll bring the leprosy with them. You've heard what the people have said about them living with the lepers in their caves."

Simon 'the fisherman,' as he was known in the village, was a large, solid-looking man with a big heart. He was a little clumsy at times, but Andrew always looked up to him. Simon had recently married a young girl from Capernaum, and didn't go out in the boat as much as in the past. He supervised the drying of their fish, lining them up daily on coarse cloths that he staked down to the beach. He, Andrew, and a sometime colleague named Philip, were the only commercial fishermen in Bethsaida. This was probably because of the proximity of the village to Capernaum, which had become the lake's principal fishing center, but the fact that Bethsaida village was not itself right on the waters of the lake might have been a contributory factor. The area between the village and the shore was thick with date palms and the commercial enterprise of the inhabitants had centered more on these than fishing.

"Do these wandering Nazirites actually believe that they are immune from leprosy?" Simon asked.

"They wash away their diseases in the lake," Andrew answered; then looking up, he said quizically, "I've heard that they believe that all their sins and diseases are washed away."

Simon was picking up dried fish and placing them in a large, reed basket. Andrew had started to help him make his selections. They heard the faint buzz of conversation. They could see the expected crowd walking along the beach toward them.

"There are the Nazirites!" Andrew announced. "Do you think we should hide the fish? That crowd is probably ravenous. They look like a pretty disorganized rabble to me."

"Smart thinking, Andrew," Simon replied. "Take the corners of the cloth. Let's carry the fish over there."

They dragged the coarse cloth laden with the dried fish out of sight, then returned to their beached boat where they sat and watched.

The crowd came nearer. Simon and Andrew could see the baptist leading them. He was carrying a large staff, which he leaned on as he turned every few steps to speak to his people. His long black beard and straggly hair gave him the look of a ruffian. He was dressed in a goatskin with a leather girdle around his waist.

"Encourage those whom you meet to come to me," the baptist instructed. "Tell them in every village that they will be cleansed of their sins if they come to be baptized. They will be made ready for the kingdom."

When they came alongside the fishing boat, Jon stopped and stared at Simon and Andrew, who were both struck by the man's penetrating gaze.

"You are fishermen?" he asked, stating the obvious.

"Yes," Simon answered. "And are you the infamous baptist?"

Jon turned to his disciples.

"You heard what this man said. Our fame has spread before us."

There was a ripple of laughter.

Jon then addressed Andrew and Simon again:

"Are you prepared for the kingdom to come? Will you live with the righteous or will you be condemned to the flames of Gehinnom? Receive the baptism of repentance and you will be with the pure in heart. You will live with the Lord in the kingdom to come."

"What kingdom?" Andrew called out mockingly.

"When the end comes," Jon explained, "there will be no time for discussion and debate. It will come like a thief in the night with no warning. Those who believe and have repented will enter the Kingdom of God, all others will be condemned like the Romans and rich men who have plenty now, but will have nothing when the Messiah comes."

"Leave us alone," Simon said, as he busied himself with his net. "We are good honest people. We live by the Law that Moses handed down to us. We have no cause to change the way we are. Take your message elsewhere."

"You'll regret that decision, you men of little faith," Jon replied. "When you change your heart, come to me. Without the baptism of repentance you can not be cleansed for the kingdom to come."

Jon and his disciples moved on, turning up the riverbed toward the village of Bethsaida. Their voices faded.

"At least they didn't find our fish," Andrew said. "We had better lay them out again to dry."

The two fishermen staked down the ground cloth. Laboriously, they laid the fish out in the hot sun again.

* * *

Joshua and his little band of followers settled in Capernaum. There was a substantial synagogue in the town, larger than the one in Nazareth. Rabbi Isaac in Capernaum was old. Throughout his ministry he had always tried to steer a middle course in heated debates over Pharisaic interpretations of the Law. It was the same with politics. He had tried to keep his people away from open support of zealots and extremists. He welcomed Joshua because of his scholarship. He was himself now very short sighted. He asked Joshua to research, read, and interpret the Scriptures to the people on his behalf. Joshua was an enormous help. In essence, the old man had retired and Joshua became the rabbi of Capernaum.

He heard how his cousin Jon was in Bethsaida for the summer and baptizing many of the poorer inhabitants of Capernaum who made the short journey to the place where the river Jordan flows into the Galilean lake. The baptist's band of followers appeared to be growing. Word also spread to the neighboring villages of Chorazin and Gennesar and farther along the shore to Magdala. Jon promised the peasants a freedom in the kingdom to come that they could not resist.

Joshua became a little disturbed by the simplicity of Jon's message. He realized that many went to the baptist on false pretences, believing that their baptism alone would give them automatic salvation and riches in the coming kingdom, without any need on their part to change their way of life and respond to the call of repentance. Bogus beggars and thieves who ran to Jon, returned to Capernaum unchanged and filled with a false hope of easy good things to come. Rabbi Isaac expressed his concern to Joshua about the baptist's influence.

"I am old and blind," the rabbi said, "but I'm telling you, no good can come out of this movement if the people don't personally repent. This Nazirite prophet is too lenient with his disciples, making them false promises of a more secure world, without instilling the true meaning of repentance in them."

"I think that the baptist's movement has become too large for him to control, Rabbi," Joshua suggested. "His message makes some sense. We must be prepared for the Kingdom of God, but in a sense it is that very preparation that will bring the kingdom about. The fruits of our preparation will spore the seeds out of which the kingdom will grow."

"How wisely put," the old rabbi commended him.

"I tell you what," Joshua continued. "Why don't you let me address this whole subject on the Sabbath? There will be many in the synagogue that day who are acquainted with Jon. What Jon has symbolically started, we can finish."

"Of course, Joshua. Your presence is the best thing that ever happened to Capernaum. I value you here so much, my friend."

The following Sabbath, when the synagogue was full, and the people had been led in their traditional prayers, Joshua walked up to the reading desk.

Slanting rays of sunlight from the square windows high up in the walls revealed particles of sandy dust showering those assembled. A musty smell emanated from the sandstone and the hard packed floor.

"My friends," Joshua began. "There are many of you here today who have been to the baptist at the river Jordan. I have been baptized by him myself. The baptist promised us forgiveness from our past sins. He washed us with water, as a symbol to cleanse us, and promised us that we will be judged with the righteous in the coming Kingdom of God. But, my friends, only God can truly forgive us our sins. What the baptist is hoping is that those of us who have been baptized will truly repent of our sins. If we live by the example of the Law and in the love and light of God, we will be worthy of life in the coming kingdom. Believe me, it will not be easy to enter the kingdom when the time comes if we are not prepared. The road is difficult and many will fall by the wayside."

There was a muttering through the crowd. The more sincere followers of Jon appeared to resent Joshua's interference with the obvious success of their movement. One man shouted back at Joshua irately:

"Go back from whence you came! Don't make trouble for us here in Capernaum!"

Others then began to speak out, and it looked very much as if the scene that Joshua had created in the Nazareth synagogue would be repeated in Capernaum.

"Listen!" Joshua said in a commanding tone, raising his arm to quiet them down, the slanting rays catching the white of his sleeve. "As I said, I myself have been baptized by Jon. I have not come to decry the message of the baptist, but rather to exhort it."

The murmuring began to stop. The curious craned their necks to watch him and listen.

"Let me put it to you like this," Joshua explained. "A farmer goes out to sow seeds in an open field. As he sows, some of the seeds fall on the pathway and birds swoop down and eat them up. Other seeds fall on stony ground that lacked any depth of soil. They sprout, but the poor soil is not able to nourish them. In the heat of the sun, those plants will die, as they will not have had a chance to develop any roots. Other seeds fall among thorns so that they grow up with the weeds. In time, however, the thorns will choke those plants, so that by the time of the harvest they won't yield any grain. Finally, there are the seeds that fall on the good soil and grow up to yield grain...some thirty times as much as the original... some sixty times as much, and some one hundredfold."

He paused and looked around with wide eyes at the now silent congregation.

"Those of you who want to learn more, listen!" he said with the same authority.

A few left the synagogue, but the vast majority stayed.

"This is the secret of the Kingdom of God," Joshua explained. "The sower is the Lord of the kingdom. The seeds that he scatters are his gifts to us. Some of us are like the path. We are trodden down and hard. The Lord's gifts fall to us, but they rest on the surface only to be swept away by Satan in the form of the birds. Such persons have hard hearts and will not listen to the word and sound of God. Some of us, on the other hand, are like the stony ground. We receive the gifts that God sends to us and excitedly respond, but our response is emotional and only of the moment. The hardness of the stones is like the hardness of our hearts. The soft earth in between is our immediate response, but it is insufficient to give the gifts of God a chance. It does not allow the seeds to develop roots, and sooner or later, we will forget that God ever sent us those gifts, just as the seeds wither and die in the hot sun."

Joshua looked up, raised his eyebrows, and glanced around the hall of the synagogue again.

"Many of you who have been to the baptist are like the stony ground," he intimated. "You excitedly accept the baptist's promises, but you have allowed the hard stones to eliminate the goodness that was in the light soil of your repentance."

He paused again.

"It will be hard for us to enter the Kingdom of God. Many of us will try, but we may be like the soil where the thorns grow. We will allow the gifts of God to develop in our hearts in all sincerity, but the cares of daily life and our desire for riches in this world will cause us to lose sight of our good intentions. We will start out on the road to the kingdom, but when we get there the entrance gates will be closed because we will have allowed the gifts of God to become strangled by the thorns we desire. There is hope for us, however, if we truly repent. That way we will become like the good soil. We are all blessed with different talents. For some, it is easier to develop the gifts of God and nurture His spirit within us to the best of our ability. God knows that we all have different advantages and skills. He knows that for some, our natural handicaps will only allow us a yield that is thirtyfold. For others, less handicapped, the yield may be twice as much. Then there are those among us, who have every advantage and can develop those gifts that God sends us one hundredfold. All of us who are like the good soil will enter the Kingdom of God, for the Lord understands our varying abilities. Jon, when he baptized you with water, asked you to be like the good soil and to open your pores to the gifts of God that the seeds of the kingdom might grow in you. When those seeds mature you will be baptized with the spirit of God, and the kingdom will be yours."

Some in the crowd started to shuffle from foot to foot uncomfortably. Joshua realised that Jon had told them that the kingdom would come at the end time when the reign of the Messiah would begin. He, however, had not linked the kingdom to the end time, nor mentioned a messiah.

* * *

Among those who heard Joshua on that Sabbath day were the Capernaum fishermen who had received baptism from Jon on the Gadarene coast, namely, Simon the Zealot, along with his partners Janus and Jonas. Judas and Thomas, their other partners, who had refused the baptist's message, were also present. The words Joshua had spoken caused discussion among them.

"This man explains things better than the baptist," Simon observed.

"He certainly gave me something to think about," Janus agreed. "I can't expect my sins to be forgiven if I don't make some effort to deserve that forgiveness."

"And that means keeping the Law as the Pharisees teach it," added Jonas.

The two burly brothers almost looked like twins—similar eyes, dark unkempt beards, wavy hair, and long hooked noses, but in reality Janus was two years his brother's senior.

"Every minute detail?" Judas asked.

"Of course, Judas. What use is the Law if it is not obeyed in full," Jonas confirmed.

"But, that becomes an impossible task," Judas said, laughing, and wiping his encrusted salt and pepper beard with the back of his hand.

Jonas looked at Judas a little scornfully.

"Only if you allow other things to get in the way like the thorns in this man's story," he warned.

"But, we all have our dreams," insisted Judas. "Things do get in the way. It is sometimes not expedient for us to obey every rule and regulation of the Law. Would you stand and watch if a storm took our boats from their moorings on the Sabbath day?"

Simon the Zealot shook his gray head.

"Of course not," he said. "Our boats are our livelihood. God made us fishermen."

"Isn't that what this man meant when he said that all of us have different skills and abilities, and according to those skills and abilities, so we can respond?" young Thomas interjected, flashing clear blue eyes from his ruddy complexion. "I understood him to say that some might only respond half as much as others with easier advantages, but that all who respond will enter the coming kingdom."

"If we obeyed every item in the Law presented by the Pharisees, we would respond one hundredfold," Judas suggested smugly.

"Quite, Judas," Thomas added, "but in your case there is no way you would ever begin to understand the Law to obey it."

"You'd have to be one of the learned scribes to understand all God's Laws," Judas replied. "What we don't know we can't obey."

"Blessed ignorance!" said Simon with a smile.

They made their way back to the beach and started to turn the dried fish on the sheets.

"Is this Sabbath labor?" Judas asked, grinning.

"Blessed ignorance!" the zealot repeated with a wink.

* * *

As the summer turned to autumn, Joshua's reputation in Capernaum grew. He taught in the synagogue with a new enthusiasm that poor old Rabbi Isaac had lost in his blindness. The crowds that came to listen to Joshua grew each time he spoke. He nearly always illustrated his interpretation of the Scriptures and the Law with human stories with which they could all identify.

"The Kingdom of God," he said on another Sabbath, "can be compared to a rich man who wants to settle his accounts with his servants. When he begins checking the debts, he finds out that one of his servants owes him a large sum of money. The man couldn't pay, and so the Master orders him to be sold at the slave market, along with his wife and children, so that the money might be raised that would pay the debt. The servant falls on his knees and begs his Master to give him more time, pleading with him that if he was given enough time he would pay back everything in full. The Master is moved by the servant's pitiful action, and lets him go. Not only does he set him free, but he also tells him not to worry about the debt anymore. Now, that same servant was owed a relatively small sum of money by a lesser servant. After he had been set free and forgiven his debt by his Master, he goes and finds this unfortunate underling and seizes him by the throat demanding payment of his debt. This lesser servant pleads with him just as he had with his master, but to no avail. The man locks him away because he can't pay his debt. Other servants hear about this and they report it to the Master. The Master then calls back the servant whom he had freed and forgiven his debt. He admonishes him in front of them all.

'You wicked man,' he says. 'I forgave you all your debt because you pleaded with me and genuinely could not pay. Why didn't you do the same for your fellow servant? I showed mercy on you, and so, too, you should have showed mercy on him.'

The Master becomes very angry with that servant. He locks him away until he can pay his debt. That's what it will be like, my friends," Joshua said, ending the story. "God will do the same to each of us if we do not forgive our fellow men from our hearts."

Some nodded in approval.

"What does the Law of Moses say?" Joshua continued. 'The Lord our God is one, and Him only should we serve. We should love our Lord with our whole heart.' I'm telling you, unless you love your neighbor as yourself you can not love the Lord with your whole heart. You will be like that wicked servant who received the love of his master, but gave none back. In the coming kingdom the Law of Moses will be fulfilled. You shall love the Lord your God and only He shall you serve. And in serving Him you will love your neighbor as yourself, on two such commands hang all the other laws that Moses gave us and all the advice that the prophets wrote."

Those who had nodded seemed astonished at the simplicity of

Joshua's teaching compared with the legalistic rambling of the Pharisees and their scribes. Joshua talked to the people as if he was one of them and yet at the same time with great authority.

Inevitably, as the popularity of Joshua's teaching grew, so the sick and afflicted came to him to seek his help in hopes of a cure. Just as in Bethany of Judea and in Nazareth earlier in the year, Joshua applied his generosity and kindness to his belief that through the power of God that he was sure that he possessed, he could cure them from their ills. At each teaching session in the Capernaum synagogue, more and more sick and injured persons were brought to him. As before, in both Bethany and Nazareth, Joshua was not always able to perform a miracle or to successfully heal or cure, but his general popularity with the people carried him through the failures.

* * *

Jethro was a baker in Capernaum. He provided much of the bread that was sold in the busy market square to the passing caravans of hungry traders coming down through Galilee from Caesarea Philippi and Damascus. It had become a profitable business with the increased traffic, and many of the townsfolk preferred to buy their bread from him, rather than bother with daily domestic baking. In the bakery, his wife, Rebekah, lay sick on her straw pallet with a high fever. She had been in this state for several days and had not responded much to the usual cooling ministrations of the women who had been nursing her. Jethro, was afraid that she was dying. He asked his friend, Simon the Zealot, if he could use Simon's boat to get word about Rebekah's sickness to their daughter who lived in Bethsaida. She had been married earlier in the year to a fisherman from there that was also named Simon.

"You may well have met up with Simon the fisherman and his brother, Andrew, from time to time when fishing those waters," Jethro said to his old friend. You'd be doing me a great favor if you could persuade him to bring Susannah home as soon as possible. Maybe my wife would stand a better chance of coming out of the fever if her daughter were with her. It doesn't look good, my friend,"

Tears welled in his eyes.

"Half the time she doesn't even know I'm there," he choked.

"What do you think of Joshua the miracle worker?" the zealot asked.

"He's managed to heal many who were sick or injured. Is there any harm in asking him to the house in the hope that he might be able to take the fever from Rebekah?"

"I find it hard to believe in miracles like that," Jethro answered. "I'm not a superstitious man. I've heard him speak in the synagogue. I rather like what he says, but I've known more than a few who have sought his cure to no avail."

"He impresses me, Jethro. There's something very genuine about that man. Why don't we ask him to come to your house?"

* * *

Jethro finally agreed that it was worth asking the miracle worker to come. Simon the Zealot set things in motion. He sent Judas and Thomas to Bethsaida in their boat, hoping that they could quickly find Susannah and Simon of Bethsaida. Meanwhile, he sought out Joshua and his followers and asked him to come to Jethro's house. Joshua agreed, and by the end of the day he had joined the women who were trying to comfort Rebekah in her weakness and misery. The poor lady was delirious, mouthing gibberish in her weakness. Her robe was soaked in the perspiration of her fever.

"How long has she been like this?" Joshua asked.

"Four days now," Jethro answered.

"Can you leave me alone with her tonight?" Joshua asked.

A ripple of mistrust went through the gathered crowd. Jethro, however, aided by a knowing look from Simon the Zealot, gave his consent. Joshua was left alone in the room with Rebekah.

* * *

There was little physically that Joshua could do. The women had done all they could to make poor Rebekah comfortable. They had bathed her and cooled her for four days, but to no avail. Joshua sat beside her for a long time just holding her hand. Rebekah didn't respond to him, it was as if she did not know he was there. She tossed and turned, and groaned from time to time, until exhausted. Then, she would just lie completely still, as the sweat of her fever poured from her. Joshua prayed earnestly to God that Rebekah might be healed and the fever die down. It seemed that his prayers went unheeded, for after the long quiet period of sweating, Rebekah again started to toss and turn, burning up what little energy her poor, racked body still had. Joshua did not give up. He prayed even more earnestly to the Lord.

At no point did Joshua sleep, although he knew that his eyelids were very heavy. He watched Rebekah throughout the night, constantly holding her hand and earnestly asking God to relieve her aching body. The periods of restlessness were followed each time by longer periods of sweating calm. Joshua noticed that each time Rebekah lay still on the pallet, her brow became a little less moist. After dawn broke, Rebekah slept peacefully for three hours. When she awoke, she smiled at Joshua whose kindly face was puffy from lack of sleep. He smiled back at her.

"Sleep on. Jethro will be with you soon," he said.

Rebekah closed her eyes. Very slowly, Joshua let go of her hand.

Quietly, Joshua left the room and made his way outside. Jethro was busy with the great throng of people that had gathered. When Joshua came out they fell silent. At first, they thought that Rebekah had died. Jethro greeted Joshua, trembling with fear.

"Blessed be God forever!" Joshua said, "Rebekah is exhausted, but the fever has left her. Please let her sleep and make sure you are there when she awakens."

He said no more. Jacob and Matthew joined him, along with Bartholomew and Thaddeus, as they quietly left the crowd to go about their business. They needed to eat, and Joshua needed to sleep.

* * *

Jethro went in to Rebekah's room. Just as Joshua had said, she lay sleeping on her pallet. He sat beside her, and, like Joshua, took hold of her hand. She seemed so calm and peaceful after the terrible turmoil of the past four days. Simon the Zealot and his partner old Zebedee with his sons, along with many others close to Jethro, crowded the room. They stood patiently, and watched as they waited.

Eventually, Rebekah awoke. She stretched her legs as she yawned, and smiling, looked into Jethro's eyes.

"Jethro," she said quietly. "I feel so much better. I need water and a piece of fresh bread."

"Of course!" Jethro shouted with great joy as he stood up and looked at his friends. "The fever's gone! Rebekah's recovering! Truly, that man is a holy man of God."

He left to fetch her water and a small piece of bread from a loaf still warm from the oven. When he returned, Rebekah ate the bread ravenously and sipped on the water that her dehydrated body so desperately needed.

"Is Susannah here?" she said, as she looked at the crowd of their friends that filled the room.

"No," Jethro replied, "but I'm hoping she will be here soon. Judas and Thomas have taken their boat over to Bethsaida to see if they can locate Susannah and Simon the fisherman. If they succeed, they all should be back in Capernaum very soon."

He picked up the water skin.

"Have you had enough water?"

"I think so, Jethro. I just need to sleep."

* * *

As Rebekah slept, Judas and Thomas beached their boat in Capernaum. They had found the fishing brothers, Simon and Andrew, mending their nets in the evening light when they arrived off Bethsaida. They had all gone straight to the village to fetch Susannah and tell her about her mother. First thing in the morning, they had set out for Capernaum in Judas' boat.

They approached the beach at Capernaum, and the bottom crunched on the shore. Simon of Bethsaida quickly helped Susannah out of the craft, and then Thomas and Andrew pulled the boat up safe and secure. Not far behind, they ran after Simon and Susannah.

They could see the large crowd that had gathered outside Jethro's bakery. Word was spreading about a miracle that Joshua, the temporary rabbi, had performed. Simon and Susannah had to fight their way through to get in the house. Judas and the others got lost behind them in the crowd.

Susannah joined her father, who embraced her and kissed her.

"Is everything all right?" she gasped anxiously. "The people outside say that Mother has been healed by a holy man."

"Your mother is asleep, but she will probably wake again soon," Jethro informed her. "She was sick with a terrible fever. We really thought we were losing her, but thanks to the miracle wrought by the teacher at the synagogue, she appears to have recovered and is doing fine. She will be really pleased to see you. You were the first person she asked for this morning."

"I'll go on in and sit with her until she wakes," Susannah suggested, moving on into the back room.

"Shalom! Thanks for coming, Simon," Jethro said, turning to his son-in-law.

He embraced him after the traditional greeting.

"It sounded pretty serious, Jethro," Simon said. "Actually my brother came with us, too, and should be here soon with Judas and Thomas, that is, if they can make their way through the crowd out there."

"It was serious," Jethro replied. "I truly believe that Rabbi Joshua brought her back from the brink of death. It was miraculous to see the change in her this morning. Last night, she was out of her mind, but today she's calm and placid, and has even asked for food and drink."

"Who is this rabbi?" Simon the fisherman asked.

"He's been teaching in the synagogue. He's rather like the baptist over your way, except he doesn't baptize. He speaks a great deal about the preparation we should all make for the coming Kingdom of God. It's almost as if he wants to carry on where the baptist has left off. Have you had much to do with the baptist in Bethsaida?"

"No, Jethro!" Simon replied emphatically. "I've listened to him once or twice, but I can't say I'm really convinced by him. I have a feeling that at heart he's a bit of a rabble-rouser. There's a whole encampment of poor peasants outside Bethsaida that are his permanent followers. Many of them are outcasts and beggars that are taking advantage of his movement for food and shelter. I must say, however, that the man himself is a powerful speaker."

"So I understand," Jethro acknowledged.

"He does have a commanding presence," Simon confirmed again. "If I was less fortunate than I am and did not have my brother to work with me and Susannah to take care of us, I might see the attraction of joining the movement. Jon takes responsibilities away from his disciples. He lets them think that the end time is about to begin and that they need not work any longer, but just be repentant so that when the moment comes they will be with the redeemed. But it all seems somwhat unrealistic and a little too easy to me. Life's just not like that."

"Perhaps that's why this Joshua man can help," Jethro suggested. "He doesn't speak of an end time so immediate, but seems much more concerned that we should use this time to improve our relationship with God and enjoy a foretaste of what life will be like in the kingdom when it comes. If I understand him rightly, he actually believes that we can create the conditions of the kingdom in our present lives."

"But, isn't that what the Pharisees believe with their rigid observance of the Law?" his fisherman son-in-law, asked.

"Yes, Simon, but this man Joshua is a lot more understanding than the Pharisees. He accepts that some of us have fewer advantages in life than others and we can't obey every part of the Pharisaic Law. The Law is interpreted by scholars for men living in king's palaces. The poor do not have the knowledge, or the means, to obey every item. Why, often, out of practical necessity in their livelihood there is a conflict with the regulations of the Law imposed by the scribes of the Pharisees."

"Where would you say we stand?" Simon asked with a twinkle in his eye that indicated he really had heard enough of this intellectual argument. "With the kings, or with the downtrodden poor?"

Jethro realized that Simon had become bored. He laughed, rubbing his hands together.

"We are in business, my son. We are somewhere in between."

They went to the back room to take a look. Rebekah was awake again. Susannah was holding her hand and talking to her quietly.

"It's a miracle, Simon. It truly is a miracle," Susannah declared through moist tears of joy.

* * *

After the healing of Rebekah, the synagogue in Capernaum was no longer able to handle the number of followers who flocked to hear Joshua teach and to seek his healing powers. As his fame spread, more and more people came in from other villages around the lake. As in Bethany of Judea, the capabilities of Capernaum were stretched to the limit in order to cope with the onslaught. The crowds moved to the beach from Rabbi Isaac's synagogue house and the town square. Simon the Zealot even offered his boat so that Joshua could address the crowds from the water. The response was overwhelming.

Many profited from the influx of visitors, including Jethro at the bakery. Joshua had become the major attraction of the lakeside, and his disciples began to outnumber those that still went to Bethsaida to receive the baptism of Jon.

Simon the Zealot's offer to give Joshua the use of his boat brought the fishing community of Capernaum closer to the holy man. Janus and Jonas, Judas and Thomas, along with Andrew, who fished with them while his brother was staying with Jethro in Capernaum, became close friends with Joshua and his inner group of Nazarenes. Simon of Bethsaida also became attracted by the magnetic personality of the miracle worker. Now that his mother-in-law, Rebekah, had fully recovered, he suggested to Jethro that they should invite Joshua, Simon the Zealot and the fishermen, to a supper at their house.

"It will be a nice way to thank the holy man for what he has done for us," Simon of Bethsaida suggested.

"Certainly!" Jethro agreed. "We have plenty of room. They would all be welcome anytime."

"Why not invite them to share Yom ha-Zikaron with us?" Simon asked. "It would be a great honor to have the miracle worker with us for the first of the High Holy Days."

"We have much to thank him for," Susannah chimed in. "The Day of Remembrance would be the ideal time."

Jethro invited Joshua, his Nazarene friends, and Simon the Zealot and his fishing partners, old Zebedee and his sons, to join with Simon of Bethsaida and Andrew, for the Yom ha-Zikaron evening feast.

Rebekah joined Susannah in decorating the house. They strewed palm fronds on the clay floor of the large living area. Jethro baked traditional challah—a sweet bread—and Susannah gathered honey for the ceremonies. Rebekah busied herself at the cooking pot, stewing enough mutton and goat's meat with traditional beans and lentils for the expected fifteen. Andrew added to the feast by bringing them salted dried fish. There were also fresh olives, raisins, dates, figs, pomegranates, and pistachio nuts. All was ready.

* * *

Joshua and the other guests arrived at Jethro's house shortly before sundown. The house smelled of the freshly baked bread. Jethro proudly welcomed them, having not met the Nazarenes—the term that Simon the Zealot had first used to describe Bartholomew, Thaddeus, Jacob, and the boy Matthew. They were not fishermen, but had busied themselves since they came to Capernaum with Joshua from Nazareth in anything where manual labor was required. Simon the Zealot came to the feast with his partners old Zebedee and his fishermen sons, Janus and Jonas. Andrew came with Thomas and Judas. For the feast, they sat themselves on the dried palm fronds at a long, low table.

Jethro gave a blessing and passed around the sweet bread loaves from which each of them tore off a hunk. When all had the bread, they dipped their pieces into the dish of melted honey that Susannah had prepared.

"May it be Your will, O Lord," Jethro said, "that the months ahead will be good and sweet for all of us like the honey that You provided for us."

"May it be Your will, O Lord," they all repeated.

After this traditional opening of the Yom ha-Zikaron feast, Susannah and Rebekah busied themselves serving the guests. Jethro had provided them with three skins of wine, which they also served in an irregular assortment of goblets.

"Joshua, we can never thank you enough for the miracle you wrought in this house," Simon of Bethsaida said. "It's as if God has sent you to us here in Capernaum. We're really grateful."

"And I can't thank you all enough," Joshua answered, "for making us so welcome here in Capernaum. In my own village there was a terrible division over my teaching and healing work. I had to leave, isn't that right, Thaddeus?"

Thaddeus and Jacob nodded.

"It was really a shame," Thaddeus said.

Matthew caught Joshua's eye with an apprehensive glance. Joshua knew the youth didn't want to go back to Nazareth. He always became nervous if Joshua began to speak of the village. He seemed to much prefer the excitement of their day to day living in Capernaum. He had expressed no interest in joining his father in those flax fields. Joshua smiled, giving Matthew the reassurance he wanted. Joshua was now well aware of Matthew's feelings.

When they had finished their meal, and had all mellowed in the warm glow of the olive oil lamps, Simon of Bethsaida asked Joshua if he would like to address them on this holy day. Joshua agreed, and still reclining at the table began to tell them a story:

"When the Day of Judgment comes," he said, "the angels of God will sit around the Almighty beside His throne. Before Him will be gathered all the nations. The Almighty will separate them just as a shepherd separates his sheep from the goats. He will put the sheep on one side and the goats on the other. He will then say to the sheep:

'Come you blessed ones, inherit the kingdom that has been prepared for you, for when I was hungry, you gave Me food and when I was thirsty, you gave Me drink. I was a stranger and you welcomed Me. I was naked and you clothed Me. I was sick and you visited Me. I was in prison and you risked your life to see Me.'

The righteous ones, who are represented by these sheep in the pen, will then answer the Almighty:

'Lord, we have never seen You before. We never knew You were hungry and that we fed You. We did not know You were thirsty nor did we welcome You. We have never seen You, so we could not have known You were naked and we never gave You clothing. How could we have ever known that You were sick or have ever visited You in prison if we never saw You?'"

Susannah and Rebekah stood behind the men and smiled as they listened. Joshua told his stories with such dynamic expression. These grown, rough fishermen, even old Zebedee, were listening to him with the same intensity as young Matthew.

"Then the Almighty will answer them," Joshua continued. "He will say to them:

'Inasmuch as you did these things to one of the least among your own it was the same as doing it for Me.'

The Almighty then will turn to the pen of goats.

'Go away from Me, you wicked ones!' he will say. 'You have no place in the kingdom and are condemned to the eternal fire of Gehinnom that has been stoked up for Satan and his demonic angels. You never gave Me food when I was hungry or a drink when I was thirsty. When I was a stranger you did not welcome Me and when I was naked you gave Me no clothing. I was sick and you never came to Me and it never crossed your mind to risk all and visit Me when I was in prison.'

The unrighteous ones represented by the goats will bleat back to the Almighty in protest.

'But Lord! We have never seen You before! How could we have ever known You were hungry or thirsty, a stranger or naked, sick or imprisoned?'"

Joshua looked around the table.

"The Almighty will give them no sympathy; He will just glare at them," he continued. "He will tell them:

'Inasmuch as you did not do these things to the least amongst you when you could have, you never did them for Me.'

After this judgment the goats will be led to Gehinnom, but the lambs will be shown into the Kingdom of God."

Joshua looked down. Nobody spoke.

"I suppose you want me to explain why I have told you this story today?" he asked.

The men nodded, still saying nothing. Joshua looked up at them and a smile spread from his sparkling eyes.

"Today is the Day of Remembrance. I will remember that all of you have done those things for me that the Almighty listed in His judgment. You took me in as a stranger. You have fed me and given me drink. You have even clothed me."

Joshua paused and looked serious again.

"If you follow me I will make you fishers of men, but it will not be easy. I will expect you to help me if I become sick, just as I have tried to help those who are sick and injured. Should I ever become imprisoned, I will expect you, as my followers, to risk safety and security in trying to find me and rescue me."

"I would follow you," Simon of Bethsaida said, mesmerized by the man.

"And you?" Joshua said, looking at the other Simon—the Zealot.

"Yes, Teacher."

"Jacob, Bartholomew, Matthew, Janus and Jonas, will you follow me?" Joshua asked.

Matthew grinned from ear to ear as the others nodded in agreement.

"You will stay with me, Matthew, then?" Joshua repeated.

"Yes!" the youth shouted.

"And you, Judas, the one called Iscariot," Joshua continued, "will you and Thomas stay with me?"

Judas hesitated. When Thomas said 'Yes,' however, he committed himself:

"Yes, Joshua, I will stay," he answered.

Joshua moved on.

"Andrew and Thaddeus, how about you?"

"Of course, Master!" they said.

Joshua realized that they were the only ones left other than Jethro, the women, and old Zebedee.

"Good," he said, "now let me continue. God knows each man's deeds and destiny, his works and ways, his thoughts and schemes, his imaginings and achievements. This knowledge, God also applies to the nations of the world, of which we have been chosen to be a light in the darkness. By trial, God will determine which of them is destined to the sword and which to peace, which to famine, and which to plenty. Remember, that when the Day of Judgment comes, the Almighty will separate the sheep from the goats."

When Joshua stopped, they all seemed a little less tense.

"Blessed be God forever!" Joshua exclaimed, and relaxing sipped on his cup of wine.

"Blessed be God forever!" Simon of Bethsaida repeated. "Susannah, pour us more wine."

Susannah filled their goblets up, while Rebekah passed around bowls of dried figs and raisins. The men lapsed into more casual conversation, and later after an evening of wonderful fellowship, they embraced Jethro with thanks and left.

* * *

After the High Holy Day of Yom Kippur, the town of Capernaum prepared for Succoth, the harvest festival when Jews traditionally slept out in booths reminding them of their desert wanderings under Moses. Joshua suggested that his chosen followers might all set up booths along the beach. They began the task of building the flimsy shelters with driftwood and palm fronds, but the weather turned blustery making it difficult. The waves on the lake increased as the waters became whipped up by a coming squall.

"We may have to give this up," Joshua suggested, as he struggled in the wind.

"We still have a day or two in hand," Jonas replied. "These squalls don't usually last that long."

Simon the Zealot had already given up. It was impossible to work with the palm fronds in the wind. He looked out at the menacing lake. He and Judas had pulled their boats well up on the beach, but as Simon looked into the squall, he thought that he could see a stranger's vessel in trouble on the lake.

The small fishing boat was heaving severely. Her mast was cracked and a crude sail flapped uselessly in the wind.

"Look!" Simon shouted.

Judas Iscariot turned into the wind and peered out at the squally waters.

"They're in trouble, Simon," he confirmed.

Judas called to Thomas:

"Get our boat in the water, Thomas! That fisherman out there is going down!"

Thomas, along with Simon of Bethsaida and his brother Andrew, ran to Judas' boat and helped to push it toward the water. Zebedee's sons joined Judas, and helped him pull the vessel out beyond the crashing waves. It was all that they could do to stand up in the raging water.

"You'll have to pull her out farther," Thomas shouted from the boat. "The winds will only push us back on the beach from here."

Jonas and Janus struggled with Judas to ease the boat out farther into the lake. Andrew and Simon grabbed the oars and frantically rowed for all they were worth. The boat eased forward, making slight headway. Thomas helped Zebedee's sons back into the boat, while Judas Iscariot clambered over the other side and took command. They eased their way through the tempest toward the floundering fishing bark.

"There's a man in the boat," Thomas announced, seeing signs of life within the stricken vessel.

A fisherman was waving his arms frantically, the torn sail flapping around him. His boat was taking in water with every whipped up wave.

"Jump!" Judas shouted. "You can't save the boat so save yourself."

The stranger took one last look. His boat was about to go under. He jumped.

Thomas fought with the steering oar, while Simon and Andrew tried desperately to move their boat closer. The stranger was thrashing about in the water as his boat finally gave up and in a swirl dove down into the shallow depths of the lake. The fish spilled out, floating with other flotsam that surrounded the struggling man.

Judas was ready with a long line of rope. He tried to throw it toward the man, but the fierce wind took the rope and it made no headway. He tied it around himself and dived in. Judas was powerful and a good swimmer. He made fast progress toward the drowning man. Reaching him, he tied the rope to the fisherman. Simon and Andrew began to pull as Judas attempted to swim while holding the man's head above the water. The man was still alive, but choking.

"Hold on there," Judas said. "We've got you now."

Slowly, they made their way to the walls of Judas' boat, where Simon and Andrew helped pull the man up over the side. Meanwhile, Judas balanced the vessel by swimming round and hanging on.

"It's Philip!" Simon shouted. "He's from Bethsaida!"

Andrew helped him haul Philip in.

Philip choked, splattered, and looked up at Simon.

"Thank God you were here," he said feebly.

"We're Simon and Andrew from Bethsaida. We know you."

"Simon and Andrew! God bless you," Philip answered, trying to smile.

Joshua and old Zebedee, along with Simon the Zealot, watched anxiously from the shore. Jacob and Thaddeus joined them, wondering what was going on and leaving Matthew and Bartholomew at'the Zealot's' house, heating up a pottage of lentils.

It was relatively easy to guide the boat toward the shore, but almost impossible to beach her. As hard as Thomas tried to control the stern, the bow swung round with the waves and the boat was thrown forward broadside to the beach. The keel hit the pebbles beneath the waves and the vessel lunged sideways, throwing its helpless passengers into the surf. Bruised and bedraggled, Simon and Andrew pulled Philip from the swirling water onto the beach, while Thomas, Jonas, and Janus helped Judas try to drag their damaged boat to safety.

Giving up all hope of building Succoth booths, the band of fishermen helped Philip to the Zealot's and old Zebedee's house where they all attempted to dry themselves off and recover from their ordeal. The pottage of lentils looked inviting as it simmered.

* * *

Every Sabbath the crowds increased in Capernaum as they came to listen to Joshua. The synagogue could not hold the people, nor could Joshua successfully address the multitude on the beach. People came from the surrounding villages just as they had in Bethany, and some from as far away as Sepphoris and Tiberias. It became apparent to Joshua that he could no longer handle his ministry on his own. It was time to bring his chosen twelve into the forefront of his work. He called them to the Zealot's house on the beach.

The twelve whom Joshua had chosen, that now included the rescued fisherman Philip in their number, met as instructed.

"I've called you all here," Joshua announced, as he shared some of Jethro's excellent bread with his friends, "because I believe our serious work is about to begin. The message preached first by Jon, and continued by me, seems to be taken seriously by the people of Galilee—The Kingdom of God is at hand."

He looked around at all twelve men. They were attentive and ready to listen to whatever he had to say.

"Most of you are fishermen," he continued. "Some of you do have sundry skills in other areas. You have all, however, agreed to follow me. We are a special group, neither baptists nor Essenes, and I will make you fishers of men. If I am to work through you, and if you are to share the task of bringing in the Kingdom of God and establishing God's spirit among men, then we will need to organize ourselves properly for the task."

Simon of Bethsaida sat closest to Joshua and looked up at him hypnotically as he spoke. Joshua noticed his gaze.

"Simon," he said. "You are very solid, a man who does not sway and you seem very dedicated to the group."

Simon made no response, but continued to stare at Joshua.

"I need a strong man to fulfil the task before us and I am asking you to be the one."

Simon didn't blink. Joshua, however, turned away from the Bethsaida fisherman and continued addressing them all:

"Simon is no greater than the least of you, and Matthew, our youngest here, is no lesser than the greatest among you," he stated with calm authority.

Matthew beamed.

"In the Kingdom of God there will be no first and no last," Joshua went on. "The first will be last and the last will be first; the least will be the greatest and the greatest will be the least. Each of us is assigned a Divine task. For some, the task may seem greater than for others, but in the sight of God all tasks are of equal importance. We are each expected to play our part."

He looked at Simon of Bethsaida once again.

"On your shoulders the Lord has placed much responsibility," he said. "I appoint you my assistant in holding us together in our task. In order to create less confusion among us, I am changing your name. You will be my unmovable support. Therefore, I will call you Cephas, the 'Rock.' I am doing this not because you are stronger than the others, but because it is confusing to have two of my 'chosen ones' with the same name."

He pointed to Simon the Zealot.

"Simon," he said firmly. "I will always call you Simon, but I will not call you 'The Zealot' anymore. The kingdom, which we are to establish in the name of the Lord, is not of this world, but a kingdom of men who will live in the spirit of God. Our kingdom will not be established through military zeal, but through the teachings that I will pass on to each of you, so that together we can build a new Judaism dedicated to the indwelling spirit of God that will be manifest in all its members."

Total silence enveloped the room as the twelve chosen disciples listened to their master.

"On the next Sabbath I am going to invite our followers to a meeting on the hillside," Joshua announced. "I want you all to be close to me on that occasion. There is a hummock, in the hillside just above Capernaum. We will lead our people out there. It will be easier to teach from the hummock than on the beach. It is hard for everyone to hear me when they are so spread out, but on the hillside they will be able to gather around us in a semicircle. It will be better."

"A good idea," Janus said with approval, for at the last beach gathering the crowds had caused considerable damage to the drying nets.

Joshua looked at Zebedee's sons.

"You, Janus and Jonas, will also be my appointed officers. Along with Cephas, you will need to be instructed in many things."

Janus and Jonas looked at each other, shaking their heads rather incredulously.

Joshua then passed his attention to Judas Iscariot.

"You are the businessman, Judas. I will need your skills to take care of our affairs. We will have to live by our wits as we travel the country, but you will be responsible for arranging how we shall eat and where we shall sleep. I am putting you in charge of my treasure. Come with me to the synagogue and I will release it to you. We have enough to take care of any emergency, but it needs to be stewarded wisely."

Judas seemed pleased with this recognition.

"Matthew can work with you," Joshua continued. "I want you to take care of young Matthew, Judas. He is a bright boy and learns things fast."

Matthew looked at Judas with his engaging smile. The lad felt truly one of the group now.

"The rest of you," Joshua indicated, "will be my missionaries. You will act as my deacons, helping me to heal and to preach the good news of the coming Kingdom of God. Men will follow your example, and so I expect you to be devoted to all that I tell you. You will spread the news of the new covenant that God will make with His people as we establish His kingdom in the hearts of all that choose to listen. First, men must repent, so that their hearts can be whole and ready to accept the spirit of God within them. Once our followers have repented, they will be able to develop the fruits of the spirit that will be the sign of the coming kingdom. The kingdom starts with us, however. You are the leaven that will raise the dough; you are the small seed from which will grow the greatest tree. When the spirit of the kingdom is manifest in you, I will send you out to preach the good news on your own."

The twelve chosen men started to glance at each other as a nervous euphoria spread through the room.

Cephas, feeling that he should now be their spokesman, was the first to answer:

"Master! Teach us!" he said. "We are ready to begin our work."

"Yes. Teach us!" the others chimed in.

"All in good time," Joshua replied. "First, however, I'm going to teach you how to pray."

"But, Master, we pray every day," Cephas replied.

"Yes, Cephas. We are all good at following our tradition. I know that all of us recite the Shema—the prayer of Moses—every evening."

Judas looked uncomfortable. Even Cephas, who had challenged the Master, seemed awkward as if he knew his own shortcomings. For most of them, except when their boats were being battered by squalls and their lives endangered, prayer was not a high priority.

"However," Joshua continued, bringing them some comfort, "I doubt very much that the God of our Fathers truly listens to our prayers or even understands what we say. That is why our rabbis tell us we must pray in Hebrew. Hebrew is the language of God. In the synagogues and in rich men's houses, it is easy to pray in God's language, but can you, who return from the lake after a hard day's toil, pray in Hebrew?"

Cephas nodded and Judas smirked.

"No, my friends. I know that most of us pray in our own language. Even if you learned the words of the Shema in Hebrew, how many of you understand their meaning?"

The twelve men began to whisper to each other. In part, their conscience had been saved, but they were also astounded at the boldness of what Joshua was saying.

"No, when we ask God for his good gifts we pray in our own language," Joshua repeated. "Aramaic was not the language of the God of our fathers, however. Do you think, therefore, that Almighty God hears the words that we use?"

Cephas shook his head in amazement. What Joshua was saying struck at the very core of all that the rabbis had taught.

"When you pray do not be like the rabbis and the rich men who love to stand in public places or in the sanctuary of the synagogue," Joshua continued. "If they pray sincerely, they will have their reward, but many of them pray in public so that they can be seen by us less fortunate men to be the pious ones. If they think that praying so publicly is setting us an example, they are mistaken, and they are losing the whole purpose of their prayers. They will have become hypocrites in the sight of God. When you pray, find a quiet and private place and open your heart to the

Lord secretly. The Lord our God is spirit. He has no visible form. But, if we open our hearts to the Lord, His spirit will enter into our hearts. Our Father who sees us secretly will reveal His will to us secretly, implanting it in our hearts. Only if we have truly repented and purified ourselves for the Lord can His spirit enter in. This we must do in contemplation and private thought."

Joshua paused, his eyes became windows of soul and he appeared to the twelve to be in a trance. He looked very serious, and yet at the same time he had left them in spirit. He had a blank look that did not seem to focus on them or anything in the room. He sat in this manner, with his glazed eyes half-closed, for what seemed a long time, only lengthened by the stunned silence of his chosen disciples. At length, he opened his eyes fully again, and carried on as if he had never stopped.

"The length of our prayers is unimportant. We do not have to repeat meaningless phrases just because that is what our tradition has taught us. We will not be heard because of our many words as some of the Pharisees think. Do not be like them, it is not necessary. God knows what you need before you ask Him. When you pray, say something like this—'Our Father who is in heaven, we honor Your name as we come humbly before You. May Your kingdom come and Your will be done, so that we can live in Your spirit now as it is in heaven. Give us our daily sustenance both in necessities and in spirit. Please forgive us our wrongdoings and may Your spirit within us give us the grace to forgive those who have wronged us. Help us to be free of the temptation to succumb to Satan's will and keep our hearts open only to Your love and the fruits of Your spirit. Hear us, O Lord God of Israel, for You are our one and only God. May we love You with all our heart, all our soul and with all our might. May these words be on our heart and may we teach them to our children. May Your divine love show forth from us when we speak, when we are at home, when we are journeying and when we lie down to sleep and wake in the morning.'"

Joshua paused again.

Thaddeus, who rarely spoke amongst the twelve, was the first to respond to the Master's teaching:

"How should we repent in order to be ready to receive the spirit?" he asked.

"You do not need to wash away your sins as in the teaching of Jon,"

Joshua replied, "although for many, such baptism is a dramatic symbol of their intent. Remember that I was myself baptized by Jon. When I was a novice in the Essenic community I was also made very aware of how much importance they stressed on the ritual of being bathed into purity. It is not wrong to be symbolically washed of our sins, but if our heart is not ready to receive God's grace no amount of ritual bathing or baptizing can remedy our plight."

Joshua looked specifically at Thaddeus.

"The answer, Thaddeus," he continued, "is in the prayer. 'Forgive us our wrongdoings and may Your spirit within us give us the grace to forgive those who have wronged us.' If we forgive those who have wronged us, God will likewise forgive us. If we do not forgive those who have wronged us why should our Father in heaven forgive us our sins?"

"Do you ask us to forgive our enemies?" Judas Iscariot asked, with skeptical interest.

"You have heard the traditional saying: 'You shall love your neighbor and hate your enemy,'" Joshua answered. "This is a political saying. It is much quoted by the zealots and false prophets who want to lead our people into conflict with the Romans. I am telling you something different. Love your enemies and pray for those who persecute you. That way the spirit of the Lord will shine from you and the Divine love will show. God makes the sun shine on both the good and bad of this world and He sends his life-giving rain on both the just and on the unjust. If you only love those who love you, how will your Divine love show? Even tax collectors love their friends. If you only love your friends, you will be no different than anybody else. Even the Gentiles share love among their friends. If our special relationship with the one God is to be manifest in us as Jews, then it must be seen outwardly in our Divine love so that we can be seen to be sons of God. The fruits of Divine love will be forgiveness and kindness and not hatred and malice."

Judas Iscariot looked down at the ground. Joshua knew Iscariot still had great difficulty in separating the coming kingdom of God from political freedom. Deep down Judas was still a zealot.

"Should we apply such love and forgiveness to those enemies whom we encounter in the Gentile world, or just to those who are the Lord's chosen people and the sons of God?" Judas asked.

"Does God only make the sun shine on us Jews or only send us the rain when it is needed?" Joshua replied, trying to be tolerant as he faced Judas' militant spirit.

Joshua's logic flawed Judas once again, and he smiled at the master, acknowledging Joshua's wisdom.

But Joshua was now less concerned about Judas' cynicism. He had recognized that Judas was the most able amongst them when it came to matters of administration. Most of the others had never had any responsibility in their lives. They were simple fishermen, taking orders from a man like Judas, or they were tradesmen apprenticed to others. *I will need Judas,* he thought. He looked around at the others to see if there were any further questions.

Nobody spoke, so Joshua continued his instruction:

"It is not the words that make the prayer. It is the action that we take on our words that becomes the living prayer," he said. "Our prayer is our means of preparing our hearts for the spirit of God so that when we have cleansed our bodies, the Divine light of God can shine through us. The spirit can not shine through us until we have shown God that we are ready to receive His light."

"But Master," Cephas interrupted. "Often we pray for God's help in distress or for our daily needs. Such prayers do not cleanse our bodies, but are direct petitions for Divine help."

"I know, Cephas," Joshua responded. "Did I not say that we should pray to the Lord that he should give us each day our daily bread, our daily sustenance in necessities and spirit?"

He turned back to them all.

"We cannot always expect God to grant our every wish. Which of you, if you had a hungry friend arrive at your house after you had eaten, would not go to another close friend's house at midnight, looking for bread? When you knock on his door and announce that you need a loaf because you have a hungry guest who has traveled a long distance to visit you and you have no bread, will you expect your friend to say: 'Go away! Don't bother me. My door is bolted and my children are asleep with me. It is too late for me to get up and give you anything'?"

"Of course not!" Cephas answered confidently, but Bartholomew didn't seem so sure.

"Be fair, Cephas," he called out. "Would you really be very pleased to be disturbed in the middle of the night? The man's friend in this story is not very considerate."

"I think I would be more likely to apologize to my visitor and rebuild the fire so that at my earliest opportunity I could bake some fresh bread for him," Cephas affirmed.

Joshua laughed. He liked the way he was getting them to think.

"That is a very good point, Bartholomew," he said in commendation. "You can be assured that the man would likely not be too pleased about being woken up in the middle of the night. But shouldn't he get up and give bread to his friend…not because he is his friend, but because he recognizes the hungry man's need? I tell you this, when you pray, ask and it will be given to you. It may not always be obvious, but in God's good time if your request is in the right spirit you will receive. Seek and you will find. Knock and the door will be opened to you. Would a father whose son asks for a fish, give him a snake instead? If he were to ask for an egg would his father give him a scorpion? God is like a father to us all. If we, who are not perfect, know how to give the right things to our children, how much more will God give us the right things through the power of His spirit? The coming kingdom is about that spirit," Joshua concluded. "When the kingdom is established that spirit will dwell within all its members. The most important and powerful fruit of prayer should be our receptiveness to that spirit. Prayer should be the moment that we share with God, allowing His light to enter our hearts. That is why I say to you that our prayers can be so much more effective if they are made in secret. They are not a sign of our holiness or of our obedience to the Law, as some Pharisees might think—they are our personal means of opening our hearts to the sound and light of God. It is not our words that are important, but the meditation in our hearts so that when the spirit becomes alive within us we can act on our words with Divine love!"

When Joshua finished, he sensed a spiritual aura in the room. His chosen men were almost in a trance, as they sat silently letting the spirit of God move into their hearts.

Chapter Fifteen

The Sermon on the Mount

The following Sabbath, huge crowds converged on Capernaum to hear Joshua. Rabbi Isaac directed them from the synagogue to a hillside off the road to Caesarea Philippi where Joshua was preparing to speak. Many sought to be healed of various conditions and ailments, and many believed, in the wake of the man's reputation, that they merely had to be in his presence to receive a cure. Few were concerned that the day was the Sabbath. It had never bothered Joshua to administer to the sick and injured on the Lord's day. Had not Lazarus rescued him from near death on the Sabbath day? Rabbi Isaac was a lot less conservative than Eliezer ben Hananah in these matters and turned his blind eyes to the work that he heard had been wrought on the Lord's day.

Joshua did his best to cure, comfort and help those who came to him in need, but as the day drew on, he realized that many of them were also hungry for spirit. He needed to give his message before the crowds left. Many had traveled a long way to come to the hillside meeting place. Some were beginning to complain.

He called together his twelve chosen disciples, and got them to form a barrier around the boulder on the hummock from which he chose to speak. The crowd of close to four thousand began to settle down. Joshua had selected this site for its acoustic resonance, but despite the natural sweep of the hillside, he had his doubts that all would be able to hear him.

He projected his voice as loudly as he could, and gesticulated with his hands:

"Blessed are you poor people, for you have come a long way to hear me. You will have a place in the coming kingdom."

A few gave a muffled cheer at his kind words.

"Blessed are those of you who are troubled," Joshua continued. "Many of you are sick, injured or distressed. I appreciate the effort that you have made to come and hear me. You will be comforted. Those who weep, now, will laugh in the coming kingdom. Blessed are the meek and humble amongst you, because in the coming kingdom you will inherit the earth. Blessed are those of you who so hunger for righteousness. Believe in what I say and you will be satisfied. Blessed are those of you who forgive others their faults, and express a love of neighbor. As you have shown mercy, so you will obtain mercy in the Kingdom of God. Blessed, indeed, are those of you who have cleansed yourselves of your sins and prepared yourselves for the coming kingdom of the Lord, for you have opened your hearts to the light of God and the Lord will be manifest in you. Blessed are all of you who seek to live in peace with your neighbor, for the Lord asks us to love our neighbor as ourselves. You peacemakers will have fulfilled all the Law and the prophets in the kingdom to come. You will be as the sons of God."

A few curious Pharisees, who had come out with the crowd, took exception to Joshua's words.

"What right has this man to refer to these undeserving poor as the sons of God?" one of them shouted. "On whose authority does this man speak?"

Such outbursts were few and far between, however, as the crowd bathed in the comforting words which the Capernaum healer and teacher gave to them. Joshua did not want to deliberately upset the established holy men, especially after his experiences in Bethany and Nazareth, so he did not confront the Pharisees, but subtely answered them in his general disertation.

"You are the salt of the earth," he continued in his comforting vein, but then he challenged them. "If salt loses its taste how can it be restored? It becomes useless and no longer good for anything, so it is thrown out to be trodden into the ground. You are the light of the world. A city set on the top of a hill cannot be hidden. So it is with a lamp. You put it on a stand so that it gives light to the whole room. Let your light so shine before others that they may see the goodness of God in all that you do. Do not think that I have come to abolish the Law and the prophets, and to offer an easy path into the coming kingdom. I am not suggesting that we abolish the Law and the prophets, but rather that we fulfill them. The Law will always be our guide, and obedience to the Law is a requirement of preparation for the kingdom. I tell you now, unless your righteousness exceeds that of the Pharisees and their scribes, you will never enter the kingdom."

One of the suspicious Pharisees turned to his friends. Some nodded. The ploy seemed to work.

Joshua continued his discourse throughout the afternoon. He gave the crowd many examples of how the Law could be fulfilled in righteousness, but his examples were always those that showed the fulfillment of the Law in an act of Divine love. He constantly reminded the crowd that Divine love is not a state of being easily achieved, and that the road to opening one's heart to the light of God makes for very close self-examination. He was not flattering. As the evening light began to catch the hillside in its golden hues, Joshua brought his long discourse to a close.

Joshua noticed that Cephas had dozed off. He smiled. *I appointed him a leader because I thought he has solid rock-like qualities, and now, he can't stay awake.*

"Not everyone who says to me, 'Lord, Lord,' shall enter the kingdom, but only he that does the will of my Father," Joshua continued, his own voice faltering from exhaustion. "Everyone who hears these words of mine and acts upon them will be like a wise man who built his house upon a solid rock foundation."

Cephas, shook his head and perked up at Joshua's mention of solid rock. He looked sheepish, slightly ashamed, as if he hoped that the Master had not seen him dozing off.

"When it rains and the floods come, and the wind blows, beating on that house," Joshua concluded, "it will not fall, because it was founded in rock. But, everyone who hears these words of mine and does not act on them will be like a foolish man who builds a house in the sand. When the rains come and the flood waters rise, whipped up by the wind, that house will float away with the sand and be lost forever."

Joshua finished. Turning from the crowd, he coughed from his parched throat. For a while there was silence. Though a few started to drift away, most stood there in awe, astounded not just by Joshua's stamina, but also by the strength of his teaching. The Pharisees and their scribes had never taught them with such remarkable authority. Many wanted to stay and just ease closer to their new hero. Some of the sick and injured still hoped for his touch to make them whole. But, the change in pace led many to realize their physical hunger and there were cries for food.

Joshua asked Judas if they had anything with them.

"I brought seven loaves for us and a few dried fish," he answered.

"That's not enough," Joshua muttered to himself.

He spoke to Judas again:

"I don't want to send these people away from here hungry. They might faint on their journey. Many of them haven't eaten all day and possibly longer."

Judas felt a little uncomfortable.

"Matthew and I only provided for the twelve of us," he said. "I didn't know that you'd want us to feed the crowd."

"I didn't anticipate it."

Joshua returned to the boulder from which he had addressed the crowd all afternoon.

"Sit down!" he commanded the people with renewed authority. "I know many of you are hungry. We only have seven loaves and a few dried fish with us, but I would like to share them with you."

There was a ripple of laughter from some.

"You'll start a riot," Janus said to Joshua. "They'll fight us for the bread."

"This will be different, Janus," Joshua continued with that same authority. "Help Judas and Matthew bring me the bread and the fish."

Judas and Matthew carried up the large basket containing the seven loaves and a pile of rotten-looking dried fish. Janus handed Joshua one of the loaves.

Joshua took the loaf and lifted it up in his outstretched arms. He blessed it and gave thanks to God for its sustenance. Then, slowly and deliberately he broke the loaf into two halves before putting it back in the basket with the others. Then, he took up one of the miserable looking dried fish and held it up, blessing it. He allowed it to crumple slightly in his hand, so that several unappetizing flakes of the dried flesh fell to the ground.

"You see this fish," he shouted down to the crowd. "It will crumble into many small fragments. So, too, will the loaves of bread. I want you all to take a crumb of either the bread or the fish from this basket. Judas and Matthew here will take the basket around to each of you. When you eat it, think about what I have been telling you today. When you live in the new kingdom, the spirit of God will be in your hearts. Just as we feed on bread and fish to relieve our hunger, so our souls need to be nourished by God's Holy Spirit. We don't have enough bread to feed you all a meal, but we do have enough bread and fish to feed you all spiritually. Just as the Lord provides us with sustenance on which we live, so He provides us also with His Divine spirit. May the Divine love of God shine forth from each and every one of us from this day on."

Joshua sat down and bowed his head. He was totally exhausted. It had been a very long and demanding day. His band of close disciples split up the loaves and fishes and started to break them into crumbs, which they distributed among the people.

* * *

Judas Iscariot counted out the gold coins from Joshua's old wooden box. Matthew watched, obviously astounded at what he saw.

"We'll surprise Joshua next time," Judas said with a glint in his eye. "I'll strike a deal with Jethro for some of this gold. We'll have enough bread to feed whoever comes to the Master's teaching next Sabbath."

Jethro was agreeable to the deal. He busied himself baking bread for Judas and Matthew. When the day came, twelve large baskets were filled with loaves. They had managed to keep the deal away from Joshua or any of the other close disciples. Secretly, they took the bread out to the hillside early and hid it among the boulders. Jethro was delighted with his reward and poured the gold coins through his pudgy hands.

* * *

The crowd that gathered was larger even than that on the previous Sabbath. Joshua spoke throughout the long afternoon. Despite discomfort, his listeners remained magnetically glued to his words. He talked to them in parables telling them stories that he knew would capture their imagination. Once he had their attention, it was easy for Joshua to interpret his stories to suit his message. Again and again, he gave them examples of how to be prepared for the coming kingdom, and always in his stories he also gave the negative viewpoint, so that the listener could see the clarity of choice. In between bouts of teaching, Joshua gave himself over to healing, and he took Cephas, Janus and Jonas with him as he wandered through the crowd bringing comfort and cure. He instructed them to observe his healing methods so that this 'inner three' could adapt them for themselves. He always stressed how important it was that their patients should believe that it was the power of God working through them as healers, and not consider them to be sorcerers or magicians of the kind he had witnessed in Jerusalem.

"You can only be made bodily whole if you will allow the spirit of God to dwell in your hearts," he said again and again. "In the coming kingdom, there will be no sickness or disease, because only those who have opened their hearts to the indwelling spirit of the Lord will be allowed in. Repent now, and purify your souls, then your bodies will heal."

In the emotion of the moment, most believed, and the remarkable rate of healing success Joshua achieved became the testimony to his methods. As in Bethany and Nazareth, however, he continued to disappoint those who sought instant healing miracles of their broken bones. It was a problem that still somewhat frustrated Joshua, who could not understand how he could raise a man from the dead and still not be able to knit together broken bones. He comforted himself with the thought that those who had broken bones could still open their hearts to God, and often with greater clarity than those who were mentally twisted in the anguish of life.

* * *

Judas waited patiently for the moment when Joshua would ask about their supplies. He could see the hungry crowd was ready. There were many there that had also listened to the Master the week before. He knew they would be expecting Joshua to share with them whatever he had. At length, Joshua asked:

"Judas, I think the crowd's even bigger than last week. What have we with us with which to feed them today?"

"Enough," Judas said secretively.

"Enough to break into crumbs for all who are here?"

"More than enough," Judas replied knowingly.

"Then, bring me a loaf that I might do the same as before. The bread is a wonderful way for me to illustrate the spiritual food of God."

Judas called Matthew and asked him to fetch a loaf for the Master. The young man brought Joshua one of Jethro's loaves. Joshua blessed it and broke it, giving the people the same instruction as the week before. But, as the disciples distributed the loaf, many other loaves appeared. There was enough bread for everyone to pull off not just a crumb but a substantial morsel. Their curiosity was roused even if their hunger was not fully abated. Joshua was astounded, and the crowd, especially those who had been with him the week before, declared the appearance of the bread to be a miracle.

"Where did that come from?" Joshua asked, somewhat irritated that his own followers had outwitted him.

"You needed bread, Master," Judas answered. "Last week you were disappointed that we did not have more. I wanted to be sure that this time nobody would go without."

Nobody did go without. Everyone who needed bread ate. Jethro had baked enough.

Later, outside Simon's house, as the moon peeked out of the silver clouds above the lake, Joshua spoke to Judas and Matthew privately.

"Now, where did the bread come from?" he asked firmly, but with a smile on his face.

"A miracle!" Judas replied, opening his hands in a gesture of false surprise.

"No, Judas. It was not a miracle," Joshua continued seriously. "You are my steward. Where did you get the bread?"

"Jethro baked it, Master."

"I can assume that, Judas, but how did you pay for so much bread?"

"Aren't you pleased, Master?" he stalled. "We fed the people."

Joshua was still smiling, but he remained firm.

"Yes, Judas, but how many gold coins did that cost us?"

"Not too many, Master. Enough to satisfy Jethro," Judas said, shrugging his shoulders nonchalantly.

"Judas, those coins are our security. We can't use them unless it's absolutely essential. Be very careful how you spend them. They were entrusted to me for a purpose. That purpose is not yet fulfilled. We didn't need to feed the multitude today. If we start doing that it will never end, but apart from that, I didn't like the way the people believed we had wrought a miracle. We can't give the people false hope, Judas. I did that once, at a wedding in Cana. I've always regretted it. The coming kingdom will be built on love and trust from within, and not on false hopes such as the zealots give. If you had only advised me of what you had done, financially imprudent though it might have been, I would have at least had a chance to explain to them our generous gesture. Instead, we have now increased our problem. You were unwise Judas. Try to be a more careful steward."

He turned to Matthew, who was surprised at Joshua's change of tone.

"Learn from Judas' mistake, Matthew," Joshua advised. "Both of you have a very important task, but don't abuse it."

Matthew nodded his head and glanced uneasily at Judas.

Joshua did not dwell further on the subject. They joined the others for the stew that Zebedee and Susannah had prepared for their meal.

Chapter Sixteen

The end of an idyll

Flavius Septimus was proud of Linus. Obviously Questus must have been impressed with his abilities to appoint him as aide to Pontius Pilatus. He was pleased, too, that Linus had taken the trouble to visit the villa, and introduce Copernia and himself to the new prefect. Linus and Pilatus had only stayed a couple of days before continuing on to Judea and Jerusalem, but they were two days that Flavius and Copernia proudly would not forget.

Knowing that Linus was now settled, Flavius decided to fulfill a promise to Copernia that he would take her back to Rome and Tuscany for another prolonged visit. He entrusted the care of the property at Magdala to Demetrius, and sent a message to Linus in Jerusalem, informing him of their plans.

They had barely left home, when they encountered a group of itinerant peasants moving down the road from the high ground above Madon. The band of men didn't look like thieves and robbers, but it was beginning to concern Flavius that there were so many such wandering groups of peasants in the country these days.

"You know," he said to Copernia, "we can never trust these Jews. As much as I love it here, you have always got to be on your guard. There's nothing more dangerous than unemployed peasants. There are too many of these itinerant bands around today. If I were to follow my instinct from past experience, I'd say that Galilee is about to break out in turmoil again."

The wagon came alongside the wandering group. The man who appeared to be their leader, greeted them in the traditional Aramaic way:

"Shalom!"

Flavius replied with the same greeting, looking down at the men from the height of the wagon. Their leader was dressed in a simple, white robe, and looked about Linus' age. There was something about him that seemed familiar...perhaps it was the light color of his beard, compared with the darker curls of most of the others. When the man smiled, Flavius got the impression that he recognized him, too. Flavius' driver whipped the oxen on, and the wagon passed the group, who stood for a while watching them.

"I know that man," Flavius said. "The leader of that group was very familiar. I think he was one of the men we used from Sepphoris to rebuild the villa."

"Really," Copernia replied, not in the least bit interested. Her thoughts were on the journey ahead and going home.

"He was a good worker," Flavius continued. "I would have thought he would have made a good career as a builder. I really trusted those men at that time. They did a wonderful job."

"Flavius! You're too soft! Remember, it was Jews that burned us out in the first place."

"I suppose you're right," Flavius agreed. "This country's so volatile. That group looked harmless enough, but you never really know what they are thinking. Nevertheless, Copernia, I still think that was the same man. Couldn't you see how he wanted to talk to us?"

The wagon rolled on. Flavius called out to the driver:

"Why don't we take the new road past Mount Tabor and through the valley? It's less of a climb than going up to Sepphoris and Nazareth. It will be easier on the oxen."

"All right, sir," the man replied. "I'll take the new road."

The sun was already setting when they reached the junction with the highway running from Caesarea to Sebaste and on to Jerusalem. They stayed at a recently built inn that had been erected there to accommodate the increase in commercial traffic now traveling these Roman roads.

Judea and the Levant was indeed a gateway into the empire. Flavius felt proud that his son, Linus, had played a part in increasing this traffic. The Palmyra agreement was bringing nice profits to Rome.

* * *

Delilah held Maria close to her. In the mornings, while Antonias taught the boys, Maria and Delilah could share time with each other. Often, they walked up the hill behind the villa and sat in a pleasant niche between the rocks where they could look out over the blue water and admire the view. They had been living at the villa for nearly three years, and although they had fallen into an easy lifestyle, they both missed the challenge they had known in their former lives.

Delilah kissed Maria's ear lightly and whispered to her:

"How much longer do you think we can live here with Antonias?"

Maria felt the warmth of Delilah's lips on her lobe. The soft touch sent tingles through her whole body. Her ears were so sensitive, something which Delilah had long ago learned to exploit.

"Why do you ask?" Maria replied. "Do you want to leave?"

Delilah was silent for a moment. She dropped her head and let it rest in the softness of Maria's breasts.

"You have Marcus," she answered. "Antonias has been very good to you both. He's given you a home and the stability that your child needed. It would have been difficult to continue the way we did before Antonias came into your life. It was all right when Marcus was a baby, but at his present age we would never have managed."

Delilah looked up at Maria's face.

"You need to stay with Marcus and Antonias, Maria," she continued, "but I need to go back. Maybe the matron at the brothel will let me return, and if not in Tiberias, maybe I can go elsewhere, perhaps to Sepphoris."

Maria stroked Delilah's hair gently:

"You're part of our family," she insisted. "You can't leave us. I love you Delilah. We need each other."

"I know," Delilah agreed, as she took Maria's hand and guided it to her left breast. "I need you, but you have Antonias. You have had us both."

Delilah felt her breast responding to Maria's gentle touch. Her nipples hardened beneath the flimsy material of her homespun shift.

She arched her back with pleasure and turned to kneel on the grass in front of Maria. She stared at her and tenderly touched her face with the tips of her slender fingers.

"Does Antonias know about our secret?" Delilah asked.

"Of course, Delilah," Maria said, chuckling to herself. "Why are you suddenly so concerned after all this time?"

Maria held Delilah and lightly kissed her with the softness of her full lips.

"Antonias is a very sensitive man. He understands the way we feel about each other. He knew right from the beginning. He knows how close we are. I believe he even wrote a poem about us, but it was hard for me to understand. He wrote it in Greek and tried to translate it for me. Somehow, it didn't quite come out right."

"He's so kind to us," Delilah observed once more.

"He loves us both in his funny way," Maria said, hugging Delilah, holding her tight. "He loves me because of the physical love that I have been able to bring into his life, but he also loves you because he knows you make me happy. We have a triangle of unselfish love between us, Delilah. You are as much a part of that as I am."

Delilah thought for a moment.

"I was afraid to tell you before," she said. "There was an occasion about a year ago when Antonias found me alone. It was one of those beautiful evenings with the golden light streaming down to the lake. He held me that evening and kissed me. I let his hand touch my little breast and I could feel his excitement. He was so gentle."

Maria looked at Delilah curiously.

"He is, Delilah. He is so different from all the men that I have had before. He is always more concerned about my feelings than his own. I think that's why I have not tired of him."

"You don't mind, then?" Delilah asked, somewhat surprised that Maria had shown no resentment over Antonias' actions.

Maria looked away.

"No, Delilah. You don't have to explain to me. That's probably not the only time he's held you, is it?"

She paused, chuckled, and then turned back toward her paramour.

"Actually, I'm glad Antonias has shown you some affection. I'm glad you have been able to share in some of my joy. Goodness, we had to share enough men in the past, how beautiful it is that we can share real love."

Delilah was comforted by their discussion, and she expressed it in a tight embrace. The truth was that Antonias had paid her close attention more than once, and each time she had felt a great joy at his touch. Never, however, had Antonias fully betrayed Maria. He had only tenderly touched Delilah and held her in his embrace.

"I love you," was all Delilah could say. "Maria, you are a real friend."

"I love you, too," Maria replied, before kissing Delilah ever so tenderly again.

She stood up.

"You're not going to leave us, are you?" she asked.

"Not as long as both you and Antonias want me to stay," Delilah replied.

"Good, then you're staying and that's the end of this talk. Now, let's go back down and see how Marcus is doing with his lessons. Antonias tries to teach me Greek, but I just don't seem to be able to learn. Thank goodness Antonias speaks our language."

"It helps," Delilah agreed, "but remember that I always spoke some Greek. You really should make more effort. If we're going to stay with Antonias we really should speak Greek. Anyway, you have a Greek name—Maria. If my name was Greek, it would be similar to yours—Delia."

"My mother used to tell me she named me Maria rather than Miriam because she was sure my father was Roman. I gave Marcus a Roman name for the same reason."

"Because you think Linus was his father?"

"Yes."

"It is hard, living in Antonias' villa, to really understand why there is so much hatred between certain Jews and the Romans," Delilah said as they walked down the hill. "It's never really been a problem for us, has it?"

"No, Delia," Maria teased her friend.

Antonias had finished his class when they arrived at the villa. Marcus ran to them and showed them his waxen tablet. His letters looked good.

Delilah took the tablet and slowly translated:

"My name Marcus and this my house. We live on hill looks out on lake."

"You have good time this morning?" she said in her very basic Greek.

Her accent was so bad that Marcus had difficulty understanding her, but when she repeated the sentence, he nodded and laughed.

Maria looked at Delilah. They both started laughing, too.

* * *

Maria and Delilah enjoyed the sun as they sat in the grass on the hillside above Antonias' villa later that summer. They saw some of his students leave the building, having finished their morning lessons. A little later, two wagons came into view and pulled up in front of the villa.

"Who are they?" Maria said. "It looks like Antonias has guests."

Delilah squinted her eyes.

"It looks like four people to me," she said.

They both stood up instinctively, as if such action would give them a better view.

"I think I'd better go down," Maria said, as she brushed the dried grass from her shift. "Marcus has finished his lessons."

Both of them made their way toward the villa curious to know whom the visitors might be. By the time they arrived, Antonias was already in conference with the strangers.

The two men were both rather portly, and seemed decidedly pompous. The third man must have been their driver as he had disappeared. The Roman lady accompanying the gentlemen was slim and good-looking, wearing a colorful purple dress with a gold trim. Maria and Delilah arrived just as one of the portly gentlemen was introducing the other man to Antonias.

"Dracchus, this is my son, Antonias," he announced.

Then, addressing Antonias, the stout gentleman continued:

"Dracchus is buying the estate, Antonias. Your mother and I will be moving back to Rome. Our work in Antioch is finished. I think Dracchus would like to look around. Perhaps you would be so good as to show him the house and vineyard."

Marcus, who had been playing with two of Antonias' other students, ran into the room. He stopped short when he saw the strangers.

"Antonias," remarked the portly gentleman, "who is this child?"

"Father, this is Marcus," he said slightly flustered. "Marcus is one of my students. I've been running a school. It's really gone very well, Father."

"Good, good," Antonias' father muttered. "I'm glad to know that you've been doing something useful. You can't spend your whole life trying to be a poet. We can travel back to Italia via Athens, and set you up properly. When you've completed your studies, maybe you would be interested in founding a school."

At this moment, Marcus saw his mother and Delilah hidden at the back of the room from the strangers. He called out to them in Aramaic. Antonias, along with his father and Dracchus turned to see who was there.

Marcus ran to Maria. She held him to her side.

"Father, this is the boy's mother and her friend. They are my guests here at the present time."

"Oh!" interrupted Antonias' father, obviously not so happy. "Aren't they Jews?"

"Yes, Father. Does that really matter?"

Maria and Delilah could see Antonias' father's face quiver. Maria remembered only too well how Linus' father had reacted to her presence in his house.

He raised his voice:

"Are you telling me that these two Hebrew women are living in my house?"

"Why not, Father? Marcus is a Roman boy!" Antonias countered in defense.

"A Roman boy! Whose boy? Hardly yours, Antonias. He's too old to be your bastard child!"

Antonias' father looked at his wife for support in his anger.

"Portia! Do you hear what Antonias is saying? He's invited these two Hebrew women to live with him and bring up one of his erring friend's brats."

"That's not what I said, Father," Antonias responded bravely. "I don't know Marcus' father, but I can tell you one thing, I am more of a father to the boy than his real father will ever be."

He called Maria to him.

"Maria, this is my father, Antonius Syllus," he explained in Aramaic. "He's not very happy you are here, but I'll explain everything to him."

With Maria at his side and Delilah holding Marcus at the doorway into the room, Antonias explained how he had met Maria in Tiberias and they had become friends. He did not reveal that she was working in a brothel at the time, but he did declare his love for her and how he had been able to help her by giving her Roman boy the basis of a Greek education.

Portia stood close to her husband and seemed sympathetic to her son's story.

"They will have to go," Antonias' father said. "They can't stay."

"Later, Syllus," Portia said. "We must show Dracchus around.

* * *

Meanwhile, Dracchus had stood there bemused by the whole scene. This domestic crisis was of no real concern to him. He was anxious to buy the villa and retire to this desirable area, which was fast becoming one of the most fashionable places in all Syria. His years of wheeling and dealing in the counting houses of trade had won him respectability. He felt a future pride as he eyed the comfortable surroundings in which he now stood.

After Portia's pleading, her husband gave up chastising Antonias. There were more important things to do. Syllus instructed Antonias to show Dracchus around.

Maria returned to Delilah and her son.

* * *

"I'll leave right away," Delilah suggested when they were alone again. "I can go back to my former life in the town. I'm sure the matron will take me back. I was one of her best girls."

"You were, Delilah, but you were also four years younger," Maria reminded her. "I'm sure they have recruited nubile replacements for us a long time ago."

"Younger maybe, but not better," Delilah stated. "Many of these Roman youths need a more mature woman to show them the way."

"Aren't you a little out of practice?" Maria needled.

"Not entirely," Delilah said rising to the bait. "Haven't we indulged our senses just a little over the past four years?"

Maria squeezed Delilah's hand as they walked out toward Antonias' vineyard.

"I suppose it was all too good to be true," she said as the reality of their situation began to sink in. "We're not Romans, Delilah. We'll never be Romans. We can only live on the fringe of the Roman world. To the Romans we'll always be Jews. We come into their lives for a brief sweet moment, and then crawl away like lepers when our time is up. I suppose you'll have to go back to Tiberias and I suppose I shall have to take Marcus back to Magdala. I should see my mother again. I owe her that much. Marcus should meet his grandmother if he's going to have to be a Jew after all."

Marcus, who had not been paying attention to them, but had been helping himself to some of Antonias' ripening grapes, looked up when he heard his name. Maria smiled at her son nervously. The arrival of these strangers at Antonias' house was about to dramatically change their lives.

Delilah left the villa later that day. She realized that there was no future for her there and sought to return to her former life. She kissed Maria tenderly before she left, hugging her with tears in her eyes.

"I will never forget you," she sobbed. "You took the hardness from me. I've loved you, Maria, like I have never loved a man. Don't forget me."

She turned and left, determined not to look back, tears in her eyes, a lump in her throat, knowing that Maria had changed her life.

* * *

Antonias made no suggestion to his father that he should take Maria and Marcus with him to Athens. Syllus agreed to Antonias' only request. He offered space in his wagon for Maria and Marcus on the new road from Tiberias to Magdala. At Magdala, Antonias let them off. With no more than a weak smile, he bade his lover farewell as Antonias' portly father looked on. It was apparent that their destinies were not to be intertwined. Maria and Marcus stood in the square as the wagon drove away. Antonias went out of their lives.

In less than a month, Antonius Syllus concluded the sale of his

Tiberias property. Maria and Delilah were rarely mentioned. It was a foregone conclusion that the sale of the property was the natural end to this undesirable liaison. They were correct. In the presence of his parents, Antonias reverted back to becoming the shy young Roman whom Maria had first met in the brothel. He lost his initiative and bowed to his father's every wish. His passion seemed lost along with his freedom. Dracchus became the master. Antonias' school was closed. The young man then traveled with his family to Ptolemais where they set sail for Greece.

* * *

It was very difficult for Miriam after Joshua left Nazareth. The majority of the villagers quickly forgot the healing miracles that Joshua had performed. Rabbi Eliezer ben Hananah was fully in control once more, and the people tended to shun the mother of the troublemaker. Joshua's real followers had left with him and taken young Matthew Levi with them. That caused ill feeling, even within the family. Benjamin Levi rebuked his son for allowing Matthew to go.

"The boy is barely eleven years old," he had said.

David rarely spoke to Miriam. Ruth isolated herself amidst the Levi family. Only Jonah was left at home, and his popularity in the village had likewise declined.

Jonah joined Miriam in the back part of their old house behind the carpenter's shop. He looked disheartened. Miriam could sense that the pressure of their isolation was taking its toll.

"Jonah," she said, plucking up courage and knowing her own feelings, "I've been thinking a lot about our situation here in Nazareth. I think we should leave. Maybe we should go down to Judea and live with James and Rachel—make a new life in Jerusalem as they have."

"I know," Jonah responded. "I've thought about that, too. We could go to Cana, of course. That's actually more what I had in mind. It's a lot closer and I could work there with my brother, if he's still in the building business."

They sat in silence for a moment.

"You know, we haven't seen Amos since his wedding," Jonah continued. "You would think that he would have visited us at least once and given us all his news. Cana is not all that far away."

"True," Miriam agreed, "but then I suppose we could equally say that we never visited them at Cana. What with Joseph's blindness and caring for my father, there never seemed to be any opportunity to travel."

"Well, let's do it now," Jonah suggested. "Let's go to Cana first, and at least find out how Amos and Salome are doing. They could have children by now." Jonah looked down for a while and then smiled up at Miriam.

"No Jonah," Miriam replied. "They would have come here with a baby. They would have brought the baby to his grandfather."

"I would have thought so. Look, if they're not willing, and there is no work for me, we'll travel to Judea. We might do that anyway. I know I'll be able to work in Jerusalem. Even Jon was able to work in Jerusalem."

"Won't we need to get a donkey and cart?" Miriam asked seriously.

"I'll build us a cart," Jonah said, laughing, "but you may have to buy the donkey. You still have some of the silver vessels that Joachim left us. It should be enough to buy us several donkeys."

"That sounds so strange," Miriam said. "You know, all my life I've never really known whether I was rich or poor. My father always took care of us all, but we never did have anything of our own."

"Well, maybe now is the time for us to make a new start," Jonah agreed. "I'm glad you suggested this. I'll begin work on the cart tomorrow."

Part Two

The Judas Triangle

Chapter One

Magdala

Maria watched as Antonias drove away. Suddenly life seemed a haze—her security gone. She felt frightened and incredibly sad. *It's Linus and his father all over again,* she thought. *They can't be trusted—even the good ones.* Taking Marcus by the hand she walked toward her mother's house. Unsavoury thoughts of her Magdala childhood returned. As they approached, Maria could tell that there was something wrong. The old square house seemed too well kept. Its walls had been restored with fresh plaster, and when she went inside the furnishings were different. There were more lamps and some colorful hangings, and the sweet musky balm of the brothel was missing.

"Is that you, Merab?" a voice called out from the back room.

Maria's fear increased. A good-looking man emerged from what used to be the brothel chamber. He was well dressed and did not have the sheepish grin of a client. He peered at Maria and Marcus and looked somewhat confused.

"Shalom! Who are you?" he mumbled.

"I'm Esther's daughter and this is my son," Maria replied. "Is my mother here?"

"Your mother?"

"Yes...Esther," Maria repeated.

"Oh! Esther. Esther's been dead three years or more," the man replied. "You're her daughter, you say?"

Maria felt a lump in her throat. Her worst fears had been confirmed. Her mother was dead. She regretted that they had never been able to patch up their quarrel. Her mother had died disowning her. Tears welled and broke in her eyes and she strengthened her grip on Marcus' hand.

The man came closer. He reached in his garment for a clean linen cloth and handed it to Maria for her to wipe her eyes.

"I'm sorry," he said. "So, you are Esther's daughter. Come over here and sit down."

Maria followed him to a bench. Marcus sat on the floor as the man comforted his mother.

"My name's Reuben," the stranger revealed. "I moved into your mother's house with my wife Merab about two years ago. Nobody wanted this house. I don't know why. It is a good, solid building with a large rooftop."

Maria looked at Reuben. He seemed a genuine man. She could even detect some of the past kindness of Antonias in him.

"I used to work here with my mother," she said.

Reuben raised an eyebrow.

"Oh!" he said.

He was silent for a moment and then asked her where she had come from.

"We were living in Tiberias. Marcus was born in Tiberias."

Reuben looked at the boy with his short Roman hair.

"You were married there?" he asked his mother.

"No. I'm not married. Marcus' father was a Roman."

"Oh, I'm sorry," Reuben replied slowly.

"It's nothing to be sorry about. Marcus was conceived in love."

"Well, it must be difficult for you. What is your name?"

"Maria."

"That's also a Roman name," Reuben observed.

"Yes."

Maria looked at her son. She felt uncomfortable.

"I think we'd better go, Marcus. This isn't our house any more."

She turned back to Reuben.

"Thank you," she said. "We'll be on our way."

Maria and Marcus left the house leaving Reuben staring after them as they went toward the beach. It was a long time since Maria had slept rough, but she realized that she was now on her own again. As they walked along the pebbled shore toward the olive groves to find a place with some shelter, Maria surreptitiously stole a couple of dried fish from a laid out stack.

* * *

Jerusalem was a lot more exciting than Damascus as Linus enjoyed a feeling of importance as Pontius Pilatus' aide. Jerusalem was not as stuffy, but it was a lot less secure than Damascus. There was always a sense of challenge in the prefect's office. There was intrigue with plots and counter-plots in a very mixed cosmopolitan society. The Jews in Jerusalem needed to be under constant surveillance. While Linus' parents were on extended leave in Rome, however, Linus felt it prudent to visit their property in Galilee—the villa above Taricheae that the Hebrews still insisted on calling Magdala. After a year in Jerusalem, he left for a month's furlough.

He was glad he did so, for on arrival at the Taricheae villa, he found the family's steward, Demetrius, to be very sick with a high fever. The man was delirius and Leah, the Hebrew maid and now the steward's wife, was quite incapable of comforting him. It was apparent that this fever had been a recurring condition that Demetrius had experienced throughout the winter, and as a result, much of the agricultural work at the villa was behind schedule. Spring tares were rampant in the normally clean soil between the neat rows of freshly sprouted vines.

The fame of a Capernaum miracle worker had reached Magdala and Leah's ears. When Linus was buying fresh fish in the village, thinking that might benefit his delirious steward, he noted a commotion surrounding one of the boats pulled up on the shingle. Being keenly alert to commotions among the Jews from his Jerusalem training, and with his astute ear for Aramaic, curiosity overtook him. He joined the crowd of onlookers who had surrounded the boat. A black-bearded fellow surrounded by anxious faced men was negotiating prices for transport to Capernaum.

It became apparent that the man, one named Judas Iscariot, and his henchman, a younger man named Thomas, were well known. Linus learned that they were from Capernaum and that they regularly ferried sick and injured persons from Magdala to be cured by the famous Capernaum miracle worker—Joshua the Nazarene. It occurred to Linus that it might be worth his while to travel to Capernaum himself to witness the healing work of this Jewish holy man. Possibly, Joshua the Nazarene might be able to help Demetrius. Either Demetrius must be restored to his former vigor or Linus would have to replace him, and, therefore, Leah, too. Linus had a certain respect and admiration for Demetrius. The steward had been surprisingly good to him during those awkward days when he had fallen out with Gladius over his relationship with Maria, the sultry and voluptuous Hebrew beauty whom he had dared to bring into the villa as his lover. He hadn't thought about Maria for a long time, but the smell of the fishermen and the provincial scene reminded him of that long and glorious summer he had spent with her along the shores of the lake.

I wonder if she is still here? Linus asked himself. *I wonder what happened to her, and if her child…possibly our child, was ever born?*

"I have room for one more," the black beared fisherman called Judas shouted, breaking Linus' reflections. "Who will give silver for one more passage?"

There were several who shouted out pathetic sums of money to which the wily Jew shook his head. Linus reached into his tunic and pulled out three denarii. The silver coins were way in excesss of the value of the bronze leptons that the others were offering.

"Jump in!" Judas commanded Linus. "Thomas! Make ready to cast off!"

His henchman shouted to some of their fishing friends as together they pulled on the rope while others pushed from behind. The boat eased out into the shallows of the lake and started to float. Thomas climbed back in and worked the steering oar as Judas pulled up the sail. The fishing boat, laden with four or five sick persons, two on cripple's pallets, set sail for Capernaum.

Judas rubbed his hands in glee.

"This cargo is proving more profitable with each voyage," he said to his young partner. "We win both ways. We sell our catch to the middlemen in Magdala and return with patients for the Master."

Linus wondered if he was doing the right thing. *These men seem opportunists,* he thought. The smell of dead fish eminated from the bowels of the boat, but fortunately as the wind picked up it wafted away. They beached in Capernaum before the sun was down. Linus, asked Judas for directions to an inn and found himself a room for the night.

As he sipped on a goblet of wine in the shady grape arbour of the inn, he overheard local gossip.

"Are you taking your daughter to Simon's house tomorrow?"

"Yes. I believe in Joshua the Miracle Worker. Why don't you come, too."

Linus felt more confident.

* * *

Maria found it very hard to adjust to a nomad's life after the ease and comfort of her years in Tiberias. She had a responsibilty to Marcus and she could see the boy's bitter disappointment in his baffling change of circumstances. She considered taking Marcus back to Tiberias where she could return to her old lifestyle at the brothel. Marcus, especially now that he could communicate simply in Greek, might usefully serve a boy's apprenticeship with a craftsman in the city. In that way, they might survive.

Maria watched the merchants carefully as she came to the market stalls that had sprung up along the beach at Magdala. When they were not looking, she would try to steal bread and fruit. She reached out for two pomegranates. A hand clasped her wrist. She looked round and saw the smiling face of Reuben.

"Don't steal, Maria," he said without admonishing her. "You don't need to steal for your sustenance. I've been watching you. I think you and your boy could do with a decent meal."

Maria relaxed as she realised that she was not in serious trouble.

"Come back with me," Reuben continued. "I have plenty for you to eat."

Reuben was a man who sounded like he was used to getting what he wanted. He had a magnetic charm, too, and it was easy for Maria to be swayed into his trust. She and Marcus followed him back to her mother's old house. Once there, Reuben called to his wife:

"Merab! We have guests."

Reuben's wife came out to meet them.

"Merab, this is Maria and her boy," he said. "Maria used to live in the village."

He avoided stating that their house had been her home or that she was Esther's daughter. Reuben was too smart to be caught out so easily.

"Maria and her boy are hungry and homeless so I thought we could give them a meal," he said.

Merab looked Maria and Marcus up and down, then looked back at her husband scrunching the furrows in her brow.

She did not seem too pleased with Reuben's suggestion, but acknowledged that they had enough bread and that there was a large pot of stewing vegetables on the fire.

"There should be enough for all of us, if they really need it" she confirmed begrudgingly.

After they had eaten, Reuben intimated that he knew of a vacant house in the village where Maria and Marcus could possibly stay.

"Let's take a look at it and see," he suggested.

Merab glared at her husband.

Reuben was right, however. Just beyond the square and beside the dovecote there was a small, single-room, square house that had recently been vacated.

"I think you could stay here for a while," Reuben said. "I can settle with the owner. It's better than sleeping rough on the beach. I can provide you with food for a day or two until you get settled."

Reuben looked at Maria intently and she instinctively interpreted his gaze. She realized with her astute feminine recognition of the male mind what he was thinking. She did not really relish going back to Tiberias if she could somehow settle Marcus in Magdala, at least for a while. Those old feelings pulled at her. Reuben was going to take care of her, but it made her nervous. *His wife already doesn't trust him*, she thought, but she had Marcus to think of.

The following day Reuben called at the house with some fresh fruit and bread and suggested to Maria that he might introduce them to a rug-maker and weaving friend of his.

"Old Zachary might take you both on. He doesn't pay much, but he's very fair and it would make a start for you," he said, enhancing his recommendation.

That sounded like a good idea. *Perhaps Reuben is genuine*, she thought.

Zachary had three looms at his house. Two of them were set up in a lean-to tent of pungeant goatskins supported on a couple of slanting poles that ran out from the sidewall of his house. Two boys were busy passing shuttles through the strings of the looms as they worked on some bright orange cloth. A slightly older girl sat inside the house where she was knotting crude wool into a rustic rug. Behind her stood the rugmaker.

"Zachary, would you have a vacancy for a strong boy here?" Reuben asked. "I can make arrangements with you for his apprenticeship. We can talk business."

Zachary looked up a little surprised at the earnest nature of his friend's request.

"I should think we can come to some terms," he said, shaking his head quizzically as he saw Maria.

Reuben caught his reaction.

"Maria might be able to help you, too," he suggested.

Zachary looked knowingly at Maria, as if somehow he recollected her.

"I could use the boy," he suggested. "I'm going to need another weaver very soon. Has he any experience with a loom?"

"Not yet," Reuben replied, "but under your guidance he'll learn, he even speaks a little Greek so he might make a good dealer for you. You know how the Romans flock to us for our goods these days."

"All right, Reuben, you don't have to say anymore. I'll take the boy, but not the woman. Leave the boy with me. I'll send him home at sundown."

Zachary introduced Marcus to one of his boy weavers.

Reuben left with Maria, Marcus looking back at her.

The sun was reaching its height and felt warm as they made their way back to the small house by the dovecote. Reuben stood in the entrance after Maria had gone inside. The room was very sparsely furnished. Two mats were on the earthen floor as pallets and a single, unlit lamp was placed on a stand against the far wall. In one corner were a small clay oven and an open hearth where hung two cooking pots and water skins.

"I'll be back later with some bread for this evening," Reuben said. "I can probably also bring you some lentils for the pot. Don't go out stealing from the merchants. You won't need it. I'll take care of you, Maria."

The truth was out. Maria knew his intentions. It was all too familiar. *Men,* she thought.

He grinned at her in a supercillious way.

"I will expect some favors in return," he added.

Somewhat flushed, Maria seductively placed her hands beneath her breasts pleased to know that in her hard times she had not lost the ability to attract. She didn't need to speak; Reuben had won his way. The man walked out, obviously happily anticipating his return later in the afternoon. Although still wary of Reuben, Maria felt a little more secure.

* * *

Reuben's self-assurance was not diminished in his encounter with Maria. He wasted no time in fulfilling the animal instincts that her charm had aroused within him, but at the same time he was surprised by her responsive sensuality. He was not used to giving in his lovemaking, but only to taking. His wife always accepted his domination giving herself to him in passive obedience. She never responded to his movements, but performed a domestic duty. But, now, Merab was pregnant. She was in her third month. Her pregnancy had made her even less exciting in her wifely duty, and Maria had walked into Reuben's house at precisely the moment when he had most felt his curtailment and frustration. In the crude comfort of their hideaway, Reuben pumped into Maria, releasing his frustrations and feeling his dominance over her.

Maria arched herself in response and allowed Reuben to massage her breasts in his frenzied action. Reuben was surprised. Her obvious pleasure actually baffled him. Maria became not only a means for relieving his frustrations, but also an interesting challenge to his self-centeredness.

Spent, and temporarily relieved, Reuben left the rather uninviting house of his chosen tryst knowing that he would return.

"Tomorrow, I'll bring you some cushions," he said, as he finished adjusting his dress. "You deserve something better than these hard mats."

"When do you want to come?" Maria asked.

Reuben didn't want to be pinned down.

"I'll come when I feel like it," he replied. "You'll be here."

Chapter Two

The Miracle Worker

Judas Iscariot had directed Linus to come to a solid square house that the fisherman had pointed out to him at the far end of the Capernaum beach—Simon's house, the same as the gossips at the inn had mentioned. As Linus approached, he found a large crowd had already gathered including a sundry collection of sick and injured persons who were patiently waiting their turn for a miraculous cure. Among them were the two crippled persons who had shared passage with him in Judas' boat.

It was impossible to get anywhere near the entrance to the house and Linus felt somewhat disappointed. He was curious. He needed Demetrius in good health. Time was not on his side. But in his frustration, he left and walked along the beach feeling that he might have been foolish to embark on this idea of a miracle cure for his steward, besides he was the only Roman there among so many Jews, and uneducated Jews for the most part, too. As the day wore on, the crowd did not diminish and some of the sick suffered from exposure to the warm sun. There was a growing sense of frustration. Linus became skeptical. Then, he heard a cheer, and looking back he saw some from the crowd had climbed up onto the roof and appeared to be chipping away at the mud and wattle. Others were holding up a man on a pallet—they looked like part of the group with whom he had traveled the day before in Judas Iscariot's boat. The men above then started to shout triumphantly and pulled the pallet up onto the gently sloping roof.

Two burly men came out of the house screaming up at them angrily:

"What are you doing? Stop immediately! Come down!"

The frustrated men worked even harder. It was apparent that they had broken through and it was easy now for them to pull away great hunks of the palm wattle and mud that lay across the rafters. Linus heard shouts from within the house and the two burly men, seeing that the intruders had paid no attention to them, climbed onto the roof themselves. A fight started. One of the defenders fell back from a blow to his head. *He's lucky he didn't fall from the roof,* Linus thought. The other continued the struggle, but he was outnumbered, and by now the hole in the roof had itself become a danger to them all.

All of a sudden, the scuffling stopped and a surprising unity came between the defenders and attackers. They gently started to lower the paralyzed man on his pallet into the house through the hole between the rafters.

I want to see this, Linus thought with renewed interest. He nudged his way past the onlookers and slipped through the door into the house where he could see the pallet with the crippled man being lowered down from above. Men reached for it as it swung, and lowered it to the ground where it rested on the earthen floor among the roof debris in front of a man with a light brown beard and deep set eyes, and wearing a rather dirty white robe.

Following Linus, others now pushed in from outside and pressed him forward until he was almost face to face with the healer—the man Linus assumed must be this Joshua, the famed miracle worker.

This Joshua, looked at the paralytic staring up at him.

"How did this happen to you?" he asked at length.

Looking fearful, the man timidly answered:

"It's my curse."

Joshua smiled and stretched a hand toward him.

"Don't touch me. I was a sinful man and this became my curse," the cripple repeated. "I lost the use of my legs."

There were tears in both men's eyes.

"I was a thief and a robber," the man continued. "One day I stole silver from the synagogue in my village. The rabbi and some of the scribes and other Pharisees chased after me. I tripped and fell and when they caught me they beat me. I could not move my legs and they told me I had sinned against God."

"This man should be stoned," a man close to Joshua shouted.

"Yes!" others echoed.

Mildly, the cripple stammered:

"I...I was wrong, have mercy on me. I...I was taught to steal because my family was poor. It...it was the only way we could live."

"Where was your village?" the miracle worker asked.

"Nain..." the man sobbed back. "I know it was wrong to steal the silver of God...but I was asked to do this by a rich man who promised me many good things."

He looked up pathetically at Joshua.

"I never saw the man again. He...he never came back to me."

Joshua momentarily raised his eyes to the opening in the ceiling. The cripple's friends as well as the two burly men, one bleeding from his head wound, were peering in from above.

Complete silence returned to the room. Joshua looked down at the paralyzed man again.

"My son, your sins have been forgiven," he said slowly and deliberately.

Choking on his sobs, the cripple said faintly:

"I know."

Linus was moved, his mind, frozen in the moment. He sensed a power in the room. It was not part of his Roman code to be sentimental, but he could see that this paralyzed man was pinning every hope in his life on the miracle worker's compassion. It was as if this paralytic man believed he was in the presence of one of the gods. There was no religion in Linus' life other than his emotive attachment to the empire, but he felt Joshua's spirituality. He knew that he was not in the presence of a soothsayer or a magician, but a man of sincerity and integrity. He quietly watched, mesmerized by the healer as he continued his task.

* * *

Joshua knelt down beside the cripple and examined his legs carefully. It seemed there were no broken bones, but his legs were cold. He gently massaged the man's thighs and calves and then sitting him up maneuvered his hands up and down the man's spine. There was not a single sound from the waiting crowd. Gently lying the man down again, he took his feet into his lap where he rubbed them briskly, bringing them some warmth. He gouged his thumb into the palm of their soles asserting pressure.

The crippled man appeared to feel no pain. He didn't appear to feel anything, but that was the way with paralyzed men. Then, all of a sudden the man's left knee jerked. The cripple let out a yelp.

Joshua asked the crowd to stand back, except for Linus, who was closest to him.

He looked straight at Linus with those pentrating eyes.

"I will need your help," he said. "Help me raise him and take hold of him when he gets up. He will be in pain now."

A Roman, Joshua thought. *What does he want with us? Still, he understands our language, that's more than most, and little does he suspect that I can understand his Greek.*

"Heal me, Master!" the cripple yelled out fearfully, as Linus went to reach for him.

Some of those standing behind Joshua began mutterring. From Linus' expression, he obviously sensed it was hostile.

Joshua looked down at the cripple.

"Sit up," he said gently.

Slowly, using the strength in his arms, and assisted by Linus, the man, wincing, raised himself into a sitting position. Then, appearing to feel sudden pain he fell back.

Joshua repeated:

"Sit up."

"I...I can't..." the man stuttered.

"We will slowly raise him together," Joshua said to Linus. "Very slowly, right."

The men behind started muttering again.

Joshua turned and silenced them with a glare.

"Why do you question that this man's sins are forgiven?" he asked them. "Which is easier to say to this man, 'Your sins have been forgiven' or 'Get up and walk?' This man will be healed."

Slowly, Joshua and Linus raised the man to his feet, taking his weight on their shoulders.

"Now walk," Joshua commanded.

The man shuddered.

"I…I can't," he pleaded.

"I tell you in the name of God, walk!" Joshua repeated.

Holding on to Joshua and Linus for all he was worth, and with terror in his eyes, the man gingerly moved his left leg forward—and then his right leg. He winced, he screamed, but he walked—slowly, step by step, the man walked to the door, hanging on to Joshua and Linus for all he was worth. Once at the door and out into the light, he walked a little faster, and gradually Joshua released his hold on the man. But the man clung to Linus in weakness and agony.

Meanwhile, those who had brought the cripple, climbed down from the roof.

After a step or two more, the man pushed Linus' hands away.

"I…I can walk!" he shouted at the top of his voice, as the crowd ran out from the house to witness the miracle. "I…I can walk!"

But after taking two steps on his own, he faltered and his friends came to his aid. Slowly, they helped him along the beach. Step by step, he then appeared to gain strength.

Linus turned his gaze from the progress of the cripple back to Joshua. They smiled at each other as extreme intensity left Joshua's face and revealed compassionate warmth that Linus was compelled to believe in.

"I must talk to you," Linus said.

To Linus's obvious surprise, the miracle worker answered him in Greek.

"Of course, but first I have more work to do."

* * *

Joshua went back into the house. The crowd followed him. Linus sat on the beach and watched as the once crippled thief disappeared with his friends. Then, he stared out at the lake—the lake of his childhood—waiting for his opportunity to speak directly to the miracle worker. *This man will heal Demetrius,* he thought. *This man will heal my father's steward.*

A group of peasants passed by.

"Roman!" they shouted.

One threw a pebble in his direction. It fell short.

Linus stood up, anger welling within him. *When will they ever learn,* he thought. He wanted to rebuke them, show them who was in charge, but he couldn't. He saw the face of Joshua, the miracle worker, in his mind. There was something in Linus' gut that made him believe in this man. Besides, if Demetrius died it would be very inconvenient. *I don't have time to take care of my father's estate. I need Demetrius,* he repeated to himself.

The peasants jeered at him, but seeing him stand, ran.

"Cowards!" he muttered, and seated himself down again to stare out over the water.

He sat patiently waiting, watching the changing light and mood of the Galilean lake. He could not stop thinking about the remarkably calm authority that Joshua had shown in the healing of that paralytic man. The whole experience was made all the more moving because of his own involvement. Through the miracle worker's instruction, he himself helped to make the man walk. He realized that he was the closest person to Joshua at the time, but he was nonetheless astounded that Joshua asked him to assist, inasmuch as he was obviously Roman and almost certainly not a Jew. Those in the crowded room were all Jews. The miracle worker could just as easily have called on one of them.

It was close to sunset before the crowd started to diminish. Finally, Linus, who had observed all day, and felt a little self-conscious around this motley collection of Hebrew peasants besieging the house with their petitions, had his opportunity to speak with Joshua.

Joshua stepped out of the house with the two burly men who had assisted in lowering the paralyzed man from the roof earlier in the day. A third, robust and rough-looking fellow was also with them. Linus stood up and walked toward them. Joshua caught his eye and said something to the others that Linus couldn't quite hear. The miracle worker then broke away from the group and came to Linus.

"You waited for me!" Joshua exclaimed, again in Greek.

"Yes," Linus replied. "I need to talk to you."

Joshua looked back at his friends.

"All right," Joshua said rather deliberately and with a whimsical smile, then reverting back to Aramaic he continued:

"Let's walk along the beach. So, you sought me out?"

"I came from Taricheae," Linus explained. "I was in the same boat as that man you healed this morning—the cripple."

"From Magdala," Joshua repeated slowly, stroking his beard.

"Yes...as you say. I am...or at least I spent my childhood close by. My father still has a villa there, but I myself am now posted in Jerusalem."

"Might I ask what you do in Jerusalem?" he asked.

"I'm in the prefect's service there," Linus answered, not wishing to reveal any more or any less.

"You are in a position of authority then, sir?"

"Yes, I suppose I am," Linus responded.

Joshua stopped walking. He turned and faced Linus.

"Well, what can I do for you?"

Linus looked into the healer's eyes.

"My father's servant has fallen very sick. He has had a high fever for some time and doesn't seem to respond to the usual herbs that his wife has tried to give him. My father's away, and I am only up in Galilee for a short visit. If Demetrius...that's his name..."

Linus paused, wanting the reassurance that this strangely powerful man was really listening to him.

"If he doesn't recover soon, I may have to replace him with a new steward," he continued. "I hate to do that. Demetrius has worked in our family for a number of years. I believe you can heal him, especially after what I have seen today."

* * *

Joshua warmed to Linus. It was rare that Romans actually came to put their trust in him and he was more than a little flattered that Linus believed in him. *Demetrius... That sounds familiar. What if this is the same place that I worked on as a building slave?* he wondered. *What was the name? Flavian, Flavius?*

Joshua had never seen either his healing powers or his message as being for Gentiles...his work had been exclusively with his own people, *but why not?* he thought. This determined Roman presented a challenge to him.

As he turned and they started to walk back along the beach the way they had come, Joshua momentarily wondered how his chosen disciples would react to such a broadening of his ministry. It did not take him long, however, to make up his mind which way he wanted to go.

"I will come and heal your steward," he said. "You say he is still in Magdala?"

"Yes!" Linus answered earnestly. "However, it may be sometime before you can come. I've seen today what demands are made on you. I am a man used to authority. I have men under my command and I know how valuable time is."

Linus thought for a moment and then continued:

"When I give an order it's obeyed. Soldiers come and go at my command and slaves fulfill my requests. I know what it is like to have authority, and in you, sir, I have seen authority. I don't wan't to take up your time, but I believe in your power, sir. Whenever you say that my father's servant is healed, I will believe you."

Joshua again felt flattered. No Roman had ever addressed him as 'sir'.

"You have great faith," he answered. "Would you believe me if I were to tell you that your father's servant is healed as of this moment?"

Linus had been trapped by his own words. He really had no choice but to follow his statement through. Not quite sure whether he believed that Joshua could actually perform a healing miracle from so far, he nonetheless let him think so.

"Yes..." he stammered.

"Demetrius has been healed," Joshua confirmed. "Return to Magdala and you will find it so. Your faith has healed him."

Linus looked a little stunned. The shadow of doubt increased. He wanted to believe that this could have happened, but doubt and reality was setting in.

"I will travel back to Magdala with you," Joshua said, reassuringly smiling at Linus. "I would like to visit the village again and from there I can travel to other parts of Galilee before returning to Capernaum. We will take all three of our boats tomorrow. It will be the quickest way."

Linus felt more reassured. He felt the need for Joshua to heal Demetrius in person. Besides, this made him feel in charge. After all he had summoned the miracle worker.

They were almost back at Simon's house at the end of the beach. The two burly men and the other heavy man were anxiously waiting for Joshua's return.

"Shall I meet you here on the beach then?" Linus inquired.

"Certainly. Be here early. By the way, what is your name?"

"Linus, sir."

"Was your father a commander in Sepphoris?"

"Er...Yes."

"I might have met him...Linus, your faith has saved your servant."

He called out to his friends:

"Jonas, Janus, Cephas, we will go with this Roman to Magdala tomorrow."

Then, turning to Linus he said:

"You are welcome to join us for the evening meal. I expect Zebedee has enough."

"Master, others are waiting for you," Cephas said impatiently.

Linus looked up at Joshua. He smiled knowingly:

"I had better be going. I have a room at an inn," he said. "I'll be back here early after the sunrise."

Joshua lightly embraced Linus in the Hebrew fashion, which made Linus a little self-conscious. Linus retraced his steps back to where the boats were beached in front of the way into town.

* * *

"That was a Roman official," Joshua said slowly to the sons of Zebedee, and Cephas as they entered Simon's house. "I can honestly say to you that among those who have come to us sound of body and mind, I have found few who have had such faith as that man. It is easy for a sick man full of hope to believe I can cure him, but it takes remarkable faith on the part of a man who has been shunned all day and yet waited to ask if I can heal his servant."

"Where is his servant," Jonas asked.

"Sick in Magdala."

Joshua seemed in deep thought.

"There may be a lesson for us here, my friends," he continued. "Gentiles will approach us in our healing ministry. Some may even come to live in the spirit of the new kingdom when it comes, whereas among our own there may be many who will never accept the spirit of God and be rejected from the coming kingdom."

Cephas raised an eyebrow.

"Tomorrow," Joshua repeated, "we will go to Magdala, to a house of gentiles. Cephas, let Judas Iscariot know. Janus and Jonas, we will need to take your boat with us as well."

Simon, once 'the Zealot', had already cleared the debris from the broken roof and was busy affixing temporary palm fronds over the gaping hole.

Chapter Three

Healing and Stoning

It was well into the afternoon. Reuben had visited Maria rather earlier than the previous day. After he left, she felt a certain release and freedom. In her heart, Maria knew that she couldn't stay with this man. She enjoyed his physical presence during its moment of intensity—the man was a strong lover—but his arrogance destroyed the pleasure when he left her feeling abused and used. Maria felt somewhat trapped. She could not deny that she had quite enjoyed obliging a dominant lover after such a long time of knowing only the gentleness of Antonias and the tender caresses of Delilah, but at the same time she despised Reuben's arrogance. She saw the bread and fruit that he had brought her, however, and realizing her responsibility to Marcus, she knew that at least for a while she would continue to oblige him.

She walked out into the sunlight wanting to take a long stroll beside the lake. When she arrived at the water's edge, she heard a commotion. Three boats from Capernaum had just come in and there were about thirty strangers crowding around them on the beach. She stood and watched for a moment as they unloaded some provisions and set them out above the shoreline. She thought she recognized the apparent leader, a man with a heavy black beard who shouted the orders as he fussed over their few possessions and basic provisions. There was also something familiar about the other central figure in the group—a man with a gentler face and lighter beard. As the crowd built up, Maria's attention moved from the two leaders to a third man whom she knew she recalled. He was Roman, and unmistakably, despite his increased maturity, was the man she had loved during that last, long summer that she had spent in Magdala—the man who had found her naked in the olive grove. *That has to be Linus, Marcus' father*, she thought.

Maria was too stunned to call out Linus' name. So often she had wondered what this moment would be like. Now, she just stood gazing at him, frozen to her spot. A well of forgiveness flowed up from her loins as she remembered only his love, totally forgetting the cold manner of their parting, and his failure to uphold his promise that he would 'find a way' and that he would take care of her and their child.

Linus never looked Maria's way. He became engrossed in conversation with the light-bearded man who was wearing a well-worn, white robe. The two of them led the group into the village and disappeared from her sight. For a moment, she doubted her observations, but the memory was too strong. *That was Linus*, she confirmed to herself. *That was Marcus's father.*

Filled with an inner glow that uplifted her after her post-coital letdown, she followed them at a discreet distance. Outside the village, just beyond the ring of Cypress trees, the man in the white robe spoke to the group once they were seated comfortably in the grassy glade. Then, he and Linus began to climb up the hillside, taking the short cut to the Roman villa that she remembered clamboring up so many times in her childhood ramblings. There was no doubt in Maria's mind, now. She had seen again the man whom she had first truly loved.

* * *

Joshua's suspicions were confirmed as he clambored up the hill with Linus. The Roman villa, which he could now see above them, was, indeed, the one he had helped to rebuild when he and Amos had been in the forced service of Flavius Septimus, the Sepphoris garrison commander.

"I've been here before," Joshua said to Linus, as he panted during a pause for breath on their steep climb. "Your father was that Roman soldier in command at Sepphoris!"

"Yes…So you did know him?"

"I worked for him in forced labor," Joshua replied quietly.

"I'm so sorry," Linus answered.

"It's all right. There were about ten of us. We rebuilt your father's villa. It had been badly damaged by fire."

"I was here the night of the fire!" Linus exclaimed. "Gladius, my old servant fought the blaze with me. We saved the villa. We were attacked by a mob from the village."

"Is Gladius the same man as your Demetrius?" Joshua asked, as he thought back on those days of forced labor.

"No...Gladius was always with us, but my father brought Demetrius to the villa when he retired from Sepphoris. He had been his Master of Works when they rebuilt the city after the rebellion. Gladius and I were in Rome then with my mother."

"I know this Demetrius," Joshua said calmly. "I worked under him here, but in Sepphoris, too."

Linus seemed a little awkward.

He probably thinks he's made a big mistake entrusting Demetrius' life to me, Joshua thought. *He must think I hated Demetrius as his taskmaster. He believes that I was one of the rebels.*

He looked at Linus straight in the eye.

"It will be interesting to see Demetrius again," he said, reassuringly. "He was good to us when we worked for him at your father's house, but it was very different in Sepphoris."

"I know," Linus replied sullenly, as he took on the race guilt of the Roman world. "I find it hard to think of you as a rebel."

"I wasn't. They dragged me and my brother from my father's carpenter's shop in Nazareth because they needed craftsmen, but many I worked with had been freedom fighters."

They walked on in contemplative silence, rejoining the track and walking to the gate.

Joshua broke the silence. On entering the little court outside the vestibule, he looked up as if he were a foreman inspecting his laborers' work.

"I remember how we replaced those roof beams," he remarked.

A matronly maid came out when she heard them coming. She was smiling.

"Master Linus! It's you!"

"Yes, Leah. How is he?" Linus asked.

"Master Linus, Demetrius seems to have recovered. The heat left him yesterday. He's eating again and seems to have finally shaken the fever. He was up for a short while today, but he is very weak."

Linus caught Joshua's eye. The miracle worker wore a mysterious expression of impish joy.

"Isn't that what I told you?" he said

"It's a miracle!" Linus exclaimed.

"It was very frightening after you left," Leah revealed. "Demetrius had a particularly bad night. He was completely out of his mind, speaking utter gibberish until he became unconscious. I thought he had died. He lay very still all the next day until close to sunset, when all of a sudden he regained consciousness and took a little water."

Linus looked astounded.

Joshua smiled. Just before sunset was precisely the time that he and Linus had spoken about Demetrius as they walked along the Capernaum shoreline.

"After that," Leah concluded, "he steadily improved. All traces of his fever were gone. But like I said, he's still weak. Don't let him work for a while."

They could both see the joy in Leah's eyes—this Hebrew maid who had crossed the racial divide, taken up with Demetrius and married into the forbidden race.

Linus put his hand to his chest as if in salute.

"Thank you, sir," he said, knowingly.

Leah took them in to where Demetrius lay on his bench bed. The steward failed to recognize Joshua—too many years had passed, but he allowed the bearded man dressed in white to place a hand upon his forehead. Then, Joshua stood back, stretched out his arms and said in Hebrew:

"Blessed be God forever."

A tear ran down Leah's cheek as she, too, muttered the shema in Aramaic.

Linus stood at the foot of the steward's bed.

"Praised be the gods, praise be to Caesar," he said.

Demetrius nodded.

Linus and Joshua left to sit in the Atrium.

"The fever has, indeed, left him," Joshua said. "Your faith has done this thing, Linus Flavian."

"Leah! Bring us some wine!" Linus shouted.

It was getting dark when Joshua left. Linus embraced him at the gate and gave him a lighted torch to see his way back down the grassy track to the village below. Joshua's followers and the chosen disciples were waiting for him at their camp behind the cypress trees.

"The servant is healed. A Roman's faith in our work allowed this miracle. Now, you must have faith that you, too, can perform miracles," was all he said.

After a good night's sleep they made plans for their overland travel and struck camp to move over the hills toward Nain and other villages to the southwest.

* * *

Although there was no synagogue in Magdala, there was a Pharisaic group that saw themselves as the lakeside community's custodians of the Law. Heading them was a particularly narrow-minded and rather miserable man named Obadiah. He and his small group of 'Pious Ones' did all they could to fight the increasing commercial spirit of the villagers. The Roman influence over the fishing trade in the marketing of pickled fish abhorred these 'Pious Ones', and the ever-increasing invasion of fishermen from elsewhere with their rough manners and basic needs was also a cause for their alarm.

The 'Pious Ones' were relieved when the men from the three boats that arrived from Capernaum stayed only one night before moving on elsewhere. They had heard about Joshua, the miracle worker, and although many reported to them on genuine healings that the man performed, they also received word about his abuse of the Sabbath rules and his generally lax interpretation of details surrounding the Law.

But foreign fishermen had been invading Magdala for a number of years now, and Obadiah in the past had waged a campaign against the growth of vices that these rough men encouraged. He had been in the forefront with his criticism of the thriving brothel of Esther. It was also well known to the 'Pious Ones' that Esther's daughter, Maria, had favored and given her services to young men in the Roman villas—even more unclean foreigners. Obadiah had personally been delighted when Maria had mysteriously disappeared and Esther had passed away. Reuben, the outsider who had moved in to the old brothel and made the dwelling respectable again, seemed a man of principle. He had encouraged the trade of carpet weaving and brought some dignity to the village. Reuben's wife, Merab, appeared to be very devout and certainly observed all the domestic requirements in her food preparation and appropriate use of cleansed utensils. Reuben's household, once the place of the whores, was an example for the whole village. Oabadiah had it in mind to court Reuben into his circle of 'Pious Ones'.

It upset Oabadiah, however, to learn that Esther's daughter, Maria, had returned to the village. He hadn't seen her himself as he didn't venture out much for fear of polluting himself among the evil sinners who seemed to frequent the waterfront. But, he learned that this shameful woman was back and that she appeared to have a boy with her, who presumably must be her son. The child was possibly a Roman bastard. That certainly was rumored. The 'Pious Ones' reported that Reuben had placed the boy in Zachary's weaving shop. Zachary overseered the looms, but it was Reuben who had control over the sale of their products. Some of the rugs woven in Magdala the previous year had been sold as far away as Jerusalem. Obadiah didn't blame Reuben for putting the boy to work at Zachary's looms, but "that Maria" needed to be watched.

Obadiah prepared himself for Sabbath prayers. It was his custom to meet with the 'Pious Ones' on the rooftop of his house at the north end of the village every Sabbath.

"She's living in Laban's old house," one of Obadiah's spies whispered to him as the self appointed leader strapped on his phylacteries and tefellin.

"Who?" Obadiah replied.

"Maria. You know...Esther the whore's daughter. You asked me to find out where she is living."

"Yes, Joab, I did," Obadiah said patronizingly. "So she's in Laban's house. We should watch the house. You can be sure she will be practicing her old profession soon. If we can find a way to expel her, we should. She's a wicked woman."

They were shortly joined by others in the group of 'Pious Ones' and made their way up onto the flat stone roof. With arms outstretched toward the gathering Sabbath observers below, they began to recite the shema and the more familiar Jewish prayers.

* * *

Reuben was very regular in his visits to Maria. He always came in the early afternoon at the time when Merab took a rest during her confinement. He usually told his wife that he was going to Zachary's house to check on the business, and, indeed, he often did. Even in his lustful longing for Maria, Reuben never forgot that he was a successful businessman. He never stayed very long with Maria, just long enough to satisfy his male ego and rid himself of his lustful desires.

* * *

It was less than a month since Maria and Marcus had arrived in Magdala, but a month was plenty of time for the 'Pious Ones' to seek out the evidence that Obadiah hoped to find. The little house, set back from its immediate neighbors, was under close surveillance. At first, Reuben's movements had not seemed suspicious, but they became a little too regular and aroused the curiosity of Joab. He watched Reuben come and go during those early afternoon hours. At length, he could not let his imagination play upon him any longer. He followed Reuben to the house, and after a suitably timed interlude, hearing Maria moaning, he crept in upon them. His suspicions were correct. Reuben was on top of Maria pumping into her like a crazed animal while his hands roamed over her voluptuous breasts. Maria was completely naked whereas Reuben was still partially clothed, his white tunic pulled up above his buttocks. It was some time before they realized that Joab was there. Obviously neither of them heard him open the heavy wooden door. They were both spent almost as soon as they had begun. As Reuben pulled out from Maria and stood up to straighten his tunic, he saw Joab watching them.

Maria screamed.

"You traitor!" was all Joab said.

He turned, leaving them both trembling in their separate fears.

Reuben slapped Maria.

"Why do you make so much noise?" he shouted.

"Leave me alone!" was all she could say in reply.

Reuben left.

* * *

When Obadiah received Joab's report he was both pleased and surprised. He was surprised at Reuben for his infidelity—the man he had marked out to join the 'Pious Ones' had shown himself to be unworthy. However, immediately, it looked as if the problem of Maria, Esther's daughter, was resolved.

"She's an adulteress!" he cried out. "We must rid the village of this evil whore."

"What do you suggest, Obadiah?" Joab asked, knowing his own opinion.

"She qualifies for death!" Obadiah replied. "She's a proven adulteress, as you have witnessed. She has broken the sacred Law. It's within our rights to put her to death."

"Are you sure we can do this?" Joab asked nervously.

"Stone her!"

"There are others who have broken our sacred Law and we have not taken them out for stoning—just expelled them—run them off."

"Maybe this will be an example to them," Oabadiah answered confidently. "Joab, call the 'Pious Ones' together. We need to be rid of this woman. She and her mother before her, have been nothing but trouble for this village, taking God's favor from us. Gather up a stoning party. We need to accomplish this tonight, before it becomes dark—before she escapes with that bastard boy of hers."

"What will become of him?'

"Who cares? He's a Roman brat."

Joab nodded.

"We can bury her in the morning at which time we should turn our attention to Reuben, don't you think?"

"We will run him out of town—the traitor."

* * *

I must escape from here with Marcus tonight, Maria decided. *It was a mistake to come back to Magdala.* Feeling cheap, she cried and clothed herself slowly.

She waited for Marcus to come home.

The door burst open. A crowd of rough men seized her and dragged her out. She struggled. One man grabbed her long dark hair. Another pulled at her arms.

"What are you doing? Where are you taking me?" she screamed.

"Adulteress!" was all they replied.

"Where's my son? Where's Marcus?" she shouted.

"Let the Romans take care of their own bastards!" one of the 'Pious Ones' henchmen yelled. "You're an adulteress and an evil woman fit only to die. You'll find your reward in Gehinnom."

The crowd grew as the men dragged Maria down the street, past Reuben's house, and on toward the stony beach south of the village.

Maria saw Merab standing at the doorway of her childhood home. Their eyes met as the growing crowd yelled:

"Aduteress!"

"What's going on?" Merab asked one of the mob.

"A stoning!" the excited man replied, although he gave no reason as to why Maria was condemned.

"Where's my husband?" she yelled at Maria.

"Where's my son?" Maria screamed back.

Not far out from the village, where the olive groves came down to the shore, the leaders tied Maria to a tree. They gagged her to cease her screams.

The crowd drew back.

The 'Pious Ones', seemingly well dressed men, had joined their henchmen.

"Stone her!" one of their leaders commanded.

A henchman picked up the first stone and hurled it at Maria.

The stone had a rough edge and cut her arm. It stung. Another stone winded her in the stomach. She could hear her own muffled cries as she fought the gag in her mouth. A third stone whistled past her head. *They are going to kill me!* she thought. *Marcus! Marcus!* she tried to cry out, gagging on saliva sodden cloth. Then, out of the corner of her eye she saw a motley crowd of travelers approaching along the beach from the south.

* * *

The group was led by the Capernaum miracle worker. The scene that they came upon horrified Joshua. He had only witnessed a stoning once before, and that had made him nauseous. It had been outside Jerusalem at the common criminal's ground, a barren place of execution known in the city as Golgotha, the place of the skull—so named because the vultures picked the flesh off the dead corpses that were denied burial. When he saw the stones hitting Maria, bruising her arms, drawing blood, and winding her stomach, he stepped into the circle. Amid shouts from the crowd, a stone hit him on the shoulder. He ducked, winced, then yelled at them with much more authority than their leaders.

A stone hit his back almost knocking him off his feet.

The crowd shouted abuse outraged by this interupting stranger.

More stones flew, hitting both Joshua and Maria.

Cephas and Judas Iscariot picked up stones and hurled them at the ruffians as they came to the defense of the Master.

"Stop!" Joshua shouted, throwing out his arms.

"What has this woman done to deserve this?" he cried out.

"She's an adulteress, a wicked woman!" one of the 'Pious One's' shouted back.

"That's the miracle worker from Capernaum!" a henchman yelled.

The well-dressed leader stepped forward:

"Who are you to interfere with the justice of God?" the man challenged Joshua. "This woman is an adulteress, who was caught in the very act. She has broken God's sacred Law and we condemn her in the name of Jehovah."

"You are right, sir," Joshua replied firmly. "This woman, by your account, has broken the Law."

Slowly, he looked around at the full circle of the crowd with a penetratiing glare.

"Whoever here has never broken any part of the Law," he said with clear authority, " be the next to throw a stone."

With that, he knelt down and cleared some pebbles from around his knees.

* * *

Maria watched in amazement. She knew she had seen this man before. He was the man who had been with Linus when she had seen him come in on the boats about a month ago. He'd seemed familiar even then. He reminded her a bit of a shy young man who had once fled from her at her mother's house. *Could it be?* she wondered. She wanted to cry out to him, but the gag in her mouth continued to impede her.

The crowd stood in silence, waiting to see what would happen next.

The man looked up. He spoke to her attackers again, not with anger, but with even greater authority:

"You heard what I said, if there is any one of you without sin, go ahead and cast your stones. If, however, any of you have sinned, and I suspect that applies to most of you, please disperse and leave this woman alone. Rest assured that your Father in Heaven knows what this woman has done and He will be her judge."

There were a few muffled jeers.

Two or three stones flew, one grazing Maria's cheek.

It stung and drew blood.

But, many in the crowd seemed frightened by the power of the intruder's words. He seemed to be in complete charge, despite his peasant's dress. They began to disperse. At length, protesting loudly about "meddling wandering holy men," the leaders also left the scene. When they had all gone except those who were traveling with the miracle worker, the stranger turned to face Maria. He walked to the stake and released the cloth that gagged her mouth.

"Woman," he said, "where are those who had condemned you?"

"They've gone," she whimpered in amazement, her eyebrows arched high.

"It seems then that you are not condemned. I don't condemn you either, but let this be a lesson to you. Whatever you have done against the Law of God, see that you don't do it again."

He unbound her bruised and somewhat lacerated arms.

"Come with me," he continued. "There is more joy in heaven over one sinner who repents than over ninety-nine just persons. I can make you whole."

He looked into Maria's eyes.

"What's your name?" he asked.

"Maria," the woman stammered.

The stranger winced.

Maria's suspicions were confirmed. *I do know this man. I think it was him,* she thought. *The shy man, too scared to touch me.*

"Who are you?" she asked.

"Joshua from Nazareth," the stranger replied. "Now, we need to bathe these wounds."

"Whoever is without sin," Joshua repeated slowly to himself, "let him be the first to cast a stone."

He took Maria's hand and called to one of his followers.

"Judas, let's camp in the olive groves tonight, away from the shore, and I don't think we should venture into the village until things have quieted down. We'll need to move on from here first thing in the morning."

Maria looked at Joshua.

"My son!" she pleaded. "I need to find my son!"

"Where is he?" Joshua asked.

"In the village. He works for a weaver—a man named Zachary. He should be home now. I must find him," Maria sobbed.

"What is his name?"

"Marcus."

"We'll find him. Don't you worry," he reassured her.

"Bartholomew, Matthew, and Jezebel," he called. "Go into the village and find this woman's son. Find out from Maria here where he should be and what he looks like. His name is Marcus."

Bartholomew and Matthew spoke with Maria and left for the village to search for the youth as darkness fell. They did not return for some time.

Maria felt anguish. She couldn't sleep and her body ached, but a woman named Susannah bathed her wounds and tried to comfort her. She appeared to be the wife of one named Cephas.

Then, Maria heard voices. *Could it be?*

"Lay still," Susannah whispered. "They might be coming back."

There was a deathly hush in the camp.

Maria then heard a young boy's cry.

"It's Marcus!" she shouted, and started to sob with joy.

Jezebel approached, pulling Marcus.

Seeing his mother, Marcus let go of Jezebel and ran to her.

"We found him crying in the street, near the place you mentioned," Jezebel said.

"Marcus! Marcus!" Maria sobbed, the pain momentarily leaving her bruised body.

Susannah fetched water for them both.

Early the next morning, the fishermen, brought the boats round from Magdala and beached them in front of the olive groves. Joshua and his followers boarded. Maria and her son left with them to set sail for Capernaum.

Chapter Four

Salt Tax

Herod Antipas, the tetrach of Galilee, moved his center of government from Sepphoris to Tiberias. He had built a comfortable palace on the hillside with tiered courtyards at different levels. In many ways, the move to Tiberias could be seen as a bid for partial independence. The Roman government remained in Sepphoris, and although Tiberias was a totally Roman town, it was an independent place of rest and recreation. Antipas hoped that the move would foster a better feeling for the tetrarchy, showing the Galilean Jews that Herod Antipas truly was their ruler and not an officer of the Sepphoris militia. Those who moved with him, to form his semitic court, unquestionably felt this new freedom, but the populace at large had other ideas. The project was not paid for out of Roman coffers. Herod Antipas made the mistake of believing that the mass of his people would support this move because of its social implications and that they would overlook the nominal tax on salt that was imposed to finance the building.

Herod had miscalculated. The Galilean peasants were indifferent to the move of the tetrarch's seat of government, but bitterly resented the salt tax. Jon the Baptist, who had lost many of his followers to Joshua the Nazarene because Joshua's miraculous healing powers had a more immediate appeal, seized on this opportunity to take up a new cause. More of a firebrand than ever, the baptist became a hero once again.

With a growing band of followers commited to the disruption of the salt tax and further ostracizing the unpopular tax collectors, Jon moved from Bethsaida, roaming the countryside, speaking out against the greed of the Herodians. He gave authority to his cause by linking this tax to his message of the end time? The action of Herod Antipas was another symbol of the abomination.

A great crowd had gathered around the baptist on his way from Madon to Cana.

"Salt is the greatest need that we have," Jon declared. "Without salt we can not preserve our produce and most of what we eat becomes like bitter herbs. This tax cuts at the very heart of living and goes against the laws of God."

Jon paused on a hummock and looked down at the crowd.

"You are the salt of the earth!" he shouted with great emotion. "Those who have repented and believed in my message will be the inhabitants of the Kingdom of God! But we don't live in king's houses nor should we subscribe to such riches. He, who builds up treasure for himself on this earth now, will find it hard to be accepted in the Kingdom of God when it comes. It is harder for a rich man to repent and prepare himself for the kingdom than for us who are poor. It will be easier for a camel to pass through the eye of a needle than for Herod Antipas to enter the kingdom to come."

There was a shout of approval.

"This tax must be resisted in all your villages," Jon instructed. "Refuse to pay. Bind yourselves together in resistance against those wicked men who accept to collect such taxes only for the profits that they can make for themselves. The tax collectors are the scum of the earth. Cast them out. There will be no place for them in the Kingdom of God."

Villagers flocked to the baptist. The tax was resisted. The dreaded agents of the Herodians found themselves lynched, stoned, and run out. Inevitable retribution then followed. Detatchments of the Herodian guard were sent out to seek the baptist's arrest and bring him to Tiberias.

* * *

Joshua's healing ministry continued to garnish followers. The success of his journey over the Galilean hills to Nain, where earlier he had come as close to fulfilling the powers displayed in the raising of Lazarus from the dead as at any other time in his ministry, only added to the numbers. Joshua encouraged by these excursions decided to leave Capernaum and make a grand journey south to Jerusalem.

Rabbi Isaac was upset to be losing him. Now, he had to find a replacement and he discussed the matter at length with Joshua.

"I think it most important that we choose a successor here who will continue what we have started," Joshua insisted. "You have been a wonderful patron for me. Without your generous acceptance of my work, I could never have reached these crowds which now throng the streets of Capernaum. Rabbi Isaac, you gave me my platform."

"I believe in you," the old man said, shaking as he fumbled to embrace Joshua in his blindness. "You have truly prepared us for the coming kingdom."

"The kingdom has come, Rabbi," Joshua replied with a twinkle. "The kingdom lives in us all if we allow the spirit and light of God to shine from us. It shines from you, Isaac. You are already in the kingdom."

Joshua thought for a moment and then continued:

"I used to believe that Jon the Baptist, my cousin, was the one sent by God to prepare us for the kingdom. You know that I was myself baptized by Jon," he confirmed, returning to deep seriousness. "I saw him as the incarnate Elijah ready to herald the kingdom to come. I'm not sure about that any more, Isaac. Elijah comes to us all individually. He is the herald of the spirit within. You have been Elijah to me. Without your support from the day that I came to Capernaum, I could never have inspired these crowds, which now have opened their hearts to the spirit of God. The kingdom is well established here in Capernaum, Isaac. I suggest that we appoint one of those who has been closest to me through all this as your successor."

"Who do you have in mind?" the old man replied.

"I would like to leave Thaddeus in Capernaum," Joshua recommended without hesitation. "He is a little older than some of the others and very level-headed. He seems to have grasped the basis of my message—namely that the kingdom comes to each of us when we accept the spirit within us as our guiding light. Thaddeus is quiet, but the spirit shines from him. I think he's our man, Isaac."

"That sounds all right to me, Joshua. You know that whomever you put in your place will have my full support." Then, he added as an afterthought, "Thaddeus reads, doesn't he?"

"Yes, Isaac. That was another reason for my choice. He and young Matthew are the only ones among my chosen disciples who can read."

It was arranged, and before Joshua led his group south, Thaddeus was officially appointed as Joshua's successor as the Rabbi of Capernaum. Joshua also appointed seventy of his followers from the Capernaum congregation as deacons to continue to preach the good news of the coming kingdom as it had been taught to them. He instructed them to go out to all the outlying villages in the Galilean hills as well as those around the lake.

"To do this," he said after he gathered them together, "you will have no visible means of support other than the love of the rest of us. Remember that love in the spirit of the new kingdom spreads visibly from you. When you try to comfort and heal the sick, try to feel the power of that inner spirit radiating from you. You won't always succeed. I don't always succeed. But the fire of God lives within all, yet most men cannot feel it. If you believe in that power of love, you will surprise yourselves how often it can be ignited in others. Your humility will also help to show the spirit of the kingdom. Travel light. Don't take any money, carry no bag, they are only hindrances asking for you to be robbed. Remember, I learned that the hard way myself. Those whom you will meet will take care of you in just the same way as you have taken care of us."

To his chosen twelve, now, actually eleven, since Thaddeus had been appointed Capernaum's rabbi, Joshua gave a similar message:

"We will travel the breadth of Judea," he said. "You are my right hand and it will be by your example that others will train for the work ahead. Along the way, I will reveal many things to you. I will teach you daily." Joshua then continued with great confidence. "The kingdom has begun to show in you and in those whom we have touched. It will grow in the days ahead. May the spirit be with us."

Within a day or two, Joshua left Capernaum and set out on the road southwest toward Mount Tabor. In the village of Madon, he and his followers encountered a large group of Jon's disciples who were protesting the salt tax of the Herodians. They were violent and and appeared to be assaulting one of Herod Antipas' tax gatherers. They had grabbed the man. Some were pulling on his outstretched arms. Others kicked him brutally. They were shouting angrily:

"Extortioner! Traitor! Enemy of the people! Your reward for your collaboration will be death!"

Joshua stepped forward.

"Stop!" he yelled at the top of his voice.

Some of Joshua's disciples caught in the emotion of the moment were drawn into scuffles with these disciples of Jon.

"Stop!" Joshua yelled again. "What has this man done?"

"He's one of Herod's tax collectors!" one of Jon's disciples, kicking the accused, yelled back. "Scum!"

"What are you doing with him?"

"Taking him to the death he deserves!"

"And on whose authority do you do these things?"

"The authority of Jon the Baptist," the man answered, as if Joshua was stupid.

"And how does the baptist have the authority to condemn this man?" Joshua said, looking around at the mob, which now cowered at his commanding presence.

Then, Joshua specifically addressed himself to the captured man, who had not taken his pained gaze off Joshua since the confrontation of the two groups had begun.

"What is it you have done to so upset these men?" he asked.

Trembling, the man whispered:

"I collect the salt tax in the name of the tetrarch."

At his reply, the mob began to shout again:

"Traitor! Extortioner! Enemy of the people!...Stone him!"

Two of Jon's disciples then grabbed Joshua's arms. Janus and Jonas, the burly sons of Zebedee, stepped to his aid.

"Let them be," Joshua cautioned his disciples. "They think that they are right to act in the name of Jon, but soon they will know that I am acting in the name of God."

Joshua's restrainers became scared, not only by his words, but by the calm authority that he imbued. They loosened their grip. Joshua again addressed their victim:

"Are you sure that you have only collected the tax on the salt as laid down by the authorities? You have never asked for more in order to gain extra for yourself?"

The man hung his head, averting his gaze from Joshua. It was the custom of both the Herodian and Roman tax collectors to feather their own nests at the expense of the people. They took the risk of unpopularity against the ease of financial comfort.

"What is that to you? It is how I live," the man replied feebly.

The crowd listened intently. The man had condemned himself.

"I have the power to forgive you," Joshua said. "But I can only do so if you give me your word that you will only collect what is due to the authorities."

Joshua looked up:

"Has anyone a coin?"

A man came forward with a Roman denarius.

Joshua looked at the coin, examining it carefully, rubbing his finger over the image of Caesar. He held it up so it glinted in the sun.

"Give to the rulers what is theirs, but I am telling you to give to God what is His. A rich man can store up treasure on this earth, but it will be of no advantage to him in the kingdom to come. If you live by the spirit of the Lord you will not care about the comfort of such treasures, but the Divine love of God will shine forth from you in all that you do. If you believe in that spirit, he who has little faith can find great wisdom, and he who is dishonest can discover great truth."

Joshua put his hand on the tax collector's shoulder and addressed him:

"If you have not been faithful in your dealings with your fellow men, who is going to trust you with true riches? Will your king trust you any more than these men here?"

The man looked chastened.

Joshua had the crowd sit down.

"No servant can serve two masters. Either, he will hate the one and love the other, or he will be devoted to the one and despise the other. You can not serve God and yourself," he preached.

Joshua looked around the quietened crowd, Jon's disciples now sitting with his own. He had a playful gleam in his eye.

"There was a rich man who had a steward," he began. "Charges were brought to him that this man was wasting his goods. He called the steward in and said to him:

'What is this that I hear about you? Turn in the account of your stewardship for I'm going to dismiss you.'

The steward was upset because he knew no other lifestyle. He couldn't dig because he was too weak, and he was ashamed to beg. He decided what to do, however, in order to provide for his security so that his fellow men would receive him favorably when he had left the rich man's service. He summoned all his master's debtors one by one. He said to the first:

'How much do you owe my master?'

The man replied:

'A hundred measures of oil.'

The steward then changed the debt by writing up fifty measures of oil."

There was a ripple of laughter from the listening crowd.

Joshua paused, showing the same child-like amusement. Then, he continued:

"He said to another:

'How much do you owe?'

The man replied:

'One hundred measures of wheat.'

The steward likewise changed his bill marking down only eighty measures in debt. So it went on with all the debts. Now, the moral of this story is such that not only were the debtors pleased because the steward had helped them, but the master was also impressed with the steward's work. The master had gained a good part of that which was owed to him, which he had not expected. How many of you if you had lost your stewardship would have continued in those last days to try to serve your master? The master, however, was also impressed by the prudence that his unjust steward had shown in providing for both of their futures without upsetting those around him in the present."

Joshua's challenging grin changed back to a look of penetrating didactic authority:

"Who among you would not have done likewise if you had only had the sense to think this through? Let the tetrarch have at least a part of that which is his command. It will gain him nothing in the end. But, for yourselves gain the spirit of God in your dealings with men. The fruit of the spirit is life in this kingdom. Serve God first and man second."

Joshua again placed his hand on the tax collector's shoulder:

"What is your name?" he asked.

"Judas Matthias, the son of Janus the weaver," the tax collector replied.

"You are the unjust steward," Joshua said. "Reduce the burden of these men's taxes. Pay back all that you have taken in excess. Give to your master what he thinks is his due and then come and follow me."

Now, there was a cheer from the crowd! But Joshua was not yet finished with his teaching. He turned on them with a sense of wrath in his eyes.

"There can be no place in my kingdom for men of violence," he shouted. "Violence can not be met by violence. This man is your brother—not your enemy. Repent of your actions and your sins will be forgiven. Don't rest only in the baptism of Jon for your forgiveness, but in every loving action of your lives. Unless you allow the love of God to show forth through you in your dealings with your fellow men—even with tax collectors and sinners—there will be no place for you in the kingdom despite your baptism! The kingdom is already within you, but you must unlock the door to let the light of God shine forth. Go back to your homes and leave this man alone. He will return to you what you deserve, no more and no less."

The crowd did not cheer further, but nor did they shout abuse. Joshua's charisma seemed to have carried the day. Those who had held Judas Matthias, released him, and walked away with thoughts to meditate upon.

Joshua called Cephas over.

"Judas Matthias will be one of our group, Cephas," he said, never taking his eyes away from Judas' face. "Take care of him and introduce him to the others. We will camp out here above Madon while he repays that which he now owes. Once his accounts here are settled and he has handed in the taxes that are due, we will move on."

Cephas obeyed and embraced Matthias.

* * *

Unaware of Joshua's differing approach to the salt tax, Jon continued his campaign, taking his followers south over the hills. He was unaware that the Herodian guards were seeking opportunities to arrest him, but he avoided Tiberias, suspecting that this might be the case. They moved toward Nain. Many who came to listen to Jon in this region had witnessed or heard of Joshua's miraculous ressurection of a young man thought to have died in the village some months before. At that time, others had then heard of the celebrated raising of Lazarus from the dead. Some asked Jon if he was familiar with Joshua the Miracle Worker. Jon answered in the affirmative. He had always spoken favorably of his cousin, although it had reached his ears that Joshua had spoken against his methods of recruiting disciples for the kingdom on more than one occasion. Jon still believed that he had been called to his ministry in order to prepare the way for the living messiah who was to come. In his ministry, he had always considered his cousin Joshua to be that messiah—the man who was to be the final teacher before the Day of Judgement.

Jon's feelings were further confirmed when the people recounted the story of the miraculous raising of the young man from the dead, which Joshua the Miracle Worker had performed in Nain. Apparently, the man had been declared dead and was being carried to the burial ground. Some even said that the man already stank, although he had not as yet been embalmed. Whatever, it was apparent that at Joshua's command, he sat up in his own coffin and began to ask where he was and why. The story seemed to be the most exciting thing that had happened in Nain in years, but unfortunately, neither the young man nor his mother, who was a widow, were there to explain the whole story. They had left Nain and moved to Hammath, a Hebrew village of relative obscurity just south of Tiberias. Jon had to rely on the excited claims of the crowd, and no two versions of the story seemed to tally.

But Jon's disciples increased in Nain as the gullible crowd learned of his admiration for Joshua. They were also sympathetic to his more recent cause—the salt tax—and promised to withold and reject any further taxation on salt that might be imposed by the Herodians. Jon, during his stay, having listened so many times to the story of the miraculous ressurection of the dead man from Nain, sought to move on to Hammath where he might actually speak to this man who had been raised.

Word quickly got back to Herod Antipas in Tiberias that the baptist was so close. Before Jon had time to find the widow from Nain and her resurrected son, Herodian guards had seized him in Hammath and took him in chains along the new coast road to Tiberias. There, he was brought before the tetrarch.

* * *

Herod Antipas could not help but be impressed by the appearance of this man about whom he had heard so much. The baptist was rough and he stank, but the peasant had a fascinating face. Jon looked hauntingly confident with his piercing blue eyes that seemed to peer out from a face otherwise dwarfed by his mass of matted black hair and the length of his straggling beard. He wore only his goatskin garment, which revealed his weather-beaten flesh.

"I have been waiting to meet you," the tetrarch said, circling around his prisoner. "You have caused me a lot of unnecessary trouble. What is your problem? What does it matter to you, who lives roughly off the food of the land, whether I tax the quantities of salt you use? Rich men use far more salt than peasants and yet you have incited the poor throughout the land. Why?"

"Rich men can afford to pay," Jon answered. "I was brought up in a rich man's house, but I have learned that riches stored up on this earth do not bring a man close to God. It will be harder for you, with your trappings of wealth, to enter the kingdom than for a poor man."

"What kingdom?" the petty king commented with a smirk.

He had heard that the followers of Jon were preparing for some sort of new kingdom—a kingdom that might replace his? He was naturally curious.

"The Kingdom of God," Jon replied, staring straight into Herod's eyes.

"And is not my kingdom a kingdom of God?" Herod Antipas asked sarcastically. "Is not Galilee in the bounds of the lands of the Jews?"

"Your kingdom can only be a kingdom of God if you repent of your sins and accept my baptism in the same way as the poor and downtrodden persons upon whom you have imposed this impossible tax," the baptist bravely announced.

The Herodian guards, who had relaxed their hold on Jon as he stood before the tetrarch, tightened their grip on him in fear of a major confrontation. But, Herod was still mesmerized by Jon's hypnotic gaze and earthy confidence and was not yet ready to dismiss his curious prisoner. At this point, Herod's wife, Herodias, entered the royal chamber.

"Herodias!" the tetrarch said excitedly. "Look who we have here."

He circled around his prisoner again.

"This is Jon the Baptist, the leader of the salt tax rebellion."

Herodias glanced at Jon and scrunched up her nose.

"He stinks, Antipas," was all she said.

Jon spat in her direction.

Once again the guards tightened their hold.

"I don't like this man!" Herodias announced haughtily.

It had been rumored in certain Pharisaic circles that Herodias had formerly been married to Philip, the tetrarch's brother. Jon was aware of these rumors, but did not consider the marriage laws of the Levitical priesthood to be so very important. He had bided his time in drawing attention to this matter in his campaign against the Herodians, but he became angered by Herodias' attitude. He continued to hypnotically gaze at the tetrarch, as if he felt that he was now within his power.

"Your marriage to this woman would be one of the sins from which you would need to repent," Jon said, testing how far he could go.

Herod Antipas rubbed his hands together nervously. He knew that his marriage was contrary to the Law of Moses and that the Chief Priests and the Pharisees in Jerusalem had advised him against it. In Galilee, however, he had felt secure in his breach of the Law. Galilee was very independent of the Jerusalem priesthood and there was the mantle of Rome always there to protect him. It was no concern to the Romans that he had taken Herodias as his wife. Besides, all this had happened some years before. The baptist was raking up old sins that seemed to have no bearing on the present, except in this man's message concerning this Kingdom of God. The baptist's eyes had not left him, however—*those damned penetrating eyes*—and Herod was fearful of him, becoming impatient and angry.

"What do you propose then, holy man of God?" he asked in a mocking voice that betrayed his fear. "Do you suggest I divorce this woman?"

Herodias now glared at her husband, astounded that he wasted his time even speaking to this man who had proven to be nothing but a rabble-rouser.

Momentarily, Jon turned his gaze on Herodias and then back to the tetrarch.

"You are the tetrarch," he said. "Do what you think you should do? But know this, unless you come to me and receive the baptism of repentence, there is no way that you will enter into the Kingdom of God."

"Herod!" Herodias shouted. "Send this man to the dungeons! Why are you listening to him? You have the power to rid Galilee of this madman. That's what you have to do and you know it!"

Herod did not pursue his dialogue with Jon any further. He ordered his guards to lock the baptist up, but he refused to commit the prisoner to an immediate death sentence. Secretly, the man still fascinated him—*those hypnotic eyes,* he repeated to himself—and he felt afraid of Jon's mysterious power.

During the months that followed Jon's imprisonment, the tetrarch on more than one occasion was drawn to the dungeon where his prisoner languished. He did not speak to him again, but he looked at him through the grill as if inspecting the progress of a beast being fattened. Jon would gaze at him from his unkempt face, and Herod Antipas would wrinkle up his eyes in curiosity and contemplatively stroke his well-manicured beard.

Herodias became only more and more bitter in her feelings about the baptist, however, and continually asked Herod Antipas to sign the baptist's death warrant. In her own vendetta, she totally misconstrued her husband's genuine concerns about the man's hypnotic holy powers.

Chapter Five

Women in the Camp

Maria had every reason to be grateful to Joshua for saving her life and expressed this in her devotion to him as she listened to his every word. Her enthusiasm for his simple discourses was not totally approved of by those who had been Joshua's most faithful disciples from the earliest days of his Capernaum ministry. These included several women, including Jezebel who had found Marcus the night of Maria's rescue. She was tall and slender and pinned up her hair in the Hellenist style. Her clothing was brightly colored and of finer quality than the other women, for she was a high-born lady who had been married to a Herodian steward. In Maria's presence, as Joshua was about to teach them, Jezebel challenged him.

"Why do you always favor sinners?" Jezebel asked the miracle worker. "You rarely speak of the rewards for those of us who have faithfully ministered to you from the beginning."

She pointed at Maria.

"This woman is always close to you. She rarely helps us take care of the menfolk in domestic duties and she was an adulteress—even a prostitute—possibly a follower of Lesbos, too! You have made this camp a haven of tax collectors and sinners of the worst kind. It's not that I don't understand your forgiving nature, but what about the rest of us?"

Some of the other women nodded in agreement.

Maria felt nervous.

"Jezebel, you will have your reward…the rest of you, too, who are already close to the kingdom," Joshua answered. "Look at it this way. What woman among you having ten silver coins, if you were to lose one coin would not light a lamp and sweep the floor of the house, searching everywhere until you find it? If you were lucky enough to find it, wouldn't you call in your neighbors and friends and rejoice with them? So it is with God. There is as much joy in heaven over these people, whom you have mentioned, than over those of you who were not sinners. They were lost and they've been found. You must welcome them into our midst with your love."

"And that is our reward?"

Jezebel scowled haughtily at Maria.

"Yes. Forgiveness creates it's own rewards," the Master said wisely.

He told them a story about a shepherd who lost one sheep out of an hundred. This loss was of little commercial importance, but this shepherd rejoiced more when he found the lost sheep than he did over the eventual sale of the whole flock.

"You see, there was more joy in finding that wayward sheep and bringing it back into the fold, Jezebel, than in the sale," Joshua explained. "True rejoicing is a spiritual experience—a oneness with the spirit of God. The financial reward of selling the flock is just the sating of commercial greed—not necessarily bad, but not spiritual."

Maria thought of Reuben. *Perhaps I can forgive him,* she mused. *Without Reuben I would never have encountered this holy man, at least, not unless he was that young man at the brothel all those years ago. I still think he was.*

"My half brother was a good man—the rabbi of Nazareth," Joshua continued. "He got very upset when my grandfather, a fairly rich man, offered to provide my father, who was only a relatively poor carpenter, with a village feast to welcome his grandson, my other half brother, Jonah. Jonah had run away many years before and we had taken him for dead. Suddenly, he came home. He was my father Joseph's prodigal son—my prodigal brother. My father disagreed with my older brother's attitude and openly expressed his spiritual joy that his wayward son had returned. What's more, Jonah the prodigal, actually turned out to be my most considerate brother, and even now, I believe, is looking after my mother."

They were all listening, spellbound.

Maria, who had felt slighted by Jezebel's remarks, felt the power in forgiveness. *I can truly forgive her, too,* she thought, *in the same way as Joshua, my savior, forgave me.*

"Once again, I tell you," Joshua concluded, "there will be more joy in heaven over one sinner who genuinely repents than over ninety-nine just persons who need no repentence."

Joshua then left them to mull over his words. He took himself apart, into the olive groves, to pray.

As they broke up, Maria approached Jezebel and Susannah, offering to play her part in assisting with whatever domestic chores were needed about the camp. Their differences were made up, but problems of favoritism and rivalry amongst those closest to Joshua continued to surface as they all, men and women, came to realize that their leader was more than a great and compassionate healer, but a spiritual master who now guided their lives.

* * *

With Judas Matthias' return, Joshua and his disciples traveled southwest from Madon. They followed the bed of a wadi that ran into the River Jordan just south of the Galilean Lake. From there, they made their way down the Jordan valley toward Jericho in the hope that they would reach Jerusalem by the High Holy Days. Joshua wanted to allow enough time to spend a week or two in Bethany, visiting those to whom he had first ministered nearly two years before. He particularly wanted to see Lazarus, who had been the most important revelation to him of his self-awareness—the man whom he had raised from the dead through the power of the Almighty.

News spread through the villages of the lower Jordan that the Bethany miracle worker was on his way. The name of Joshua had not been forgotten. As they came closer to Jericho, so the numbers of casual followers grew. The crowd was excited, and there was a feeling amongst them that this was a triumphal march that heralded the start of the kingdom.

* * *

Sitting beside the road outside Jericho was a man in disheveled rags. He was blind, but his sense of hearing was astute and keen. He had heard about the crowd that was gathering around Joshua and he had taken up his position on the roadside in the hope of receiving a miraculous cure. It was not long before he could make out voices and the shuffling of feet down the path. When the blind man sensed that they were really close, he shouted out at the advancing crowd:

"Joshua! Joshua! Have mercy on me!"

Judas Iscariot and others close to the man, who had not noticed his blindness, shouted him down:

"Don't trouble the Master now. It's been a long day and we have many to feed and shelter here."

The blind man would not take 'No' for an answer, however, and stood up waving his stick frantically so that it actually hit some of those passing by with the leaders.

"Joshua! Joshua! Have mercy on me, miracle worker!" he cried vehemently.

Joshua, who was a little behind the leaders, turned toward him. Not having heard what Judas had said, he went up to the man:

"What do you want me to do for you?" he asked.

"Holy man, let me receive my sight again."

Joshua held the man's forehead and prayed, while the disciples stood around in silence.

The blind man felt warmth between his eyes generated by the pressure of Joshua's fingertips.

"Receive your sight," Joshua said to him quietly before releasing the pressure. "Your faith has made you well."

The blind man thought he could see a dim gray light, and smiled. He deliberately threw down his stick, looking upward at the bright noon sky. Then, gingerly he offered his hand to a woman, who happened to be beside the healer.

The voices of the crowd started to whisper and rise.

Joshua left the blind man holding the woman's hand.

The crowd started to move on.

"Take the man's other hand, Marcus," the woman said to a boy close by.

The blind man felt the smooth skin of the hand of the youth grasping his gnarled flesh.

The woman picked up the blind man's stick and put her arm around his waist.

"Can you see a little?" she asked him.

"I can see the light," the man said.

"Soon you will see more," the woman said, as she and Marcus guided him along the road into the shuffling crowd. "My name's Maria."

"My name's Bartimaeus," the blind man replied.

The disciples and their gathering crowd camped that night outside Jericho.

* * *

Judas Matthias thought that he recognized a small man in the increasing crowd the following morning. The man was jumping up and down excitedly. He was well dressed, but those around him paid little attention to him. Judas Matthias had taken moneybags to the Jericho palace of the Herodians during his earlier years as a tax collector. This man looked like the king's agent there, but he lost sight of him.

Matthias didn't think any more about him until later in the morning when Joshua led his disciples into the city. He caught sight of the little man again, running ahead of them. Matthias was close to Joshua at the time.

"I know that man," he said. "He's Herod's agent. I used to work with him."

"Why is he running from us?" Joshua asked.

"I expect he's afraid, but I saw him earlier before we left the camp. He's curious about us, Joshua."

"Or a spy?"

"Maybe."

Joshua stopped and put his hands on Matthias' shoulders.

"If he is a friend of yours, spy or otherwise, we should welcome him," he said. "Ask him to join us?"

The crowd became disturbed and Judas Matthias lost sight of the man yet again.

Three desperate lepers were forcing their way through, causing turmoil.

Many shouted abuse at the lepers—contagious and dangerous people. Most, however, shrank away from them, fearful of their plague, thus clearing a path for them to make their way to the miracle worker. The lepers then clung to Joshua's robe.

"Help us, Master!" one of them cried, looking up desperately from his blotched face.

"Don't touch them!" the portly Cephas warned Joshua.

"They're unclean!" Judas Iscariot echoed.

Maria, guiding the blind man Bartimaeus, whose impaired vision seemed to be slowly returning, also called out to Joshua:

"Don't touch them, speak to them and they'll be healed!"

Joshua turned toward Maria:

"I am not afraid, Maria. I am not here to be protected from the evils of this world, but for your sake I will not contaminate myself."

Judas Iscariot spat on the ground.

Joshua looked down at the kneeling lepers pulling at his robe.

"You know the cure," he said. "Go and bathe in the sulphur waters south of the city. The minerals will cleanse you."

"Master we have," they cried pitifully. "We have bathed ourselves in the sulphur pools many times. It has had no effect. Look at our skin. The leprosy only increases daily."

"I am commanding you in the name of God to bathe in the pool again," Joshua said with that great authority that had become so much a part of his magnetic appeal.

The men continued to pull at Joshua's garment.

Cephas intervened:

"You heard what the Master said," he retorted gruffly. "He has commanded you to bathe yourselves again in the name of God. Now, leave us. Do what the Master says. If it's God's will, He'll make you whole."

Joshua expressed surprise at the manner in which Cephas spoke—such assuredness and confidence.

"Leave now!" Cephas repeated.

The lepers, somewhat disappointed, obeyed.

"Be sure to come back and see me when you are healed," Joshua added as they loped away. "You will be. It is God's will."

Joshua and his disciples moved on down the street toward the center of Jericho. Along the way there were many trees that grew in lush groves in the fertile soil of the Jordan valley. Some of the curious crowd had climbed into these trees to get a better view of the famous miracle man. Amongst them was the short Herodian steward whom Judas Matthias had noticed earlier.

"That's my friend again," he said, pointing toward the branch of an olive beside the road ahead.

"The Herodian tax collector?" Joshua asked with an interested smile.

"Yes, Master."

"Call him down to us," Joshua commanded.

Judas Matthias hesitated.

"Call him down," Joshua repeated.

"Zacchaeus!" Matthias shouted.

Zacchaeus didn't answer.

"Perhaps he is afraid of us, Master. He is not like us. His position is high-ranking. Most of us are rural poor."

Now, almost under the tree, Joshua looked up.

"It's all right, Zacchaeus," he said. "I'm not going to harm you. Come and join us. I understand you know my friend Judas Matthias here. You must join us for our meal tonight. I would like to meet you."

Zacchaeus picked his way out of the tree. Climbing trees was obviously not an every day pastime for the little man in his fine clothes. When he reached the ground, he brushed off his hands and straightened his Roman style tunic and cloak.

Matthias stepped forward and embraced him.

"Who is this man?" Judas Iscariot muttered to Cephas.

"Some friend of Matthias," Cephas answered.

"Another of these tax collecting leeches," Iscariot retorted. "What is the Master's fascination with these men?"

Matthias listened.

"You've heard the Master's teaching," Cephas replied. "The Master is not here to condemn such men. We can be judges of their integrity in their unpopular profession. Remember that there will be more joy in heaven over the one sinner who genuinely repents than over the ninety-nine just persons. Joshua made it plain to us that it will be harder for a rich man, like this Herodian steward, to enter into the Kingdom of God than for a poor person."

Judas Iscariot backed down and the two appointed leaders returned their attention to Joshua and Zacchaeus.

* * *

The little man seemed to be in awe of the Master. Zacchaeus looked up at Joshua with intellectual pleading.

"I have been fascinated by the stories that I have heard about you," he said. "In particular, I am curious to know how you raised a man from the dead?"

"With God, all things are possible," Joshua replied.

"You have mysterious powers, sir," Zacchaeus continued.

"My powers are no greater than yours. If you live in spirit you can work miracles with spirit. My power is no less than yours."

Cephas pondered Joshua's words as he watched Zacchaeus' response. More and more, he sensed the Master's claims, and he noted them with mixed feelings of awe and fear. The claims were becoming more Godly and yet more blasphemous at every turn. *Who is our Master?* Cephas thought. *Is Joshua the Messiah?* He wondered what Zacchaeus was thinking. *What if he is a Herodian spy? This man could be dangerous.*

But Zacchaeus' response was a benign smile.

"Come back with me to my house," Zaccheaus suggested to Joshua. "I would like to discuss many things with you."

"Now?" Joshua asked.

"Tonight. Judas Matthias knows where I live. Why don't you both join me after the sun sets?"

Joshua said nothing. He just nodded in acceptance.

"What if they steal him away from us?" Cephas whispered to Judas Iscariot.

"I don't like this," Judas whispered back.

The little man winked at Judas Matthias.

"Let me go and make the necessary preparations," Zacchaeus continued.

He turned and went his way.

Judas Iscariot looked at Cephas and rolled his eyes upward in further disbelief.

"What if this is an Herodian plot to arrest our Master," he said.

"Pray that it is not," Cephas responded.

* * *

After Zacchaeus left, Maria and the blind man shuffled up to a position closer to the Master. Maria felt important—Blind Bartimaeus was her charge. The Master had entrusted him to her. Bartimaeus' vision was definitely improving. The shadows of light that had signified the start of his miraculous healing had developed into hazy sight. She knew he could now make out her face and that of her boy. In fact, he could now see his own arms to feel his way rather than swing out with his stick. But the more important she felt her role to be the more she could feel the cold attitude of some of Joshua's leaders toward her, especially Iscariot. Led by this Judas, there were those who seemed to resent her presence in their midst. But she knew the Master had truly forgiven her over that affair with Reuben. She now, only wanted to serve Joshua.

She walked beside Bartimaeus and encouraged him with congratulatory phrases as he stumbled on his way, so obviously relishing the reality of his partial cure.

When they came to the central market in Jericho, Bartimaeus took Maria off to a place that smelled of sweet gum. It was a small stall set up outside a cavernous hole in the wall that was separated from the street by a heavy awning of colored wool.

"I often come here to enjoy the fragrance," Bartimaeus said. "It helps me to appreciate that there is still beauty in this world even though I can not see it. But, look, now I can see that orange awning. Wow…! I have a friend here. His name is Ephraim. He will be so surprised that I can see!"

He thumped his fist on a table at the stall.

"Ephraim!" he shouted.

A man peered out from the cavernous interior when he heard Bartimaeus' voice.

"He often gives me wine to drink," Bartimaeus confided to Maria.

"I can see!" Bartimaeus informed Ephraim joyfully.

Ephraim was thin and bony with an angular face and very little hair.

He was certainly not attractive, but Maria could tell he was kind in the obvious joy that came over his face when he could see that Bartimaeus was so improved.

"I can see!" Bartimaeus repeated, as he sniffed the familiar scents of Ephraim's stall.

He reached out and stroked one of the jars lined along the back shelf.

"Joshua the Miracle Worker is restoring my sight!"

Bartimaeus went along the shelf touching every jar in turn, stopping in front of a small vase of precious nard.

"It's wonderful to see you like this!" Ephraim exclaimed. "How did this miracle man cure you?"

"He touched my forehead and pressed his fingers against my flesh," Bartimaeus answered. "Nothing really happened at first, but he spoke to me gently, saying that if I believed he could cure me, then my sight would return. It was not long before I saw dim shadows of gray light. Maria, here, took my hand—she and her boy, Marcus. They've guided me ever since. Over the past two days, my vision has returned. I can see, Ephraim. I can see all your jars. I can see you, Ephraim. You look thin!"

Ephraim laughed.

"Would you like wine?"

Bartimaeus nodded.

Ephraim brought out three goblets of crude new wine and some dates. He offered a goblet to Maria. The two men quaffed at the sickly sweet liquid that always surprised them with its strangely bitter after taste, but Maria only took a couple of sips and then joined Marcus at the dates. The wine had reminded her of Antonias. She felt homesick for Antonias' villa. Antonias had always served them his best wine. He had been most particular about his selections, and had always informed Delilah and her that good wine inspired his best poetry. He had shared that poem with her that he had written about them, and even though she understood little of the Greek, she could tell, like everything about Antonias, that it had been filled with a tender love. Maria could see that same tender love in her new mentor. Joshua had made no overtures to force himself upon her any more than had that shy young Roman. Antonias had courted her with his tenderness, and in many ways Maria saw those same qualities in the magnetic miracle worker who had rescued her from probable death. Those tender beginnings had led to a beautiful relationship with Antonias. *Maybe it will be the same with Joshua,* she mused. Her sexual desires that were never suppressed for long, pulled at her.

Bartimaeus returned to the jar of nard. He sniffed at it, breathing in the balm deeply.

"This is my favorite," he said, passing the jar to Maria to share the scent.

Maria inhaled the sweet odor. Often she and Delilah had massaged each other with such balms in their more intimate and sensual moments. She missed those tender moments, too, especially now, in the loneliness of her rejection by Joshua's closest associates. *They will never let me anywhere near him if they have their way,* she thought. She handed back the jar, almost in a trance.

"It's lovely," she said.

Ephraim put down his goblet.

"Take the jar," he said to Bartimaeus.

Bartimaeus laughed.

"With what shall I pay you?"

"Nothing, my friend. You have come here for many months and enjoyed this small thing in your blindness. It's the least I can do to show you my joy. Take it. I can get more."

Excitedly, Bartimaeus tried to pick the vase from the shelf, but his actions were still clumsy. Ephraim helped him. The jar wasn't very big, but the balm did have an extraordinary perfume.

Joshua and his disciples had moved on, so Maria, Marcus and Bartimaeus turned back to the camp. Bartimaeus clutched his jar of nard each step of the way like a treasured possession.

After they left Jericho's gates, Bartimaeus became silent and subdued. On reaching the camp, he placed the precious jar into Maria's hands.

"For you," he said. "You have done so much for me."

Maria smelled the fragrance again.

"Are you sure you don't want to keep this?" she asked.

"What real use have I for it? When I was blind it fed my senses, but now I can see. You keep it."

Joshua had not returned, but many of the disciples had gathered to eat together as the evening drew nigh. Some were grumbling that the

Master had gone off to eat with that Herodian agent and the favored Judas Matthias—the tax collector.

When Joshua returned, he sensed their grumbles and disappointment. He told them a story as they sat around the ebbing fire:

"There was a rich prince who had to travel to a distant city to become the king. Before he left, he called together his three principal servants. He gave them each a talent of silver.

'Trade with these until I return,' he instructed them.

When he came back as king, he asked his servants to account for their talents. The first said that he had increased his ten times in active trading. The king commended him and gave him rule over ten cities. The second servant came forward and showed that he had traded his talent and gained five times its value. He also was commended and given rule over five cities. The third man came forward rather sheepishly. He had hidden his talent of silver in a napkin stored in a safe place at his house, so he could be sure to still have it on his master's return.

'I know you to be a hard man,' he said. 'I was afraid that I might lose what was yours so I hid it.'

He pulled the talent from the napkin and laid it before the king.

'It's yours,' he said.

The king was not grateful, however, and chastized the man for his action:

'If you were afraid of losing the silver through your poor ability to trade it, why didn't you take it to the moneylender and have him pay you interest on your loan? If you had done that, I would have at least gained the interest.'

The king then took the talent of silver and gave it to the man who had traded his silver ten times. Those standing around thought this to be unfair and questioned the king's action. The king, hearing their murmuring, replied:

'I tell you, that to everyone who has, more shall be given; but from him who has not, even what he has shall be taken away.'"

Joshua's disciples looked at each other. The moon was rising up from the horizon making silouettes out of the olive branches and fronds of the Jordan valley. As usual these days, it was Judas Iscariot who was the first to speak:

"But, Master, that's unfair. Why should the rich get richer and the poor get poorer. Aren't you always teaching us not to lay up treasure in this life?"

Cephas joined with him.

"Yes, Master. That seems contrary to everything you tell us. You have always said that the poor will find it easier to enter the kingdom than the rich."

"Cephas," Joshua said, "and all of you," as he looked around at their puzzled faces brightened by the rising moon, "listen to me. I had my evening meal with Zacchaeus today. He invited Matthias and me to his house. Zacchaeus is a rich man. If you have riches, it is hard to give them up. You may not know it, because you are blinded in prejudice against Zacchaeus because he is a tax official of the Herodians, just as was Matthias, but Zacchaeus is already in the Kingdom of God and that is more than I can say of some of you."

A tense silence fell over the grumbling group, and the sound of crickets and bull frogs became paramount.

"Zacchaeaus has promised me he will give half of his wealth to the poor," Joshua continued. "He has also promised, as did our brother Judas Matthias here, that if he has defrauded anyone in his financial dealings he will repay them, and not just what is due, but four times what he owes them."

Joshua looked at Judas Matthias for confirmation of what he had just said.

Matthias nodded in agreement.

"Zacchaeus sought us out. He approves of what we are trying to do. In many ways, it is harder for a rich man to enter the Kingdom of God. A rich man has greater temptations than we do. A rich man has more opportunity, however, to increase his talents for the common good, just as Zacchaeus has done. We can't afford to discriminate against the rich. They will have their place in the kingdom, too. When I come back here and find you all grumbling in this way, I know that I have failed, and that the spirit is not in you. Without the spirit, there is no kingdom. Don't let me hear you grumbling again. We are all sons of Abraham whether rich city-dwelling Herodians or simple fishermen and craftsmen. It's up to all of us to use our talents to the best of our ability. Talents are not always of silver—they are the fruits of the Holy Spirit."

Cephas expressed shame:

"Forgive me, Master. I failed to understand."

"I don't have to forgive you, Cephas. I don't have to forgive any of you. If you want to join Zacchaeus in the Kingdom of God you do not have to seek forgiveness, but simply open your hearts to the spirit of God. The key to the kingdom is in you."

Joshua's stern disciplining face melted into his charismatic warmth.

"You are my sheep," he concluded. "Follow each other in spirit."

His eyes caught those of Maria. Her hair was illumined by the increasing moonlight and the light of the fading fire glazed her wide sultry eyes.

Maria was mesmerized by Joshua and knew from his look that he had some feelings for her, but he was always so busy, and the others never seemed to leave him alone.

Iscariot looked away.

"We need sleep," Joshua said. "Tomorrow we have to climb the difficult road up to Bethany. It's rough going and dangerous, but I know there will be a warm welcome waiting for us when we get there."

* * *

When news reached Bethany that Joshua and his entourage had been sighted coming up the Jericho road, Lazarus and his sisters were among the first to leave the smelly village and go out to greet them. Mary was particularly excited. She had so longed to see Joshua again.

"I wonder if he's changed," she said to her sister, but Martha remained her cool, calm self.

"Why should he look any different, Mary?" she replied. "It's only a couple of years since he was here."

"Well, you don't know," Mary continued like a young girl. "He's probably met all sorts of people in between. He might have even fallen in love."

"Oh! Mary! I'm sure he will be very busy while he's here and he may well not be able to spend any time with us."

Noting the growing crowd of curious onlookers gathering along the track leading down to Jericho, Martha firmly reminded her sister of their responsibilities:

"You see all these people—they all want to see him about something. Don't think you're going to waste Joshua's precious time. When he is with us, you and I are going to be busy. There will be lots to do taking care of those traveling with him."

Mary became silent and stared down the road. *Maybe…I wonder,* she thought. Her heart was fluttering with internal excitement, but she controlled her inner feelings as she pondered on her sister's harsh words.

Her disappointment and Martha's practical advice were lost when the moment came and Joshua and his band of over thirty people were in view. Memories of those hectic days, when Bethany had become the place of miracles, took over. Despite the tanning odors, there was euphoria in the air.

* * *

Joshua saw Lazarus, and a beaming smile came across his face. Lazarus had been the inspiration for his healing ministry, but he was also the only real friend, outside family, that Joshua had ever known. There was something about the simple tanner, who always reeked of those foul odors, which had become eternally endearing to Joshua. He was a walking symbol of natural goodness—the light of the kingdom shone from him.

If anyone I have ever met is possessed of Divine love, thought Joshua, *it is this man.*

He walked up to him and embraced him warmly.

"Joshua, welcome home!" Lazarus said in response. "We've missed you."

"Yes," Mary joined in. "Me, too!"

Joshua looked at Mary with her doting eyes. He could see that her infatuation had not changed. He didn't want to disappoint her and hugged her warmly.

"Mary, my devoted little Mary," he whispered in her ear. "What's Martha got in the pot for us tonight?"

Martha glared at Mary.

"There's enough for you, Joshua, but this is a big crowd. You're all going to keep Mary and me pretty busy."

Joshua looked at Judas Iscariot.

"How many of us are there?" he asked.

"Thirty-eight, Master. We have enough flat Matzoh to take care of our own, but if the crowd grows much more locally, we'll have to rely on customary donations in the village."

"Don't worry about such matters, Joshua," Lazarus interrupted. "Everyone here will help out. We've been waiting for the day of your return. It's so good to see you."

"And you, too, Lazarus, and you, Mary and Martha. Now, tell me, how have things been?" he asked as they all started back up the hill toward the village.

Lazarus took Joshua back to his house, along with Joshua's 'chosen ones' that now seemed to include Judas Matthias, and Maria and her boy—all except Iscariot. Judas Iscariot organized Jezebel, Susannah, and the other women in preparing food for the crowd that milled around outside. They set up a campsite on the edge of a grove between Bethany and Bethphage.

Nothing had changed in Lazarus' little house. Martha quickly set about preparing the stew. Mary felt mixed emotions as she watched the voluptuous Maria. *Who is she? Why is she a chosen one?* she mulled. Sensing her sulks, Martha scolded her.

After the evening meal, there were so many, who wanted to catch a glimpse of their hero that Lazarus and Joshua had to move outside so that Joshua could greet them. Mary followed and sat on the bench beside Joshua while the chosen disciples tried to control the crush of the crowd. Maria held on to Marcus, carefully watching Mary.

Joshua began to address them.

His message, as nearly always, told them of the Kingdom of God, and how they could all enter the kingdom through open hearts. He taught them about the fruits of the spirit that would create the fabric of life in the kingdom. First, however, he advised them that the spirit must be awakened in each individual:

"All of us have this Holy Spirit within us," he explained. "Some of us, however, suppress this spark of God through our concern with things of this world. Things of this world will be far better executed if they are achieved through the fruits of the spirit. In that way, they will be uplifted from this world into the Kingdom of God. The kingdom is within this world, but it is not of this world—it is of God. No political principalities and powers can create this kingdom, only you in your humble acceptance of God's indwelling Holy Spirit can create it. Some of you, like my good friend Lazarus, here, are already living in this spirit of Divine love. Some of you are already in the kingdom."

Joshua paused. Without really understanding why he felt the way he did, his eyes lighted on Maria. Her eyes caught his. *I rescued you from a cruel fate,* he thought, *which many would say you justly deserved, but I see the spark of God in you.* He had sensed this more and more as each day had gone by. He could feel it in the gentle way that she treated her boy—the young Marcus—and recently in the manner in which she had helped out blind Bartimaeus; but most of all he had seen it in her eyes, as he did now.

Mary noticed him looking at Maria, and she felt the pangs of jealousy.

* * *

Maria had observed Mary ever since they had arrived. She related to the woman's obvious infatuation with Joshua, but could clearly tell that the feelings Mary felt were immature. *Joshua raised Mary's brother from the dead—this was his great miracle. It is only natural that Mary has this deep fascination for him,* she thought.

Maria prided herself on her understanding of relationships between men and women—even women and women. She had known young girls in the Tiberias brothel who had fallen under the spell of infatuation only to learn the harsh reality of their mistaken love. In some ways, she had felt similar emotions when she had taken compassion on Antonias in his feeble fumbling when he had first encountered her. Fortunately, however, their joint fascination had grown into respect and love. Perhaps she had recognized the fruits of the spirit, to which Joshua now referred, in Antonias when he had taken Marcus into his care that happy afternoon on the Tiberias shore. Perhaps Antonias, a Roman and not a Jew, was already in Joshua's Kingdom of God. When she saw Joshua look at her, she sensed those same feelings that she had felt that day on the beach. *Has he singled me out like he singled out Lazarus?* flashed across her mind. There was a mature longing in her heart to share her soul with this remarkable man—more even than her body. Her response to Joshua's knowing glance gave away her every thought.

She watched as Mary instinctively pulled on Joshua's arm seeking her hero's attention.

Joshua responded with a generous smile and one quick side-glance back to Maria. He put his arm around Mary's waist and then continued addressing the crowd.

After a while, Martha came out and sat with her brother and sister beside the Master. At length, Joshua stood up and recited the Shema. One by one, the others all stood and joined in the sacred words before he turned to follow Martha and Lazarus back into the house. Mary looked back at Maria before she went in. There was a smug look of satisfaction on her face. She knew that Maria, along with the other 'chosen ones', was now left behind.

The crowd made their way back to the campground.

* * *

Deep in her heart, Maria believed that there was a tangible bond between the Master and herself, but she could not help feeling isolated when Joshua was taken away by his hosts and she was left to the reality of sharing camp duties with Jezebel, Susannah, and the other women. The feeling of isolation persisted. In her loneliness, the foul smell of the tanneries filled her nostrils. In time, travelers became impervious to the odor, their senses absorbing it as a natural phenomenon, but if the mind was not occupied in daily living, somehow the smell became more obvious and obnoxious.

"This place stinks!" Marcus said. "It's worse than the rotten fish on the beach at Magdala."

"I agree," his mother replied, "it's awful."

She paused for a moment, and then looked at Marcus with a playful smile.

"Go and fetch that jar of sweet smelling balm that the blind man Bartimaeus gave to us," she said.

Marcus picked out the jar from their few meagre possessions and brought it to his mother.

Maria worked at the stopper until it freed. The strong, sweet smell of the nard wafted up.

"Smell this, Marcus," she said.

Marcus sniffed at the fragrance. He grinned, showing the clean white teeth of his youth.

"That's much better, Mother."

They both drank in the fragrance. They felt elated and began to laugh.

When Joshua returned to camp, he sat down with Judas Iscariot, Cephas and Zebedees' sons, not far from where Maria and Marcus were seated. At length, Joshua caught Maria's eye and there was that same mutual feeling of intangible emotion. But then, Joshua turned away as if he was bothered—not sure what to make of it.

Maria realized, now that the jar of precious ointment had been opened, that it would not be easy to keep it. Instinctively, she picked it up. Joshua's look had charged her with emotion, not to mention her natural curiosity as to his feelings for Lazarus' sister Mary. Maria did not understand her own emotions. She walked up to Joshua and poured the liquid over her Master's head and with uncontrollable tears knelt before him and kissed his feet.

* * *

Joshua felt the liquid slowly trickle down his body. The sweet perfume of nard pervaded the air. Lost for words, Joshua looked down only to see Maria's eyes gazing up at him in a mingling of fear and love—what had she done?

Jonas and Janus were already restraining her as Judas Iscariot shouted:

"What are you doing, woman? Such precious ointment could have been sold for up to three hundred denarii. How dare you..."

"The proceeds of such a sale could have been used to feed this crowd—to help the poor in many ways," Cephas added.

Joshua stood up, holding his hand out to Maria.

"Leave her alone!" he shouted.

Jonas and Janus, astounded by Joshua's voice, and still holding onto Maria's arms, looked at their Master.

"Let go of her," Joshua repeated. "The poor you will have with you always. What this woman has done to me may seem a waste to you, but she has expressed a deep love in her action. She will be rewarded for what she has done because she is closer to me in spirit than most of you. Judge not, and you will not be judged; condemn not, and you will not be condemned; forgive and you will be forgiven."

Joshua looked around at his closest associates and those now gathering around, while Maria bowed, hiding her head in fearful shame and emotional tears. His authoratitive voice changed to warmth again:

"Do not think I am being harsh on you, but rather on your behavior. You are my closest friends. You can learn from this experience. Now, listen to me."

Jonas and Janus sat down again.

Judas Iscariot glared at Maria, and he, too, sat on the ground.

"A certain creditor had two debtors," Joshua said. "One owed five hundred denarii, and the other fifty. When they could not pay, he forgave them both. Now, which of the debtors will show the greater expression of love and thanks?"

"The one, I suppose, to whom he forgave more," Cephas answered.

"So it is with this woman," Joshua said, putting his hand on Maria's shoulder.

Cheeks still moist with tears, Maria looked up. She looked ashamed as if she knew she had allowed her emotion to take over from her self-control.

"I forgave this woman, and rescued her from condemnation," Joshua reminded them. "Her persecutors were no better than she! The greatest sinners still have the capacity to open their hearts to the spirit and radiate its Divine love. We should not concern ourselves with condemnation, but only with forgiveness. As we condemn others, we are blinded to our own faults. It is as if you see the speck that is in your brother's eye without noticing the dirt that's in your own eye. Can a blind man lead a blind man? If he tries, they will both fall. You are to be my leaders. You must, therefore, understand the importance of forgiveness and the realities of the blessings of love that true forgiveness brings. The good man, out of the treasure of his heart, produces good, and the evil man, out of the wickedness of his heart, produces evil. We speak according to our hearts. If our hearts are forgiving and filled with the Holy Spirit we will speak and act on the fruits of that spirit."

Joshua wiped the tears from Maria's cheek. Marcus stood back. He seemed puzzled and a little afraid.

"Marcus needs you," he said softly to Maria. "What you have done is a beautiful thing and I'll remember this for a long time, but right now I need to talk to my disciples. Wash my robe tomorrow, Maria. The Holy Spirit dwells within you. You have a great capacity to love."

The tears welled up again as Maria choked in her muddled emotions. She hugged Joshua and kissed him lightly on the cheek.

"See that!" Judas Iscariot whispered to Cephas.

The sweet smell of the nard filled the air couteracting the smell of the tanneries.

"I love you," Maria whispered, without really knowing what she was saying.

Joshua pushed back her hair with his hand lightly caressing her forehead.

The highly charged emotion passed as Maria silently walked away with Marcus holding her trembling hand.

The disciples stared at them, not knowing what to say or think. Obviously this woman, whom most of them regarded as an intruder, meant a great deal to their Master.

Joshua called his inner circle closer and continued his teaching.

Chapter Six

The Head of the Baptist

Pontius Pilatus received Herod Antipas' messenger in Caesarea Maritima. The tetrarch sent his traditional greetings to the Roman prefect and invited him to visit with him at his new provincial palace in Tiberias. Pilatus sent a messenger back with his acceptance, and within the month Linus Flavian had made arrangements for their journey.

Pilatus was impressed by his first view of Tiberias. As the prefectural party approached from the west, the sight of the gleaming new city spilled down the hillside in front of them opening out onto the flawless blue of the Galilean lake. Out of a haze, beyond the water over to the east, rose the high hills of the Decapolis country. The fringes of the city were verdant with palms and cypress groves. Spacious looking Roman villas stood in patches of vines and olives. There was something decidedly civilized about this place. It was obviously not a garrison town, but a living symbol of the 'Pax Romana'. Pontius Pilatus felt at home.

"This could be Tuscany or even Capri," he said to his aide.

"That was why my father built our villa along this coast—further north at Taricheae," Linus agreed proudly. "There is great beauty here."

The prefectural party was well received by the citizens, and even the Hebrews seemed friendly. The prefect transferred from horse to bier. He waved at them as he was carried down the hill toward the great new Herodian complex. Linus rode a white stallion ahead of the bier and at times had to use considerable equine skills on the steep street with its ocasional steps. The chariot slopes were quite slippery and they progressed slowly. The canopy of the prefect's bier bobbed severely at each step. However, the sturdy men that supported the staves were always quick to correct the angles and kept the bier horizontal throughout. They reached the middle level of the city and turned south on a wide, well paved street that led out to the new road that gangs of slaves were constructing to link Tiberias with the Jordan valley at the southern end of the lake. Eventually, this road would connect Caesarea, Sepphoris and Tiberias with the Decapolis just like that from Sepphoris up to Caesarea Philippi and on to Damascus, even on to Palmyra. Together, with the Jerusalem road, these made three trunks through the Herodian tetrarchies and the prefecture, radiating out from Caesarea Maritima, Herod the Great's seaport that was now Pilatus' prefectural capital—three great roads traversing the Syrian Province, linking them to Rome and Pilatus' power—three routes bringing the goods of the Orient to the empire. *Yes, this prefecture is important—Syria is important,* Pilatus thought, as he looked out of his bier at the gleaming new stones not yet worn by the wheels of countless carts and chariots. The section between Tiberias and Hammath was virtually finished, receiving its final touches in roadside statues and periodic water troughs, which were essential embellishments to such imperial building projects. Off this road, south of the city, spilling down the hillside in three distinct terraces, lay Herod Antipas' palace.

At the entrance, Herodian guards greeted the prefectural party, and Linus went on into the palace's upper court to meet with Herod's agent. A messenger was dispatched to the tetrarch to inform him of the Judean prefect's arrival, and in a short while a troup of Herodian trumpeters were stationed in the upper court to officially welcome Pontius Pilatus. At the sound of the trumpets, the prefect was ceremonially carried up through a massive arch and flight of stairs into the inner sanctum of the tetrarch's palace. The bier was laid down and Pilatus got out to be greeted by Herod Antipas. The petty king was dressed elaborately in jewel-encrusted Semitic robes and wore his simple crown of gold, pinned into his thick, black hair. Herodias looked like a Roman matron and had a haughty air. Herod's scribe read a formal greeting in both Aramaic and Latin. Linus then nodded to the prefect's appointed secretary, who likewise unrolled a leather scroll, and in a loud and pompous voice gave the prefect's tribute in Latin, expressing the prefect's pleasure at Herod Antipas' kind invitation to visit him in Tiberias. There was ceremonial bowing at the end of the greetings and a joint "Hail, Caesar!" after which Pontius Pilatus and his entourage were taken to their guest quarters. Once they had settled in, Herodian servants arrived with sweet meats and citrus drinks to refresh the travelers, and showed them to the baths, before Pontius Pilatus, dressed in a fine purple and gold trimmed toga—almost above his station—had his first ever official meeting with the Galilean ruler.

There was not much other than strengthening ties that needed to be discussed. They spoke together in Greek. Pilatus was able to assure Herod that to the south in Judea there was peace and prosperity, but he briefly mentioned his concerns about large gatherings of excited peasants around the village of Bethany just southwest of Jerusalem. Apparently, there was a miracle worker in Bethany, some sort of holy man, who among other things, it was rumored, had raised a man from the dead. Pilatus was not critical of the miracle worker and could not even remember his name. His concern was merely with the large crowds that the man seemed to attract. Herod Antipas agreed about the danger of such crowds. He, then touched on the subject of Jon the Baptist.

"I have him locked away now," the tetrarch explained. "He's a very strange man. In some ways, I rather like him. I really don't think he means any harm, but his followers become fanatics."

"That's what bothers me about these rabble rousers," Pilatus agreed. "Crowds so easily get out of control, especially if there's religion, superstition, or magic involved."

"These followers of Jon the Baptist are deliberately disrupting my collection systems up here. Several of my tax officials have been attacked by their mob. I really had no choice but to put their leader away, but he's interesting to look at—mysterious. I can show him to you while you are here."

Herod expressed a triumphant leer. It felt good to him to be able to point out to the Judean prefect that he had things so well under control. He was smugly satisfied that he could say that he had as famous a prisoner as the infamous baptist.

"Show me this trouble-maker whenever you like, my dear Herod," Pilatus returned. "Such broken men can be interesting, even revealing."

He leaned toward the tetrarch.

"It sounds to me like you are administering the region quite adeptly. Damascus must be pleased."

Herod called out to his guard:

"Convey to the jailor our wish that we should bring the Judean prefect to the dungeons to visit our baptist prisoner."

The guard left.

* * *

The penetrating eyes of the imprisoned baptist did not particularly move Pontius Pilatus. He was more impressed by the hefty hulk of the man.

"Have you considered exhibiting him at the games?" he asked.

"No, strangely enough that hadn't really crossed my mind," Herod answered as he caught Jon's hypnotic stare.

"He'd be good in the gladiatorial ring," Pilatus continued. "Maybe you'd be interested in selling him to us in Judea?"

Herod Antipas hardly heard him as Jon cast his customary spell on the tetrarch. The man continued to fascinate him—he had such power—mystical power.

Pilatus looked at Linus.

"What do you think?" he asked.

Linus could definitely see that Jon had the physique for the gladiatorial arena.

"Why not?" he answered.

"All right, Linus Flavian. You make the negotiations with His Majesty. I'll pay good money to have this prisoner transferred."

* * *

In the evening, Tetrarch Herod Antipas gave a feast for his honored guests. It was the most elaborate feast that he had yet staged in Tiberias. It took place in the Great Hall of the palace that was flanked with Corinthian columns behind which were numerous serving niches. Low tables and comfortable couches were set in place in front of the columns on either side. Herod Antipas and his queen, Herodias, took their seats centrally along the northern flank. The prefect, Linus and two high-ranking bodyguards sat with the tetrarch. Opposite them, the rest of Pilatus' officials and advisors seated themselves. On either side of both parties the officials of the Herodian court and their ladies took their places. It was a colorful gala occasion. Pilatus was dressed in his prefect's toga and Linus wore the full tribune's uniform of his rank.

Apart from the obligatory flat fish of the Galilean lake, the serving slaves passed platter after platter of Semitic dishes down the long tables, including many of fowl that had only recently been incorporated into standard fare. Then followed traditional dishes of whole lamb wrapped in herbs. The tender meat broke as easily as that of a succulent goat. To accompany the dishes, Herod's wine stewards kept the guests' goblets filled. The tetrarch served nothing but the best. The royal cupbearer ceremonially tasted each new jar. Mountains of fresh fruit, the finest that the garden tetrarchy of Galilee could provide, followed the main dishes—all manners of citrus fruits, dates, and pomegranates, nuts of all kinds, along with figs, raisins, and succulent fresh bunches of Tiberian grapes. There was watermelon, field melon, and all manners of dried beans. And as if that was not enough, the serving slaves came back with honey baked sweets to tempt the palate further.

The best came after this feast, however, when Herod Antipas entertained his guests with the most exotic and beautiful dancers that he could assemble at his court. On this particular occasion, in honor of the Judean prefect, the king included the sultry Salome in their midst—his step-daughter.

Herod knew that Salome was a temptress that could excite the passion in the most impotent of men. Since she had turned twelve years of age, she had been a constant source of palace gossip. Now, at seventeen, she had blossomed into the most sensuous woman whom Herod had ever seen. He found it hard to believe that this living goddess was his wife's daughter—his own brother's daughter! If there was nothing else that Pontius Pilatus was going to take back to Caesarea and Jerusalem from this visit, it was going to be the memory of Princess Salome.

There were some twenty girls dancing in flimsy, gossamer garments to the music of lyres, gongs and cymbals, who had been amusing the tetrarch's guests with their sensuous movements when trumpeters heralded Salome's arrival. The girls stood to the side as Herod's sensuous step-daughter gyrated her way down the middle of the Grand Hall. Mouths of courtiers dropped. Linus stretched his neck to get a better view. Pilatus stared. The girl was beautiful. She was as good as naked, clothed only in jewelry and gossamer veils that she swirled. She had gold rings around her neck and bracelets on her arms, but it was the narrow, jewel-encrusted, golden girdle piece on which all male eyes fastened. The piece accentuated her gyrating hips, but it hid nothing. Imaginations were fed on Salome's most intimate secrets.

After generally locking the attention of her entire audience, Salome concentrated on the honored guests. She gracefully stepped up onto the table in front of Linus and Pilatus. Her form was now immediately in front of them as she moved her hips. Her musk and perfume filled their nostrils. Linus and the astounded prefect were forced to follow the line of her smooth thighs up to their point of meeting and beyond to the nipples of her dancing breasts. The dance seemed to last an eternity, and in their excitement, Linus and Pilatus tried to catch the swirling gossamer of Salome's veil. Each time they reached out for it, Salome adeptly pulled the floating material away from them, taking it up and waving it above her head thus giving the enchanted men a full view of her bejeweled nakedness. Her eyes flashed in time to the Semitic rhythms and her sultry lips revealed her tongue as she rotated her head in slow tittilating movements. Her hands fell back down and lightly caressed her breasts as she pulled the veil across her torso and finally discarded it in front of the Roman prefect. She shook her whole body and rotated the muscles of her stomach that sensuously moved the sparkling golden girdle at the height of their eyes. It was her final gesture before she stepped down from the table. Gracefully, she fell into a split pose upon the floor. The music ceased.

Thunderous applause followed from the tetrarch's guests and Herod Antipas felt well satisfied with the entertainment he had provided. Pontius Pilatus and his aide seemed mesmerized, almost dazed by the specatacle. He was sure that his reputation as a monarch must have increased in stature before the Roman officials. He called Salome over.

"You were magnificent, my dear!" Herod Antipas said, congratulating her on her sensuous performance. "You were so sensational that I will reward you with anything that you ask. What can I give you, my precious princess—rubies, emeralds or even a palace? What is your pleasure?"

Salome seemed self-conscious. It was one thing to dance to the sensuous sounds of the musicians, but quite another, now, to stand almost naked in front of the tetrarch and his guests to answer such a serious question—riches, rubies—what? Flustered and flattered, she didn't know what to say. She looked at her mother.

Herodias had been somewhat embarassed by her daughter's sensuous dance—too erotic—and she had liked her husband's leering looks even less. She saw in the tetrarch's request, however, a golden opportunity to reap the revenge that she had held bottled up over the preceeding weeks. She beckoned Salome to her side and commanded her with a beady eye that looked down the hook of her nose:

"Ask for the head of Jon the Baptist on a silver salver."

"What!" Salome gasped.

"Do it for me, your mother," Herodias continued.

Salome looked back at her stepfather, the tetrarch king. He did not appear to have heard what they had said and was still purring in his own personal satisfaction as he grinned back at her naked form.

"Your Majesty…Give me the head of Jon the Baptist on a silver salver," she shouted clearly across to him.

There was a buzz in the Great Hall and the tetrarch's face changed to one tested by fear.

"The head of Jon the Baptist?" he repeated, a furrow forming between his eyes.

"Yes," Salome confirmed deliberately.

"Right now?"

Salome turned back to her mother, who nodded surreptitiously.

"Immediately!" Salome shouted, enjoying the power that she now sensed she had over her stepfather and his court.

Herod Antipas hesitated for a moment. This was not the way he had planned things. He glanced at Pontius Pilatus. The Judean prefect did not look too pleased either. They both realized that if he bowed to Salome's request there would be no deal on selling the baptist for the gladiatorial arena at a good price. What was he to do? This sale was his gift to Pilatus. And, now, his whole court was assembled in his presence, awaiting his answer. If he did not honor Salome's request he would publicly go back on his word. He was also acutely aware that almost everyone in the room hated Jon the Baptist, regarding him as a troublemaker who had long deserved to die. It was only through his personal fascination with the prisoner and the baptist's hypnotic power that he had allowed him to live. Herod Antipas had no choice.

"So be it," he said quietly, and then with authority he called his guards.

"I hereby issue the death warrant on our prisoner Jon the Baptist," he declared. "He is to be executed by decapitation. I want his head delivered to this feast dressed on a salver as witness to all here present that I have kept my word. Do it!"

The guards left, excitedly muttering to themselves. There was a ghastly silence in the Great Hall. The tetrarch clapped his hands and beckoned the musicians to play. The strains of the Semitic sounds returned, and the dancers resumed their exotic movements. Wine was poured. Herodias beckoned Salome to sit beside her, and placed a silk shawl around her daughter's shoulders. Pontius Pilatus and Linus Flavian became engaged in deep conversation.

* * *

Jon heard the commotion as the guards clambored down the stone stairs to the dungeons. He heard the movement of furniture and a lot of shouting. There was not much, however, that he could understand from inside his locked cell. For a moment, the noise abated, but within minutes, started up again. Bolts were withdrawn. Guards seized him. Two of the Herodians held him. One more tied his hands behind his back. Another strapped his legs. The four of them dragged him from the cell. In the middle of the dungeon hall, Jon saw a low wooden table of heavy boards. The guards forced him to kneel and pushed his head down on the table. Jon tried to raise his head again, but all he saw was the glint of a polished axe. Sudden, momentary, incredible pain, and he felt no more.

* * *

Herod Antipas was becoming nervous. His courtiers were impatient. They anticipated the drama. Then, the music stopped. Four of the Herodian guard entered the Great Hall carrying a bier on which was placed a large silver salver. In the center of the salver was the head of Jon the Baptist, the blood still draining in semi-congealed form from the shredded and torn tissue that was once his neck. His eyes were bulbous, no longer penetrating, but set at crazy angles within those deep sockets whose muscles had contracted. Only the great mass of black straggly hair and the ferocious beard that hung over the edge of the silver dish from the baptist's chin, gave credence to whom the head had once belonged. The guards lowered the bier in front of the tetrarch. Herod called over to Salome, feeling disgust in his stomach.

"Receive your gift," he said quietly.

Salome, stood up and peered at the spectacle, still naked but for her exotic rings and bejeweled girdle beneath that silk shawl. She gagged.

"I give this gift to my mother!" she cried out, and with one fierce look at her stepfather, she turned and ran from the room.

The guards carried the bier round to the inside columns and placed the gory object in one of the serving niches.

Herod Antipas rose and bade Pontius Pilatus and his entourage to follow him out. The feast had ended.

Chapter Seven

Galilean Odyssey

Joshua and his followers were on the move again. The Master had become wary of staying at any one place for too long. There was an uncanny revival of unrest in the country, which only increased with the news of Jon the Baptist's death. Word about his decapitation had spread swiftly down the Jordan valley that had been the scene of Jon's early triumphs. Some greeted the news as a sign that the end time really had come and preached a message of doom to those who had not heeded to Jon's call for repentence. Others reacted with anger, as the brutality of the baptist's execution became known. The peasants, who had rallied around the Nazirite in his stand against the salt tax, sought revenge for the loss of their hero.

As the crowds poured into Bethany to seek miraculous cures from Joshua, so he became ever more conscious of the dangers that arose from attracting such gatherings. When open rebellion broke out in Jericho under the leadership of a ruffian named Barabbas, Joshua became afraid. He was well aware of the Pharisaic spies from Jerusalem, who watched his every move, and he thought twice about going up for the High Holy Days. Then, Roman soldiers passed through Bethany on their way to Jericho to quell the riot there and several loud-mouthed peasants from among Joshua's followers shouted abuse at them. The wrath of the whip followed. Some were arrested. It was at that point that Joshua decided to move north again into the less conspicuous villages of Galilee.

The Master deemed it safer to travel through the middle country of Samaria rather than to return up the Jordan valley where most the trouble seemed to be brewing. It was coming into winter, and the glow of their campfires was a welcome sight after a hard day on the road. Maria, who had longed to be close to Joshua in Bethany, but had always felt a tension between Lazarus' sisters and herself, was sensitive to the Master's increasing loneliness—loneliness in a crowd. In her boldness, as they camped not far from Sebaste, she sought him out. He had separated himself from the main group as was his custom for evening prayer, but when she found him, he was lying on the ground wrapped in his blanket not far from his own small campfire. The orange glow of flame made his eyes glint. He was far away in deep thought.

"Joshua!" she whispered.

The Master looked up. The firelight caught his full face, picking up the weatherbeaten lines on his forehead and highlighting the sandy streaks in his light brown hair and beard. His long nose became exaggerated, giving him a look of distinction.

"Can I sit with you?" Maria asked.

Joshua looked around furtively. There was nobody else close by. He beckoned to her to be seated.

"You're afraid, aren't you?" Maria said.

Joshua smiled nervously.

"Afraid of what?" he said.

"The Romans," she whispered.

Joshua took both Maria's hands in his.

"If we're not careful, Maria, we'll get caught up in all this unrest. I'm concerned, but I'm not afraid. Actually, I'm more afraid of our own."

Maria looked into Joshua's eyes. She could see that he was troubled and she squeezed his hands reassuringly. Joshua smiled and kissed her lightly on her forehead. Maria felt a shiver down her back as she hunched her shoulders in response.

"Let me stay with you awhile," she suggested. "Why don't you put your head on my shoulder."

The question was very direct, but Maria had asked direct questions all her life. To her joy, Joshua responded.

Maria lightly stroked his hair as he lay back relaxing on her shoulder looking up at her face in the firelight.

"That's better," she whispered softly. "Let me caress you. Just relax and let me take away your worries."

The Master smiled, letting Maria soothe his brow as he nestled into her warmth. He became drowsy, turned and snuggled up to her, falling asleep on the softness of her breasts.

Maria felt the pangs of passion, but she instinctively knew that she must hold back her feelings. Joshua was different. A great peace descended.

When the moon, now waning, rose to join the canopy of stars, Joshua stirred and woke. He looked at Maria tenderly.

"You must go," he said quietly. "I treasure you, Maria, but you must go. The others…they don't understand. You must go."

He kissed her lightly on her brow.

"Go back to Marcus. I must stay alone to pray."

* * *

Barabbas attempted to make his escape west out of Jericho and turned across the River Jordan into the country of Tetrarch Herod Antipas. Forewarned that soldiers of the Roman prefecture were close to Jericho, he thought it unlikely that they would pursue him beyond the river into Peraea. He took stock of his small band of rebels. They were an unruly and undisciplined mob. Most of the men were from Jericho. They had heard his firebrand speeches and sought the excitement of rebellion, fleeing the city with him as soon as they felt the danger of retribution. There was not a leader among them.

Barabbas rose to his full height. He had the proportions of Goliath amongst this motley crowd.

"Who knows this country?" he asked. "We can't go back to Bethany on the river, it's too close to Jericho. Are there any villages further south?"

"That's wilderness country," one of them replied. "There's nothing there but salt."

Barabbas laughed.

"Isn't salt exactly what caused some to rebel? Wasn't it our brothers to the north who first struck a blow against their authorities in revenge for a tax on salt? Didn't Jon the Baptist die for salt?"

He looked at his feeble followers contemptuously.

"Well, may God protect us. We'll travel south to the safety of the salt."

Armed only with sticks and staves, the men headed toward the mountains and the salty wilderness that overlooked the deep-set lake into which the Jordan flowed. There was no road or track for them to follow. The landscape was barren and the searing sun beat down upon their backs.

* * *

Meanwhile, Joshua's band of disciples and followers pushed on from Samaria, entering Galilee to set up their next camp not far from the village of Nain. Across the prosperous valley of Esdraelon they could see the golden light catch the eastern slopes of Mount Tabor, and to the left, the vineyards on the slopes that led up to Nazareth—golden green against the brown hillsides. Joshua had his arm around Maria's waist as he looked toward those distant hills. They seemed closer in the clarity of this evening light.

"I came from those hills," he whispered. "We're almost home."

Judas Iscariot and Philip were watching them.

"Joshua's lost his drive since this woman came. Look at them always together now," Judas muttered. "Who does he think she is? She was a whore, an adulteress and a sinner. Has the Master no shame?"

They watched as Joshua kissed Maria lightly on her forehead, then gently, but fully, on her mouth. They craned to hear what the lovers were saying to each other.

"Tomorrow, we'll camp below that mountain," Joshua said, pointing at distant Tabor. "I've been there before. It's very peaceful. At the top of that hill there's a lovely grove of olives surrounded by clumps of cypress trees standing guard around a sacred haven. It's a very special place Maria—very silent except for the sound of the breeze rustling through those olives. It would be good for me to take Cephas, Janus, and Jonas up there. We can regenerate our souls."

Maria looked up at Joshua, pleading with her sultry eyes.

"Can I come, too?" she asked.

Joshua looked down at the ground and thought for a moment.

Judas craned to listen. *Surely not,* he thought. *And why not me? Am I not one of the Master's inner circle any more?*

"You're never out of my thoughts, Maria," the Master answered, "but I need to spend tomorrow with my leaders—Cephas, Janus, and Jonas. They're not ready for you to join them. We have to be careful. There are some among the 'chosen ones', especially Judas Iscariot, who are jealous of our friendship."

He nudged her waist gently and turned her toward him.

"We'll find our moments, Maria, but tomorrow I must be with my leaders," he repeated.

"But I want to be with you in that peace and beauty that you have described," she pressed.

"Only at a distance, Maria," the Master said. "Tomorrow, my destiny will be revealed."

They let go of each other.

Maria left to join Jezebel and the others in preparing for the evening.

Judas and Philip watched as Joshua stretched out his hands in prayer.

"Why does he no longer include me?" Judas questioned. "Why does he now always favor Cephas and Zebedees' sons over me?"

* * *

The next morning they rose with the sun, and passing through En-dor with its stately oak trees, followed a track down into the valley, with its threshing floors, millstones, and dovecots, crossing to the lone hill that Joshua had pointed out—Mount Tabor.

At its base, he called his 'chosen ones' together.

Maria followed them, seating herself and Marcus at a discreet distance behind them.

Joshua continued to teach about the indwelling spirit of God:

"Your bodies are all temples of the Holy Spirit," he suggested. "All of you have the potential to be messengers of God's Divine love. The Holy Spirit is that essence dwelling within you. The miracles that I perform are not performed by my body, but by the Holy Spirit dwelling within my body. If you can only believe that you also have this Divine power, you would also be able to perform these same miracles."

Cephas was looking down. He began to nervously stir the earth with his staff.

"I will not be with you forever," Joshua continued. "There will come a time and it might be closer than we know, when I will be taken from you and you will be on your own."

"By whom?" Iscariot asked.

Cephas looked up.

"We live in uncertain times, Judas. Who knows?"

Judas' eyes flashed fearfully and caught those of Cephas, looking for assurance.

"Go on, Master," Cephas said, leaning on his staff.

"When that time comes," the Master continued, "you must be ready to recognize the power of the Holy Spirit within you. I pray daily for you that when that time comes you will be ready and that you will understand this Divinity."

"But, Master," Cephas said, "you have already asked us to perform healing miracles among the crowds that flock around you. Has any one of us yet succeeded, at least without your help?"

"Cephas, at times you are a man of little faith. If I can not rely on you, how can I expect the others to follow? Simon of Bethsaida, didn't I name you Cephas? You are my rock. Who do you think I am, Cephas?"

Cephas blinked with surprise.

Judas Iscariot listened intently, knowing that it was he who had been the first to be chosen.

"Some say you are Elijah and others that you are one of the prophets," Cephas replied, failing to look his Master in the eye in his uncertainty.

"Yes, but who do you say that I am?" Joshua deliberately challenged.

Maria, from her vantagepoint, felt pangs of anguish as she listened to this exchange. She knew Joshua as a loving man, who had touched her senses. When she heard Cephas challenged in this way, she felt challenged, too. *Who is this man?* she thought. *Did he not say to me only yesterday that today his destiny would be revealed?*

"Master," Cephas replied. "You are our spiritual leader. You have taught us not to fear the Day of Judgment because God's kingdom has already come."

"Cephas, some things you understand and other things are beyond your grasp. I want you to come with me now—you, Janus, and Jonas."

Joshua turned from Cephas and addressed the others:

"Stay here. Watch and pray and wait for us to return. We will be back before sundown."

Judas rose, but caught the Master's eye and an arm that beckoned him to remain seated.

Joshua then led Cephas and Zebedee's sons away up a sheep trail through the oaks.

Judas Iscariot immediately assumed leadership over those left behind.

"Why are they favored?" he asked. "Why didn't he take us all? Why does the Master favor some of us more? We are all his 'chosen ones.'"

Some agreed, adding their own observations. Others, like Judas Matthias, made no comment.

"And what of the woman from Magdala?" Iscariot continued. "He pays as much attention to her as to us."

Philip nodded.

Maria tugged at Marcus and pulled him away from the group into the trees. She looked around.

"Marcus, stay close to me," she said, and she put her finger to her lips. "Keep very quiet."

At a discreet distance, she pulled him along the same path.

The sheep trail wound its way up the hillside out of the oaks and on past outcrops of rock to a stony grove of olives surrounded by stately cypress trees. *That must be the place?* Maria thought as she watched Joshua and the other three disappear. Carefully, passing through the open area, she and her son sought refuge behind a group of boulders close to the top of the hill.

The high afternoon sun lit up the gaps among the cypresses and the old olive trees in great shafts. The leaves rustled in the light breeze.

"Stay here for a while," Joshua said to the others, who were now seated in a grassy verge among the rocks. "Pray this afternoon that you might know the truth. Ask God to illuminate the Holy Spirit within you."

Joshua then walked away from them and stood looking upward to the heavens in one of those splashes of sunlight. The white of his old Essenic robe caught the light and took on a sheen. There, he prayed in earnest.

Maria and Marcus stayed hidden behind their boulder just downhill from where Joshua now stood. It was a cool spot in the shadow of the cypress trees. They could observe Joshua in that brilliant shaft of sunlight. He was quite close.

* * *

If the kingdom has now come, the end may follow, Joshua considered as he took his thoughts to God. *If only I can inspire Cephas, Janus, and Jonas into believing that they share in my Divinity. If only I can bring out that same spark of God in all those whom they touch. But, I am not sure that they really believe this, and yet time may be running out. If I am too bold in what I say, I could be taken from them, just like Jon. The Romans are losing patience, just like Herod. If I openly say that I am God's chosen Messiah, both the Herodians and the Romans will become afraid of me and will probably destroy me. It is better that the authorities only see me as a healer, but it is essential that Cephas and the others see me as the Messiah. They must believe this if they are to continue my message. What if I am taken from them? They must believe that they share in my messiahship. They must believe that in the kingdom we are all 'sons of God'.*

* * *

Maria lay on the ground, peering around the rock, never taking her eyes off Joshua. Then, she saw Joshua lose his concentration, as if he was distracted. A warm smile crossed the master's face and with an outstretched hand he made a shooing motion. Maria looked around, taking her gaze off Joshua and saw her son. *It's Marcus. He must have become bored and has set off on his own adventure.* He had strayed from their hiding place and was staring at Joshua as if mesmerized by the brilliance of the man's robe in the sun. *He's out in the open.* She called out to him in an exaggerated whisper:

"Come back here! Marcus! You must stay here with me!"

Marcus took no notice and continued to stare at Joshua.

Joshua winked at the boy and gestured with his hand, pointing to the large boulder where Maria was hiding.

He knows we are here, Maria mused.

Marcus looked back at their hiding place, and seeing her mother's expression of concern, ran back to her.

"Joshua looks strange," he said softly. "He shines."

"I know," Maria replied. "Today he is going to tell us something important, but we must stay hidden. We are not supposed to be here."

"But he knows we're here. He saw me, Mother."

"Yes, Marcus. He was suspicious we might come here, but we mustn't let the others see us."

"Why not, if he knew we were going to be here?" Marcus whined.

"It's a secret between Joshua and me," Maria replied. "Joshua wants me to be here, but he doesn't want the others to know."

Marcus remained silent for a while as he looked at his mother quizzically.

"Why do you always want to be near Joshua?" he asked eventually. "Are you going to marry him?"

Maria put her finger to her lips.

"Shsss!" she whispered. "They'll hear you," but her heart was racing.

She looked out toward Joshua again. He did look different. The shaft of sun surrounded by the shade of the glade caught all the fair strands in his light brown hair, giving it a luster. His robe was indeed shining in the brightness, and she could almost swear that there was a glow around him. Maybe it was just caused by the way the afternoon sun's rays silhouetted his form in the olive grove, but somehow it stirred her. Joshua was her savior and hero, but he had become her closest friend. *I washed his robe,* she thought. She longed to rest in his arms and feel his caresses and tender care. But, at the same time, she was afraid of him. There were moments like this when he seemed detatched. He looked different, surrounded in this glowing light. He appeared to be in a trance when in his still posture of contemplative prayer. He was so close to her and yet so unobtainable. She turned to Marcus and smiled: *If only I could share with you the strange feelings that this man arouses deep within me,* she thought, as she pulled the boy to her side.

* * *

Joshua stood alone for a long time. In his meditation, he had felt the energy of God surge through him. He left all thoughts behind as his prayer progressed to become a union with God. He became immersed in the light of Divine union and was overwhelmed by the sound of God's music above the stillness of his mind. He glowed in the sunlight.

Joshua's contemplative peace and the eerie aura that seemed to surround him, also mesmerized Cephas and Jonas. Wishing to share in his experience, they stepped forward to join the Master in that mysterious shaft of now gilding light. They stood on either side of Joshua, joining him in prayer; they, too, illuminated in the strange light. In his trance, it was a moment or two before Joshua realised they were there. When he did, he spoke out loud, as if intending Maria to hear him.

"Today, Elijah and Moses have come. Today, is the beginning of the end time. I will not be with you forever, but when I am gone, you and those you teach must carry on with my work. The end time is only the beginning of a new world when the Divine spirit that is manifest in me will be seen in all of you and those whom you enlighten. The 'Prince of Peace' may suffer many things in these difficult times, but what I may have to sacrifice as a man, will be redeemed in you."

Cephas and Jonas made no reply. Cephas seemed hypnotized by the Master's appearance. *Is this glowing light just from the sun in the trees—or is it emanating from the Master's very body? Is this a manifestation to the burly fisherman of the power of God—mysterious?* Maria wondered.

Janus broke Cephas' trance. He had approached the shaft of sunlight in the olive grove more cautiously than the other two, hanging back on the fringe. When he heard the Master's words, he rushed forward with practical excitement, seemingly unaware of the spiritual metamorphosis that was taking place.

"Master!" he shouted. "If Elijah and Moses have come, shouldn't we build two altars here like our forefathers?"

Cephas turned to Janus in deep thought:

"No, Janus," he said. "Let's build three altars, one for Moses, one for Elijah, and one for Joshua, the 'Prince of Peace.'"

"No!" Joshua said emphatically. "Remember the commandment, 'Thou shalt have no other gods but me.'"

Janus and Jonas stared at Cephas, awaiting his response.

Momentarily, a late afternoon cloud passed over the sun and the brilliance disappeared from Joshua's robe. The reflected aura that had surrounded him was no longer evident. Joshua looked quite normal again.

"Joshua is the Messiah!" Cephas said to the two brothers. "Listen to him! Now, I believe him. He is the Messiah!"

The sunlight returned along with the aura.

Joshua smiled. He looked down toward the boulder where he knew Maria and Marcus to be in hiding. Then, he turned toward Cephas.

"Today you believe," he said deliberately, "but there will be many moments when you will doubt. For the moment, all of you, keep these things to yourselves. This troubled world may destroy us, but it will not destroy the spirit that is within us. What is of God cannot perish."

* * *

Maria clung to Marcus as she stared up from her vantagepoint.

"He says he is the Messiah!" she whispered. "That's what makes it so impossible. He is not a man like all the others. He is God's annointed one."

"Is that why he shines so brightly?" Marcus asked. "Is that why he is a magic man who can heal sick people and animals?"

Maria hardly heard her son. She didn't answer him as her own body ached with mixed emotions that mingled fear and awe with that inner longing to bathe in Joshua's light and share his love and Divinity.

The sunlight faded again. The aura was gone.

In silence, Joshua and the 'inner three' disciples left to follow the path down the hill to the place just above the followers' camp where the other 'chosen ones' had stayed. The light was truly golden now as the sun returned from its rest behind those evening clouds. Momentarily, a breeze rustled through the olive trees, making the sunbeams dance; the columns of light fused in the movement of the branches. Then, a serene peace fell on the grove. Birds began to chirp their evening song.

"It's time to go back," Maria said to Marcus as the turmoil of her emotions subsided. "We must follow them down, but at a distance. They must never know that we were here."

"Good. I like secrets," the boy answered.

Holding hands, they threaded their way through the rocks and down the sheep run. The vale of Esdraelon lay golden before them as the shadows of the tall cypresses lengthened.

* * *

The following day, Joshua led his disciples through the vale of Esdraelon up the familiar road to Nazareth. Matthew was particularly excited to be returning home and walked with the Master—his Uncle Joshua. He was still young enough to look forward to that reunion with his family. Soon, the old landmarks came into sight for them both. Joachim's vineyards and groves were on their right. They still looked fairly well kept, unlike those on the left—Joshua's own vineyards of the past. Joshua, however, had another mission, now. His family, other than his sister Ruth, who with Matthew's father now lived in old Joachim's house, had all left the village to live in Jerusalem. Joshua's prime intent was to visit Joanna's grave.

They made their camp at the lower end of the ramshackle vineyards on their left that once Joshua and Jon had tended with such care. Now, there were tares growing among the vines and twisted columbines clung to the unpruned arms of the past season's growth.

Joshua sought out Maria.

"I used to work this vineyard," he confided. "This was my home."

He pointed up the hill at the little house he had built for Joanna. Nobody was living there now and Joshua reminisced in sadness. He put his arm around Maria's shoulders and they slowly walked toward it.

"I was married once, Maria," he said. "My wife, Joanna, died here when the plague came to Nazareth."

Maria saw tears welling in Joshua's eyes, but could not reconcile herself to her own emotions, let alone his. She had no idea that Joshua had been married, but this revelation in itself gave her rising hope. *Even in his Divine calling he is one of us,* she thought. *But, then, that is what he is trying to teach us—we are all Divine.* As she saw his sadness, she realized someone else once held her hero's heart and her feelings of compassion became mixed with excitement. *Maybe it is possible, after all. But he is so remote most of the time, so inaccessible in this crowd.* She felt she knew she had his trust and friendship, but could she unlock his heart? So many men had fallen at her feet throughout her life, but not Joshua. He remained an enigma. *Is it because he is some sort of mystical son of God?* she considered in her mind, *or is it because he already gave his love to this woman? He accepts my caresses of comfort and he treats me with deep respect, but I cannot arouse his passion. He spends ever more of his time with me, at least when he is not with the 'chosen ones', but the union for which I so long seems constantly denied me. Perhaps this is the reason. Perhaps this old vineyard and its memories are what stand between us.*

Joshua peered into the gloom of the little house. The earthen floor from which he had dug up his treasure still revealed the hole where it had been buried. There were a few alien pots and jars in the room, and some broken shards that showed that the place had periodically been used by itinerent peasants or hired workers for the vines. But there was nothing to reveal the happy memories of Joanna's laughter and their brief life together. It was all eclipsed by the memory of Joanna's painful struggle to hold onto their world as her fever rose and her life was sapped.

When they emerged back into the daylight, Joshua pointed up the hill at the vineyard wall.

"I buried her up there," he said.

A few wild flowers—blue cornflowers—grew among the weeds running along the base of the wall.

"Do you mind if I pick some of these and leave them at her grave?"

Seeking the prettiest blooms, Joshua plucked them and placed the small bouquet on a ledge in the wall.

"For you, Joanna," he said quietly. "It was not God's will that we should stay together. God set me a different task, which is yet to be fulfilled."

Tears ran down Joshua's cheeks.

"I loved you," he whispered, before he turned, seeking comfort in Maria's arms.

He looked over her shoulder.

"I think Judas Iscariot is following us. He's down there in the vines," he said quietly.

Never had Maria felt closer to Joshua. *If he is a son of God he is certainly vulnerable to the emotions of men,* she thought as she felt his embrace. She responded with all the love that she could muster, a harbinger of her heart opening to the breadth and depth of his Divine love as every twinge of plausible doubt left her. She cried with him as he shared his grief, and she sensed the growing of a total trust that she hoped would become the foundation of their future love.

* * *

Joshua and Maria stayed by the little house for a long time. If Judas had followed them, he made no approach. He appeared to have decided to leave them alone.

Meanwhile, Matthew had run across to Joachim's old house and sought out his parents. When Joshua and Maria went back to the camp, they found David ben Levi and Ruth with Matthew. Even though his parents had cautioned against Matthew joining Joshua and his disciples at the time he had left home, they were deeply pleased to see him and know that he was fit and well. Matthew was no longer a boy, but a young man with a spiritual purpose. Ruth and David ben Levi felt reassured. Joshua and his followers appeared to have been a positive influence on their only son. Later, Matthew's family joyfully prepared several baskets of bread for Joshua and his friends, along with fruit and vegetables from their garden. They also brought skins of good Galilean wine. The following day, there was a relaxed atmosphere at the camp. It was not long before they were all singing songs, inspired by David ben Levi's bounty…even Judas Iscariot. Their camaraderie seemed restored. Maria put aside her longing for Joshua as she clapped hands with Marcus, adding percussion to the questionable melodies of the merry crowd.

They all slept well that night and their snores were heavy, but no one overslept. In the morning, Joshua gathered his disciples around him as usual to teach them. The vineyard had inspired him. He looked back on his happy years as a vinedresser and winemaker and addressed them as such:

"Before we leave this camp and travel on, my friends, I would like to share with you a truth, which I now feel you are ready to receive."

There was a hush among them.

"When I lived here, I was a vinedresser. I took care of these very same vines."

He looked at the unkempt straggling shrubs.

"I think I did a rather better job than those who are now the husbandmen."

There was a ripple of laughter.

"I worked these vineyards with my cousin, Jon the Baptist, whom they beheaded. Now, some of you still follow me because of the healing miracles that I am able to perform. What I would like you to understand is that those miracles can only be performed because of the Divine power that is within the soul that gives me life. I am like a vine. God is the vinedresser. Every branch of mine that doesn't bear fruit, the vinedresser will take away and those that do bear fruit he will prune so that in their bleeding they will bear even more fruit. The sap in the vine is the Divine spirit within me, which is strengthened by the vinedresser's loving care. I am preparing you for the Kingdom of God. Follow the teachings I have given you and you will be like a dressed vine. My strength, which comes from God, will then be in you. The indwelling spirit of God within you will be like the sap that rises in the dormant vine to produce fresh new growth and an abundance of fruit. I am the vine, and now, you are the branches. Together, we grow, fed by the sap of God. We are spirit. We are Divine. We are of the essence of God. If you follow me and take note of all that I have taught you, then the Divine love lying within you will shine forth from you. We are co-workers with the Creator. Know that in you, God will be glorified and you will bear much fruit and prove to be worthy disciples with the power to do what I do, even more than I do. As God loves me, so do I love you, and will always! Let your Divine love also show forth in all your dealings with each other."

Maria felt sadness in her heart even at these words of encouragement to them all. There seemed to be a finality in what Joshua was saying. He spoke as if he was going to leave them. It was hard for her now to conceive of a life without Joshua. This mysterious man was becoming her whole being. Later in the day, when she found a moment to sit with Joshua up at the little house where they refreshed the graveside flowers, now wilted in the hot sun, she spoke of her concern:

"When you taught us this morning you sounded as if you would be leaving us. Is that true?"

Joshua thought for a moment, aimlessly flicking small pebbles from the rough ground in front of him.

"I don't know, Maria," he said at length. "Jon was arrested and killed. I always felt responsible for Jon. His destiny always seemed wrapped up in mine. The authorities do not look favorably on many of the things I do and say. Remember how it was in Bethany? The High Priests and some of the Sanhedrin Pharisees sent men to the village to challenge my authority. That's partly why we left—that and the rebellion in Jericho stirred up by Barabbas. The authorities fear me because they feel threatened. They know I had the power to raise Lazarus from the dead.

Who knows…maybe they have turned on Lazarus since I left. The very life that I restored might now be in danger."

Joshua paused for a moment. He stopped picking up the pebbles and just stared straight ahead.

Maria put her arm around his waist.

"You really are afraid, aren't you?" she suggested.

Joshua turned and looked at her. There was no smile on his face, only a forlorn sadness.

"Don't you think they will try to destroy me, too?" he asked.

"Why, Joshua? All you have done has been to help others. What have you ever done that could upset anyone?"

"Maria, you are a woman who has seen all sides of life and yet at times you are so naïve. There are some, even among our own group, who condemn me just because I share private time with you."

"Judas Iscariot?" she said.

"Maybe. He…they…have forgotten what I said when I found you about to be stoned to almost certain death. Do you remember what I said?"

"I'm not sure, Joshua," Maria answered. "It was very confusing for me. I didn't know who you were. You simply saved my life."

"Maria…I said to your accusers: 'Whoever of you is without sin let him be the first to throw a stone.' I think they were shocked that I dared to be that bold, but at that time they did not know who I was. You were on the top of Mount Tabor the other day."

He smiled.

"My goodness, Marcus nearly showed the others you were there! But, you heard what Cephas said?"

Maria remembered the scene very well. In recollection, as she sat alone with her arm around Joshua's waist and her head resting on his shoulder, her fears returned. Cephas had acknowledged him to be the Messiah.

"Yes," she answered slowly, looking down at the ground, almost shamefully. "He said that you were the Messiah, and that means you are God's annointed one."

"No more so than anyone else, but it is hard for our holy men to understand that."

Joshua squeezed her and looked into her eyes.

"It is hard for some of them to understand that if you are a 'son of God' you should forgive the sins of those who have broken the conventions of the Law. The Law is good, Maria, but I am telling you that in the kingdom to come there will only be the law of love—a love that can only spring up from the sap of God that dwells within."

He cupped Maria's face with both his hands.

"You have that love. You will share in my Divinity," he said as he drew her lips lightly to his.

Maria felt a burning sensation in her stomach as a surge of emotional power passed between them. He had acknowledged her love for him, but he had also shared his most imtimate spiritual secret with her. She felt the pain of pure joy as she gave her love to him in that brief moment and shared in his Divinity.

"Remember the vine," Joshua said, looking into her eyes. "It will produce its best fruit when pruned. The grapes are small on the unpruned stock—the sap less concentrated. The divine vines are pruned. Sacrifices are made."

* * *

Joshua and his disciples only stayed a short while in Nazareth. The Master was anxious to return to Capernaum. Along the way, he continued to instruct his 'chosen ones' on the importance of understanding their own Divine power. He compared himself to a shepherd who knows his sheep and is prepared to lay his life down for them, as opposed to a hireling, who has no personal attachment to the sheep. He again suggested to them that he was of the essence of God, and just as the shepherd had an integral bond with his sheep, so, too, did he have a spiritual bond with each of them—his 'chosen ones'.

"My Divinity is, therefore, also your Divinity," he declared.

This generated much discussion amongst them as to how they could prove their Divinity.

"Did you choose us because you could sense a greater Divinity within us?" Janus asked. "Have we three—my brother, Cephas and me—greater power than the others."

Before Joshua had time to answer, Cephas challenged the sons of old Zebedee:

"What makes you think we are any greater?" he shouted. "Aren't we all fishermen? Wasn't it me who gave you your start? Weren't your father and I partners?"

"Quite right!" Judas Iscariot shouted in agreement. "If it hadn't been for Simon the Zealot and old Zebedee, none of us would have formed the fleet. What commercial success we have had we owe to that. This talk of Divinity is beginning to make me sick."

"Judas, you, too, are no less than Cephas, Janus, and Jonas. You are all equally Divine," Joshua interrupted. "Remember, however, that your Divine love finds its greatest expression in humility. The first among you will be as the last and the least among you can, in his Divinity, be raised to the greatest."

At the Master's bidding, they stopped their bickering, although Judas Iscariot continued to mutter under his breath at their folly.

On arrival in Capernaum, Judas Iscariot and the inner three forgot their differences in their common bond of fishing. It felt good to take the boats out again, and from Judas' viewpoint as treasurer of the group, it was a necessity in order to replenish funds to sustain these wandering journeys that The Master now liked them to take.

Over the winter weeks they spent in Capernaum, however, an opportunity arose to test the reality of their power. Joshua spent a day healing and preaching to a large crowd on the beach. About midafternoon, after most of those seeking the miraculous healing had left, a shy young man, who had a terrible impediment of speech, pulled at Joshua's robe. As he tried to speak, the man pointed toward the town. Joshua could not understand a word that the young man was saying, but it was obvious that the man was desperate for him to go with him. The Master turned back to his disciples, some of whom, led by old Zebedee and Simon the Zealot, were busy gathering up the dried fish to sell at the evening market while the fishing group prepared their boats for the evening catch. Zebedee and Simon still shipped the majority of the fish off to the Roman markets in salt and brine.

"Wait for me," Joshua called out to Judas Iscariot and Cephas, who were habitually in charge of the boats. "I'll join you as soon as I can."

Joshua left with the anxious young man who had the speech impediment.

As the afternoon drew on and there was no sign of Joshua's return, Iscariot ordered the boats out so they wouldn't lose their day's catch.

Zebedee, old Boanerges, named after his thunderous bad temper, stayed behind as usual, and Simon and the women, including Maria, exchanged dried fish at the late afternoon market for flour, goat's meat, lentils, and spices.

By the time the women returned, the three boats were gently bobbing in the water. Their nets were cast a little way from the shore. The sun had begun its slow descent heralding early evening.

When Joshua returned from town, he, too, could see the boats were out and the men fishing. Old Zebedee was quick to explain why Judas Iscariot and Cephas had thought it best to start without him.

Joshua looked at the boats silhouetted against the evening light.

"I will join them," he said.

"But, Joshua, all three boats are out. Andrew has my boat," Zebedee said.

"I know," Joshua replied with an impish grin, as he caught Maria's eye.

They stood and watched, wondering what was going to happen next. Obviously, Joshua had meant something by his deliberate response, but he did not reveal to them what.

Joshua walked along the beach until he was a little way out from the town and Zebedee and Simon's house. For a moment, he leaned back on a boulder by a little cluster of beach palms and looked intently at the still waters of the lake—a perfect fishing evening. Then, deliberately, he started walking out into the lake. He walked slowly, and it appeared from Zebedee's house, where Maria and Marcus were watching, that he was actually walking on the water. The golden light of the dwindling evening sun caught his white robe and highlighted the flesh of his face and hands.

"Joshua looks strange—glowing…like that time…you know, our secret," Marcus said, as he watched with his mother.

Steadily, before their eyes, Joshua walked out toward the boats. Andrew's was the closest.

* * *

Young Matthew was the first to notice the Master coming toward them. He tugged at Andrew's arm.

"Look! There's someone out there on the water!" he said.

Andrew dropped his net.

"God Almighty! You're right"

He called to Thaddeus:

"There's a man on the water! He might need help!"

Thaddeus also dropped his net to look at the phenomenon. He waved his arms frantically and called out to the other two boats.

"It's the Master," Cephas shouted back. "He's walking on the water. The Master is walking out to us."

"Holy Moses!" Andrew retorted.

Judas Iscariot and Thomas heard Cephas from their boat, too, and looked up from their tasks. Assuredly, the figure of a man was moving toward them across the water.

"Impossible," Judas muttered.

"No, Judas. It is possible," Thomas replied. "There's a narrow ridge that runs out into the lake shallows from the beach west of Capernaum. Jonas and Janus warned me about it. More than once we were grounded on it when I was in their boat."

They stared at the figure coming closer to them, calmly walking on the water.

"It's him all right," Judas said at length. "It's Joshua walking toward us."

He took the steering board and gave his commands:

"Pull in the nets, Thomas! Philip and Bartholomew, put out the oars!"

They began to guide their boat toward Joshua. The others did likewise. As Jonas and Janus' boat came closer, they saw James, the son of Alpheus, normally the silent one in the group, stand up in the prow and shriek:

"It's a spirit!"

"Sit down!" Jonas yelled. "You're rocking the boat!"

But, the son of Alpheus screamed only the more.

* * *

As the boats came closer to Joshua, the Master could clearly hear their cries.

"Don't be afraid!" he yelled back. "It's me, Joshua—the Master. I told you I would join you."

Cephas and Matthew stood up in Andrew's boat, their jaws still hanging open in disbelief.

"Master, if it's really you on the water, let me join you," Cephas shouted.

"Don't!" Matthew said emphatically. "You can't swim."

"That's true, Matthew," Cephas replied, "but if the Master is walking on the water through his Divine power, then, so can I through the same power."

Cephas began to clambor out of the boat.

Jonas and Janus looked at each other skeptically, their boat now very close to Andrew's.

"He's on the ridge!" they shouted. "There's a ridge out there and he is walking on the shallows! You can't swim, Cephas!"

Cephas did not heed them. The others watched in amazement as the burly fisherman sat gingerly on the side of the boat.

Judas' boat joined them.

"What are you doing?" Iscariot shouted. "You can't swim."

But the Master's voice came calmly across the water:

"Come to me, Cephas."

Cephas pushed himself away from the boat and fell into the water. He floundered and thrashed out with his arms and legs as he tried to swim. He couldn't raise himself up to try to walk—he began to flounder... choke...to sink.

Judas Iscariot leaped into the water and swam a few bold strokes toward Cephas, while Thomas, Philip, and Bartholomew steadied their boat. Judas caught hold of Cephas and held up his choking head. Then, assisted by Philip and Bartholomew, pulled the heavy man from the water. Thomas stove off a collision with his oar as the boat lurched toward that of Andrew.

Meanwhile, all three boats drifted toward the Master. With a light crunch Judas' boat reached the shallows first. The Master clambored in. Thomas pushed off with his oar.

Cephas recovered as they headed back toward the Capernaum beach.

"Master," Thomas asked, "were you really walking on the water?"

Joshua had a mysterious look.

"Any of you could have walked on the water," he gently replied. "Only

Cephas, here, from among you, tried—Cephas, who can not swim. To that end, he showed greater faith than all of you. Why do you still doubt your Divine power?"

Judas Iscariot scowled.

"Master! Cephas could have drowned!"

"Judas, have you no faith?" Joshua calmly asked.

They silently rowed.

* * *

Maria and Marcus along with some others, who thought that they had seen Joshua walking on the water, were waiting for them as the boats beached. Back at Simon and Zebedee's house, Janus spoke up:

"Master, tell us the truth? You were walking in those shallows above the ridge, weren't you? We know these waters. Why do you want us to believe that you were walking on the water?"

"Yes," Thomas agreed. "We have been grounded there in the past. We always avoid that area now."

Joshua remained evasive.

"Why do you all continue to doubt?" he said firmly as they sat down to eat. "If you truly have faith in the spark of God that can be ignited in you, all of you can have God's power. The power does not come easily, however. You must train yourselves in your faith and open your minds to the indwelling Divine spirit. I can help you discipline yourselves into this state of being, but first you must have faith in me."

"So, we really can walk on water?" Jonas asked quizzically.

"When I was an Essene at Qumran, I learned to walk on water," Joshua said. "When we go south again, I will teach you all to do the same. But, remember what I said. It was only Cephas who had the faith. If we have that faith, one day it will manifest—we will be able to move mountains."

After saying this, Joshua had a faraway look. Maria sensed that something was bothering him as she filled a pouring vessel with wine from a skin. Joshua caught her eye, but he didn't smile. He was wrestling with his own conscience as he considered how he had used the illusion of miracle. *It is like the water jars in Cana,* he thought, *the jars I filled with my best wine. It saved the day at Amos' and Lila's wedding three years ago. Maybe it did herald my work for the Lord, but it was deceptive.* He knew he had walked on the shallow bar, and it bothered him in the same way that in using this illusion to teach a lesson he had allowed some of them to think his action a miracle. *Is it right to lead them on like this,* he asked himself, *even if it does give me a chance to teach something profound? Cephas might have drowned—the only one of them who can not swim!* Then, he chuckled. *We really did walk on the Salt Sea at Qumran!*

As Maria filled Joshua's cup she whispered:

"I have faith in you."

Joshua broke from his thoughts and smiled. *It was worth it after all,* he concluded.

Later, when he was alone with Maria out on the beach under the stars, he described to her how he had walked on the waters of the Salt Sea many times when at the Qumran monastery.

"It was amazing there," he explained. "You really can walk on the water, and if you fall you can not sink. It is actually impossible to swim, as your legs just fly up out of the water. You can actually sit in the water without touching the bottom."

They laughed together and gently embraced. Maria felt, as they kissed, a deeper desire for a more intimate relationship.

"I love you," she whispered in his ear. "One day you can take me to this mysterious sea and we can walk on the water together."

"I will," Joshua replied, holding her closer.

The next day, after selling the remainder of the fish that they had caught, Joshua and his 'chosen ones' left Capernaum. They followed the fringe of the lake to the fertile area known as Gennesaret, about halfway between Capernaum and the village of Magdala. Here, during the mild winter months following the autumnal rains, two substantial streams tumble down from the hills, bringing fresh water to the lake. It is an area of great beauty. For a while, they settled there and Joshua started to teach them how to meditate—how to open their souls to the indwelling spirit of God.

Chapter Eight

Barabbas

"His Majesty theTetrach of Galilee!" the Roman secretary announced.

Linus adjusted his toga, while Pilatus sat back comfortably in his audience chair.

Herod Antipas entered the Jerusalem audience hall, followed by his royal guards.

The administration in Caesarea Maritima and Jerusalem had taken on a very official look during the prefecture. It was hard to believe that they were on the outskirts of the Roman Empire in this magnificent reception hall with its marble columns and Italian frescoes. All traces of Semitic or even late Hellenistic influences had given way to the central grandeur of Rome. The room was sparsely furnished except for two lines of wrought iron lamp stands and traditional Roman camp chairs evenly spaced at the base of each of the marble columns. On the dais, was the prefect's gilt and ebony chair and several smaller chairs for his entourage, including that for his principal aide—Linus Flavian. Two additional chairs, with comfortable yellow cushions edged with golden tassels, had on this occasion been placed just below the shallow dais. They were for Herod Antipas and his chief scribe. Behind the prefect and his aide stood four Roman guards in full dress. Two more guards stood at the entrance. They saluted Tetrarch Herod Antipas as he came in.

"Hail, Caesar!" echoed through the vast, empty hall.

When Herod was about two thirds of the way up to the dais, Pilatus stood to greet him.

"Welcome your Majesty," he said in a superior tone. "Greetings from His Imperial Majesty, Tiberius, the Emperor of Rome."

The vassal king stopped, placed his hand to his forehead and then gestured toward Pilatus with a flourish. Like his grandfather, the tetrarch clung to his Semitic ways in this Roman world. He was dressed in a scarlet outer garment edged in gold that covered much of his green, and further gilded, robe. He wore a small crown that was little more than a headband, but boasted three elaborate jewels, which had once graced King Herod the Great's crown. The crown held back his thinning, black hair, which slicked with oil swept down to his shoulder. His face was clean-shaven, and his eyes were dark and deep. Pilatus had never treated him quite as an equal, which Herod Antipas resented, but the tetrarch was not nervous, because the Roman prefect of Judea had always worked with him as an ally, and these occasional audiences called by Pilatus were ususally cordial and with purpose.

Once Herod Antipas and his chief scribe were seated, Pilatus began their business.

"Your Majesty," he said seriously, and with an air of confidentiality as he leaned forward in his chair, throwing his toga surplus back over his shoulder, "I need to enlist your help in tracking down a rebel who threatens the peace in both our territories."

Herod looked up at the prefect with interest.

"A certain Barabbas has been whipping up unrest in the border towns and villages of the Jordan valley, most notably in Jericho itself, a city that I know we both hold dear to our hearts."

Herod Antipas took his gaze away from the prefect at this reference to Jericho. It was a sore topic with the tetrarch. Jericho had once been such a stronghold of Herodian rule, with its magnificent palace and sub-tropical delights. The palace was still his to enjoy, but the fact that Archelaus had politically lost this important Herodian seat to the prefecture of Rome, still hurt his family pride.

"Yes, Your Excellency," I have heard of this Barabbas," Herod eventually replied, his hurt pride swallowed. "He encouraged many in the Jordan valley to support the salt tax rebels, even to challenge my authority in Peraea."

"Quite, Your Majesty, but it is more than the matter of salt," Pilatus cut in. "He incited those in Jericho to rise up against my authority—Caesar's authority. He is an impressive firebrand and a giant of a man—a fighter—but his followers don't amount to much. I am sure you would be as pleased as I to see this man a prisoner of Rome. Unfortunately, when I sent men to Jericho to bring about Barabbas' arrest, the rebel escaped. He's crossed the Jordan and is hiding in your territory of Peraea. I think it would be in our joint interest to flush him out and remove this potential menace to us both."

Herod nodded, then consulted with his chief scribe.

"We agree," he replied. "Your Excellency, I will send a detachment of my own guard down to Peraea. We could join forces at Bethany beyond the Jordan."

"Fine," Pilatus agreed, "but under Roman command.

"In my territory!" Herod retorted.

"Yes, Herod, in your territory, and the prisoner when captured is to be handed over to our authority. It's in your interest to be rid of him, is it not?" Pilatus cynically reiterated.

The powerless tetrarch capitulated.

"So be it."

* * *

Barabbas was impatient. He was not the sort of man who could remain in hiding for long. The wilderness did not appeal to him and the weakness of his followers bothered him. It was not long before he moved from the salty terrain of Machaerus back up to the Jordan valley to recruit new reinforcements and begin his campaign again. He traveled as far north as Pela in the Decapolis and successfully added a few dissident rebels to his cause, but it was not long before the combined Roman and Herodian force became aware of his movements. They waited for him on the borders of the Decapolis and Peraea.

Barabbas fell right into their trap. Unsuspecting, he moved his men back south, thinking he was safe in the lush vegetation of the Jordan valley. At his camp, the men were enjoying the valley's good fruits and the marauding freedom that most of them could never experience in the daily round of their native village lives. There were no guards and nobody stood on watch. The forces of authority surrounded their camp as evening fell, and in that twilight, they moved in to the kill.

The Roman and Herodian soldiers butchered most of the peasants with ease, but Barabbas was to be taken alive to be kept in the Praetorium at Jerusalem. Those were their instructions. There was no escape. The attack was so swift and sudden that Barabbas had no chance. He made an attempt at escape, jumping into the Jordan. He struggled to cross the shallow waters. Three of the Herodian guards quickly tackled him and held his head down so that he choked to submission. What little remained of his ill-prepared mob fled for their lives. Barabbas was handed over to the Romans, bound, gagged, and escorted to Jerusalem. On the way to his captivity, the rebel was paraded through the streets of Jericho to the jeers of many of those who just a few weeks before had rallied to his cause. In this volatile world of the Roman occupation, such was the reaction to the failures of false prophets and messiahs.

* * *

In Bethany, Lazarus looked up from his tanning vat as the soldiers passed by. Silently, he spat in their direction. After they had gone, most the village men gathered outside Lazarus' house.

"That was Barabbas," one of them said.

"Are you sure?" another asked. "Barabbas from Jericho?"

"Another bid for freedom crushed," Lazarus stated resignedly. "I wonder if Joshua is safe?"

"It was wise of him to leave when he did," one of the older men said. "They'll get him one day, Lazarus. Don't feel too comfortable yourself. You are seen by many to be the very cause of Joshua's power. People flocked to Joshua when he was here because he raised you from the tomb."

Mary heard them. She stepped forward and stood beside Lazarus for comfort.

"What harm can they do to a man who knows only how to heal and help?' she challenged.

"Wait and see," the older man replied. "Anyone who draws a crowd can seem a threat to the Romans these days."

Martha came out from the house, rubbing her dough-covered hands on the folds of her shift.

"What's going on?" she asked.

"The Romans have captured Barabbas," Lazarus informed her.

"What's that got to do with us?"

Martha looked at the crowd that had gathered.

"Have none of you anything better to do but gossip around these vats?" she scolded.

Martha was always so practical, but she was also protective. She became wary when the villagers gathered around her brother. Deep in her heart, she realized that Lazarus could be a rallying point for ignorant support against the authorities. His resurrection from the dead had brought them mixed blessings.

"Be off with you," she said sternly.

The crowd began to disperse.

Lazarus said nothing. He picked up a hide and continued his work.

Chapter Nine

Youthful recall

It was an unusually warm, springlike, winter day. Birds chirped as Maria sat dabbling her feet in the Gennesaret stream. Her long hair hung freely, blowing lightly in the breeze. Her wet robe clung to her legs. She watched as Joshua stripped off his robe unabashedly, and wearing only his loincloth, waded into the water. His body was beautiful and unblemished. He was in the right proportions. His waist was trim. His shoulders were broad. His calves and thighs were muscular from many days of wandering. Then, he sat in the water. He splashed its coolness over his body. Maria felt those familiar urges of physical attraction. She jiggled her feet in the excitement of her silent observation. *Will he ever give himself to me in total freedom?* she asked herself. *I know how much I could soothe him with my love.*

Joshua lay back and soaked his light brown hair. He rotated his head so that all of it was bathed in the water, and as he sat up again, he brushed the now dark wet hair back.

"All right, Maria," he called out. "You can wash it now."

Maybe this is the moment, Maria thought, taking the box of sticky ointment that she used for washing her hair. Years ago, her mother had taught her how to mix the white pods of the lye flowers with olive oil and powdered hearth ash. The lye would foam into a soapy substance as it was rubbed into the hair. Esther had always taught her from earliest days the importance of a woman's hair. "The Roman boys like clean hair," she used to say. In their profession, it was vital that those silky locks should remain fresh and clean to attract the men.

Maria waded into the shallow stream to where Joshua sat, her heart pounding with anticipation. She began to rub the lye ointment into his hair.

Her loving hands felt powerful as she massaged his scalp. Her fingers worked the sensitive areas in order to relieve the pressures that harbored his tensions. As the lather built up, some of the soapy mixture flew into his eye. It stung, and Joshua shook his head with momentary pain. Lovingly, Maria took the wet hem of her garment and bathed his irritated eye. When the pain diminished, she returned to her task.

When completed, Maria sat in the water behind him. At first, it felt clammy and cold as the stream rushed past her buttocks and lower back, causing her skirts to float in folds before her, but the feeling soon passed.

"Lie back now," she said softly to Joshua.

He obeyed and lay his soapy head in her lap as the brook babbled around them. Maria scooped up water on either side and rinsed his hair. The soapy mixture eased into the stream.

Joshua looked up at her face as she leaned over him.

"Thank you," he said. "You do this so well."

Maria smiled with pleasure and excitement.

"I would do anything you ask of me," she said. "I love you, Joshua."

Joshua obviously felt the same excitement as he gazed at her in affection.

"I know," he agreed.

Taking his head in her hands, she eased back so that it rested between her knees, deeper into the rushing flow. He lay there in the stream stretched out in front of her as the last of the soap washed out of his hair. She sat back in the water, leaning on her elbows with her face turned upward to the surprisingly warm winter sun. It was such a clear and beautiful Galilean day. Her heart glowed with contentment.

* * *

After a while, Joshua sat up, shook his head like a dog, then swept back his hair squeezing out the water. It hung like a donkey's tail from his hands. Maria reached forward gently pulling it back, releasing the last drops as she squeezed it in her hands. Slowly, almost teasingly, she let it go and Joshua stood up, his back still to her, as the water fell from his loincloth. Then, he turned and smiled, gently offering her his hand, and pulled her up from the stream. As she rose, her soaking garment clung to the folds of her voluptuous body and exaggerated the form of her breasts and buttocks. Hands clasped, they stood looking at each other in the stream, holding similar thoughts centered on their first encounter—the back room at Esther's. They could have given themselves to each other then, in that sordid musk, but they did not. Neither that place nor that time was right, but now, on this heavenly springlike day…maybe? But more than desire—the spark of God leaped between them as they savored this simple moment of love.

* * *

Ecstacy mingled with the mystical in the power that flowed. Joshua felt Maria's love, rising from her physical attraction to him, to a deeper, more spiritual love. But, he knew she was holding back. Perhaps she was afraid of losing him if she became too passionate. Joshua remembered how it had been that first time. He had held back. Then, he was in awe of her—now she was in awe of him. They had rarely spoken of that time, and possibly Maria had no recollection of it other than his recall. Joshua had felt ashamed and had left her unfulfilled. Only for a brief moment had he allowed her to take his hand and rest it on her breast. He could remember the softness and the warmth, but he could also recollect the fears that this had brought upon him. There had been a sense of betrayal. *But, betrayal to what?* he thought. *Is it really a sin to savor the beauty of a woman? It certainly didn't bother the other men who visited the brothel in Magdala—Amos hadn't been able to get enough.*

* * *

Maria knew how Joshua had reacted when he had shown her Joanna's grave. He had obviously loved Joanna deeply, and she felt sadness that his joy had been so short-lived. But, the very fact that he had loved Joanna gave her hope. This mystical, spiritual leader was not incapable of a loving relationship. She longed for his touch and yearned for his tender caresses. They had enjoyed some precious moments together, but for some reason Joshua had not yet quite let himself go. *Was this to be their moment?*

There was a waterfall above the shallow waters of the stream in a fertile grove where stately willows leaned from the banks. Most of the year, only a trickle fell from the rocks, but now, with the mild winter rains, the overflow was full.

"Why don't you wash my hair, too?" Maria suggested as they clambored upstream in their wet clothing toward the tumbling water. "There's enough lye left."

Maria looked up at Joshua with her wide, appealing eyes. The statement was as daring as she felt she could be. She awaited his answer.

Joshua stopped and took her in his arms. He kissed her lightly on the forehead, and with tenderness in his distant look, answered her:

"You've always managed without me before."

"I know, Joshua, but today is our day. We are alone here in all this beauty—just you and me. Could you not, just this once, wash my hair? It would give me such joy!"

"Maria, if it will really please you, I will anoint you with lye and water. You once anointed me with oil; it is the least that I can do. You anointed me in spirit, Maria, because you understood me. You understand me more than all the others, even more than Cephas. Because you have faith in me, I will anoint your head as I wash your hair. It will be a cleansing of your soul. I will give you the power of the Holy Spirit."

Maria clung to Joshua in a long silent embrace. He patted her back as she pressed against him releasing her mixed emotions. *My savior, and yet so unobtainable. My best friend, and yet will he ever be my lover? Who is this man?* she thought. Then, looking up at him, she smiled serenely.

"It is just as it was on the mountain, Joshua. You are a son of God, aren't you?" she said.

"There is only one thing that is different about me," he replied. "I know that my soul is the spirit of God. One day, you will know that yours is, too, Maria; but sometimes I wonder if the others ever really will."

For a moment, Joshua remained silent, almost in a prayerful trance. Then, he laughed and started to pull off her heavy wet robe.

"You won't need this when that soap foams in your hair, will you?" She helped him, shamelessly revealing her nakedness.

"No," she answered.

They waded toward the falling water. The stream tumbled down from about ten feet. Standing close to the waterfall, they embraced. Joshua kissed Maria gently on the lips and felt the warmth of her body against his flesh. Slowly, she pulled at his loincloth, which loosened and fell. They stood together in a silent embrace for which they had both longed. Maria felt a powerful surge of emotion within her, but it was a new sensation that she had never experienced with any of her many lovers, not even Linus. She felt the presence of God. They stood there for what seemed an eternity and then, ever so gently, Joshua led her into the waterfall and let the free flow wet her hair in preparation for the lye anointing. Their bodies touched in anticipation of the harmony of natural union, and it all seemed so right.

* * *

Flavius Septimus had been in Rome for a couple of years and made the acquaintance there of Antonius Syllus.They discovered that they had a common interest in Galilee. Antonius' wife, Portia, also became firm friends with Copernia Flavian. They moved in the same circles within the patrician society of the Palatine hill. Flavius invited Syllus and Portia to visit with them when they returned to Taricheae on the Galilean lake. Both couples traveled together from Rome.

The port of Caesarea was now half a century old. It had lost some of its gleaming impact compared to the days of King Herod the Great. Nonetheless, it was still an important gateway to Judea, Galilee, and Syria, and the late king's vision had brought its rewards. The two middle-aged Roman administrators stood in the bright sunlight as a flat barge brought them into the inner harbor.

"Trade looks good," Flavius commented, as he noted the bustle on the quayside.

Syllus nodded in agreement.

"The air always smells so good here," he remarked, sniffing the coastal breeze.

For these two men, despite their important connections with Rome, the Levant was home. They happily anticipated their return to Galilee.

After they landed, they left their boxes for the Caesarea agent to forward on to Taricheae. Copernia had taken this opportunity to ship more family treasures to their villa. Once all arrangements had been made, they bought a wagon and continued their journey up into Galilee, chattering to each other. They stopped in Nazareth.

The inn there was small, but they were able to share a room, and the Jewish family that took care of them fed them well and seemed friendly. The daughter of the innkeeper waited on them. Her appearance brought back to Syllus a flood of memories. *She reminds me of that sensuous Hebrew girl Antonias brought to the villa,* he thought. *I can't blame him, but he's better off in Athens.*

"Some of these Hebrew girls are very attractive," he said confidentially to Flavius.

"I've always found something exotic about these Jews," Flavius agreed. "I can understand why so many of our people who have settled here have fallen to their charms."

"Do you think that's a good thing?" Antonius Syllus asked rather pointedly.

"No, not really," Flavius answered slowly.

Syllus looked at him. He sensed something was bothering him.

"Why not?"

"No reason really, if you think about it, but we had an awkward situation with my son a few years ago."

"Linus?"

"Yes. Linus became involved with a pretty girl from the village of Magdala as they call Taricheae. He had an affair with her and she became pregnant. I don't blame him for his fling—she was a very lovely girl—but she was totally unsuitable. She was the daughter of the village whore! She was probably one herself."

"Really!" Syllus exclaimed, amazed at this revelation so similar to his own experience with his son. "What did you do?"

Flavius flinched as he fought with his memories of Esther, who had brought him warmth and love even if he had paid for it in silver. Deep in his heart, he felt sure that he had also given her Maria.

"I sent her back to her mother," Flavius answered at length. "There was no way that I could allow them to stay together."

"And the child?" Syllus pressed.

"Who knows? She probably aborted the child. In that profession, they have their ways of dealing with such matters."

But an inner voice gnawed at him as if he knew that somewhere his grandchild lived.

* * *

The next day brought them to the lake. Syllus was driving the horses as they first saw the water below Tiberias and the city's Roman villas, Roman streets, and so many citizens in Roman dress. It made them all feel at home again. It looked much like any place in Tuscany.

"It's so delightful to have such a civilised Roman community on the lake now," Copernia said. "It really makes life so much easier than when we first built our villa above Taricheae."

"And hasn't Tiberias grown," Portia agreed. "In many ways, I wish we still had our villa here. It was such a peaceful place."

Syllus turned to Flavius who sat beside him on the driver's bench.

"It's funny," he said. "You know what we discussed last night?"

"About my son?"

"Yes...Flavius. I had a similar experience here in Tiberias with my son. Antonias wanted to write poetry and start a school for Roman boys here. That wasn't exactly the life that I had in mind for him, but you know how it is, the young never seem to quite follow the path that we plan for them."

Flavius raised an eyebrow, feeling a certain pride—even one-upmanship. His son was now following exactly the path that he and Copernia had hoped for him—now aide to the Judean prefect—and one day he could even be the governor of Syria, just as they had dreamed. But, he nodded in polite agreement as Syllus continued:

"Well, while we were away, he started his school all right, but he also brought two Hebrew girls into my house. One of them had a child. His name was Marcus, if I remember correctly. The boy seemed very fond of my son, but there was no way we could allow those Hebrew women to stay when we returned. I later heard that they were from one of the brothels here! They probably still work the brothels." Syllus chuckled, "Mind you," he said poking Flavius in the ribs, "that's not something that I would know."

Portia gave her husband a haughty look of disapproval.

"What did Antonias do?" Flavius asked.

"He accepted our decisions and went back to Athens. He runs a school there now. He may return here one day. He writes that he misses the peace of the lake, but I think it is these attractive Hebrew women that he misses more."

Syllus pulled on the horses. They were well into the streets of Tiberias now and he needed to concentrate on driving the wagon. Traffic had increased in Tiberias during the past decade. There were chariots, carts, donkeys, horses, and numerous pedestrians, all vying for space in the streets. Skillfully, Syllus maneuvered the wagon through this throng. He turned his horses into a less congested street that ran out to the vineyards and villas to the north. The square façade of his old villa came into view.

"It looks just the same," Portia commented as they slowly passed the estate. "Do you think Dracchus might still be there?"

"Who knows?" Syllus replied. "Properties change hands fast these days." He whipped the horses on. "It's not much further to Taricheae."

They drove down to the new road north linking Tiberias and Magdala. In no time, they arrived at the Flavian villa. It looked well kempt, and Demetrius was there with Leah to greet them.

"I'm delighted to see you looking so well," Flavius noted. "Linus had told us how sick you had been."

"It was like a miracle," Leah said. "All of a sudden one day he came out of his fever. Then, a healing prophet from Capernaum visited him with Master Linus. He was cured. But all that was some time ago, now."

Chapter Ten

Jew and Gentile, rich man, poor man

Refreshed from their retreat at Gennesaret, Joshua and his close followers moved back down the Jordan valley with the purpose of making a pilgrimage to Jerusalem for the Passover. The spring weather was warm in the lush valley. Along the way, wandering nomads joined them and told them of Barabbas' arrest and how they had themselves escaped the wrath of Roman revenge. Judas Iscariot befriended the nomads, curious to know more about the story of Barabbas and how most safely to move Joshua's group through this dangerous terrain. He was after all, responsible for Joshua's entourage—the steward of the group. Judas, still a zealot at heart, sympathized greatly with what they told him of Barabbas' hopes. Cephas, on hearing of Judas' leanings, and hearing the nomads himself, was disturbed.

"These men could put us in danger," he expressed to the Master. "Judas now talks freely with them like a rebel. I fear for your safety, Master—our safety."

After warning Judas Iscariot, Joshua called them all together addressing the nomads along with them.

"You give to Caesar what is duly his," he advised. "We do not make the laws and if the Romans did not rule this land, someone else would make the laws, not us. Has it not always been that way? Besides, when did ordinary humble people like us make the laws—even in the time of King David or under the Hasmoneans? Some things we just have to accept. You give to the Romans what they ask, but you give to God what they can not give. You give your whole selves to God. You surrender your spirits to God."

"So, was it right for the Romans to seize Barabbas?" Iscariot shouted.

"I didn't say that, Judas. I do not know enough about this Barabbas. It seems that he was one of Jon's supporters and that he campaigned against the salt tax. Has the salt tax really affected us very much?"

He plucked a pomegranate, took a bite, spat out the pips.

"Did it require salt for me to eat? The salt tax affects rich men more than poor men. You should know, Judas, you're our provision master."

"We needed salt to pickle our fish," Iscariot retorted.

"But, are we pickling fish now? Rich merchants now take care of that. Didn't we sell our fish direct to the picklers in Capernaum when we were there last? They paid for the salt, and in turn they were well paid by the Romans."

"The tax is a symbol of our oppression!" Judas exclaimed.

"Exactly, Judas! The salt tax has become a rallying point for political emotions. It is not in itself an evil thing. In God's kingdom there are no politics and no causes. Such action can only destroy the chance of us establishing the kingdom! Who needs salt! We are the salt of the earth! We establish His ways by our example and not by kicking down the temporary authorities. Caesar is our temporary overlord, but he does not control our spirit. God creates our spirit, so let the spark of God that is in you dictate who you are."

Judas scowled. He felt that Joshua had put him down in front of the others, and seeing that woman, Maria, close to Joshua, smiling at him as if in triumph, he muttered and walked away.

Maria sensed the bitterness in Judas. *Maybe he hates me because of my son,* she thought. *Marcus is a Roman.* She looked at Joshua as the others started to discuss the Master's observations.

"Marcus is a Roman," she repeated softly to Joshua. "Maybe that's why Judas hates me."

"So are you," Joshua replied. "You and Marcus both carry Roman blood. Do I condemn you? No, certainly not—nor should Judas Iscariot. Many Romans, as you know, have come to me seeking healing and comfort. Are they any different from us? We are all spirit. All of us are possessed of Divine love—Judas, too, Maria."

Maria was a little taken back by Joshua's authority. She realized that he was supporting her in his argument, but still somehow, he seemed detatched.

Cephas and Jonas had only sat in on the end of Joshua's remarks to Judas Iscariot. They still had not grasped the essential truth of the Master's teaching.

"Is it no advantage to be a Jew, then?" Cephas asked. "Is the kingdom for the Gentiles also?"

"Cephas, we are Jews," Joshua said. "Every one of us in this group has been born a Jew. We will always be Jews. We should use that privilege wisely. The spark of God within us does not make us Jews—only our birthright does. If I had been born Roman, I would still have used the power of God to heal. My message of establishing God's kingdom through anyone expressing their Divine love would still have been given. It helps that I am a Jew. It helps that we are all Jews because we already know God. The Romans have to learn about God before they can allow His spirit to grow within them. Some will, however, and some that I have met have exhibited great faith. Do you remember the Roman from the villa in Magdala?"

"The Roman whose servant was sick with a fever?" Cephas recalled.

"Yes! Do you remember how he sought me out in Capernaum just on faith that I could heal his servant?"

Maria perked up and listened intently. *I think he means Linus or his father?* She thought.

"That man," Joshua continued, "will walk in God's kingdom as assuredly as will all of us. In some ways, it is harder for us Jews who are tied to our Law than it is for Gentiles. They can allow the spirit to be kindled within them without the guilt feelings that surround us when we break with our traditions."

"What was that Roman's name?" Maria asked, seeking confirmation as her whole being tingled in retrospective fear and fascination.

"Maria, there have been so many. How can I remember all their names?" Joshua replied. "He lived in a villa above your village. He seemed to be quite a wealthy man. I had known that villa when enslaved after the Great Rebellion. As you know, I worked on rebuilding there after it was burned."

Maria did not ask for any more information, but stored Joshua's comments in her heart. She was sure that this man must have been Linus or his father. *I must ask him when we get a private moment,* she thought. Since leaving the lakeside retreat at Gennesaret, it had been hard to find such private moments.

* * *

The group moved on to Jericho, then up the steep and rugged road that led to Bethany. Joshua wanted them to visit with Lazarus and their many friends in the tanners' village again, before he took them to Jerusalem where they could base themselves at James and Rachel's house for the Passover. *Mother will be there, too, with Jonah, at least that is what they indicated in Nazareth,* he mused. He was looking forward to finally seeing his family again. *Rachel's little girl will be growing up by now. They named her after Joanna.* The thought brought a lump to his throat as it always did. *How different my life with Joanna might have been, but it was not my destiny,* he mused.

His sandals shuffled the dust as he leaned heavily on his staff and plodded on up the rocky road with his growing band of disciples. Word had spread as they passed through Jericho that the miracle worker from Galilee was back.

* * *

The knowledge that Joshua and his entourage were approaching reached Bethany well ahead of their arrival. Even before Joshua got there, the sick and the injured had descended on the village in hope of cures, some even from Jerusalem.

Lazarus and Mary prepared for Joshua's arrival. Martha busied herself with extra baking. They expected Joshua and his closest associates to stay for a while. Naturally, Joshua would stay with them as in the past. Lazarus made sure that at least a dozen straw pallets were also available for the others in an adjacent shed at the tannery.

At length, they arrived.

Lazarus embraced Joshua.

"It's so good to see you," he said. "We've all missed you."

"Is it all right for us to stay a few days?" Joshua asked, knowing well that Lazarus would already have arranged for that.

"Stay as long as you like. Our home is your home. Why don't you stay for Passover?"

"I can't," Joshua replied. "I need to spend Passover with Rachel and James, and I believe my mother and my brother Jonah are there now, too. I need to see them. Hopefully, after Passover we can return here for a while. After all, Bethany has become our Judean home. You are always so good to us here."

They embraced again.

"And you to us," Lazarus added.

* * *

It was difficult, however, for Joshua to spend much time with Lazarus. Joshua's fame as the Bethany miracle worker had not diminished. Within hours, the village was overflowing with those seeking his help, along with the curious and the critics. Joshua was busy healing.

Among those who came forward was a wealthy man from Jerusalem—a merchant with a trading empire encompassing goods from as far away as Britannia in the west and India in the east. His name was Joseph, and originally he had come from a small town north of Jerusalem called Arimathea. He was a member of the Sanhedrin Council and well respected at the Temple. Joshua noted his fine clothes—as fine as any Roman's. At first, Joshua was a little wary of him. He feared he might be one of those Pharisee spies that had been such a bother the last time they were in Bethany.

"What can I do for you?" he asked the man.

Cephas watched Joseph suspiciously as Joshua awaited the perceived wealthy man's reply.

"I come from the Sanhedrin. I've come to seek this Kingdom of God before I die," Joseph of Arimathea answered.

"But you're not old enough to die," Joshua observed, noting that the man was only about his own age.

"I look fit enough, sir," the man agreed, "but, inside, I am riddled with worms. I do not expect to live much longer. The physicians in Jerusalem expect me to die in the near future. I observed you when you were here before, but I was afraid to come forward. I believe you to be a holy man of God. I have seen many cured by your laying on of hands. What have I to lose. If you are the prophet of the end time, or the Messiah, as some have said, bring me into the Kingdom of God of which you speak… before I die. I do not ask to be cured, for if God has weakened my body, so be it. Just show me the way to the kingdom."

Joshua was astounded. He had not expected to hear such a speech. He embraced Joseph and held him for a long time, tears of emotion gathering in his eyes. *This is what I have lived for,* he thought. *This man has faith in me and in the kingdom.* He felt a great warmth for the man. Then, releasing his hold, he placed his hands on Joseph's temples and silently prayed. As he very gently released the pressure from his fingers, he then spoke to Joseph:

"You have remarkable faith. I know that many of your associates are afraid of what I teach, but my message is not from me, but from the God that dwells within me. He dwells within you, too, Joseph."

Joseph stared at Joshua and said nothing.

A Pharisee who had accompanied Joseph to Bethany shouted out:

"Joseph! That's blasphemy! Does this man believe he is above the Law?—Above the High Priests?"

"Saul, we are not debating the Law," Joseph replied, without diverting his eyes from Joshua's hypnotic face. "I have come here to be healed. I have not come like you, to be this man's critic. He is obviously a force for good. Light shines from him."

"I do not need to hear more," Saul remarked, and the Pharisee turned away and disappeared into the crowd.

"The Kingdom of God is found in that indwelling spirit, Joseph," Joshua continued calmly. "You do not have to seek God only as the Pharisees instruct, for you are of the essence of God. But, the Pharisaic disciplines can assist you in finding that still small voice within yourself that is the key to the kingdom. However, you must open your heart and allow the light and sound of God to enter in—vibrate through you—cleanse and heal you. I know that you, with your faith, Joseph…you will respond, and your body will be filled with the Holy Spirit. God's spirit of life is also the great healing power within. When I lay my hands upon you, I am only passing on the power of the Holy Spirit. If you believe that the life force of God lies within you, not only will you find the kingdom, but also, your internal bodily weakness can be healed. You do not need to die, Joseph. From this day on you will live in the spirit. Life in the spirit is life in the kingdom, both now, here, and forever."

Joseph stood back from Joshua and bumped into Marcus, who was watching with a youth's curiosity. He stepped on the boy's foot. The man had big feet and they were well shod compared to Marcus' simple thong sandals. Marcus squealed. Maria pulled her son back as Joseph turned and apologized for his clumsiness.

Maria smiled at the rich man.

Joseph of Arimathea smiled back at her, and then quietly walked away.

A hush came over the crowd.

"Who was he?" Janus asked.

"A member of the Sanhedrin at the Temple," Joshua answered.

"I think he was a spy," Jonas commented. "You need to be more careful to whom you speak, Master."

"Yes, be careful, Master," Cephas repeated. "You must be very careful what you say to the Pharisees of the city. You heard what his friend just said."

"Saul," Judas Iscariot said to himself.

Joshua answered them:

"It is harder for a rich man to enter the Kingdom of God than it is for a camel to squeeze through the eye of a weaver's shuttle. This man has succeeded where many have failed."

He looked at the ground, and then, in a softer voice, concluded:

"He is one of us."

Marcus looked up at his mother.

"That man had heavy boots," he grumbled.

Maria laughed.

There was no time for Joshua to continue a philosophical discussion on his teaching. There were many others crying out to be healed, yearning for his touch in hope of a cure. The Bethany miracle worker returned to his arduous but heartfelt task.

Chapter Eleven

Triumphal Entry

Lazarus wanted to do something special before Joshua left to celebrate the Passover with his own family in Jerusalem. Azariah, a friend of his from neighboring Bethphage, had tried to sell Lazarus a donkey. The beast was now nearly two-year's old, but somehow Lazarus had never felt he could quite pay the price. Azariah was anxious to sell the donkey and came to Bethany to try to conclude the deal. Had Joshua not been visiting at the time, Lazarus would probably not have agreed to the purchase, but he decided he would make this ass his gift to Joshua. He concluded the deal while Joshua was ministering to the crowds.

Azariah touched his forehead in salutation as he took the prescribed number of coins from Lazarus.

"Shalom! Many thanks to you," he said, quite surprised that he had finally talked Lazarus into the deal.

"When can I collect the donkey?" Lazarus asked.

"Anytime you choose, Lazarus. You will find the ass usually tied up outside my house. You can send someone to Bethphage to collect the beast whenever you like."

"I'll send someone tomorrow."

The deal concluded, Azariah left.

When Joshua came home that evening, Lazarus broke the news to him.

"We've found a donkey for you, Joshua," he said excitedly. "We want to give the beast to you as a gift."

"What!" Joshua replied, overwhelmed by his simple friend's generosity.

"Lazarus is serious," Martha added in support. "The donkey's nearly two-year's old. You can collect it tomorrow from Bethphage. It will make your traveling so much easier. You deserve it."

* * *

Mary kept quiet. She had made her own plans. She had heard about Maria of Magdala's anointing of Joshua with the ointment from the jar of the blind man. She did not want to be outdone by this intruder into Joshua's intimate group. She had spent almost all that she owned on a jar of scented nard herself. Just before their evening meal, while Joshua was at the well, Mary presented her gift. She rubbed the ointment on his weary feet massaging it into the roughness of his flesh.

"That feels so good," Joshua admitted.

"Nothing is too good for you, my dear sweet Joshua," Mary said, kneeling before him and looking longingly into his eyes.

The fragrance of the nard drifted up from Joshua's feet.

"You see, Maria is not the only one who can annoint you," she said softly.

Joshua looked around.

His chosen disciples, including Judas Iscariot, were busy washing their own feet.

Maria was not in the vicinity.

"Thank you," Joshua acknowledged.

Then, Maria appeared, carrying an empty water jar. She could smell the sweet odor.

Mary saw her coming and her helpless passion showed great jealousy emanating from her knotted stomach.

"She's not the only one who loves you," she repeated. "I love you. I love you with all my heart. Stay with us here, Joshua. Don't go to Jerusalem. Let me be the one to take care of you."

She pressed her hands on the flesh of his feet and began to weep.

"Mary," Joshua whispered. "I thank you for your kindness and love, but I must do what I have to do. I can't stay here with you. I can't stay here with anyone. You must try to understand. However much you may admire the work I do, I have never made any promises to you or to anyone, not even Maria."

He took her face between his hands and looked at her.

"I can't give you more, Mary. All I can give you is the love of God."

Mary felt the pang of shame.

"I'm so sorry," she said as she wiped her eyes, causing them to sting from residue of the precious oitment. "Please forgive me."

"There is nothing to forgive, Mary," Joshua comforted her. "You are both very special people and the light of God shines from you. Do not shine that light just on me but give your light to all whom you meet."

Maria filled her jar from the well, casting a suspicious eye in their direction. Marcus joined her.

"Can I help you carry it?" he asked.

"Not this time. It will be easier for me to carry it on my head," Maria said.

Mary smiled awkwardly, then slipped away.

"Women! Now Mary! That sister of Lazarus! What did she do that for?" Judas asked, as the men finished their ablutions.

* * *

Maria started to ask Joshua what had been going on, but she realized the time was not right and hoisting up the water jar, she took Marcus with her free hand and left for the camp.

"Many who love me shall come to hate me," Joshua replied to Iscariot. "The boundaries of love and hate are very close."

"Women!" Judas repeated.

Then, he looked back at Joshua.

"Watch these women, Master, they are making you soft."

He spat on the ground and stood up.

"The one use they do have is to cook for us. Now, if all women could be like Martha, and not emotional like her sister or your friend Maria, we would all live together better. Let's hope there is something good in the pot."

"Judas," the Master said quietly, "there is no bitterness in the love of God."

"So be it," was all Judas Iscariot replied.

* * *

The following day, Joshua sent Philip and Bartholomew to Bethphage to collect the donkey from Azariah. When they returned with the beast, Joshua had to admit that it pleased him. The animal looked as if it had been well fed and lacked the sores that beasts of burden tend to gather. Five days before the Passover, Joshua was ready to move on to Jerusalem.

By this time, a large number of the Jerusalem poor, who were seeking the help of the miracle man, had gathered around Bethany. Some were rejoicing in their healing and that of their friends, others still hoped for a chance to attract attention for a cure. The whole, motley bunch of men and women gathered to follow Joshua and his entourage along the road to Jerusalem.

Lazarus helped Joshua onto the donkey. Mary had donated a brightly colored cloth to cover the donkey's back. Joshua was wearing a fresh white robe that Martha had washed the day before. When he straddled the donkey, the contrast made an impressive sight.

"Shalom!" Joshua shouted to those gathered at Lazarus' house. "Have a wonderful Passover. We'll be back soon."

Mary stood with Martha and their brother, waving goodbye to the Master.

Joshua nudged the donkey as Philip pulled on the lead. It was a brilliant sunny day, and they began the journey through Bethphage and up the Kidron valley. As they came nearer to Jerusalem, more crowds came out to greet them. The people treated Joshua like a hero, some in adulation and some still desperate to just touch him in hope of a cure. Others were simply curious, wondering what the throng was all about and joined in the commotion just for the fun of it. As they drew closer to the city, they passed the lush area of Gethsemane. There, some in the crowd started to cut down palm fronds and wave them in front of Joshua as he rode the donkey. Others followed and they began to chant:

"Blessed is the miracle worker of Bethany! Hosanna in the highest! Blessed is he who comes in the name of the Lord! Hosanna in the highest!"

Judas Iscariot frowned at the folly. *What has happened to the Master—*

the friend of the fishermen. Now, does he think he is a king? He thinks he is God. This is blasphemy.

* * *

The sounds drifted up from the valley catching the attention of those within Jerusalem. Many in the Temple's Court of the Gentiles ran to the western wall to look out from Herod's portico on to the scene below. Roman guards at Antonia's Tower saw the people running, and raised concern over the commotion. As the crowd came nearer and approached the North Gate, they sounded hysterical.

In no time, the anxious centurion on duty at the tower dispatched his men to the gate.

"Don't take action unless it is necessary," he briefed them. "Just show our presence. We can't take any chances this time of the year. Their Passover—some rebel celebration of how they escaped from the Pharoahs of Egypt—is always a dangerous time. If we show ourselves, they will subside. They're afraid of us."

The Roman soldiers lined the street ready to quell any possible riot. At length, the noisy procession arrived. As it passed, it seemed to be joyous—not dangerous. The soldiers witnessed people waving palm fronds and laying them in the street ahead of a moderately well-dressed man on a donkey. They were shouting and singing and it was impossible to make out what they were saying. However, they did catch the repeated phrase:

"Hosanna! Hosanna in the highest!"

Peacefully, they allowed the noisy procession through, and the following crowd became absorbed in the bustle of the city.

The soldiers returned to Antonia's Tower.

* * *

Joshua led the crowd into the Temple. There, in the vast Court of the Gentiles, he sat them down, many of them still holding palm fronds. Dismounting from the donkey, the Master began to teach them about himself. He was very aware that many who had flattered him on the road to Jerusalem had only followed him as a miracle worker. His own interpretation of his role now far exceeded the simple powers of faith healing that he had practiced so successfully.

"This building is a very wonderful and spiritual place," the Master acknowledged, "but I am telling you that if it were to be destroyed tomorrow, we would be just as close to God as we are now. This building was destroyed—twice raised to the ground—but God did not disband His people. This place is only an outer symbol of the purity of the God that dwells within us all. We should make our sacrifices here, which I trust you will do this Passover. I will. It has always been my practice to make the required sacrifices whenever I come to Jerusalem and visit this sacred place. The sacrifice is a reminder to us that it is our duty to purify ourselves so that our own bodies can be temples—temples of the Holy Spirit. Outwardly, we make sacrifices to God at the altars here, but inwardly we must make sacrifices in our daily lives to allow space for God to dwell within us. We are of the essence of God. We are spirit. Spirit can only be manifested within us if our outward bodies have been cleansed through forgiveness, prayer and meditation, and through all the personal sacrifices that we must make for these disciplines to be effective."

Many, passing through the Temple court, noticed the crowd around Joshua. Some sat down with them. Joshua paused to give them time. He noted that a few of the newcomers looked like pious Pharisees who might criticize what he had to say. *So be it,* he thought. Then, he recognized one of them: *Surely that is Saul,* he concluded, *the man who came to Bethany with Joseph from Arimathea. He called me a blasphemer then—what will he call me now?* A nervous twitch cautioned him as he saw more of them moving in their direction.

While he waited for them to settle down, he instructed Cephas, Jonas, and Janus to take the donkey, find James and Rachel's house on Mount Zion and warn them that he would join them for Passover week.

"Tether the donkey there," he instructed, "so I will remember which house it is."

Obediently, his inner three disciples left. Maria and Marcus moved closer to Joshua where they had been seated.

When it seemed appropriate, Joshua continued:

"I am the way, the truth, and the life," he said dramatically.

There was a potent buzz among the crowd at these words.

"In me, you have seen the Father."

Philip, who sat closest to Joshua, spoke out clearly:

"Master. Show us the Father and we shall be satisfied."

"Have I been with you this long and still you don't know who I am, Philip?" he answered, then continued:

"He who has seen me has seen the Father, and all of you can see the Father in each other."

He looked at Philip.

"How can you say, 'Show us the Father'? Do you not believe that I am in the Father and the Father is in me as he is in all of you? We are all sons of God. I do not teach you these things on my own authority, but it is the Father, the indwelling spirit of God that is within me, that speaks these things. Are you like these others here, who believe in me only because of my miraculous healing powers?"

Philip could not look the Master in the eye. He looked at the ground shamefully. The Master had changed. It seemed to them all that he was losing some of his patience with them. These days he said such strange things.

Having admonished Philip, Joshua turned his attention back to the growing assembly of curious onlookers.

"Truly, I'm telling you that those of you who have the courage to believe in me as spirit will be able to perform the same miraculous healings and cures that I do. Possibly, some of you may be able to perform even greater works where I have failed. When I am not with you, remember what I am now saying to you. When you are required to test the strength of the spirit within you, remember me, and remember that the light of God is that strength within me. You, too, can be torches of God."

A voice shouted out:

"Does this man claim to be God?"

Joshua saw that it was Saul, the Pharisee, who was now seated beside Judas Iscariot.

* * *

Judas tugged at Saul and whispered:

"He makes extraordinary claims at times, sir. I'm beginning to think he is becoming obsessed with his power. He has great healing gifts, that's true, but this talk of being a son of God annoys me. He is not perfect, no different from the rest of us. He has his weaknesses and strengths."

"What weaknesses?" Saul asked.

"That woman close to him for one," Judas replied. "She was a sinner, a whore and an adulteress, and yet he has taken her for his own."

As Judas Iscariot and the Pharisee whispered together, Joshua continued his teaching:

"If you love me you will keep my commandments and I will see that my Father kindles the Holy Spirit within you. Remember that the fulfillment of the Law and the Prophets is in this commandment: 'Love the Lord God with all your hearts and love your neighbor as yourself.'"

Joshua looked around again with a definite apprehension and uncertainty in his eyes that his disciples had rarely seen before. His words were confident, but his physical appearance expressed his concern.

"If I am taken from you," he continued, "do not be afraid."

Maria looked up at him with fearful eyes.

"Know that I am in the Father and that you will also all be in me, as I will be in you. Those of you who keep my commandments and love me, will be loved by God, the Father. I will love you, even if I am taken from you, and I will be manifest in you, just as you, too, are sons of the Father."

Saul nudged Judas Iscariot:

"He claims that the commandments are his!" the Pharisee exclaimed.

"Like I said, he claims many things," Judas replied.

"But the commandments were given to us by Moses! They are God's own Law!" Saul stated. "This talk is blasphemy!"

Judas felt exhilerated by the Pharisee's response. *It is time that someone challenged the Master,* he thought. *It is time for the Master to stop playing at being God and to focus on being the rallying point for our people. Can't he use his incredible persuasive powers to support the cause against our oppressors, the Romans and the Herodians, or even against the sanctamonious Temple hierarchy? Why does he now have to make these absurd claims and put us all in danger with his blasphemy?*

Saul read Judas' thoughts and stood up, pointing at Joshua.

"You speak blasphemy!" he shouted.

Then, he walked through the crowd shouting:

"This man has the devil within him. Don't listen to him!"

Many in the crowd watched the Pharisee as he disappeared into the throng of Passover pilgrims shaking his head.

Judas Iscariot watched, too, not quite knowing whom he should trust—the Master, or this Pharisee, who had introduced himself to him as Saul of Tarsus. Judas was confused.

Some in the crowd, who had only stopped in curiosity, heeded the Pharisee's advice and left.

Bartholomew then asked Joshua how they would know that God's spirit was in them.

"If a man loves me and lives by my Father's word as I speak it, as you do, Bartholomew, then, whether I'm here or not, my Father will also love him. Together, we will dwell within him, igniting his soul with the light of the Holy Spirit. Listen for the sound of God, Bartholomew, you can hear it within the depths of your heart. It binds all of us together forever in spiritual light and love. But it has no power unless you truly accept it and believe in it."

Joshua called Judas Iscariot to him.

"I must join my family in Mount Zion," he said. "Take the others back into the valley to camp with the pilgrims and meet me here tomorrow morning."

"In this court?"

"Yes, in this same place."

Judas started to walk away.

Then, the Master beckoned to Maria and Marcus:

"You can come with me."

Judas looked back, scowled, and spat on the ground.

* * *

Marcus was the first to notice the donkey with its brightly colored saddlecloth. He saw it tethered to a post at the bottom of a flight of yellow stone steps leading up to a house in one of Mount Zion's small squares.

"That's Joshua's donkey!" he shouted. "Is that where we're going?"

"I think so," Maria replied.

"Yes, Cephas must have found the house all right," Joshua commented with a grateful smile.

"So, this is your brother's house?" Maria said.

"Yes, this is the place," he answered, recalling the steep flight of steps.

Joshua patted his donkey on the head and rubbed the beast's long ears affectionately.

He started up the steps:

"James! Are you home? It's Joshua!" he called out.

His brother Jonah appeared at the top of the steps.

"Come on up, Joshua. Your friends from Galilee are here."

"Jonah!" Joshua exclaimed. "You are here! Does that mean Mother is here, too?"

"Yes! Your mother is inside with Rachel. Remember...Joshua..." Jonah answered with a grin, "you instructed me to take care of her."

Rachel was soon at the top of the steps, with Cephas peering out from behind them in a happy mood.

Joshua took Marcus' hand and introduced him.

"This is Marcus," he said, looking down at the boy with an affectionate smile, "and his mother, Maria."

He pushed Marcus forward and quietly told him to go in. Joshua took Maria's hand and they all went into the house.

Inside, Jonah embraced Joshua.

"James isn't home yet," he said. "He's at a meeting of the Sanhedrin."

Jonah then looked at Maria. A quizzical sense of recognition came across his face.

"Shalom!" he said. "Welcome to our house."

Joshua saw Janus and Jonas very comfortably sprawled on a low couch, holding goblets of wine.

"You look like Romans!" he teased.

They all laughed.

Joshua then saw his mother. She was at a weaving frame where she was working intently in the dim light of one of the windows set high up in the wall of the room. Her eyes now followed every move that they were making. She completely lost concentration on her work. Tears of emotion were overwhelming her. She had really given up any hope of ever seeing Joshua again.

"Mother!" he cried out joyfully as he went over to her. "I knew you might be here and when I saw Jonah...I was sure."

Beaming, Miriam stood up and joyfully stepped right into Joshua's embrace. They remained holding each other for some time.

Rachel poured out another goblet and offered the wine to Joshua.

"Mother," Joshua said as he took the goblet, "I know you've already met my closest friends, Cephas, Janus, and Jonas, but now I want you to meet Maria and her son Marcus."

"Maria," Miriam repeated softly. "Is she your new wife?"

"No, Mother. Maria is a very special, loving, friend."

Miriam greeted Maria, but not without just a little maternal skepticism as if she might be reflecting on Rachel's younger sister—Joshua's deceased wife—Joanna.

"She is very lovely," she whispered quietly when Maria turned back to her son, "but..."

"Mother, you mustn't always think in terms of family. Maria has a soul that is filled with the love of God. She is my spiritual partner. Just as you were my spiritual inspiration when I was a child, so Maria now radiates that Divine love that is the essence of our being. I have brought her into my confidence because I believe, unlike most men in our world today, that God created us equal, male and female. Often the Divine love radiates from a woman more easily than from a man. It always shone from your heart, Mother, just as it shines from Maria."

Miriam was quiet for a moment. Then, looking up at Joshua from a face that was beginning to show the wrinkles of her middle age, she asked:

"Who is her boy?"

"Marcus, Mother," Joshua said nonchalantly, reading his mother's simple mind. "Marcus is Maria's son. He had a Roman father, which is why he has a Roman name."

"Be careful, Joshua," was all Miriam said.

She hesitated, searching within herself deeply. Then, speaking slowly, continued:

"I have had many strange dreams recently. You have been so often in them. Keep away from the Romans, Joshua. I have seen the Romans beat you and tie you up. I have seen you hanging on one of their wooden crosses of death. I'm afraid for you. I don't know what you've done, but I instinctively feel you are in danger."

Joshua pulled his mother close to him once more.

"I have only been about my Father's business," he said. "Whatever will be, will be."

He quaffed on his wine.

Rachel came out from the back of the house, holding her young daughter, Joanna, by the hand.

"Joshua, remember Joanna, the baby we named after your Joanna?"

"Of course, my goodness, hasn't she grown!"

Joshua caught Maria's eye. Maria stepped closer to him, feeling his emotions. She remembered so well that tender moment when Joshua had shown her Joanna's grave—when he had picked cornflowers and placed them there.

Little Joanna was approximately two years younger than Marcus. She looked more like her namesake than her mother. She had the fresh friendliness of Joshua's Joanna and the lengthening curly hair of a child. She latched on to Marcus and took him back to her secret world away from the grown-ups.

After Rachel had fed them sweat meats and it was becoming dark outside, James arrived.

"Joshua!" he shouted. "My goodness! We are blessed! Joshua!"

Joshua greeted his old mentor.

"Shalom, brother! Blessed be God forever! I hope you don't mind, but I was in Bethany and I felt compelled to come on in to Jerusalem to see you all again. Now, hopefully, we can stay for Passover."

They embraced.

"Of course! It's wonderful to see you!" James reassured him. "Has Rachel taken good care of you here? Now, who are the rest of your friends?"

The round of introductions started again. Jonah lit the oil lamps for the evening and Rachel and Miriam went back to make them supper.

"There was quite a scene at the Sanhedrin today," James mentioned to Joshua as he got him aside. "One of the Pharisees, a foreigner named Saul, from Tarsus in Asia Minor, announced that there was a teacher in the Temple court today claiming to be God!"

James raised an eyebrow.

Joshua winced.

"What was their reaction, James?"

"Some laughed, but most took the man seriously," James explained.

"This man Saul is well respected in the Sanhedrin. He was on the Council long before I was, and because he is a Roman citizen, he is the High Priest's special envoy when it comes to negotiating matters with the Roman prefect. There is more concern these days over claims like this. There have been many false messiahs."

Pausing, James looked at Joshua intently.

"Where do you stand on these matters?" he asked.

This was a very pointed question and Joshua knew it. He felt very uncomfortable. Joshua's hesitation confirmed James' suspicions.

"Be careful, Joshua," James said. "It was you, wasn't it? They will condemn you on charges of blasphemy. You really don't have to go that far. Watch this man Saul. He could do you harm."

"Whatever is God's will shall be," Joshua replied. "Please, James, I ask you to keep silent. We need to prepare for the Passover. Before the sacrifice of the paschal lamb I will make the necessary sacrifices at the Temple."

They returned to join the others.

CHAPTER TWELVE

Afternoon in the Garden

The following day, Joshua met with his 'chosen ones' in the Temple as he had planned. He spent the morning teaching them, and this time, taking heed of James' warning, avoided too many direct references to his belief that he was a Divine son of God. He remembered the teachings of Zadok. The leader of that Essenic type of sect looked to the end time, but his teachings showed a gentler more spiritual approach. He wondered if Zadok was still in Jerusalem. He remembered how the prophet had taught his followers much about the sound and light of God and the necessity for men to open their hearts inwardly so that the light of God could be manifested through them outwardly. It was a simple concept, but Joshua thought that maybe he could disguise some of his own, seemingly more blasphemous statements, within this concept.

"Think of me as the light of the world," he suggested. "This light can not live forever, except as soul. Walk toward the light before darkness overtakes you! In the darkness, you will not know where you are going. If you walk in the light now, and believe in the Divine radiance of that light, then the darkness can never stop you becoming sons of light. As sons of light you will have the same powers that God has given to me, or possibly greater. You will continue to be united with me in spirit. The light that you will manifest through your Divine love will be my light, and our light will be God's light. You will not always need me, and should

I be taken away from you there is nothing that you should fear. For we shall always be united in the light of God."

The statement was generally too philosophical to really register with his disciples, who had become increasingly impatient among themselves with his habit of talking to them in such riddles. But the reference to him being taken away from them had dramatic impact.

"Master!" cried Cephas. "What do you mean that you might be taken away from us?"

"Yes, Master," Jonas agreed. "Why do you say such things?"

Joshua's voice dropped.

"Because we live in uncertain times," he replied. "There are some here in Jerusalem who do not like the work that we do, nor know God as we know Him!"

He scanned their eyes.

"You have seen them. Often they came out to Bethany to watch us."

"But what harm have we ever done?" young Matthew asked fearfully, sensing the urgency in what Joshua was saying.

"None," Joshua replied. "We've done nothing wrong other than to attract large crowds. The authorities don't like large crowds. Such crowds can be the breeding ground for rebellion and unlawful behavior."

"But, when have we ever behaved in such a way?" Matthew pressed.

"We haven't, but we have to be careful."

Maria felt a deep pain within her. She sensed Joshua's uncertainty about his future, and she personally feared the possible truth in what he was saying. Joshua had changed her life, but more than that, he had become her confidant and friend. Although the climatic fulfillment of their physical union, for which she so longed, was not yet achieved, their spiritual union was complete. When they found those rare moments to touch, it was in exactly that aura of light to which he had referred—the aura she had witnessed, unknown to the others, on Mount Tabor—the aura, which she now saw around him almost all the time. With him, she felt in the presence of God. *How can this be taken from me?* she thought. *I've walked into his light; I want to bathe in it forever.* But, she kept her feelings to herself, silently listening to the others as they bothered Joshua with their questions.

As the sun rose overhead heralding midday, Joshua stopped teaching. He blessed them and announced his Passover program.

"Tomorrow, we will make our Passover sacrifices. Meet again here about the same time. Judas Iscariot, come back with us to my brother's house. I would like you to check with Rachel on our needs for the Passover. We will all eat the Passover together with my family."

Judas obeyed, and while the others dispersed, he returned with Joshua, Maria, and Marcus to James' house.

* * *

Later, Maria left the city with Joshua. Marcus stayed behind with Miriam, Rachel, and Joanna. Marcus was happy to have someone about his own age that he could impress with his stories of all that he had seen when traveling the countryside with Joshua and his followers. He told his stories to Rachel's daughter with great drama, even stories about his time in Tiberias.

Joshua took Maria back to Gethsemane—that lush area overlooking the far side of the Kidron valley. It had been a favorite place of peace and meditation for him when he had first come to Jerusalem with Jon. It was an area in a slight hollow at the foot of the Mount of Olives that gathered what little moisture there was in a shallow stream, babbling with the lifeforce of spring, tumbling over rocks before running down to join the Kidron. Here, there were date palms, fan palms, yuccas, and ferns. There were patches of lush grass in open glades between the oak and olive groves that provided areas of shade. Wildly beautiful, the vegetation provided a haven for songbirds, bountiful at Passover on their spring migration. The birds flew up from Africa over the desert wastes of Sinai and the Judean wilderness. This green oasis beside Jerusalem became a natural resting ground before they would sweep over Samaria, Galilee and Syria on their journey north to Asia Minor, Greece and Germania. Many a romantic man of the city had also rested here with his loved one, looking across the valley at the yellow stones and white marble façade of the Temple and the golden city beyond.

Joshua noted that there were still palm fronds lying on the ground from those that the crowd had cut two days before on his triumphal entry into the city.

"I love this place," he said, holding Maria close to him as they stood in the sunlight of one of those grassy glades. "Higher up, beyond the olive grove, you get an even better view of the Temple and the city, but it is prettier down here where it is so lush."

They held each other closely for some time.

Maria could feel the pressure of Joshua's embrace, and nestling her head against his shoulder was overcome with a sense of submission and inner peace.

Joshua also tried to hold on to the moment and savor it, but in Joshua's silence Maria sensed an apprehension, and could see in his gaze the uncertainty that she had noticed so much in recent days.

"Don't be afraid, Joshua," she said lovingly. "Let me soothe you and calm you. I know what you like best. Whatever is causing you to feel afraid, take this moment to relax and melt into my arms. Nobody can harm us here."

"The birds sound so lovely," Joshua said at length, releasing his hold and taking Maria's hands so that they could stand and just look into each other's eyes.

He knew she was right, that he wanted to share his ultimate love with her at least this once. The future was so uncertain. He wanted to be sure that she would understand, but he was so fearful that in this one final step he might undo all the spiritual trust that had grown between them.

As she looked into his eyes she caressed him.

"None of them can see us here," she whispered. "We can be ourselves. We can freely share our joy."

Joshua's nervous gaze melted at Maria's words, and he put his arm around her waist and walked her down to a flat part of the glade, just above the tumbling waters of the spring stream. There, they lay together. As they soothed each other in gentle caresses of love, both their passions rose. There could be no turning back. Their union became complete in the secrecy of the glade. There was no mistaking the fulfillment of Maria's dream; they became wholly one. She felt the spark of God in their lovemaking. Joshua's Divine presence had never seemed so real or so close. In the warmth of the afternoon sun, they were transported into a Divine pleasure that rose above their anxious worries, taking them to a place of heavenly bliss. They shared with each other their ultimate joy.

As their ardor cooled in the aftermath of their passion, however, worries returned.

"I love you, Maria," Joshua whispered in her ear as he stroked her hair nervously. "I have longed to be with you ever since we washed each other's hair in Gennesar. In Bethany, I despaired that we could ever again have the peace to experience the love that we began to share then. Doesn't this place remind you a bit of Gennesar. It's a little lusher here—but the babbling brook?"

"Yes. At Gennesar I somehow knew we would eventually come together. I love you, too," she answered

Joshua sat up and looked across the valley, seeing those glimpses of the Temple and the city through the trees.

"I'm not sure we should ever have left Galilee," he said.

"Why, Joshua?"

"It's dangerous for me here. I realize that now."

He continued to stare ahead.

Maria rested her head on his shoulder again.

"Jerusalem is not the same," he said slowly.

His eyes moistened.

"Don't weep," Maria said, wiping away those first welling teardrops. "What makes you cry?"

She felt nervous. *Perhaps he regrets this,* she thought. *What if he leaves me now like so many other men? Was I too much for him? He is such a gentle man.* Momentary pain stabbed her heart: *What if I am pregnant now—will he stand by me?*

"It's not you, Maria," Joshua said at length, trying to smile. "I weep for Jerusalem. I used to love Jerusalem. The city was a source of much inspiration for me. There was a sense of excitement in the learning here, like Alexandria. There was a spiritual aura at the Temple. Like the Sadducees and Temple Pharisees, I used to feel a great pride in our traditions and institutions. It was a privilege and a joy for me to teach in the Temple courts. Jon was the rebel, not me."

He looked at her, kissing her lightly.

"I sense big changes coming to Jerusalem."

"In what way?" Maria asked, somewhat relieved that he had not expressed guilt over their recent passion.

"The Temple has lost its God-center, Maria. I used to feel the power of the Holy Spirit within the Temple courts. Now, I sense only commercialism and greed. Maybe it's just within me, but the Temple doesn't seem to belong to us any more. Perhaps it's the Roman presence, the great tower fortress that now looks into its sacred courts, but equally it has to be our High Priests and Sanhedrin leaders. They've made the Temple their own. They have made our holy place into their personal powerhouse."

Joshua looked right into Maria's eyes.

"They're jealous of me," he said. "That man Saul, I fear him. James warned me to be wary of him. The Pharisee spoke negatively about me in the Sanhedrin—accused me of blasphemy. He and others see how the people flock to me, because many have more confidence in my healing power than in sacrifices at the Temple. The authorities are afraid of the power of love, Maria. They can not see that God is love—light, sound, and love. They don't hear the still small voice within because of their own conceit."

He stopped and stared across at the city again.

"It's more than that," he continued slowly. "They are so afraid of the Romans. It seems that all Jerusalem is afraid of the Romans. The Sanhedrin Council is afraid of me because they think that every time I draw a crowd, the Romans will be suspicious that I'm inciting rebellion."

"You, Joshua!" Maria laughed. "You have never encouraged anyone to rebel against the Romans. You've healed Romans!"

"True, Maria, but how do they know that? But, that Saul, he does bother me. Did you see how he was gaining the confidence of Judas Iscariot? I don't feel I can trust Judas any more."

"Judas hates me," Maria interjected.

"I think he is afraid of you, Maria, not hates. He doesn't understand. None of them understand...except, maybe Cephas."

He turned and cupped her face in his hands.

"You understand better than any of them, better even than Cephas. You are the only one, Maria, who really understands the power of this inner Divine love."

Maria's stomach pulled as her body glowed to his words.

"I've changed, Maria. I can no longer put my faith in our old ways. Tomorrow, I will make my Passover sacrifice at the Temple, but it has somehow lost its meaning. I was looking forward to celebrating Passover with my family again—with James, Jonah, Rachel, and Mother."

"And Joanna," Maria added. "It's good for Marcus to be with a young child again. He really hasn't been with children since he was in Antonias' school."

"It will be good family time," Joshua agreed. "We Jews have always been very confident in our traditions and institutions, but I'm losing that confidence. You know, Maria, outwardly I'm a Jew, but inwardly I am no longer a Jew."

"What do you mean?"

"God didn't just choose us Jews to be His people. We are all God's people. All of us have the Divine spark of God within us...the Romans and Greeks as much as us Jews. I have seen how some Romans have opened their hearts to God and allowed their Divine love to show through. Some who have come to us have shown greater faith than righteous Pharisees."

Maria smiled.

"No, but they don't obey our Law," she said.

Joshua chuckled.

"Did the Law ever mean that much to you, Maria? The Law means little to the poor and downtrodden. I've never felt that your ignorance of the Law has ever held back that inner love that radiates from you. You're a spark of God like Lazarus—even Mary. The Divine light shines from the likes of you."

Maria blushed and looked away from him.

"So are you, Joshua. When we were together just a short while ago, I could feel the power of God flowing between us. It was a sacred union."

"And so it is," Joshua confirmed, squeezing her hand.

They sat in silence for a while as the evening light turned Jerusalem from white to gold. Then, staring at its beauty through the trees, Joshua said:

"Why can't the others understand that we all share the power of God. I have spent so much time trying to teach them the reality of their own Divinity. If they can see the Divine love in me, why can't they see it in themselves?"

"Perhaps it is because they only see your God-like powers in your healing hands," Maria answered with surprising authority. "I have had the chance to see that Divine love in the intimacy of our friendship—even in our union."

Joshua took Maria's hand again, and looked at her intently.

"My powers are not a gift of God," he said seriously. "My powers, as you call them, are of the essence of God. Our Father has sent me into the world so that I can make others realise that they, too, are sons of God and possessed of these same powers. I was afraid at first, when I began to realise that we are all sons of God. But, I understand that so much better now. God showed me His power when He allowed me to raise Lazarus from the dead, but He has shown me the soft intimacy of His heart in the Divine love that I have found in you. It's the same power, Maria, but somehow the Divine love that can radiate from our hearts has a greater strength than the miraculous forces that gave me my fame. That's what the others still fail to understand. God is everywhere, Maria. He was there in the total freedom of our lovemaking, but He is also in all the little things of life that we share with each other every day. The Law sometimes strangles us so that we lose sight of our real Divine strength in search of miraculous illusion."

Maria gave a bemused smile as she looked up at Joshua in response.

"I'm not sure what you mean," she said, "but I know that if the light shines from me now, it's because of you. You have changed my life."

"I know," Joshua agreed. "What I may have awakened in you now lives."

He kissed her lightly on the lips.

"Keep feeding on me Maria, for my strength is your strength and your strength can be the strength of everyone whom you meet. Everyone who believes that my powers are from the Holy Spirit that dwells within me can bathe in the same light, and hear the still small voice of God."

"You give me such strength," Maria said, putting her arms around his neck.

Joshua responded by gently caressing her.

The waxing Passover moon appeared on the horizon in a now darkening sky.

"We must get back," Joshua said.

After they left Gethsemane, Maria brought up the subject of Judas again. She was more than conscious of the way that he always put her down, and had observed how little respect he appeared to have shown for the Master recently.

"He's dividing your disciples," she said.

"Judas finds it hard to dwell in the spirit," Joshua answered. "He is anxious to please, but he only understands the practical. I have tried to show him how to open his heart, but deep down he is not one of us; he is still a zealot. He has a deep desire to help the poor and needy, but as I have said before, Maria, there will always be poor people, whereas you will not always have me."

Maria looked at Joshua with saddening eyes. *What do you mean?* she thought, as fear of separation arose again.

"Perhaps Judas is a better Jew than I am," Joshua continued, "but I'm afraid it will take a major miracle for him to understand and believe in the light and sound of God within. He doesn't mean you any physical harm, Maria, he's a coward at heart, but I don't think he can ever understand the spark of God that is the fire of our love. He has a fixed notion of you as you were."

Maria felt a pang of guilt as she was reminded of her life in the brothels. She barely heard Joshua say that when they got back to Galilee he would probably suggest that Judas Iscariot should return solely to their fishing venture.

"It wasn't always sinful," Maria said thoughtfully. "I freely gave my love to Linus and Antonias."

"Ah! The two Romans," Joshua acknowledged. "So which one was Marcus' father?"

"It was Linus," Maria replied, "but he never knew his son."

"Linus...Was he from Magdala?" Joshua questioned curiously, their recent intimacy making him feel freer to ask of Maria's past.

"Yes."

"I think he may have been the Roman I met in Capernaum. He was the Roman commander's son, wasn't he? He took me back to his father's house to heal his steward. He had great faith in me. I liked him."

"When did you meet him?" she asked excitedly.

"About the same time I rescued you," he said with a twinkle in his eye. "His steward's name was Demetrius. I worked under him once when I was enslaved after the Great Rebellion. I helped rebuild that villa for the Sephoris commander, Flavius Septimus."

Maria stopped walking.

"That was Linus!" she cried. "Why did he never come to find me?"

Joshua looked at Maria lovingly.

"Did you really ever expect him to come and find you?" he said, holding her shoulders with both his hands.

She thought for a moment.

"No, Joshua," she replied, looking down.

"He is a good man, Maria. He believed in my powers, but he is Roman. You can't blame him for following the ways of their world. Romans and Jews are not expected to mix."

Maria's eyes reflected a moist sadness as she looked up at Joshua again.

"I know," she said, "but outside my love for you, I really cared for Linus, and he is Marcus' father. I cared for Antonias, too. Antonias softened me, Joshua. He prepared me for you. If the Holy Spirit lives in us, that same spirit lives in Antonias. He's a mild and gentle man who showed me a glimpse of the love that we now share. You would have liked Antonias, too, Joshua."

He squeezed her.

"Isn't that a good enough reason for you not to pay attention to Judas? You have nothing from which to feel shame. Our Father will not judge you any more than I do. Don't you worry about Judas."

He looked up.

"Look at the city walls, Maria. See how beautiful the light is, and the Passover moon, how big it is?"

"Can Judas harm you, though?" Maria asked.

"I don't know," Joshua answered as they approached the North Gate. "Let's get back to my mother and James' family. I wonder how Marcus has enjoyed being with little Joanna all afternoon?"

They walked back through the city. Lamps were being lit in the dark and narrow streets that surrounded the Temple. The smells of olive oil and pottage drifted on the air.

"I'm hungry," Joshua said. "I hope Rachel has something good in the pot."

Chapter Thirteen

The Moneychangers

Early the next day, Judas Iscariot and the others arrived at the Temple ahead of Joshua. Passover now being only two days away, the courts were already bustling with devoted pilgrims. Over the Temple mount, the spring sun rose upward to reflect its brightness from the white marble flagstones and clean yellow limestone walls of Herod's legacy. The most eager beggars were taking the best positions at the gates, hoping for a good day's clutch. Pilgrims flocked to the merchants, who were already selling their sacrificial animals at exhorbitant rates to this gullible clientele. Extra Passover stalls were being set up by beady-eyed opportunists, who could see quick profits in sales of simple trinkets and cheap treasures that the unsophisticated pilgrims would readily buy. For many such pilgrims, this would be their first visit to Jerusalem, and they would feel the awe of the Temple in all its glory. Judas sat with Joshua's disciples near the Triple Gate, waiting for the Master and his 'inner circle'.

He's late, Judas thought. *I suppose he's dallying with that woman again.* A sarcastic grin crossed his face. Yet, he knew his thoughts were really unfair. His real contention was that Joshua relied so heavily on him to take care of the group—to be provision master and make all their arrangements, and yet he was now rarely included in any of the privileged gatherings of this 'inner circle'—the three, and that shameless whore and her brat. *What did Cephas, Janus, and Jonas ever do to gain this honor?* he questioned, blinking at the sunlight. *They were never even as good as fishermen as I am.*

Judas' thoughts were disturbed by Thomas, who like Judas Iscariot, had become just a little disillusioned since they had moved south.

"Where are they?" Thomas asked.

"I don't know," Judas replied gruffly.

The sun rose higher and began to beat down on them as shadows shortened. A merchant approached and tried to sell them water. He also held out a tray of sweet honey cakes, tempting them.

"Those look good. Let's eat while we're waiting," Bartholomew suggested.

Judas reached into his leather purse.

"How much for the honey cakes?" he asked.

"One Temple shekel," the excited merchant replied.

Judas looked at his few coins.

"I don't have Temple shekels," he stated. "I only have Roman coins."

"Then you can't have the honey cakes," the man said, pulling back his tray. "You must change the coins at one of the moneychangers. You can't use Roman coins to trade here during Passover."

The man pointed in the direction of the shouting merchants, and the diverse pilgrims in barter and trade.

"The moneychangers are over there."

"No, my friend," Judas said firmly. "We don't need your honey cakes that badly."

Bartholomew nodded in agreement.

Two pigeons landed on the vendor's tray and attacked the sticky sweetcakes. Bartholomew broke out in laughter as the merchant tried to shoo the birds away. Other birds followed the pigeons to the feast. The vendor fumbled, dropped the tray, and the birds swooped to the ground.

"Obviously they weren't meant for us after all," Bartholomew said.

Judas laughed, too, and the vendor, leaving the debris, walked off, muttering to himself in a disgruntled manner.

Then, Thomas shouted:

"There they are!

Joshua, Maria, Marcus, and the 'inner three' were coming up through the Triple Gate. As they approached, Judas Iscariot stood up and touched his forehead.

"Shalom, Master!" he called out. "Shalom!"

Joshua exchanged the greeting in kind. Then, he sat with his disciples for a while instructing them as was his custom. Again, he dwelt on his special relationship with God and how he could transfer that to them.

Some members of the Sanhedrin Council gathered around the disciples, listening to his claims, just as they had the day before. Judas Iscariot could see Saul of Tarsus among them. The Pharisee looked skeptical and cynical.

"Tell us again, by what authority you do the things you do?" Saul shouted out, breaking Joshua's line of thinking. "Who do you say gives you this authority?"

Joshua looked curiously at the heckler. Recognizing him to be the same troublemaker—that man Saul—he said:

"Let me ask you a question. Was the baptism of Jon from heaven or from men?"

Saul conferred with those who had accompanied him—those other Sanhedrin members.

"If we say, 'From heaven', surely he will say, 'Why did we not believe in Jon?' If we say 'From men', we will upset these Passover pilgrims as many of them are convinced the beheaded Jon the Baptist was a prophet of the end time."

He turned back to face Joshua as the disciples silently awaited his reply.

"I don't know, none of us know," was his answer.

"Since you can not yet perceive the difference of that which God sends to try man's purity from that which He uses to judge men's souls," Joshua said firmly, "neither will I try to explain to you any more by what authority I do the things I do."

He then ignored Saul and continued his teaching:

"A man planted a vineyard and let it out to tenants. He himself went on a long journey. At length, he sent a servant back to the tenants and expected them to give to his servant some of the grapes and skins of new wine so that this servant could bring them back to him. Well, instead, the tenants beat the man up and sent him away empty-handed. The master then sent another servant to the vineyard, but the tenants beat him up and treated him shamefully, too. He sent a third servant, whom they also wounded and cast out. Then, the owner of the vineyard said to himself:

'What shall I do?'

'I know,' he thought, 'I'll send my son to them. They will respect him.'

He was surprised, however. The tenants showed no more respect for the master's son than the others. In fact, one of them shouted out:

'This is the heir. If we kill him, the inheritance will be ours.'

So they tethered up his son with leather thongs and stoned him to death."

* * *

Maria, painfully reminded of her own stoning, became suspicious as Joshua said these words, knowing that he was concerned about the Sanhedrin elders. Joshua had told her James had said some of them were talking about him in a negative way. *He's telling this story about himself,* she thought. *He's afraid that they might kill him!* She caught Joshua's eye.

"No!" she shouted, attracting the attention of all those listening, including Judas Iscariot and Saul, the Pharisee.

"Maria, I'm not finished!" Joshua cooly answered her interruption.

* * *

"What, then, will the owner of the vineyard do to them?" Joshua continued addressing them all.

Nobody answered. They sat waiting for the end of the story.

"He will come and destroy those tenants," Joshua said. "He will give the vineyard to others."

He looked around at the sparkling Temple court.

"All this splendor that you now see here, may count for nothing. The day may come, and soon, when there will be left here not one stone standing upon another."

"Why, Master?" Cephas asked.

"Do you remember this quote from the Scriptures: 'The very stone which the builders rejected has become the head of the corner'?"

"No," Cephas replied honestly. He never did respond well to Joshua's quotes, as his knowledge of the Scriptures, being an illiterate fisherman, was very poor.

"Don't talk to us in riddles, Master," Philip said in support. "We don't understand what you are saying."

Meanwhile, Saul had found his way to Iscariot again.

"All of you listen," Joshua said. "Believe in me and who I am. I may not be with you much longer. There are many here that are afraid of me. They do not understand, as you should, that my power is from God and that we are all sons of God. All of you can do the things that I do if only you will believe in the power of the spirit of God that dwells within you. Our authority is the authority of God. If we open our hearts to God, His power will flow through us and His light will shine from us. There are many that have claimed to be the Messiah and will continue to do so. Do not follow them. I am the Messiah. My Father owns the vineyard and I am the son whom he personally sent to the tenants. Do you not believe that I am a son of God?"

Judas and Thomas, now both standing with Saul toward the back, slowly shook their heads.

"He's out of his mind," Judas muttered.

"I agree," Thomas whispered.

"It's blasphemy!" Saul added.

"First, my Father sent you the prophets," Joshua continued. "You abused the prophets, but they pointed the way. Now, I am telling you He has sent me to you as if I was His son. Believe me!"

* * *

Maria's heart surged: *Joshua is the son whom the tenants of the vineyard might seize and kill,* she realised. She now knew that her liberator, lover and friend—her Joshua—believed that the authorities might actually kill him. Tears formed in her eyes and she held Marcus close to her side.

* * *

"Before the end time comes," the voice of Joshua said with heightened anxiety, "expect the authorities to lay their hands on you, too. They will bring you before these Temple authorities and before synagogue councils. Some of you will be imprisoned. You could even be brought before the

Herodians like my cousin Jon, or accused before the Roman prefect. Now, is the time to confirm the things that I have taught you. Are you ready to defend my claims?"

"So, he is a cousin of Jon the Baptist?" Saul whispered to Judas.

"Yes," Iscariot replied.

Meanwhile, in blind faith, Cephas shouted out:

"Yes! I'll defend your claims."

But, none of the others were so brave, fearfully looking around at each other.

Maria held Marcus close and wept in the folds of the boy's tunic.

"Well said, Cephas!" Joshua acknowledged. "But you always support my words. Do you really believe? I doubt it. I would venture to say here and now that you would deny knowing me if I should be taken from you."

Cephas hung his head in confused and shameful fear, too.

Then, Joshua's severity softened:

"Should you come to believe in what I say, the Holy Spirit will protect you. Despite all the hardships, which you may suffer, you will be sons of God, too. You will be raised from this life to higher things."

One of the Sanhedrin Saducee observers, who like most in his party, still supported the claim that there was no resurrection, unlike most Pharisees, then shouted out:

"Teacher!"

Joshua looked around to see who spoke. He knew it was not one of 'the twelve'.

The well-dressed Sadducee challenged him:

"Moses wrote that if a brother dies, having a wife but no children, the man must take the wife and raise up children for his brother. Now, can you answer what would happen if there were seven brothers who all are married in succession to this one woman, because she never had children, and all of them died before her? After she finally dies, whose wife will she be at the resurrection?"

Joshua smiled, amused to see how these learned men kept trying to trick him with their scheming questions.

"People marry in this life, but should they be selected by God to be worthy of resurrection they will neither marry nor be given in marriage in the end time," he answered. "They will be spirit equal to the angels. They will all be as sons of God, bathing in His light, which is eternal."

The Sadducee shook his head.

They don't all agree, Joshua realised. *The Pharisees, like Saul, do believe in some form of resurrection.* He looked back at that Pharisee, now in deep conversation with Judas.

Joshua also saw that some of the Sadducees and Pharisees had started to discuss among themselves as if he had opened their internal divide.

"Moses also said," one of the Pharisees declared, "if a man takes his brother's wife, it is impurity; he has uncovered his brother's nakedness, they shall be childless."

As they argued, Joshua noticed a poor woman dressed in rags coming up the steps at the Triple Gate. Rich Pharisees and Sadducees had been dropping silver coins into the Temple treasury boxes that the Temple authorities placed at the gate during the High Holy Days and festivals. This wizened old lady also dropped coins into the coffer.

"Truly, I tell you," Joshua said, "you see that poor woman coming in now. She has just dropped money into the coffers, probably all she had, maybe two mites, coins of almost no value, whereas rich men have been putting in silver coins all morning. That poor woman has probably contributed more than all those rich men who have passed through the gate today. The rich Sadducees and Pharisees contribute a portion of their wealth, but I believe that this woman probably gave everything she has. Beware of rich men, who like to go about in long robes and love salutations in the market places. They like the best seats at the synagogues and the places of honor at feasts. They make long prayers, but they are not from the heart. Few of them will see the light of God, but this poor woman may."

Joshua watched the poor woman pass them by.

The Sadducee wrapped his cloak around him and whispered to his scribe. He pointed at Judas Iscariot:

"Find out who that dissenter is," he said. "Follow him until you get a chance to talk to him on his own. I think we should engage him. This teacher is dangerous."

The well-dressed Sadducee walked away, but the scribe elbowed his way in the direction of Judas.

"Now, we should make our sacrifices for Passover, just as that poor woman has made her sacrifice," Joshua suggested.

* * *

The disciples moved off toward the crowded stalls where the merchants were busy selling their wares. There was a lot of shouting and it seemed that a scuffle had broken out. Some of the pilgrims seemed very angry, yelling at one of the moneychangers who stood, waving his arms. The bright sun caught the gilded thread of the elaborate border of the excited man's garment.

"You scum!" the moneychanger shouted. "You pay my price or you go without!"

"You're cheating us! You're demanding more than is fair!" angry pilgrims returned.

"You are robbers! You think you can charge whatever you like, knowing that we will have to pay," a tall man yelled.

An over ripe juicy pomegranate then flew through the air, hitting the moneychanger squarely in the face, exploding in pips. More pomegranates followed, and the crowd pressed against the moneychanger's table, hammering on the wood.

"We won't pay!" pilgrims yelled. "No! We won't pay!"

Some other moneychangers came to their colleagues' aid. They tried to kick the pilgrims away. Others started to beat them back with their waist ropes, yelling obscenities.

"What's going on?" Joshua asked stridently as they came closer. "What's all this fighting about?"

"These moneychangers are thieves!" one of the onlookers yelled. "They are charging excessive rates on Roman coins. I know, because I'm here every week. They put up the exchange just to rob pilgrims at festival times."

"It's true!" another feisty man answered, fending off one of the moneychangers. "Their rate is more than double its worth. They are taking the robes off these pilgrim's backs. Everything is more costly here this week. It's not only these moneychangers, but those merchants, too. The pigeons are selling at three times their normal price."

The scuffle increased.

Joshua, suddenly, walked boldly into their midst. He raised his hands and gesticulated.

"Listen to me!" he shouted as loudly as he could.

Those in the crowd closest to him stopped their shoving and looked around to see who was this stranger with the commanding voice.

Joshua pointed at the moneychangers.

"You robbers!" he shouted. "You have made the Temple of God into a den of thieves! Don't you know it is written in the Scriptures: 'My House shall be called a house of prayer?' You are not worthy to serve in my House!"

Someone recognized Joshua.

"It's the miracle worker from Bethany!" he shouted.

Others took note and started to shout Joshua's name. In a few seconds, it became a chant before the startled moneychangers:

"Joshua! Joshua! Joshua! Hosanna in the Highest!"

When one of the moneychangers retaliated, lashing out with his waistcord at Joshua, the crowd went to protect their hero. They pounced on the man, seizing his self-made whip. Then, started to attack the moneychangers and merchants alike with renewed vigor.

Tables overturned. Coins spilled. Moneychangers and hapless merchants retreated from their stalls. Awnings ripped. Ropes snapped, and tents fell. Pigeons found freedom from broken cages. Tethered oxen broke loose. Goats ran wild. A gaggle of geese hissed. Jewelry was smashed. Trinkets fell. Joshua and his followers being at the head of the crowd were bourne forward, swept along in the passionate joy of the mob. The mob finished what they perceived the miracle worker of Bethany had started—a bid for freedom—a blow against authority—a cry for justice. They whipped and beat both moneychangers and merchants so that they fled from the Temple. The mob's victory was complete. The stalls of the Temple court lay in battered and tattered ruins, along with the bodies of the injured. Animals wandered aimlessly.

His robe torn, Joshua gathered up his 'chosen ones' as the crowd dispersed in pursuit of the moneychangers. They collected up three unharmed cages of doves. There were four birds in each cage, cooing in fear.

"We will take these to be sacrificed, now," Joshua said calmly. "My Father's house should not be a house of unfair trade."

As they crossed to the inner court with the doves, men from the High Priest's Temple guard arrived at the scene of devastation, followed by Romans from Antonia's Tower. The soldiers were too late to stop the melee. The High Priest's guards picked up the wounded, taking them prisoner.

The brilliant white marble slabs of the court were strewn with debris, straw, and the glint of coins.

The Roman soldiers moved out into the surrounding street and wrought their harsh discipline on those they found still embroiled in brawling.

Joshua and his disciples presented their doves for sacrifice in the Court of the Jews and as they watched the smoke rise from the pyre they could still hear distant cries from outside the Temple precinct:

"Joshua! Joshua! Joshua! Hosanna in the highest!"

"Don't you think you've taken your claims a bit too far?" Judas Iscariot asked.

"In what way?" Cephas chimed in, wanting to defend the Master from one of Judas' potential attacks.

"The Master said that the Temple was his house," Judas stated. "He didn't just say that it was God's house."

Joshua's mind flashed back to all those stories his mother used to tell—those stories about the 'Prince of Peace' and the treasure that the merchants had left for him at his birth. Her belief that an angel, Gabriel, was his real father or some priest of fanciful Davidic blood. Then, he thought of kindly old Joseph in the Carpenter's shop. *Fantasy or myth,* he thought. *No, I am the Messiah. I need to be about my Father's business. Like my cousin used to believe, I am the one whom God has appointed to bring in the end time—the Kingdom of God—the kingdom that understands the Divinity of us all.*

"My Father and I are one," Joshua insisted. "If you believe in my Divine spirit you also believe it to be the same as the spirit of my Father—your Father. The Temple is our House, our Divine sanctuary, just as individually we are each temples of God's Holy Spirit."

"You do claim to be God, then," Judas said cynically.

"You could claim to be God, too, Judas," Joshua said. "All of you could claim to be an aspect of God, but you're not ready. All of you are soul, all of you have the spirit of God within you."

"Then, why am I only a simple fisherman?" Judas chuckled.

"Why was I a carpenter and a vinedresser?" Joshua answered.

He looked over at Maria and silently thought to himself: *Only you, my beloved, really understand. With you, I can feel this union of spiritual power, but with the others, that bonding of soul and spirit is still missing. I may be running out of time. After all the things that have happened in the past two days, it may be too late. If my life, like those of the prophets, is now in danger here in Jerusalem, the others may never come to understand.*

"Master, you go too far!" Judas repeated. "I can not take on the presumption that I am God. When you make such statements, don't you realise that you endanger all of us? Do you really think that the Temple leaders will believe what you say? We'll all be arrested because of you! You heard what Saul, the Pharisee, said. He's a member of the Sanhedrin."

"So is my brother, James," Joshua answered.

"I agree with Judas, Master," Thomas said. "They will never believe you, any more than we can."

"You take me too literally," Joshua said, slightly exasperated. "I said an aspect of God. Anyway, it is in His hands, Thomas. You must believe what you believe, but I chose you—I chose you all to change the direction of our beliefs. Are you up to it? Are you with me?"

No one spoke as they looked from one to the other in silent fear.

Joshua looked up at the last of the rising fatty smoke of their little sacrifices.

"We should go to the Mount of Olives now and prepare for the Passover in prayer and fasting," he said. "This is the festival of our deliverance—our freedom."

He turned to Maria.

"Take Marcus back to my brother's house. We will join you all tomorrow, but tonight I must spend with my disciples."

Joshua took the others out of the Temple, along the bustling streets that led to the North Gate. The Sadducee's scribe followed at a discreet distance. Soon, they were on the familiar road into the Kidron valley with the Mount of Olives rising to their left.

* * *

Maria left the Temple with Marcus. She feared for Joshua, and felt helpless that she could not be with him when he might need her most. *He's right,* she thought, *the others don't understand, especially Judas.* The Roman soldiers were marching away the last of their prisoners from the affray below the Triple Gate. *Soon, they will march him away,* she felt. *I know it. He knows it.*

"Joshua said he was God," Marcus commented, quoting Judas as they walked toward Mount Zion.

"We are all sparks of God," Maria replied, squeezing his hand.

Chapter Fourteen

Judas and Saul

High Priest Caiaphas leaned back in his chair and adjusted the heavy phylactery that covered much of his chest.

"You say that this riot was instigated by a man named Joshua?"

"Yes, my lord. The people were chanting the miracle worker's name," Saul of Tarsus replied.

"Joshua, the miracle worker from Bethany—the Galilean?" Caiaphas continued. "This man is beginning to be a problem. The people flock to him, believing that he raised that Bethany tanner from the dead. We know the man has charisma, and some definite powers, but these appear to have gone to his head. His claims are outrageous. You are right, they are blasphemous. He seems to think he is the personal agent of God."

"He has said as much," Saul agreed. "He speaks of God as his Father and calls himself God's son."

"Such talk is very dangerous, especially during Passover or other festival seasons. You know how ignorant the pilgrims are, and how gullible—illiterate peasants. We need to silence this Joshua. Can we use the doubting disciple of whom you speak?"

"I think so," Saul answered. "His name is Judas Iscariot. He looks like he's about to break away from the group, he and a young man named Thomas." He paused for a moment. "He's also somewhat disgruntled over the love this Joshua shows for one of the women in their group."

"Ah! Nothing like a woman to fire a man up. If your man, Judas, could lead us to the miracle worker outside the Temple precinct, away from these pilgrims who so dote on him, we might be able to arrest this Joshua, at least for the duration of the festival. Rome's watching us, Saul."

"Rome's always watching us, my lord."

"Do you think you and your associates could get the doubter away from the group?"

"I think it's quite possible, my lord," Saul replied, stroking his black beard pensively.

Caiaphas sat forward in his chair, slowly rubbing his hands together.

"Offer him silver if need be," he suggested.

"Very good, my lord," Saul agreed. "Let me see what I can do."

He left the High Priest's chamber, crossed the Sanhedrin council room and walked out into the bright sunlight of the Temple court.

* * *

Caiaphas' appointed Sanhedrin spies were out scouting the Temple court early. There was no sign of the miracle worker and his group. The sun rose and the pre-Passover rush of Temple business got underway. The debris had all been cleaned up and the moneychangers were back in business, but at more reasonable rates. Pilgrims came in through the gates, swarming around the Temple stalls, continuing to buy souvenirs, trinkets, baskets, sundry utensils, and the inevitable sacrificial fowl and livestock that were required for purification prior to the holy day. Most were unaware of the recent disturbance. This was always the busiest day before the Passover.

After their night of prayer and fasting on the Mount of Olives, Joshua and his band arrived at the Temple mid-morning, where they continued to fast throughout the day. They might not have gone to the Temple at all after the experience of the previous day, but Joshua, knowing how busy the Temple would be the day before Passover, felt compelled to return to heal the sick among the travel weary pilgrims. It would also be good practice and training for the others, too, especially Cephas, Janus, and Jonas.

Cephas noticed the reduced rates at the moneychangers' tables.

"You scared them, Master," he commented.

"Yes, but it's still business as usual," Joshua commented. "My, they cleaned up that destruction fast."

* * *

In the Sanhedrin chamber, Saul of Tarsus met up with the Sadducee who had followed Judas to the Mount of Olives.

"They will be back at the Mount of Olives again tonight," the Sadducee said. "I'll observe them again."

"Good, we need to get Judas away from the group, somehow. Maybe I can get him on his own this afternoon."

Saul left the chamber. It was not long before he spotted the group.

A large assemblage had gathered around the Galilean, pressing and shoving for a glimpse of the man they were sure could cure them of their ailments. Joshua the Miracle Worker appeared to have Cephas, Jonas, and Janus assisting him.

Saul gathered that they had enjoyed some measure of success exercising their own healing powers, but some of the pilgrims also expressed bitter disappointment. One or two openly declared the miracle worker and his assistants to be charlatans. Saul moved closer as a commotion seemed to be erupting. A particularly dissatisfied paralytic was yelling abuse at one of Joshua's disciples. Judas Iscariot was trying to hold the man back.

"What's the commotion about this time?" Saul asked.

"Janus doesn't know what he's doing," Judas muttered, without taking his attention off both Janus and the angry paralytic.

Meanwhile, Joshua looked up, disturbed by the paralytic man's anger.

"Have you no faith?" he called out. "How can you expect a miraculous cure if you are not prepared to open your heart to the healing power of God? If you believe that my power comes from God, you must believe theirs does, too. Believe your healing to be an act of God, but first, you must open your heart to His healing spirit."

"From you, maybe, but not from these men. They don't have your power," the paralytic said, spitting at Janus.

Joshua's eyes met Saul's. Then, a desperate man pulled at Joshua's robe that was still torn from the day before. He turned to help the man.

Saul looked at Judas.

Judas laughed.

"He set himself up for this," he said. "His 'inner circle' don't have his way. I don't know why he favors them so much. They are no better than the rest of us, and certainly contribute less to the group than me. He never lets me try to perform miracles, but he would be lost if I did not take care of their camp."

"Could you perform such healing miracles?" Saul asked, partly curious and partly needling him.

Judas sniggered.

"Well…I doubt it," he said softly, hoping the others couldn't hear him. "To be honest, I'm suspicious of the whole thing. The favored ones don't seem to have much success and there are times when even the Master fails. It's a lot of luck if you ask me."

"It's not luck if your Master truly is the Son of God," Saul said pointedly, beckoning Judas away.

"Well, so he says," Judas replied.

"You are not convinced, then."

"He is a great teacher, sir, and he's a good story teller. He has certain healing gifts—definitely—but he also has his weaknesses. As I've said before, I don't think he has ever been quite the same since he brought this woman into our group. She pulls him down, sir. If he were God, he would be above these sins of the flesh."

"Where is she?"

"She's not with us today, sir, but she's usually hanging around distracting his purpose with her sensual snares. She was a whore and has a bastard Roman boy. She was caught in the very act of adultery! She doesn't deserve all the favors he heaps upon her. If he were the Son of God he wouldn't fall into this trap! We were a more cohesive group before she appeared."

"I understand your thinking," Saul said, nodding his head in agreement. "I would like to talk with you more. Do you think you could break away for a while?"

Judas looked nervous, but he felt the man's seeming friendship.

"I'll know where to find them if they leave without me," he said. "We're camped out at the Mount of Olives."

"Good. Now, you're quite safe with me, but there are several people who would like to talk to you," Saul suggested. "Follow me across the court."

Judas furtively looked around. None of the disciples were paying much attention to him. All eyes now centered on Joshua and the desperate man seeking to be healed. Judas slipped away, following Saul of Tarsus.

* * *

Judas Iscariot felt uncomfortable in the presence of the High Priest. Part of this feeling came from the fact that Judas had never before been exposed to such regal splendor. Caiaphas wore a dark, dome-shaped crown, encrusted with precious stones. Its great size gave him a false height. Seated beside the High Priest, was his father-in-law, who was also his predecessor and still carried the High Priestly title. Often he sat with his son-in-law on Temple business, adding his advice as he felt fit.

Caiaphas spoke in a deep voice that echoed in the dark emptiness of the chamber.

"You are acquainted with the miracle worker from Bethany?" he asked.

In discomfort, Judas was slow to answer, so the High Priest repeated the question:

"You know this man, Joshua, the miracle worker from Bethany, don't you?"

Saul of Tarsus, who had brought Judas to the High Priest, smiled at Judas and nodded.

"Yes," Judas replied nervously.

"Are you one of his followers?" Caiaphas continued.

"Well, in a way," Judas answered. "I take care of his practical needs. I don't necessarily agree with everything he says. I'm a fisherman by trade. I run a fleet of boats for him in Galilee."

"But you don't agree with everything he says?" Caiaphas repeated, looking at Saul for confirmation. Then, leaning forward in his large chair, this giant of a man pointed at Judas.

"Nor do we," the High Priest said.

Judas suspected that he was falling into a political trap, but there was no way he could escape the High Priest's presence, now. He tried to look Caiaphas back in the eye.

"What do you disagree with him about most?" the High Priest asked.

Judas didn't really know what to say. The things that he most disagreed with Joshua about were not things he could really share with this man. *What concern is it of the High Priest that Joshua shows favoritism to certain disciples of their group over and above himself? Why should he tell the High Priest about Maria?* Suddenly, he felt very small and scared. In his indecision, he remained silent.

"Does the miracle worker say his authority is from God?" Caiaphas asked.

"Yes," Judas replied. "He has healing gifts and he believes they are from God."

"This is quite a claim," the High Priest commented. "A peasant with healing powers from God."

"My Master can certainly perform miraculous cures," Judas explained. "He truly believes his power is from God."

"Does he claim to be one of the prophets, then?" Caiaphas continued. "Does he think he is Moses or Elijah?'

"I don't think he has ever made such a claim, although others have made such claims about him. He is a remarkable man, sir."

"So it seems. The other day it was reported to me that your Master, as you call him, actually claimed to be the Son of God. Is that true?"

"He often talks of God as his father," Judas answered a little evasively, sensing the trap closing in on him.

"But does he claim to be God?" Caiaphas pressed.

"I sometimes find it difficult to follow his teaching. He says we can all have the power of God."

"That's blasphemy!" Saul shouted, having remained silent all this time. "What more evidence do you need?"

Caiaphas stroked his beard and sucked on his lips.

"That is blasphemy," he agreed at length.

Judas didn't really know what they meant, but sensed the urgency of their remarks, and it sent a tremor of dread through him.

"We need to talk to your Master," Caiaphas stated.

"You know where he teaches," Judas replied.

He looked in the direction of Saul.

"This man knows where he teaches."

Caiaphas stood up to his full height. In his deep gravelly voice, he addressed Judas:

"It must be more subtle," he said. "We need to speak to him privately. Your Master is treading a dangerous path. We believe he incited that riot in the court with the moneychangers. The people were chanting for him; they flock around him. Indeed, if he persists in this path, you could all be in danger. It will only be possible for us to discuss this blasphemy privately."

The High Priest walked toward Judas.

"What is your name?"

"Judas Iscariot," Judas replied, now with real worry as Caiaphas began to circle him, dwarfing him:

"Well, Iscariot, how can I make you understand how important it is that we talk to your Master? He has by all accounts performed some wonderful healing cures, but he has also gathered around him large crowds. Such crowds are potentially very dangerous, as we saw yesterday. The Romans do not like to see such gatherings. Yesterday, was not pleasing to the authorities. We believe your Master, as you call this supposed miracle worker, was an instigator of this riot. Temple business is my business, Judas. Joshua the Miracle Worker should not interfere in my business, especially if he claims his authority is from God. I am God's authority here!"

"What do you want from me?" Judas asked, now plain scared.

"Your cooperation," Caiaphas boomed.

"What do you mean?" Judas pleaded, looking up at the High Priest's towering frame.

"You must lead us to your Master at a time and place when the crowd can not be incited to rally around him in dangerous support. We may have to arrest him to question him. This is the Passover, Iscariot, a time when the Romans watch our every move. It's the festival of our freedom and freedom is a word the Romans don't like."

Judas felt the fear take root in his stomach. He was being asked to betray Joshua. *I don't agree with everything Joshua says,* he thought, *but I am not ready to betray him, to get him arrested.*

"I can't" Judas said pathetically.

"You will," Caiaphas said, nodding to his Temple guards, who had stood quietly at the entrance to the High Priest's chamber throughout this interrogation.

The guards stepped forward and circled Judas. They were not heavily armed and wore simple leather tunics unlike the more resplendent uniforms worn by the Herodian and Roman soldiers.

Caiaphas addressed his father-in-law:

"Annas, make sure that Iscariot here agrees to our wishes. Make it worth his while. It is very important to me that we talk to this, Joshua, the so-called miracle worker."

"Agreed," Annas said, as he adjusted his own phylactery.

As Caiaphas left with Saul of Tarsus, Judas shook his head. He knew he had trusted Saul too much when sharing his confidences. *Betray the Master?* he thought. *I have been betrayed!*

Annas instructed the guards to bring Judas Iscariot to his rooms behind the Sanhedrin.

"I will join you there in a moment," he said, looking at Judas quizzically.

* * *

Annas left and picked up a substantial bag of silver—Temple shekel coins from the treasury. When he arrived at his rooms, Judas was comfortably seated and chatting with the Temple guards who appeared to be treating him well and were seemingly quite friendly.

"Good," the High Priest's father-in-law said, "you are more relaxed. Rest assured that no harm will come to you if you cooperate with us. Our guards here will protect you should your own people turn against you."

Judas gave a false smile of gratitude as he wrestled with his conscience and concern.

"Do you know where your Master will be tonight?" Annas asked.

"I'm not sure," Judas replied. "I suspect that he will be outside the city, probably on the Mount of Olives. We are in camp there prior to the Passover."

"Is that certain?" Annas continued.

"No. He might go back to his brother's house on Mount Zion. He'll definitely be there tomorrow. We will all be there to eat the Passover meal."

Annas grinned with the satisfaction of knowing that Judas was cooperating. He held out the bag of silver coins, clinking them.

"Take this. Let this be your reward."

Judas took the bag and felt its weight. It was heavy. *Maybe this is worth it,* he thought.

"Most generous," he said cautiously, satisfaction beginning to overshadow his conscience.

"It's nothing, Judas," the retired High Priest assured him. "Your information will be a lot more valuable to us. Now, what is your Master's pattern? Can we expect him to return to the Mount of Olives after the Passover meal?"

"Again, I can't be sure," Judas answered. "I will know, however, as I am the one he always tells about his movements. I have to make provisions and set up camp for him. In these matters, I am his principal steward."

"Good, Judas," Annas commented excitedly. "I have an idea. Why don't you show the guards here where the house on Mount Zion is situated? We can wait for you there on the Passover evening. We can then follow you all when you leave the house. I would much rather we arrest the miracle worker outside the city. It will be less noticeable to the crowd. We don't want any trouble. Hopefully, he will lead you all out to the Mount of Olives. That would be ideal."

Judas felt a piercing pain of remorse as he heard Annas mention arrest.

"What do you mean by 'arrest' my Master?" he asked, confusing emotions reverting to anger. "Are you asking me to betray my Master for some crime he has not committed?'

"Not exactly, Judas, but we must be careful. Your Master is dangerous to us at this time. He could embarrass us with the Romans. We need to arrest him, possibly in order to protect him—protect us—from further incidents during the Passover festival that he might innocently bring about because the people flock so to him."

Annas was pleased with his line of argument, but to his surprise, Judas threw the bag of coins down on the floor. Many spilled out, glinting at Annas' feet.

"Take back your blood money!" Judas shouted. "You've tricked me!"

The guards took hold of Judas again.

"Don't be so hasty, Judas," Annas retorted, as he picked up the bag and most of the spewed coins. "I have not said your Master will come to any harm. We would just like to keep him away from the Passover pilgrims. I'm sure that will be all."

He proffered the bag back to Judas.

"Here, take back the silver. Think how much you and your friends can help the poor if you don't want to take it for yourself."

Judas took the bag from Annas begrudgingly as the guards released him again. *He has a point there,* he thought.

"All right, do you want me to show your men where the house is on Mount Zion?" Judas asked.

"Yes. Take these men there now. They will then wait there tomorrow evening. When they follow you to the Mount of Olives, give us a sign. Walk up to your Master and embrace him."

Still feeling most uncomfortable, but obligated, Judas led the guards from the Temple the short distance to the square on Mount Zion.

"It's the house with those steps," he said, pointing at James' property.

Then he gave each of the guards five shekels from the bag.

"Now, you won't harm me," he said with a nervous smile.

The soldiers touched their foreheads in salutation, and left.

Stringing the bag of silver to his belt, Judas then made his way back out of the city to the Mount of Olives.

* * *

Speculation as to where Judas Iscariot might have gone broke out amongst Joshua's disciples.

"He was talking to that man Saul," Philip said, "the Pharisee with the Greek accent."

"Yes, perhaps he left with him," Thomas agreed.

Joshua felt an ache in his heart. He knew that something was definitely wrong. He had sensed Judas' antagonism for several days. He knew how much Judas mistrusted his relationship with Maria, and he felt the man questioned his leadership.

"Where do you think he is, Master?" Cephas asked. "He has been very shifty lately. Do you think he has abandoned us?"

"I don't know, but if so, Cephas, he is free to go," Joshua replied, cooly repressing his own concerns. "None of you are bound to me, but it is my hope that you should recognize the spiritual bond that we have. This includes you, Cephas, because I pin much of our future hope on you. Indeed, you are not bound to me, but you are bound to my Father's spirit, which is in me and in all people."

He looked his protégé squarely in the eye.

"I'm not sure you quite understand that, yet," he said.

Cephas didn't. Joshua's recent claims were beyond his grasp. *How much simpler things were in Galilee,* he thought. Tears of failure welled in his eyes and he diverted his gaze.

It was dark when they got back to the campsite at the Mount of Olives.

When Joshua left them to pray, Cephas asked the Master if he could go with him so they could pray together.

They walked in the light of the Passover moon to the higher ground on the mount, where there were just a few gnarled olive trees silhouetted against the rocky skyline. There, they knelt in silence, taking their troubled thoughts to God. Joshua lifted up his fear and uncertainty for his future, while Cephas contemplated on his failure and asked for strength. The stars were bright and the night air had the coolness of spring.

Both Joshua and Cephas were pleased and surprised when they came back down to the camp to find that Judas Iscariot had returned. Perhaps their prayers had been answered.

Chapter Fifteen

Passover

Rachel and Miriam were busy baking the unleavened bread for Passover. For Maria, this was a new experience. She had never celebrated Passover. Religious festivals had not been part of her life in Magdala. Her mother had never taught her any of the sacred rules and regulations of food preparation. The procedure for the normal baking of bread for their family use was as much as Esther had ever taught her. Maria had learned more from Delilah in Tiberias than she had ever learned at home. That meant little, though, because in the Roman world that she and Delilah had shared, the Jewish holy days had no place.

"Marcus and Joanna will have to find the matzoth," Miriam explained. "The youngest are always asked to do this. It can be fun."

Maria had no idea what Joshua's mother, Miriam, was talking about.

"Joanna seems to like having Marcus around," she noted.

Miriam smiled.

"Yes, he's very kind to her. Your boy really has a sweet nature."

Miriam thought for a moment as she smeared the pliable substance of their breadmaking onto a flat tile to push into the oven: *I wonder if Marcus will become my grandson. It would be nice if Joshua could become a settled family man once again.* She could see only too easily how Joshua had singled Maria out of the group as his confidante and companion.

They looked good together, and Maria seemed to have a great calming effect on Joshua. She warmed to her.

"Do you think Joshua will ever come to Jerusalem permanently?" she asked.

Maria could easily sense the drift of Miriam's thoughts. She would have loved to settle down with Joshua and give him a family, but deep down she knew him rather better than his mother. She knew from what Joshua had told her that Miriam had been very close to him throughout his childhood, but she had not been with them, traveling the countryside and witnessing his healing ministry. She had not heard him teaching his followers, and did not know how dangerous some of his claims might be. Maria reflected again on Miriam's question, paused, and then said deliberately:

"I doubt it, I think it would be difficult for Joshua to stop his roaming life."

"James might be able to get him an appointment here in Jerusalem," Miriam suggested practically. "He has influence in the Sanhedrin. Joshua could teach with the learned rabbis here. He would reach more people that way than as a wandering healer."

Rachel, who had stepped out, came back to their food preparation just in time to hear Miriam's suggestion.

"A great idea," she concurred. "I could speak to James tonight."

Maria remained silent. Her heart told her otherwise. The only settled life she had really known had been spent with Antonias. Those years seemed far away now. She had become accustomed to Joshua's way of life and she really enjoyed the countryside more than the bustle of the city. She thought of the waterfall at Gennesar and the nights under the stars in the lushness of the Jordan valley. In many ways, she felt that their closeness to nature had fostered the love that had grown between her and Joshua. The presence of the Divine that they shared together seemed more obvious in the flight of the birds and the beauty of the wildflowers on the spring hillsides than in the bazaars of the city or the stones of the Temple. This reflection on their life together, however, hurt in other ways. Much though Maria dreamed of living with Joshua, she was acutely aware of Joshua's concerns for his own safety at the present time. She longed to get him away from Jerusalem and back to the peace and safety of Galilee where he belonged. It was not important to her that they should be gathered in the Holy City to celebrate Passover—a festival about freedom. *Freedom from what?* she questioned incomprehensibly.

* * *

In the dark kitchen area at the back of James' house, Rachel checked on the portions of lamb that she had drained and prepared for the Passover meal. Miriam washed the wooden platters Maria handed to her. The clay oven glowed with hot embers waiting to bake the matzoth, a thin twirl of smoke rising upward into a cloud above them before seeking escape through the small opening in the roof.

"There will be so many of them at the table this year," Miriam said, making sure that they had sufficient bitter herbs to dip into the brine. "There will be nineteen with all Joshua's disciples."

Maria seemed in deep thought.

"I don't think Joshua is ready to change his lifestyle," she said at length.

Miriam looked at Rachel. She could tell that Maria was not happy. She reflected on the past: *I set him on his course,* she thought. *I set him on that path because God had chosen him for a special task. I was only the instrument for bringing this son of God into the world.* She turned to Maria with her warm smile.

"No, Maria. You are probably right," she said. "Joshua has always been very independent. Whatever is the will of God, so be it."

Maria then joined with them in baking the matzoth.

* * *

Joshua and his disciples spent most of the next day on the Mount of Olives. It was a warm spring day, and the gnarled trees gave just enough shade. Across the valley, the sandstone walls of the Temple mount merged into the white marble of King Herod's portico, shimmering in the bright sun. The Master felt anxious about continuing to be a presence in the Temple. *There are just too many spies, especially that Pharisee named Saul,* he thought. *What is he up to with Iscariot?* He observed Judas. The man was very subdued around the camp, distant and quiet, but they had all slowed down from their meditative period in fasting and prayer and the peace and serenity of their surroundings.

Joshua could not help recalling his recent passion in this same peaceful place, just a little further down in the lush area of Gethsemane. *I wonder how my mother is getting on with Maria?* he thought. *I wonder how she is getting on with Rachel? Rachel can be quite demanding. I remember how she used to boss her sister Joanna when preparing for the Passover.* He realised Maria would not know what was going on, but he drew comfort from the knowledge that they would all be celebrating Passover as a family again. It had been four years now.

In the mid-afternoon they all returned to the city, stopping at the pool of Siloam on Mount Zion to make their ablutions. Judas Iscariot took water from the pool and kneeling before Joshua began to wash his feet. Three or four silver shekels fell from his pouch and chinked on the pavement. Wiping the Master's feet, he looked up shiftily into Joshua's eyes. They could both sense the dismay in each other—the mistrust.

"Temple shekels for the poor?" Joshua asked.

"Yes..." Judas stammered.

Joshua stared vacantly for a moment.

"You should not be washing my feet, rather I should be washing yours," he said at length. "There are times when the master becomes the servant. You have always served us well, Judas. Tonight let me serve you and the others."

Joshua took the water basin and poured some of the cool liquid over Judas Iscariot's feet. Judas remained speechless as foreboding gripped him all the more, while Joshua gently wiped his feet with the rag. When he had completed the task, Joshua picked up the shekels.

"For the poor," he said giving them back to Judas Iscariot.

He put both his hands on Judas' shoulders and looked him directly in the eye. Judas could not return the gaze and looked away as a tear of remorse slid over the rough skin of his ruddy cheek. When Joshua released his hands from Judas' shoulders, he took the basin to Cephas where he began to wash and wipe the burly fisherman's feet.

Cephas was astounded.

"Master!" he cried. "You can not wash my feet. I am not worthy of this!"

Joshua looked up.

"You are all worthy of this. My Father did not send me into this world to live in king's houses and to be waited on like a rich man. A son of God must be like Isaiah's suffering servant. The first shall be like the last, Cephas, so that the last can be spiritually raised to the first. In me, you are all united."

"But, Master!" Cephas protested.

"Cephas, you must try to understand," Joshua interrupted. "Remember that I am really going to need your help."

Cephas shook his head.

"I don't understand," he said. "Surely, I should be the one to wash your feet."

Joshua smiled at Cephas, took up the water basin and moved on to Janus and Jonas.

In turn, Joshua washed the feet of all the others, none of whom questioned him after Cephas' protest. In this way, they were all prepared for entry into James' house for the holy meal.

* * *

Rachel and Miriam had everything ready. James and Jonah welcomed Joshua at the top of the steps that led to the upper room of James' house. Maria was in the back, taking care of Marcus and Joanna. Both the children had been dressed in clean white tunics for the festival. Maria, much aided by Marcus who loved to tell his stories, tried to keep Joanna amused, but when they heard the noise from the large upper room, they lost their attention and excitedly moved to the doorway.

"They're here!" Joanna shrieked. "Can I look for the matzoth now?"

"Stay back here," Maria whispered, gently putting her fingers to her lips to beckon silence.

Marcus stepped forward to restrain Joanna in her enthusiasm.

"We have to wait until they call us in," he said, like a protective big brother.

Joanna turned to him, beaming all over:

"I know where they've hidden it," she wispered confidently. "I know I'll find it before you do. You don't know where it is, do you?"

Marcus shook his head. He looked back at his mother. He was a little mystified by all this talk about the matzoth.

Maria smiled back. She didn't really know what the matzoth was all about either, but she did know where she and Miriam had hidden it.

Joanna continued to show her superior knowledge of Passover. This was one area where she did seem to know a lot more than Maria's son.

"I'll answer the questions," she said to Marcus. "You can open the door for Elijah."

Marcus thought for a moment. He wasn't too sure what Joanna was talking about, but he did know about Elijah.

"I've seen Elijah," he said proudly, looking back to his mother for support and confirmation.

Joanna was wide-eyed.

"I saw him on top of a mountain. He was with Joshua. Moses was there, too."

Maria put her finger to her lips again.

"Shsss...that's a secret," she whispered.

"Moses!" Joanna shrieked.

"Yes," Marcus confirmed in a serious tone. "They were there, weren't they, Mother?"

"That's what Cephas said," Maria confirmed. "They stood there in the sunlight. It was difficult for us to really make them out. It was hard to see them from where we were because the shafts of sunlight were so bright among the shadows of the trees. We could hear their voices, though."

"You talked to Moses and Elijah?" Joanna continued excitedly.

Their new story eclipsed the excitement of all that was about to take place in the upper room.

"We didn't," Marcus explained, "But the others did."

"Which others?"

"Joshua, of course," the boy said.

"And who else?"

"Cephas, Janus, and Jonas."

He looked to his mother for help.

"It's just a story, Joanna," she said, and put her finger to her lips yet again.

Their attention was now drawn to the action in the upper room.

Joshua arrived.

Maria had not seen him for two days. It was the longest she had been separated from him for some time. She was excited, and it was not long before their eyes met across the distance of the room as she stood in the doorway at the back with Marcus and Joanna. She had a green cloak over her white shift and her recently washed wavy dark hair fell over her shoulders. She was no longer interested in pursuing this discussion about Moses and Elijah.

Joshua's robe was dirty and still torn, but James provided him with a clean one for the feast. Rabbi James then began to organize the seating of the men for their Passover meal. It was not long before they were all sitting on the benches around the long table that Jonah had set up for them. Rachel had set it with an assortment of bowls and goblets. A large dish in the center held the lamb shank and bitter herbs. After they had all taken their places with Joshua at the place of honor, Maria and Miriam started to pour the first cup of wine. Rachel held Marcus and Joanna back, waiting for James or Joshua to invite them to look for the matzoth.

James started the Passover ritual by recounting the scriptural story of Moses and the escape of their ancestors from their taskmasters in Egypt. He described terrible plagues sent by God, and ultimately the threat of extermination through the slaughter of all first-born sons in Egypt, but how they, the Hebrews, were spared the ordeal by marking the lintels of their doors. The Lord God of Abraham, Yahweh, passed over them, and their households were saved. Then, Moses led them across the sea, and the sea became dry land, but after them the sea returned and drowned the wicked Egyptians. After that, Moses led them on a wandering journey through the desert to their promised land.

Marcus listened to the story enthusiastically, while Joanna tried to whisper embellishments.

Eventually, the moment came. James asked Joanna to come into the middle of the room and he asked her the Passover questions. She had been well schooled by her father. Marcus was impressed as she rattled off the answers. Maria felt just a little embarassed—inadequate perhaps—because Marcus did not share Joanna's knowledge of these things, but Maria herself was still mystified by the whole ritual surrounding Passover. This was a new venture for her just as much as for her son.

"Good," James said to Joanna in a kindly manner, "now, you and Marcus look for the matzoth."

Maria pushed Marcus forward and the boy began to look around the room, following little Joanna. He only searched for the unleavened bread where she had looked, as he had no idea what he was doing.

Joanna found the flat bread quickly, squealing with delight as she picked it up to bring it to her father. Miriam and Maria really hadn't hidden it very well. It was in a linen cloth at the foot of one of the lampstands.

James took the matzoth from his daughter. Rachel took Marcus' hand and led him to the doorway at the top of the outside steps.

"Open the door for Elijah," James instructed. "We always leave the door open for the prophet because in our tradition we believe that Elijah will come to us before the end time. We must always be prepared, for we do not know when the end will be. In opening the door, we are showing that we are ready, and Elijah can come in at any time."

Marcus pulled on the latch and eased the door open.

Joshua's donkey bayed from his tethering point in the street below.

"He's not here!" Marcus shouted back.

"Maybe he will come later, or even next year," James reassured him. "We will save some wine for him just in case. Now, you must go back to the other room with Joanna."

Marcus didn't move. He stood at the open door. He could see some soldiers across the square, and a well-dressed man. The man turned and looked up at the open door. *Maybe he's Elijah?* Marcus thought, but when the man did not advance toward the house, he shut the door and returned to Joanna.

* * *

Maria observed Joshua and the 'chosen ones' as she stood by the wall. All of them, except Thaddeus, whom they had left in Capernaum, were there. Judas Iscariot looked very subdued tonight. Maria remembered what Joshua had said to her. Judas hardly seemed a threat to her, now. He seemed to have lost his outspokeness. *Perhaps he and Joshua have sorted things out,* she thought. *It looks as if they have confronted each other in some way.* Judas Iscariot was definitely the loner. With James, Jonah, and Judas Matthias, there were fourteen around the table.

Rachel and Miriam were busy filling the goblets for the next celebration. James invited those assembled to take matzoth from the center of the table and dip in a bowl of honeyed berries and spices, which Rachel and Miriam had prepared. They all tasted the sticky sweet mixture before he asked them to join him in drinking the second cup.

When this official part of the Passover celebration was completed, James handed his authority over to Joshua.

Joshua reached for the dip again. Seated closest, Cephas, Janus, Jonas, and Judas Iscariot were all easily able to dip in after him. Joshua, with his hand still on the broken piece of matzoth, looked around the table with a tired and sad expression.

"There are some among you," he said, "who have dipped in this bowl with me tonight, who will disown me and betray me."

The air stilled.

Cephas and Jonas pulled their hands sharply back from the dip.

"Not me!" they shouted almost simultaneously.

Janus was slower to respond, but also withdrew his hand.

Judas was left, staring straight at Joshua with his hand fearfully frozen on the matzoth. All his muscles had tightened at once. He was almost in a state of shock as penetrating guilt swept through him.

"Am…I going to betray you?" he asked in trepidation.

Waiting, Joshua said nothing until Judas withdrew his hand from the dip.

"Only you know, Judas. If it is you, then do what you have to do."

Every eye in the room turned upon Judas. He seemed deeply afraid as if he knew that the Master knew something he was not supposed to know. Visible sweat beads formed on the back of his neck and over his hands. The piercing gaze of the other disciples forced action. Slowly, he stood up, and staring at Joshua one last time, he turned and left the room.

Cephas got up, yelling abuse, setting out in pursuit of Judas.

"Don't!" Joshua shouted. "Leave him! Let him go!"

Cephas sat down.

"I knew something was up with him," Bartholomew said to Simon the Zealot. "What's he going to do?"

"Try to turn the Master over to the authorities," the Zealot answered.

"For what?"

"At heart, Judas has never agreed with Joshua's passive ways," Simon continued. "Judas Iscariot was once a freedom fighter. Once a freedom fighter always a fighter. That's the way it is. I should know. Perhaps the Master is too passive. What have we really achieved?"

"What about Joshua's attack on the moneychangers?" Bartholomew reminded the Zealot. "That was hardly passive."

"No, but only because of the crowd forcing him," Simon noted.

The others joined in, adding their easy criticism of Judas Iscariot. The discussion rose from suppressed muttering to open argument. Joshua tried to quiet them and finally said with dignified authority:

"That's enough! This is the Passover! Save your opinions until later."

Silence descended on the shattered group.

Joshua picked up the last remaining flat matzoth on the table. He held it in front of them and broke it in half. Then, taking a further small piece for himself, he passed the two halves around to his disciples, asking them to each break off a piece for themselves. He called to Rachel and Miriam:

"Fill the goblets one more time."

Maria joined Rachel and Miriam in the task.

Joshua smiled weakly, and looking over his shoulder at James standing behind him said:

"Thank you, my brother James, for allowing us to join with you for this celebration of the Passover."

When the wine cups were filled, he nodded to Rachel, his mother, Jonah, and Maria, beckoning them closer.

"Listen, all of you..." he said very seriously. "I feel I might not be with you much longer, yet I want you to understand one thing if I should be taken from you. For this may be the last time we are all gathered together."

The disciples, including the 'inner three', were now mystified as to what Joshua was going to say. They could all sense the tension in the room, but also the authority of the Master.

"This bread that we are holding," Joshua continued, "is the bread of life. It is our basic food. Whether we bake it as unleavened bread like this matzoth or as leaven with yeast to raise the dough, doesn't matter. If we become wanderers in the wilderness, the chances are that we will bake locust cakes like the prophets. What's the difference? What matters is that bread is a symbol of that which we need. Without this basic food, none of us would live. Every time you eat, whether it is bread, fruit, meat, or lentils, remember that without this bounty from God you can not live. To eat and to drink is essential to life. Remember, too, that every time you pick up bread to eat, that just as God the Father feeds your bodies with these good things, so, too, my Father feeds you spiritually. Remember me when I am gone, for I will still be your bread from heaven. Just as this food enables you to live, also remember that in this same way my teachings have been placed before you to open your hearts so that my Father can breathe life into you. I will ask my Father to revive your spirits that you may grow in the Father even as I have, for we are all sons of God!"

Cephas looked at Joshua and then at the others.

"Master, give us this bread that we may live anew," he said, and following Joshua he bit into the flaky matzoth.

The others did likewise.

Joshua picked up his wooden goblet.

"It is even more important to drink than to eat," he continued. "Elijah stayed many days in the desert without food and survived just on drink."

Joanna looked at Marcus, wide-eyed.

"Elijah!" she shouted in her high pitched voice.

Joshua smiled and then carried on with his teaching:

"The thirst of our bodies must be quenched in order for our bodies to live. It is even more important, therefore, that every time you drink you remember what I have just said. I am the true vine. Drawing from the roots of God's life force, whenever you drink, remember that just as God enables your bodies to live through this simple action, so, too, I am feeding you spiritually with the essence of God's eternal life. God's spirit is everlasting. I am trying to show you the way to this eternal life. When the spirit of my Father is awakened within you, my spirit will be in you and with you forever. I am the sap in the vine and you are the grapes. Grapes are only with us for a season, but the sap rises again each successive year. Remember that my powers, which are the powers of my Father, can be yours also. Wait for the spirit of God to be ignited in your hearts! You will then be able to move mountains in His everlasting light."

Joshua then drank from the cup.

Cephas and the others followed his example.

"Good," Joshua continued as he put his goblet back down on the table. "Every time you eat and drink, remember these words that I have just spoken. You are all sons of God."

Maria was listening to Joshua's words intently. This all seemed to make far more sense to her than the Passover—some celebration of a story from long ago about deliverance from bondage. *We are fed and watered by the spirit of God so we can pass that spirit on to all whom we meet,* she thought. *We are then sons of God—the sound and light of God. I know the spirit of God dwells in Joshua. I saw it in his very being. I felt it in his passion.* She paused in her thought for a moment. *His passion—what if I conceived? What if I have his child? What if he has passed his son on to me?*

"Has Elijah come?" Joanna squealed again, tugging on Maria's robe.

"I think so," Maria replied vacantly. "I think Elijah has come, and more."

Chapter Sixteen

Betrayal and Arrest

Judas Iscariot spotted Saul and the High Priest's guards when he ran down the steps from James' house. They challenged him as he tried to make an escape.

"What's happened?" Saul asked.

Deathly pale, Judas looked at Saul, then, spat at him.

"Nothing that is of any concern of yours!" he said.

"Oh, yes it is!" Saul shouted.

The guards seized Judas.

"Leave me alone!" Judas yelled. "You've got what you wanted!"

Judas wrestled with them, and knocking one of the slower unarmed men to the ground, he broke away. Two of the four guards raced after him. It was easy for them to catch him in the narrow street running toward the Temple. The men pinned Judas to the wall. He kicked and struggled, but they punched him in the face and stomach until he capitulated. Dragging him back to the square, they took the rope that tethered Joshua's donkey and used it to bind Judas. They gagged him, and then retreated with their prisoner to wait in the shadows of the side street as it became dark.

The donkey ran off, braying.

Not long after, Joshua and his disciples appeared in the doorway at the top of the steps. Judas wished that he was still with them and felt his world closing tightly in around him. The guards held him back, and periodically his eyes met the curious penetration of Saul's.

Cephas appeared to be leading the disciples as they came down James' steps. Joshua stayed back by the door. His mother came out and embraced him. Maria joined them. They were silhouetted by the warm light of the oil lamps within the upper room and surrounded by a deep orange glow. It highlighted Maria's hair and the straggly strands of Joshua's beard. They hugged each other. Maria's boy was right behind them, peering out from the upper room.

Judas spat again, in personal contempt. *That woman has ruined us,* he thought.

He heard Cephas call out:

"The donkey's escaped."

Joshua then parted from Maria, and followed them into the court, only looking back when half way across the square. Miriam had gone back in, but Maria was still there with her boy. Joanna appeared. She brayed like a donkey, but there was no response from below. Rachel reached for her daughter, then, Maria, all of a sudden pulled at Marcus and ran down the steps.

Now, they were following the others.

Saul ungagged his prisoner.

"So, where are they going?" Saul whispered to Judas, twisting his arm.

"Probably outside the city," Judas answered.

"Where do they usually go?" Saul pressed, as they followed Maria and Marcus.

"Follow them, and you might find out," Judas answered cynically with minimum cooperation.

As Joshua and his disciples made their way through the narrow streets beneath the Temple's walls and out to the North Gate, Saul and the High Priest's guards forced Judas to follow along at a discreet distance. It was very dark, but by the time they reached the Kidron Valley the Passover moon was beginning to peek above the surrounding hills. As Judas suspected, Joshua and his chosen disciples returned to the camp in the old garden at Gethsemane on the lower slopes of the Mount of Olives.

"Shall we go on in immediately?" one of the guards asked Saul.

"No," he replied. "Give them time to make themselves comfortable. Just make sure the Galilean miracle worker stays with them."

They took up positions behind the boulders of the garden to wait for the right moment.

* * *

Pontius Pilatus sat on the terrace of the Jerusalem Praetorium Palace with his wife, Lavinia, and Linus Flavian. They watched the Passover moon rise behind the cypress trees. The moonlight silhouetted the arches of the new western aqueduct.

"So far, so good," the prefect said to his aide.

"I'm glad," Linus replied. "I was worried after that incident in their Temple the other day. There are so many visiting Jerusalem. This is definitely a dangerous time."

A slave brought them all a fresh goblet of wine.

"Quite right, Linus," the prefect agreed. "That could have developed into something."

Pilatus picked up his goblet and sipped.

"I'll be glad when their religious festival is over," he continued. "We can concentrate on other things, such as entertaining your father and mother when they come down from Galilee with Antonius Syllus. I remember Antonius from Rome. He's rather too intellectual for me. Actually, he's a mind dulling bore."

"I like his wife," Lavinia said in Syllus' defense. "We need a little culture here. I believe their son is quite a poet—schooled in Athens. He might be back from Greece, in which case we might have quite a gathering here next month."

"They're harmless," Pontius Pilatus agreed. "I suppose it'll be nice to have someone here for you."

He turned back to Linus.

"But your father…he is most interesting. I'll enjoy a good chat with Flavius Septimus. I love it, too, the way your mother always gives that Tarquin viewpoint."

"My father really has become quite the Galilean," Linus commented. "It's funny how a soldier can become so settled. He just loves his vineyards and his livestock. We really should call him 'Gracchus' Flavian."

They laughed, relaxing for a while, until Pilatus brought up the subject of Barabbas.

"Should I free this rebel?" he asked.

"Why?" Linus replied.

"It's one of those diplomatic customs that has grown up with the prefecture—you know, a gesture of good will—hearts and minds at times of potential tension. Once a year, at the Jewish festival of Passover—a festival that celebrates a freedom movement from their past, so potentially always dangerous—it is suggested that we should release at least one relatively harmless prisoner. There has been some pressure for me to release this Barabbas."

"The Jericho troublemaker?"

"Yes. He was as much Herod Antipas' problem as ours, but that seems often to be the way. As far as I'm concerned we should let him go if it creates some goodwill. He's a firebrand, but somehow he never really got many behind him—just a rowdy rabble of peasants. He was easy to track down. I would say a small fish."

Pilatus looked at Linus in a superior sort of way.

"Of course, I don't have to release anybody; it's just a custom," he affirmed.

"Are you asking my opinion?" Linus said, wanting to make sure that he had the prefect's confidence.

"Yes. I value your opinion. You are very astute in these matters."

"Barabbas bothers me," Linus replied. "The man is a symbol of resistance to authority. He is not in himself a dangerous prisoner. To my knowledge, the jailors have not had any problems with him. But, he could easily become a rallying point for rebellion here in Jerusalem. You are right, those who rallied around him in Jericho were mostly spineless peasants—not truly rebels—but you have a more organised underground here. Barabbas has charisma. He could rouse them up."

"True," Pilatus said, grinning with patronizing approval as he saw how his aide held his own real viewpoint.

"Well, that's important, sir," Linus continued. "Many followed Barabbas because of his charisma and not really because they agreed with him. Charisma is dangerous."

"Then, I will not release him. You're right," Pilatus concurred. "This year the Jews can do without my charity, unless Herod Antipas persuades me otherwise. He's arrived here for Passover—a token gesture to appease his subjects, I presume."

* * *

Joshua lay on the grass with his 'inner three'.

"Master, if you think you are in danger, why don't you leave Jerusalem?" Cephas suggested.

"Yes," Jonas agreed. "Why don't we go back to Bethany? We can go with you tonight while the others stay here. If Judas Iscariot comes, he will find them, and not us."

"Are you afraid, too, Jonas?" Joshua asked.

Jonas didn't answer, but looked at Cephas for support.

"We can all sense the potential danger of Judas, now," Cephas commented. "It is more than likely that he'll bring the authorities here if he wants to destroy us. We should go, Master. We don't have to take the road along the valley through all the pilgrim camps. We could take that path over the hill to Bethphage, and then the road to Bethany. If the authorities find we are not here and follow the road south down the Kidron, they will be delayed searching through those pilgrim throngs. We will have more time. Our pledge is to make sure you're safe, Master."

"What about the others?" Joshua retorted. "Do they not need to be protected, too?"

Cephas looked back at the main body of Joshua's disciples. They were lying everywhere on the grass. Some were sleeping and others whispering to one another.

"Surely, no harm will come to them," he said. "Do they look like trouble, and what have they ever done to upset anyone; besides, Thomas, Philip, and Bartholomew have always been pretty close to Judas."

Joshua leaned toward Cephas.

"Cephas, if you are truly to follow me in the days ahead, you must be prepared to suffer all things that I might suffer. You may be beaten or imprisoned because of me. It is the same for them, too. All of you may suffer because of me, and not because of anything any of you might have done to upset the authorities. If you believe in me, and in what I have tried to teach you, then you will suffer with me. I can not leave any of you. I am your shepherd and you are my sheep. Without me, you will be lost and I will not be able to achieve what God has asked me to do."

Joshua looked at Janus and Jonas to assure them that what he was saying to Cephas applied just as much to them.

"Stay here and watch," he instructed. "I need to pray in private."

Joshua walked up the hillside from the glade of Gethsemane to the area of loose rocks above where the ground was flooded in the eerie light of the full Passover moon. Here, olives clung to the poorer soil, their roots running out like spider's feet as they searched for stability. It was these determined trees that gave the mount its name.

* * *

Saul and the High Priest's guards saw Joshua leaving the group.

"That's our man leaving now, isn't it?" the leader of the guard suggested to Judas Iscariot.

"Maybe…I think so," Judas answered hesitantly.

Exasperated by Judas' lack of real cooperation, Saul siezed Iscariot by the throat.

"Well, is that our man or not? It looks like him to me!"

"Ye…eess! You know it is," Judas choked.

Two of the High Priest's guards stayed with Judas while Saul and the others discreetly skirted the unknowing disciples and followed Joshua.

They got close enough to the Galilean to make out that he was praying. Joshua looked helpless, earnest, and sadly desperate. Saul was Pharisee enough to know that arresting a man in prayer was not a good idea. They watched, and creeping closer, listened, as they heard Joshua speaking out loud:

"My Father! Please hear me, now! Never have I felt less sure of myself. What have you done to me? I can not feel the same power. My closest disciples are skeptical. Iscariot has left me. Am I to be abandoned? Do not let them arrest me, Lord. My work has not been completed. My disciples are not ready. Please help me now, in my greatest time of need!"

Joshua looked down at the ground. He hung his head in silence for a while and then looked up at the Passover moon.

"Has it all been for nothing?" he continued. "Speak to me, Lord! Help me! Help us! Why have You abandoned us? I do not hear You any more. Even my donkey is gone."

* * *

Joshua stared at the moon. *Is it a face or a rabbit on its side?* he thought. It was a source of comfort to him. Looking up at its face through the olive branches reminded him of those nights in his childhood when he had sat with his mother. Miriam had always told him that God was there in the moon. Somehow, God felt closer in the comfort of the moon. The spiritual gulf that he had begun to feel receded in its light, and he felt the power of Divinity well up within him again.

"Father, far be it for me to understand," he prayed, "but I won't doubt you. You are my strength, You are the Lord. I am your servant, one with You in spirit and love, and therefore I give my whole being to You. Let not my will be done, but only Yours."

He stood up without taking his eyes off the moon.

"Whatever is Your will, let me have the strength to do it," he continued. "Forgive me my weakness. Like Cephas, there are times when my spirit is willing, but my body is weak. Forgive me, Lord!"

He bowed his head and knelt in silence for a while.

Then, getting up, he turned and slowly walked down the hill.

* * *

Saul and the guards skulked behind him in the shadows.

Back in the garden of Gethsemane, Joshua found that Cephas, Janus, and Jonas had fallen asleep, along with most the others, but Maria and her boy were awake and waiting.

Joshua was surprised to see them.

"What are you doing here?" he asked. "Why aren't you still at James' house. You shouldn't be here. It's dangerous!"

Joshua's voice woke Cephas.

"Who's that!" the burly fisherman shouted.

"Cephas, couldn't you stay awake just this short while?" Joshua said, chastising him. "I asked you to watch out while I went to pray. Look at you all. Jonas and Janus are sound asleep."

Cephas then saw Maria and Marcus.

"I thought you stayed behind," he said. "Why have you come?"

"Something just told me I needed to be here," Maria replied. "Maybe it was the spirit of God. I couldn't leave you all after what happened at supper."

She turned back to Joshua.

"Are all the others asleep?" Joshua asked.

"Yes, Joshua, all but us and Marcus here."

Joshua put his hand on the boy's head.

"You should sleep. This has been a long day for you," he said affectionately.

"I might miss Elijah," the boy said sleepily.

At that precise moment, two of the High Priest's guards, startled them, running out from the shadows. They seized Joshua's arms. Two others followed, pushing Judas Iscariot forward. Saul then showed himself.

"Judas!" Saul shouted. "Identify this man! Is this your master, the miracle worker from Bethany?"

Judas looked at Joshua, the soldiers still holding his bound wrists behind him, and then he turned and faced Maria.

"You are the cause of the Master's downfall!" he shouted,

His voice roused some of the others.

He went up to Joshua.

"Forgive me, Master!" he said. "It was never meant to come to this."

Joshua said nothing, nor could he push Judas away, while his own arms were being held.

Janus, now fully awake, took his old fisherman's knife from his belt, and thinking the guards to be Romans, pulled the knife and hacked at one of the men holding Joshua. The man jumped with pain, releasing his hold on Joshua's arm. The guard's ear started to bleed profusely.

"Master, I fell asleep," Janus pleaded. "What's going on?"

"Put away your knife!" Joshua commanded. "No good will come from violence!"

Janus obeyed.

The guards pulled Judas away from Joshua and threw the coward to the ground. Then, one of them seized Janus.

"Leave him!" Saul shouted. "We have our man. Make haste!"

They tightened their grip on Joshua, leading him away from the speechless disciples as the moon passed behind a cloud, enshrining the grove in darkness.

* * *

Cephas kicked at Judas and beat him with his stick, but Iscariot managed to slither away, scrambling for his life.

Cephas, and Maria, pulling Marcus, then tried to follow the soldiers and the Master.

"What about the others?" Maria shouted, trying to keep up with Cephas.

"We can't worry about them now, Maria!"

Along the rough path, Marcus tore his tunic and lost his loincloth as it caught on a thorn bush. The moon peeked out again, and as they reached the Kidron valley they could just make out the sillhouette of Saul and the guards, rushing Joshua back toward the city.

Chapter Seventeen

Denial and Trial

Caiaphas was becoming impatient. The evening was dragging on and there was no sign they had captured the Galilean miracle worker.

"What do you think has happened?" he asked his father-in-law.

"I would have expected them sooner than this," Annas agreed.

Annas did not want to reveal his true thoughts, but he realized that they had not found a very reliable man in this Judas Iscariot. The man was still too involved. He had not detached himself from the group in quite the way that they had at first envisaged.

"Perhaps Judas was late meeting the guard," he replied.

In dimming light, a slave replenished the braziers that burned in the large hall of the High Priest's old Hasmonean Palace. There was little furniture, and nothing of opulence. A large, orange, woolen drape hung behind the High Priest's throne on the end wall, providing the only color. Four guards waited outside with instructions to bring in the miracle worker of Galilee—this Joshua—immediately on arrival.

Time passed.

Caiaphas wrung his hands nervously over the possible failure of their plan.

Eventually, their silent vigil ended. There were sounds in the courtyard.

"They're coming!" Annas reassured his son-in-law.

* * *

The guards, followed by Saul of Tarsus, escorted Joshua into the great hall. Protecting each exit, they released their hold on him.

Caiaphas stood up and adjusted his crown and phylacteries.

"My lord. This is the miracle worker who claims to be God," Saul announced sarcastically.

"Come closer," Caiaphas commanded Joshua.

Joshua stepped forward into the light between the braziers.

"I have been wanting to meet you," he continued. "So, you're the miracle worker from Bethany?"

Joshua felt momentary relief. Perhaps the High Priest needed him for some special healing. Maybe, he had misread all the signs of the previous day. *Perhaps I'm not in as much trouble as I fear,* he thought.

"Yes, I am he," he answered clearly.

"What is your name, miracle worker?" the High Priest asked.

"Joshua, sir."

"They tell me you raised a man from the dead. Is that so?"

"Yes. Unfortunately, many people only believe in my Father's spirit, and His coming kingdom, because of that miracle," Joshua replied slowly.

"And who is your father?"

"The very same who is your Father."

Caiaphas laughed and his tall crown wobbled.

"So, we are brothers then," he said.

"We are sons of God," Joshua corrected him.

"Sons of God!" Caiaphas repeated, looking at Annas. "What do you mean by sons of God?"

"Are you not the High Priest of the Jews?" Joshua replied. "Should I have to explain to the Lord's servant such things?"

He could see Caiaphas' anger mount.

"Mind your tongue!" the High Priest shouted.

"Are you the Son of God?" Annas asked cooly.

"Is that who you say that I am?"

"No, Joshua of Bethany," the old man retaliated sarcastically, "but that is what others have said to us. Have you spread this message that you are the Messiah and the Divine Son of God Almighty?"

"Have you heard me preach this message?"

Caiaphas and Annas both stared at Joshua.

"Are you questioning us?" the High Priest bellowed.

"I do not question anyone or anything. I know who I am, and I know my God is my Father," Joshua answered forthrightly.

"Then, you are saying that that you are the Son of God?" Caiaphas repeated enthusiastically.

"If you say so," Joshua answered again, "but no more and no less than you."

Saul smirked.

"That's enough to condemn you," Annas added in support. "Caiaphas, you have now heard the man's blasphemy. This nobody has collected up a veritable army of peasants who follow him as the Son of God. He would like to set himself up above us, and above our Temple. This is blasphemy, Caiaphas! We must silence this man before his teaching gets out of hand."

Turning, Annas conferred with the High Priest in a whisper. Caiaphas nodded in agreement, then stepped toward Joshua.

"You were the man who instigated the Temple riot the other day. It was you who attacked the moneychangers, wasn't it?"

Joshua looked down at the tiles on the floor—*patterns,* he thought.

"Speak to me!" Caiaphas yelled. "It was you, wasn't it? What rights have you to interfere in our Temple affairs? You caused the Romans to bring out their guard. We don't need that. On that charge alone I can lock you up. For blasphemy, I could have you stoned!"

Joshua looked up momentarily, a scowl on his face.

"Do whatever you have to do, High Priest of the Temple, but know that whatever you do to me, you do to God," he said calmly.

"That is blasphemy! Take him away!" Caiaphas screamed.

Obediently, the guards ran forward.

"Lock him up. The man is dangerous," the High Priest ordered.

The High Priest's men grabbed Joshua and hustled him away, leaving Caiaphas and Annas to discuss their intentions with Saul.

Joshua was led to a dank room below the old palace, which had been prison to countless Hasmonean princes during the previous century. It was dark, with a cold, stone floor, and foul air. He was locked within this dungeon space with no knowledge of his fate. In the silence that followed, he thought only of Maria, seeking comfort in the deep recesses of his human love.

* * *

Cephas and Maria sat against a mounting block, close to a brazier, in the forecourt outside the Hasmonean Palace. Marcus, having finally fallen asleep, had his head in Maria's lap. Cephas put his arm around her.

"Where do you think he is?" Maria asked.

"I've no idea," the fisherman replied. "I imagine they are still questioning him in some way."

"Who are they?" Maria asked, still mystified as to who had arrested her lover and friend.

"I don't know," Cephas answered, "but, judging by this building, they are working for important people, possibly the Temple authorities. They didn't look like Romans or even Herod's guards. They didn't appear to be carrying any weapons. But that was Saul with them—that Pharisee. He got to Judas."

"Judas Iscariot was never very happy with us," Maria suggested. "He hated me."

"I think he was always a little jealous of Janus, Jonas, and me," Cephas agreed. "He was a freedom fighter at heart, Maria. I don't think he should ever have really been in the group, but he was efficient and he had the best boat."

"What will happen to him? Do you think Joshua would ever take him back?"

"I hope not. He betrayed the Master. I really don't care what happens to him."

They sat together in silence for a while.

Maria reflected much on Judas. It bothered her that she might have been the cause of his bitterness. She remembered his stinging words at Gethsemane, and it hurt. *Perhaps I am the cause of Joshua's downfall?* she wondered. *Did I let my love for Joshua weaken his spiritual strength?* She thought about it a long time, while Marcus slept. *No!* she concluded. *Our love is only a manifestation of his spiritual strength. I see God in him most when we are together alone, even more than when he is teaching or healing. The spark of God is in the warmth that glows between us in those most sacred moments that we share.* Comforted by her thoughts, she, too, drifted into a shallow sleep, leaving Cephas to watch alone.

* * *

Neither Annas nor Saul could understand why Caiaphas was hesitating to condemn the Galilean troublemaker.

"He's declared obvious blasphemy," Annas insisted. "The man has set himself up as God."

"I know," the High Priest admitted, "but if I condemn him to death on charges of religious blasphemy, I fear we may open up a bigger problem than this man's blasphemy. There are many Pharisees, especially outside Jerusalem, who are critical of our Temple hierarchy and who would rally around his case. Then, there are zealots. They will follow anyone who attacks authority. Look how they flocked around Barabbas! They were not really concerned with his cause—I don't know what his cause was—it was Herod Antipas' matter—but zealots certainly supported him. This Galilean miracle worker could become an equal rallying point. Annas, I don't think I can risk condemning him to be stoned."

"Why not send him to Pilatus, then?" Annas suggested. "Let the zealots blame Rome for the removal of this rabble rouser. Rome's more afraid of the zealots than we are."

"The prefect isn't concerned with blasphemy, Annas. I don't have a case to present."

"Yes you do," Annas insisted. "This was the man who instigated a riot in the Temple that could have been very dangerous. It spilled out into the streets. It was Roman soldiers who put it down. You can flatter Pilatus, Caiaphas. Tell him that it was only because of the careful watch and swift action of his soldiers that the city was saved from spreading chaos."

Caiaphas closed his eyes and played with his phylactery.

"Good thinking, Annas," he agreed, "but that's hardly enough for Pilatus to have him put to death. If Pilatus could condemn him, however, the wrath of the rural Pharisees and those who follow this Galilean would fall off our shoulders. There might be some bitter condemnation of the Romans, but it would dissipate almost as soon as it would happen. The days of Archelaus are long since over. Rome's in charge now."

He paused for a moment, then looked at his father-in-law confidentially.

"Perhaps we should add that he preaches of a new kingdom," Caiaphas suggested. "The last thing Pilatus wants is for a man to set himself up as a rebel king!"

"My lord! The miracle worker does speak of a kingdom," Saul interjected. "I have heard him refer to this kingdom as 'my kingdom' just as he refers to God as 'my Father'. Actually, he's another of these Scripture quoting prophets of the end time. We could probably use this 'kingdom' talk against him. The Romans are not sympathetic to any messianic ideas, especially if they allude to 'kingship'—the Herodians neither, for that matter."

"Good point, Saul," Caiaphas agreed. "Let's send him over to the Praetorium first thing in the morning. Annas, have a document drawn up in Greek, explaining why we feel this case should go to the prefect. Concentrate on this claim of 'kingship'. Pilatus won't like that. We will have to act fast, though. If we are to get our prisoner condemned, we will need the action completed by the Sabbath."

Annas smarmed with approval.

"The right decision, Caiaphas. We still make a good team."

"Would you like me to take the papers to the Praetorium?" Saul added.

The High Priest nodded.

"Yes, you are what Pilatus would call 'a Greek Pharisee'—a Roman citizen. It will lend even more authority to our case."

Swiftly, Annas' scribes drew up a document.

* * *

Marcus was the first to awake in the open court in front of the High Priest's old Hasmonean palace. A dark gray dawn smoldered in the sky and a horseman was clattering out. Somewhere, not too far away, a cock crowed. The boy pulled at his mother's arm to wake her. He was cold in his torn robe and without his loincloth.

"Where are we?" he asked, with a mixture of sleep and fear.

Maria opened her eyes and looked around.

After their nightime race, following the guards, she didn't know where they were any more than Marcus.

"We're in Jerusalem," she said, and looking around, noticed two girls in rather ragged clothing, starting to brush the courtyard with long bundles of reeds.

The cockerel crowed again.

Cephas awoke.

Before they had time to rub the sleep from their eyes, their attention was drawn to further action in the court. Guards were hustling a prisoner out of the building. There was shouting.

Maria craned her neck.

"It's Joshua!" she cried, recognizing him in the first light of dawn.

Cephas stood up. He could clearly see that six men were escorting the Master, whose hands were tied behind his back.

Then, Joshua saw them.

"Cephas!" he shouted in a loud voice.

The guards looked over in their direction, but Cephas remained silent and looked away in fear.

"He's calling us!" Maria said, pulling on Cephas' garment.

"Keep silent," Cephas whispered. "Pretend that you have never seen him. It's dangerous for us here."

While Cephas looked away, Maria stared in Joshua's direction. Momentarily, their eyes met. She knew that he knew that she was there. *I must stay with him,* she thought. *I must be there for him.*

The sweepers came close to Cephas, Marcus, and Maria. They gestured for them to move, so they could sweep the debris from the base of the now extinguished brazier.

"Did you know that man?" one of them asked Cephas in Aramaic.

"The prisoner they just took out?" Cephas asked, stalling a response.

"Yes."

"No," Cephas answered, looking down at the ash beneath the brazier. "Who was he?"

"I've no idea," the sweeper answered.

"He was brought here last night," the other girl said. "They say he's a Galilean and a miracle worker."

"Really," Cephas muttered.

Maria could not believe that Cephas, of all people, was actually denying knowing the Master. But, following his instruction, she remained silent.

"You don't sound like you're from here," the sweeper continued. "You must be a Passover pilgrim?"

"Yes, from Galilee," Cephas answered in his obviously rustic Aramaic.

"Then, are you sure you don't know who that man is? He's a Galilean. Why are you here in the High Priest's court?"

"Why are you so persistent?" Cephas asked angrily, as his conscience caught up with his lie. "I've told you, I've never seen that man!"

Maria held Marcus tightly as she stared at Cephas. His lie was so deliberate and final.

The sweepers continued with their task.

The cockerel crowed again.

Maria saw tears forming in Cephas' downcast eyes. *The fisherman's lost his heart,* she thought. He could not look her in the eye. Still staring at the ground, he said to her:

"Go Maria! Leave me alone! I am no better than Judas! Go! Go, while you can! It's not safe for you here."

Maria remembered what Joshua had warned at supper the previous night. *There are some among you, who have dipped in this dish with me, who will disown me and betray me.* The words rang in her ears. She could hear Cephas and Jonas's response: *'Not me!'* Now, before one day had passed, Cephas had denied ever knowing Joshua, and Jonas was nowhere to be seen! *What has happened to us,* she thought. *Is there no stability, no truth, anymore?* But in her compassion, she felt sorry for Cephas as he slumped against the mounting block, sobbing. She stretched out her hand to him.

"He will forgive you," she said. "He forgave me."

"Leave me Maria!" Cephas repeated. "Go back to James! It's not safe for you here."

Afraid, and more alone than ever, she backed away, and pulling Marcus with her, ran across the court to the street. The guards were just in sight. Her heart raced. Maria and Marcus followed them.

Early vendors were setting up their stalls, jeering as the guards hustled Joshua along. The dawn had broken. The city was waking up.

* * *

Linus rose early as was his custom. When he came down the marble steps of the Praetorium he was surprised to see action at the gate. The prefect's guard seemed to be in some sort of interchange with leather tuniced men of the Sanhedrin guard. *I wonder what all this is about?* he asked himself, crossing to the gate at a brisk pace.

The captain of the prefect's guard saw Linus coming. He broke away from his inquiries.

"Good morning, sir. We have a prisoner from the Sanhedrin. He looks pretty passive. Papers were delivered a short while ago by one Saul, a citizen of Tarsus. I have him here."

The captain and Linus rejoined the soldiers. The prisoner, with arms tied behind his back, was of medium height with long, light brown hair and a natural beard. He had hypnotic eyes and Linus was almost positive that he was the Galilean healer whom he had begged to visit his father's villa. He stared at the man for a moment curiously. He was moved by the charisma of the man's eyes: *This man has got to be the same person,* he thought. *He's the man who cured Demetrius of the fever.* A well-dressed Jew was at the gate, his horse tethered.

"May I present The High Priest's messenger," the captain said.

"What's the prisoner's name," Linus asked.

"Joshua, sir. He has proclaimed himself a 'King of the Jews,'" Saul said in excellent Greek. "Here, let me pass over to you the High Priest's case against this man. My lord seeks a hearing before the prefect with a view to condemning this man."

"And your credentiuals, sir?"

"Ambassador to the High Priest, Saul of Tarsus, member of the Sanhedrin Council."

Linus took the scroll, while looking suspiciously at the man. He glanced at the content written in perfect Greek.

"Can the prefect hear this case today?" Saul asked. "It's the Sabbath tonight and my lord, the High Priest, is anxious that should this man be condemned, his execution should be completed before the Sabbath. There are still going to be many Passover pilgrims in the city. The Passover Sabbath could be a very dangerous time for us. It is expected that many could rally around this self-styled king."

Linus looked at the guard; an anxious furrow scored his brow. *Joshua,* he repeated to himself. *That was his name...Joshua.* He did not want to believe what he was hearing and reading. *How could the Jews want to rid themselves of such a good man? What do they know about him that I don't? The man healed my father's servant, and showed great kindness to me, even though I am Roman.* Linus felt uncomfortable standing there. *I hope he doesn't recognize me,* he thought.

"Bring the man in," he instructed his soldiers.

The High Priest's guard handed Joshua over to the Roman guard. The prisoner was then led across the courtyard to disappear in some strange corner of the white marble palace that was the Praetorium.

* * *

Outside the gate, Maria and Marcus waited. They had not witnessed the exchange, and Maria had not seen that it was Linus who now seemed to be in charge of Joshua's fate. Not being able to follow any further, she felt hopeless. The sun was up now, and the early morning rays caught the gilt of golden eagles that were mounted atop the pillars of the Praetorium gate. She looked up at the eagles to try to hide her tears from her son, but Marcus knew that his mother was crying. He put his arms around her, and looked up, too.

"Look at those golden birds," he said. "This place is like a king's palace."

Maria warmed to her son's attempt to console her.

"We will have to wait for Joshua here," she said.

They sat on the marble paving outside the Praetorium and began their vigil.

* * *

Pontius Pilatus was not too pleased to be woken up and hear that his aide was waiting for him so early in the day.

"What does he want?" the sleepy prefect asked his slave.

"He says it's urgent, master. Can you come to the ante-room as soon as possible?"

"All right, Hector. Tell him I'll be out as soon as I can."

He yawned.

"But, first, pass me my linen cloth and shave my face."

He stretched and sat in a chair.

"I hope there's no trouble. These Jewish festivals tend to create trouble," he said, as his slave brought Pilatus oil and a silver basin filled with warm water.

With a sharp blade, Hector scraped the oil over his master's stubble.

When his face was smooth and clean, Pontius Pilatus sent Hector back to Linus. The prefect then got dressed in his toga, picked up a silver glass and looked at himself. *There is no point in disturbing Lavinia or putting off this meeting with Linus any longer,* he thought. Confidently, he left his private apartment to join his aide.

Linus saluted him.

"Hail Caesar!"

Then he stated calmly:

"We have a prisoner, sir. I have the charge here. It's from the Jewish High Priest, Caiaphas, and was delivered by a Roman citizen from the Sanhedrin Council—Saul of Tarsus."

"Oh dear! Not trouble in the Temple again," Pilatus asked impatiently.

"Not exactly, sir. Actually, I think I know the prisoner. He couldn't possibly pose a threat to us. He visited my father's villa at Taricheae and healed our servant. He has done many wonderful things in Galilee, not only for Jews, but also for Romans. I think this charge is probably trumped up, maybe he's even being framed."

Pontius Pilatus screwed up his forehead.

Linus unrolled the scroll and read the Greek:

"To His Excellency the Prefect of Judea, Greeting! I Caiaphas, High Priest of the Jews along with the Sanhedrin Council, beseech you to hear our case against the prisoner, Joshua, known as the miracle worker of Bethany. The man is a Galilean, but has caused us severe problems here in Jerusalem. I am asking for your consideration in making necessary condemnation and judgment on this man that he might be put to death to preserve the sanctity of our Temple, the peace of our city, and the safety of the province. The man has made the claim that he is 'the King of the Jews'. What kind of support he has for this claim is hard to tell. He does have a large following, created because he has exhibited certain healing powers and performed certain aspects of magic and sorcery. It is said he raised a man from the dead. Whether this is true or not is no matter to us, but it has been the cause of large crowds gathering around this man. It seems that he has now turned these crowds into accepting him as a new King of Israel. Naturally, Your Excellency, I have felt it my duty to inform you of this outrageous claim that threatens both the sovereignty of the High Priesthood and Rome. Because he is Galilean, his claim also threatens the Tetrarch Herod Antipas, who I am sure would support me in asking that this imposter should be removed. I am positive that the dangers will be self evident to you. On other counts, I have also brought him under arrest. It was this man who instigated the abortive attack on the Temple this week with further outrageous claims that his authority and kingship are from our God. Naturally, amongst us Jews, this is blasphemous, but I am sure you can appreciate the danger that such talk may have in swaying the ignorant masses to his royal claims. It is in both our interests that we should condemn this man. I ask for your assistance and swift action. I remain, Caesar's friend, Caiaphas, High Priest of the Jews."

Pontius Pilatus scratched his forehead.

"Sounds like a zealot rebel to me," he said slowly. "There can be no revival of kingship in Judea unless it is appointed through my office."

He could see that Linus was disappointed.

"You disagree, Linus Flavian?" he asked, raising his eyebrows.

"I know this man, sir. I don't believe these charges. I don't think he has political pretensions."

"But, kingship has enormous political pretension," Pilatus said, somewhat surprised by Linus' negative reaction to the charge. "You mustn't let your judgment become clouded by personal feelings."

"See the man for yourself, sir," Linus insisted. "I'm sure you will make the right judgment, and naturally, I will concur with your decision. I think, however, you will understand what I am saying."

In his heart, Pilatus felt uncomfortable. He trusted Linus implicitly. He usually believed what Linus said. During his time in Jerusalem, the young Flavian had proved to be extremely astute. However, Pilatus realized that he had to make a stand in this case. It was important that the relationship between the prefecture and the Jewish authorities was seen to be working, so that law and order could be maintained in Judea. He would have to go partway in granting the High Priest's wishes, but at the same time, it must be seen by the people that Roman justice had been done. Roman justice, even in such restive provinces as Judea, must be fair.

"You say this man is a Galilean?" Pilatus asked thoughtfully.

"Yes, sir. He was living in Capernaum when I met him. His immediate followers were also Galileans—mostly fishermen."

"Seeing the Tetrarch Herod Antipas is here in Jerusalem, what do you say to sending the Galilean over to the tetrarch for trial?" Pilatus suggested. "After all, it would seem that these charges more directly affect Herod Antipas than us. The man is challenging Antipas' throne more than Ceasar."

Linus remembered the awful scene in Herod Antipas' palace in Tiberias when the tetrarch had allowed the savage execution of the man they called Jon the Baptist. He didn't trust Herod. He didn't feel the tetrarch would be fair.

"Herod's not king here in Judea," he replied. "Jerusalem is the center of the Jewish world and we are responsible for justice here."

"Herod can't condemn a man to death in our province," Pilatus reminded Linus. "If it can be seen that we have taken action against this man and kept him away from the mob at this critical time, hopefully all parties involved will be content. I'm going to send this 'King of the Jews' over to Herod's palace. He really is Herod's case."

Linus felt that he might worsen the situation by questioning the prefect further. He agreed to inform the guard.

"Shall we send him over right away?" he asked.

"Send a messenger ahead, Tribune Linus Flavian. It's early, and I doubt Herod Antipas will be ready for such a deputation. It's well known how he enjoys these religious festivals and I expect that last night was no exception. We should warn him ahead of time that we would like him to hear this case. He may react well to the idea. It will make the pompous little vassal feel important."

Linus drew up papers for Herod Antipas and dispatched them with a messenger immediately.

To both Linus and Pilatus' surprise, the messenger returned from the Herodian palace without delay.

"The Tetrarch Herod Antipas will be pleased to receive the prisoner named 'the King of the Jews' at your earliest convenience," the Roman envoy announced. "He will hear the case."

"Good," Pilatus said. "Linus Flavian, arrange to send the prisoner over."

* * *

Joshua, who was finally dozing off in the slightly better conditions of his Roman prison compared to the dreadful confines of that Hasmonean dungeon, was disturbed again. His hands tied once more behind his back, he was removed from the jail and escorted up and out of the Praetorium by Roman soldiers. He blinked in the sunlight, which was made all the stronger by the new, white marble walls that faced the Praetorium buildings. The soldiers escorted him across the court and out into the street. Opposite the gate mounted with the golden eagles, he saw Maria and Marcus. He called out to Maria, but one of the Roman soldiers slapped him in the face and silenced him.

Maria obviously heard his cry. She looked like she wanted to call back to him, but no sound came forth. Joshua observed, however, that Cephas was no longer with them.

Marcus then shouted:

"That's Joshua! I told you he would come back."

"Yes, but where are they taking him now?" Maria sobbed. "He's still bound, Marcus, and those soldiers won't let him speak to us."

Joshua tried to look back and thought he could see Maria and Marcus following, but the soldiers tugged at him and moved him forward.

Where is Cephas now? Joshua wondered. *He was at the High Priest's palace. Have they all deserted me now? Is Maria the only one with faith in me? Where are Janus and Jonas? How can Maria complete my mission alone…she is only a woman? Is she the only one who really believes me? I realize I might have made a mistake…Was I wrong to appoint Cephas the leader? He has never really acted like one. He seizes on truth, but hasn't the courage to follow it through. Divine love shines from him, yet he can't see it. That's the difference between them—Maria knows that she is a spark of God.* He thought of the others. They all had their good points, even Judas Iscariot. *I had marked Judas to be the leader. He certainly wanted to be. He was much more of a leader in the practical things, but he couldn't grasp the spiritual things. It was such a shame, because he was the strong one! He could have made a good leader, but instead he became the one who betrayed me. So, is Maria now the leader? Will they follow her if I am condemned?*

The soldiers did not take him far. He was led into an imposing, but smaller palace built in the less ostentatious yellow limestone of Hasmonean Jerusalem. Gates closed behind him. Looking back, he saw Maria and Marcus, watching, waiting, and no doubt worrying.

* * *

Tetrarch Herod Antipas walked around Pilatus' prisoner with an air of superiority.

"So, you are the 'King of the Jews,'" he said slowly and sarcastically. "You're not as tall as me. In fact, you are rather small."

The petty king paused for a moment with his hand in the curly locks of his black beard.

"Small in stature and very small in significance," he continued.

Joshua said nothing. He might have been smaller than the pompous tetrarch but was of medium build. He just looked at the floor.

"Speak to me, 'King of the Jews'?" Herod Antipas continued.

Joshua kept his silence.

The tetrarch went back to his dais where he was surrounded by richly dressed courtiers. They were much more colorful than the smooth-shaven, clinical Romans of the Praetorium. They all wore long Semitic robes, richly embroidered in silken threads. They crowned themselves with assorted headpieces in equally fine materials, fastened by long golden pins set with costly jewels.

When Herod sat down, his chief advisor reminded him that this 'King of the Jews' bore the same name as the miracle worker who had built such a reputation around the lake in Galilee. If indeed, they were one and the same person, then this prisoner was the same man who probably conspired with Jon the Baptist to incite rebellion against the salt tax.

The tetrarch raised his dark eyebrows with interest.

"Joshua of Nazareth?" he repeated in question to his advisor.

"That's right, Your Majesty, the very same man."

Herod stood again, calling down to Joshua, who was still looking at the flagstones of the floor:

"'King of the Jews', are you also he who is known as Joshua of Nazareth, the miracle worker from Capernaum?"

Joshua looked up, bemused by the titles that were bestowed upon him.

Herod noted this response.

"So, you are the great miracle worker," he said. "I have wanted to meet you face to face. Would you perform your powers for me?"

Joshua looked down again.

"Answer me!" Herod shouted as his hereditary anger rose. "Will I have to flog you to get you to speak?"

Joshua continued his silence. It seemed that all anyone wanted from him was a miracle. *No one, not even those among my own disciples, seems to understand that it is not I who performs miracles, but my Father, who works through me,* he said to himself. He thought of Maria, and wondered if she was still waiting at the gate. He was reminded of where he was, however, when Herod bellowed again:

"Speak to me! King of the Jews!"

Joshua looked up and scowled at the tetrarch.

Herod turned around and whispered something to his courtiers. Some nodded in serious agreement. He faced Joshua again.

"I warned you, miracle worker!" he shouted. "Now, I am going to have you flogged. Maybe, you will answer me, then!"

He called his guards.

"Take this man away!" he ordered. "Give him thirty lashes. Maybe, that way, we will make this 'king' confess."

* * *

Herod's brutal guards kicked Joshua out into a dingy courtyard at the back of the palace. He landed hard on his knees, scraping his hands on the stone as he broke his fall. High walls precluded much of the sunlight from filtering down. As he looked up, Joshua saw a whipping post in the center of the court. He tried to resist, envisoning deeper pain ahead, but the Herodian guards kicked him on. At the post, two of them held his arms as another undid the short rope that tied his wrists. Then, they placed his arms over the post and retied his hands in front of him. They tethered his legs to the wood, forcing him to stand. Joshua couldn't move, and though his spirit was still free, his body was now bound to the wishes of others.

For a moment, there was a foreboding silence as the Herodian guards left him where he was. Then, Joshua saw two men, dressed in black leather tunics, approach with flails. They passed behind him and he could see them no more. The temporary peace was broken as the flails with their pointed metal studs swished sharply through the air and tore into his back. Joshua screamed. The pain was unbearable. He screamed again and again until it seemed another man was screaming.

After about the fifteenth lash, the pain seemed to subside as Joshua's body became numbed by its fate. His world began to fade in and out as his consciousness became sapped of strength. There was a rhythm to the pain, which now almost made it bearable. Joshua tried to forget his torture as he focussed his mind on the only person who could bring him any comfort—Maria. His body shuddered with the violent impact of each blow, but he kept the image of Maria's face in his mind, and felt the warmth of her body and the softness of her flesh in his senses, as he battled the terrible pain of the scourging hissing whips. By about the twenty-fifth lash, even Maria's face became blurred. It, too, dissolved in his fading consciousness. The warmth of her body remained, however, as Joshua struggled to cling to his senses. His focus became so intense that the scene in the courtyard vanished. The warmth that he imagined melted into his own flesh in a union that was not physical, but wholly spiritual—a merging of Divine love in total surrender.

All of a sudden, Joshua was jerked from that moment of bliss. His head fell forward, jarred to a stop, and hung helplessly above his tied hands as the top of the whipping post ground against his ribs. Meanwhile, the flails lashed into his bleeding pulped back two more times…then stopped.

There was no pain. Joshua felt like he was drifting into an eternal sleep, and in that state, he could see himself as if from above, soaring as a dove. Above the dismal scene, he saw his own torturers wipe his blood from the leather thongs of the flails so that it wouldn't congeal. The metallic studs in the strips of leather that had bitten so deeply into the lacerations on his back then sparkled, caught by a stray shaft of sunlight amidst the courtyard gloom. Then, he dove down from above, returning to his tortured body. The excruciating pain of his lacerations returned. Moments, became like millennia, frozen in agony. All he could see from his drooping head were the flagstones of the courtyard, and all he could hear, was the relentless slow buzzing of the gathering insects feeding on his blood.

In his agony, it seemed an eternity before anyone came back, although in reality it was not long. The Herodian guards returned with a purple cloak, which they threw over Joshua's shoulders as they released him from the whipping post. The rough texture of the material grated against the gaping wounds on his back and the bruises to his rib cage made it very difficult for him to stand, let alone walk. The guards forced him up, however, and they took him back inside the palace—back into the presence of Herod Antipas.

King Herod stood up when they came in and beckoned to a slave. A man stepped forward carrying a cushion on which had been placed a rugged tangle of sharp woven thorns. The tetrarch, himself, carefully took this 'crown' in his own hands and carried it over to Joshua. He placed it on his prisoner's head, pushing the twigs down. The thorns pressed into Joshua's scalp.

"I crown you 'King of the Jews'!" Herod said with malicious satisfaction. "Are you going to speak to me now?"

As the tetrarch pulled his hands away, one sharp thorn barbed Herod's flesh on the palm and the wound immediately bled. The king flinched.

"Heal my wound, miracle worker," he continued in his sarcastic vein. "Heal me, just like you healed all the others, and I will let you go."

There was only quiet as monarch and prisoner stood eyeball to eyeball.

Joshua said nothing. He was in a complete daze. The pain from his wounds, and the weakness that had overcome him through the flogging, had affected his senses. His vision was blurred and he could barely hear the tetrach king address him. Blood from the thorns that pierced his forehead, now ran down into his eyes. As his body softly trembled, he dropped his head in anguish.

Herod Antipas circled Joshua one more time, as if inspecting him to see if his torturers had done a good enough job.

Joshua did not have the strength to look at him

"Take him back to the Romans!" the tetrarch shouted. "Take him away! He's a fraud! He's no miracle worker! He's no king! Let the Romans do to him whatever they like!"

The guards came forward again, but before they seized Joshua, Herod Antipas stood in front of him and in that sarcastic tone addressed him one last time:

"Your reign is over, 'King of the Jews,'" was all he said.

* * *

Maria gasped as she saw Joshua stumble out from the Herodian palace. She could see and feel his pain as he tried to walk. Blood was congealed on his face, and showed in dark patches where the purple robe fell down his back. Agony in his expression was emphasized in every step he took.

Marcus, wide-eyed, asked:

"What's happened to Joshua? What have they done to him?"

"They've tortured him, Marcus," Maria gasped.

Maria boldly stepped forward in the street. Her feelings for Joshua completely overcame her caution.

"Joshua!" she called.

Joshua seemed to hear her voice but could barely turn his head. Then, as Maria came up to him, Marcus following, with great effort the Master croaked her name:

"Maria."

"You can speak then," the guard on his left jibed.

The soldier looked at Maria.

"Behold, your king!" he cried, before spitting at her.

One of the other guards then pushed Maria away, and they dragged Joshua on down the street back toward the Praetorium.

The street was now crowded with vendors conducting morning business. Many looked up to see who was passing. Some, seeing Joshua in his bloodstained purple robe, and crown of sharp thorns, jeered at him. The Herodian guards then encouraged them.

"Make way for the 'King of the Jews,'" they shouted.

Some of the merchants gave mock salutation; urchins threw garbage; others, out of maleficence, followed in procession, yelling and shouting all manner of abuse. There were a few, however, who restrained their neighbors, and some, who even started fist fights in defense of Joshua.

Maria's tears formed rivulets down her face, while Marcus watched the melee—mesmerized—almost excited. Neither of them noticed a well-dressed man approach as the escort and ranting mob moved on toward the Praetorium. The man had a compassionate face, framed by his well-trimmed beard and the richness of his headpiece. He stopped and gently patted Maria on the shoulder. She looked up into his face.

"You knew him?" he said.

"Yes..." Maria sobbed.

"So did I," the rich-looking Jew continued wistfully.

Maria noticed his phylacteries. The man was obviously a Sadducee or Temple Pharisee. She pulled away, suspicious of him, despite his kind face. She no longer felt she could trust anybody.

Marcus, staring at the man's fine clothes, pulled on a sleeve.

"I remember you!" he said, laughing. "You stepped on my foot, didn't you?"

The man looked down, as Maria grabbed Marcus.

"Really, when?" he said

"You came to be healed in that smelly village, didn't you?"

"Yes," the man replied. "I went out to Bethany about ten days ago."

"You did?" Maria asked, looking for reassurance.

"Yes," he assured her.

"What's your name?" Maria asked.

"Joseph," the man answered. "I'm originally from Arimathea, but since I was elected onto the Sanhedrin Council, I've been living here in Jerusalem."

"He's the man who stepped on my foot," Marcus repeated, laughing again.

"Ah...yes, that's right," the rich man agreed, patting Marcus' head. "I hope I didn't hurt you."

Maria's fear began to drop away. She looked at Joseph intensely.

"You believe in the Master, then," she said.

"I have faith that he has healed me," Joseph answered. "I was not expected to live long. Worms are supposed to be eating me up, but since I met Joshua the Miracle Worker in Bethany, I have felt better. I believe he has cured me."

He paused, looking up the street as the soldiers turned into the Praetorium, shutting the gates on the mob. Then, he asked:

"Why have the Herodians seized him?"

"We don't know, sir," Maria answered. "One of his disciples betrayed him, but we don't know why. All his followers have gone now. Even Cephas, his most trusted man has fled. Do you know anything? Do you know what is going to happen to him?"

"I know enough to know that many in the Sanhedrin, including the High Priest, were worried about the crowds that the miracle worker drew in Bethany. They didn't like him teaching in the Temple, either. He was described as a 'disruptive influence' and was blamed for a disturbance there a few days ago."

He looked intently at Maria.

"There was no conclusive evidence, however, only hearsay," he continued. "I don't know how he came to be arrested. The Sanhedrin doesn't meet during the Passover festival."

"Let's follow them!" Maria suggested. "Won't you come with us? I need to be near him."

"You are very close to him, aren't you?" Joseph observed.

"Yes..." Maria replied, her sobs returning.

Joseph put his arm around Maria and held Marcus' hand.

"Let's go," he said. "We'll stay with them and find out what's happening."

They moved in to the milling crowd, who, curiosity challenged, stood around at the gate grumbling. Joseph of Arimathea shielded Maria and Marcus from their rough abuses as he nudged them forward to take up a position in front of the forecourt of the Roman prefect's Praetorium.

* * *

Pontius Pilatus was more than just a little irritated when Linus Flavian announced that the tetrarch of Galilee had returned, Joshua, the 'King of the Jews'. He thought he was rid of this problem.

He looked up at the white ceiling. The Praetorium was clean and bright, unlike surrounding Jerusalem. Then, shuffling his feet he looked down at the fresh mosaic floor—chariots in black and white surrounded a central image of himself, or at least a prefect, being carried on his litter. There was little else in this spartan hall other than his chair, his aide's chair, and a small table with a tray of goblets and a flagon of wine.

"Can't we just imprison him until the festival period is over?" he suggested at length.

"We could," Linus agreed, "but unfortunately, after Herod Antipas made a spectacle of him, a large crowd has now gathered outside, and it's growing. They seem to be against the Galilean. It might at least be prudent to let them know what we are doing so they will disperse. Herod had him flogged. The man looks half dead and they've mocked him by dressing him up as a king, crowning him with a wreath of sharp thorns."

"Hasn't that satisfied them?" Pilatus muttered, irritated that he would now have to take up the matter where Herod had left off.

"It doesn't seem so," Linus replied.

Pilatus walked over to one of the windows and looked out in silence for a while. It was now mid-morning. There was not a cloud in the sky on what seemed an almost perfect day. He turned back and looked at Linus again.

"How about this?" he said. "Why don't I suggest to the crowd outside that we free Barabbas as we discussed earlier. It might be sufficient to satisfy their frustrations against the 'King of the Jews', if they even know who this imposter is. They're just looking for excitement at festival time. It's just another gladiatorial performance to them. I have the right to release Barabbas, even though it's against my better judgment. Maybe, releasing Barabbas to them will be enough for them?"

"If only we had not sent the Galilean to Herod," Linus said. "We could have kept all this quiet until after the festival—even released Joshua after the festival, quietly, without ceremony."

He hesitated, then continued:

"Maybe they will accept your gesture. Will you pronounce your decision?"

"I'll announce my pardon from the gate's guard house. Have a scroll prepared," Pilatus answered. "Meanwhile, we'll keep the mysterious 'King of the Jews' our prisoner here until this furor dies away."

Pilatus was surprised, however, when he arrived at the gatehouse to see how large the teeming crowd outside had become. Rumor had spread that a prominent person had been arrested—a king. The early crowd was more curious than anything, but as the word spread, spies of the High Priest were freely supplementing their propaganda, condemning Joshua as a blasphemous rebel who had tried to upset the festival of Passover. Pilatus felt very uneasy. The crowd was noisy. Some were shouting:

"Crucify him!"

Roman soldiers appeared above the gate flanked by those golden eagles.

The crowd temporarily hushed.

A herald blew a trumpet. The prefect and his aide came out.

Pilatus took a scroll from Linus and faced the people from the gatehouse balcony.

"Men of Jerusalem!" he shouted, although he noted there were a few women among the curious. "It is my custom at this festival season to release to you a prisoner, in the name of Caesar, as an act of goodwill and generosity. I will release to you Barabbas of Jericho at this time, a man who was condemned by us, in conjunction with the Tetrarch Herod Antipas, for subversive activity in the Jordan valley."

The prefect paused for a moment to test the reaction of the crowd.

"Free Barabbas!" a rough-looking man close to the front yelled.

Others followed, chanting:

"Free Barabbas!"

Before Pilatus spoke again, a wealthy-looking man right below the gate, looking a little incongruous in the crowd and standing with an attractive woman and a boy, shouted up to the prefect:

"What about Joshua, the miracle worker!"

Others heard the man. One or two also called for 'Joshua'; but their cries were drowned out by those who yelled:

"Crucify him! Free Barabbas!"

The chant increased with as much intensity being expressed for Joshua's crucifixion as for Barabbas' freedom.

Pilatus was worried. Some of those who had shouted for 'Joshua' were beginning to brawl with those calling for 'Barabbas'. His scheme to appease the crowd had turned into a dangerous scene. He felt he would have done better if he had ignored them altogether and maybe, in the heat of the day, they would have dispersed.

"The plebs will have their blood," Pilatus said to Linus. "They want the 'King of the Jews' to be put to death."

"Not without fair trial," Linus suggested. "It would be inappropriate to condemn Joshua until you assess him for yourself."

"Agreed, Linus," the prefect said in fustration, then, turning to the crowd, he held up his hand.

As they hushed, he gave the Imperial salute:

"Hail Caesar!"

"Hail Caesar!" the crowd returned.

"I release to you today the prisoner, Barabbas of Jericho," he said firmly, before returning inside.

"Linus Flavian, make arrangements for a proper hearing immediately. We need witnesses. We must accomplish this immediately. Should we condemn the 'King of the Jews' we will need to carry out a crucifixion before sundown. Their Sabbath starts tonight. We will only irritate them more if we break their Sabbath rules."

"Do you really think it will come to that?" Linus questioned, with deepening concern. "Please wait until you see him."

"Haven't you seen the crowd?" Pilatus replied. "Make the arrangements!"

Pilatus left Linus at the gatehouse and crossed the court into the Praetorium. Reluctantly, Linus ordered preparations for Joshua's trial.

* * *

Joshua was not taken back to the prison in the Praetorium where he had been held earlier. Instead, he was left in a small room with a high window and a marble floor. The room was furnished with a small stool and he was able to sit. That, alone, took some of the pain away from his back and legs, profoundly stressed by the burdensome trek from Herod's palace. The pain was still unbearable—very sore—but at least the quantity of flies that had harassed his wounds in the street, were now reduced. The Romans had not untied his wrists so he was unable to pull out the thorns, which he yearned to do. The sharp burrs continued to cause his head to throb. But, the flow of blood had thankfully now stopped, leaving dark red encrustations on his face and in his beard. He sat, trembling, and waited. Somehow, he felt a little more secure in the Praetorium than he had in Herod's palace.

Eventually, the Roman soldiers returned. They led Joshua out into the main hall of the Praetorium where Pilatus and his aide were seated along with four or five toga-clad Romans among whom was the Jew, Saul of Tarsus. The room was bright from the midmorning sun, which shone through high windows, catching the white marble in shafts of light. Joshua was goaded to the center of the room and left standing alone in front of the prefect and his aide. The aide appeared to smile at him.

Something familiar. I feel like I know him, Joshua thought, but had no recollection as to why. Pilatus, then nodded at Linus to begin.

The aide stood up and addressed those present in a clear voice:

"Your Excellency, Pontius Pilatus, Prefect of Judea, and to all assembled. The prisoner before us has been returned to us by Tetrach Herod Antipas on the charges of Caiaphas, High Priest of the Jews. The man is a Galilean whose powers as a miracle worker have been duly noted. He apparently claims that these powers have been given to him directly by the God of the Jews. This is contrary to the High Priest's opinion and has led to the prisoner attracting dangerous crowds, some of whom believe this apparent blasphemy. The prisoner and his followers were probably the instigators and cause of a small but bloody riot in the Temple a few days ago, which led to us having to command the release of troops from Antonia's Tower. Order, however, was quickly restored. Most significant has been the claim, allegedly made by the prisoner, that he is a new 'King of the Jews'. For this charge, which incites zealots and could have serious implications for Jews and Gentiles of this prefecture and the tetrarchies, we sent the prisoner to the Galilean tetrarch, King Herod Antipas. Herod, as you can see, has flogged the prisoner and mocked him with a crown of thorns, but wiped his hands of further sentence. Our purpose at this time is to ascertain whether this punishment is sufficient for the crimes here mentioned, or whether under Roman justice, further sentence should be made. It should be noted that the mob that followed the prisoner from the Herodian palace is generally hostile toward him, which does add to the danger. Bearing this in mind, we submit the prisoner into your hands."

Pontius Pilatus nodded again, and then stood up to address Joshua.

"You are a Galilean?" he asked.

Joshua stared at the Roman prefect.

"Tell me about your kingdom? Does your kingdom extend beyond Galilee?"

Joshua lightly and painfully bowed his head in acknowledgment. A few drops of fresh blood plopped on the floor from one of his wounds. No one saw them fall. But Joshua felt them slide down his skin, as a bead of sweat would on a sultry day.

"So, you would set yourself up as a king in the Roman prefecture of Judea?" Pilatus asked.

Joshua was more conscious of the pain, which made his body quake with each fearful heartbeat. Again, he said nothing.

"On whose authority do you claim this kingdom?" the prefect asked, becoming more concerned.

There followed a pregnant silence until, at length, Joshua assembled enough strength to reply, his head still bowed:

"My kingdom…is not of this world."

One of the Roman witnesses leaned over toward Pilatus.

"He is deranged," he suggested.

"No," Saul said firmly. "He does believe he has been called to reign over some kingdom. I have heard him say so in the Temple. I consider him to be another of these firebrand fools who incite rebellion in the name of messiahship."

"Messiahship," Pilatus repeated.

"A form of Jewish kingship, Your Excellency, heralding the end time. Not relevant during the good governance of Rome, but a distant future dream of Jewish fanatics. We, Roman Jews, do not hold much belief in messiahship, for we are used to living in the 'Diaspora.'"

"Quite," said Pilatus.

Then, Joshua continued in a faltering voice:

"Those…who enter my kingdom…enter in faith. Neither the High Priests, nor Herod, nor you Romans…have any power over me. My authority…is from my Father, who is beyond princes and powers."

"Your kingdom is not under Caesar?" Pilatus quizzically exclaimed.

Joshua merely glanced up at the prefect, drained from his reply.

"But you call yourself 'The King of the Jews'?" the prefect continued, his questioning becoming more intense with his rising frustration and anger.

"So…you say," was all Joshua whispered in reply.

"I can have you crucified!" Pilatus yelled. "The crowd outside my gates is calling for your death."

He walked down toward Joshua.

"Do you hear me? Do you understand me? That is my power. I have the power to sentence you to death!"

Joshua then condemned himself. Slowly and deliberately, he labored to elaborate on his earlier remarks.

"In my kingdom…you have no power…neither you, nor Caesar. In this time...we give to Caesar what is Caesar's, but my kingdom is not of this time. Those who enter my kingdom...enter in spirit...live in spirit. They live by the authority of God...not by that of man. You can do to me whatever you like. Some of you Romans only know brutality. You do not understand the love of the Kingdom of God—yet I will forgive you... that is my Father's command."

Pontius Pilatus realized as he heard these words that he was caught in his own trap. He had no choice but to condemn this man, who in the presence of Roman witnesses had openly defied the power of Caesar. He looked at Linus, who instinctively knew what the prefect was thinking. Joshua had condemned himself.

"I sentence this man to death by crucifixion," Pilatus said slowly. "He is condemned for enticing Jews into a conspiracy against the power of Rome."

Saul nodded in agreement. The other Romans turned their thumbs down as if sentencing a gladiator.

Pontius Pilatus called back the Roman guard.

"Gaius Cassius," he said, addressing their leader. "You are in charge of today's executions. See that all is completed before sundown. We don't want to upset the High Priest at this festival time. Take this prisoner away to join the others."

"Three all together, then, Your Excellency?" Gaius asked in confirmation.

"I believe so... this man and the two robbers that killed Martus on the Jericho road."

* * *

Gaius Cassius and five Roman soldiers hauled Joshua away from the prefect's presence. The witnesses were dismissed, including Saul of Tarsus. Pontius Pilatus was left alone with his aide.

The prefect called for Hector, his slave.

When Hector entered, Pilatus asked him to bring a bowl of fresh water and a linen cloth. When the slave came back he washed his hands and looked at Linus.

"I wash my hands of this case," he said. "I agree with you. There is something remarkable about this man. He moved me in his simplicity, but he condemned himself. Messiahship—why do these Jews mix their religion with politics? Sometimes, Linus Flavian, we have to do things in the name of Caesar for the good of the empire. This prisoner got himself caught up in something that has become politically dangerous. I do not believe that he himself is a serious threat. I have sacrificed him for expediency."

Linus said nothing, although in his heart he understood, and wondered what he would have done if indeed he had been the prefect judging this case.

"Go with them, Linus," Pilatus continued. "See that Gaius Cassius is not too brutal. This 'King of the Jews' has suffered enough already. See that they use no nails. It's not necessary. The man is already half dead."

Pilatus was obviously moved. Linus observed a moist, glossy appearance in his eyes.

"I understand. I'll go with them," he said.

"Oh, we are obligated to release that villain Barabbas," Pilatus added. "See that is also arranged."

Chapter Eighteen

Crucifixion

Gaius and his soldiers took Joshua into a dark part of the Praetorium where there was no marble. There, they removed the crown of thorns, although the action in itself only brought greater pain to Joshua's head. Linus entered as they were stripping Joshua of the purple cloak. He winced at the welts that crisscrossed the healer's back. The wounds spewed an unhealthy combination of blood and mucus, forming jellylike globules on his raw flesh.

"Go easy on him," Linus suggested. "The man is already half dead."

"Whatever you say, Governor," Gaius said with a sneer. "His back's a beauty."

Two of the soldiers untied Joshua's wrists and pulled his arms out, forcing him to bend forward.

Joshua groaned as his back muscles strained against drying blood. Another soldier placed a large plank across his shoulders while two more tied his arms to the beam with thongs. The whispy leather cut into Joshua's already raw wrists. The wood grated against the wounds on his upper back, and when he tried to walk he felt dizzy, staggered, and fell to his knees. The crossbeam hit his head, ramming his chin against the floor.

"He'll never make the journey," one of them observed as they pulled Joshua up again.

The weight of the crossbeam caused Joshua more agony even than the crown of thorns. The hard wood ground into his raw flesh.

Two others were brought in and likewise strapped to crossbeams. They had not been flogged and were better able to handle their fate. One of them vomitted when he saw Joshua's wounds. When all of them had been made ready, they were roped together in convoy with Joshua at the rear, and led out into the Praetorium court. There, they waited in the hot sun, burdened by the weight of their load, until Barabbas had been released. More flies returned to feed on the juices of Joshua's flesh in the agony of that wait.

Eventually, Barabbas was led out from another part of the building and taken to the guardhouse gate. There, he was untied and released to the waiting crowd. Cheers rose—shouts of "Barabbas!"

Roman soldiers whipped Joshua and his unfortunte companions into motion as they dragged their heavy feet across the courtyard. Linus, in his tribune's uniform, breastplate gleaming as he sat astride a white horse, ordered the gates to be opened for their passage.

* * *

Many of those closest to the Praetorium gate followed Barabbas when he was released. Maria and Marcus, however, waited with Joseph of Arimathea. They were right there when the gates opened again for the three condemned prisoners and their escort. Linus went ahead. He did not appear to recognize Maria as he rode by, but she was shocked—there was no mistaking him. The man on the horse was Marcus' father. She was so surprised, following Linus with her eyes, that she did not particularly notice the two robbers struggling with their crossbeams. It was not until Joshua staggered along in the rear, prodded on by the Roman guards, that she became aware of what was happening. Joshua obviously saw her. He looked in her direction in agony, stumbled and fell again. The soldiers kicked him and forced him up. Linus looked back to see what had happened. Joshua couldn't speak and was forced forward again. Maria screamed when she saw his tortured torso. She shared his agony. Linus drew his horse closer and stared down at her. Then, he looked quizzically at her boy. Maria wanted to shout up to him, '*Your son,*' but the words suffocated in her throat. Saying nothing, Linus goaded his horse onward, but looked back curiously one more time, before taking his place at the lead again.

"Linus!" Maria finally called out. "Have compassion. For my sake... Have compassion!"

Linus turned again. He stared at Maria as his horse pawed the ground.

"For my sake!" Maria repeated.

Linus nodded, but Maria could not hear him amid the shouts of the regrouping and excited, jeering crowd.

* * *

Linus led the prisoners down the long straight street that led to the Calvary Gate at Golgatha. They had not gone far when Joshua fell yet again. Once more, the soldiers kicked him back to his feet. As Joshua looked up in his agony, he saw a lady in fine clothes. Her face seemed filled with sympathetic love. He tried to smile as their eyes met, but the pain was too much. The soldiers kicked him on. After a few steps, he collapsed again. This time, he had no will to respond to the soldiers' brutality. He lay crushed under the weight of his beam ready to accept whatever they gave.

Linus stopped.

Meanwhile, a strong-looking man stepped forward from the jeering crowd lining the street of merchants' stalls.

"Joshua!" he cried. "What have they done to you?"

Joshua didn't answer. He was painfully and critically exhausted.

"You know this prisoner?" Linus asked the man.

"Everyone knows him," he answered, "at least everyone who has been healed by his touch."

Linus choked. In his mind's eye he saw Joshua so vividly at his father's house. He knew exactly what this man was saying. If anyone had ever had an encounter with this miracle worker named Joshua, they would not forget it.

"What is your name?" Linus asked.

"Simon, sir."

"You don't sound like you're from Jerusalem. Do you speak Greek?"

"Yes," he answered in Greek. "I am from Cyrene."

Linus called down to Gaius Cassius.

"Let this man from Cyrene carry the prisoner's beam for him. We will never get to Golgotha at this rate. Untie the condemned man's arms and give the plank to Simon here."

Simon momentarily froze and then tried to escape back into the crowd. Two of Gaius' men seized him. They held him while Joshua was released from his burden and his arms again tied behind his back.

"No harm will come to you," Linus called down to Simon. "Just carry the crossbeam for your friend. He's too weak."

The good looking woman now rushed forward and placed a cool damp cloth over Joshua's face. The guards shooed her away, but the soothing moisture had helped revive Joshua. The soldiers pulled him up, the rope jerked and the death march continued.

* * *

Maria was still in a double state of shock from the horror of observing Joshua in his agony and seeing Linus as the symbol of Joshua's oppression. One minute she screamed, and the next, she collapsed in a torrent of tears.

Marcus was more composed. He was not aware of his mother's recognition of his father and more detatched in his observation of Joshua.

"What are they going to do to him?" was all he asked as he looked up at Joseph of Arimathea.

"They've sentenced him to death," Joseph replied truthfully. "They are taking him to be crucified." He squeezed the boy's hand. "Where do you live? I think we had better take your mother home."

Marcus vaguely described the location of James' house:

"Somewhere just south of the big Temple gate where the beggars sit." Then, looking up at Joseph again, he asked: "Why are they going to kill him?"

"Because they are cruel wicked men," Maria said before Joseph could collect his thoughts. "He has done nothing wrong."

"But that Roman in the plumed helmet didn't look cruel," Marcus persisted.

"No..." Maria answered. "I don't think he is...I think he knows us."

Joseph, who knew the city well, walked them back toward Mount Zion.

"I know that woman who ministered to Joshua," Joseph said to Maria. "Her name's Veronica. She came to Bethany. Her son was sick."

At length, they arrived at the house on the square.

Jonah greeted them.

"What's happened?" he shouted, seeing how distraught Maria was.

"I am a friend of Joshua, too," Joseph of Arimathea explained. "The prefect has sentenced him to death. They're taking him out to Golgotha to be crucified."

"The murderers!" Jonah exclaimed. "You mean right now? Why? I thought you were all still at the Mount of Olives...Why?"

Momentarily, more composed, Maria said:

"They've beaten him badly. He's already almost dead. Fetch Miriam and come with us. We must go there, now!"

Then, becoming hysterical again, she screamed, and shouted:

"I must be there! I must be there!"

Miriam joined them. Jonah tried to explain to Miriam what Joseph and Maria had told him. Miriam took the news with surprising calm, almost as if she expected it. James was not home, and Rachel stayed behind with Joanna, but Marcus wouldn't leave his mother. They hastened through the city to Golgotha—the place of the skull.

* * *

Joshua was held captive by one of the guards while his cross was being assembled on the ground. The soldiers under Gaius' command drove heavy pegs into the crossbar to fasten it to the hanging post. The crossbeam was then lashed to the vertical for added security. At the same time, other soldiers prepared the execution crosses for the two murdering robbers. Golgotha was a noisy place.

What have I done that it should come to this? Joshua asked himself. *My God, why have you left me?*

When the soldiers were ready, they took Joshua and laid him down on the frame. Two, held his legs, while two others stretched out his arms. He was too weak to struggle. As they positioned him, the presssure reopened sores on his back giving him excrutiating pain.

"Help me!" Joshua cried weakly. "Help me!"

One of the onlookers, an agent from the High Priests, heard him, and shouted to the gathering crowd outside the city walls:

"He saved others, but he cannot save himself. If his authority really comes from God, see if he can save himself, now!"

The crowd responded, mocking Joshua:

"Save yourself, 'King of the Jews'!"

Joshua barely heard them. His mind was too occupied by the pain of his exposed muscles and lacerated flesh grating against the rough wood of the execution post. The soldiers tied his arms firmly to the crossbeam at his forearms and wrists. The thin thongs were so tight that they cut into his flesh, adding to his agony. Then, they bound his feet and tied them firmly to the post. Once he was truly secure, they left him strapped to his cross as it lay on the ground. They busied themselves tying up the two thieving murderers to their posts.

Joshua lay on the cross looking up at the sky. A temporary peace came over him as the pain numbed. A few, white, puffy clouds had appeared in an otherwise blue dome. There were black birds, flying, surveying the scene. If he turned his head just slightly to the right, he could see the hills of Samaria. It was peaceful and calm. To the left, however, it was a different story. Below the city wall, he could see how a crowd had gathered. *Men have such a morbid fascination with death,* he thought, as he heard them chanting their mocking abuse. He turned his head back to the tranquility of the right.

Peace was broken by screams from the other condemned men and the sound of hammering. Joshua couldn't see what was going on, but the cries gave him a fair idea. It was not long before the callous soldiers came back to where he lay. He could now see the man with the mallet, splattered in recent blood. The man carried a wooden box in which Joshua presumed were nails. Two soldiers knelt down and held his arms. Joshua winced in anticipation.

"No!" came a voice from behind. "No nails for him!"

"Why?" the man with the mallet questioned with surprise.

"These are the prefect's orders," came the answer from behind.

"If you say so," the man said.

The soldiers looked up, loosening their grip on Joshua's arms.

Joshua thought he could make out the tribune dismounting from his white horse.

"Bring me one of those wood chips!" Linus commanded.

He then wrote boldly on the chip, using a vial of dirty oil. He wrote in Greek and Aramaic: 'Joshua, the King of the Jews.'

"Where's our man with the mallet?" he asked when finished.

The man stepped forward again.

"Nail this to the post," he ordered.

The man nailed it to the cross above Joshua's head. Every time the brute hit the nail, the whole cross jarred, causing sharp, shooting pains in Joshua's wounds. The pain was too much and Joshua cried out in pure agony:

"Leave it! Leave me alone!"

"That'll do," Linus said, although the sign was only partly placed.

The soldiers then started to turn Joshua's cross around so that the bottom end would rest in the freshly dug post-hole. Whimpering, all Joshua could hear and feel as he looked up at the increasing puffy white clouds was the grinding of the gravel beneath the dragging frame. The movement pressed coarse wood splinters into the lacerations on his back. As the field of his vision changed, he could see the more tranquil scene to his right. Separate from the crowd, standing alone by an outcrop of rocks, he could make out a little group of figures. There were women in the group. He hadn't noticed them before. It was hard to be sure from the new ground level view that he had. Weeds and wildflowers impeded his line of vision and the clumsy soldiers attaching the ropes kept getting in the way, but he thought he saw his mother and Maria. *I think they are here,* he said to himself, and he smiled in his agony.

At length, the soldiers were ready to hoist the post. With two long ropes they pulled up the cross bearing Joshua's frail body. The post slid into the hole with a jarring painful thud that jerked Joshua's spine. As the cross became erect, Joshua's torso sagged. The wounds on his lower back scraped against the crude post and more splinters pierced through the light material of his loin cloth, causing him even greater agony. Pressure increased on the thongs that held his arms and they bit even deeper into his flesh. Stones were thrown in to give support as the cross wobbled. The man with the mallet swung at the stones to firm them up, again sending shudders through the frame that wracked Joshua's ruined body. For a moment, Joshua thought that he was blacking out. The landscape became blurred in tones of yellow and orange, and the new pain of stretched bare muscles and sinews added to the intense throbbing of his wounds. Below him, the soldiers steadied the post with yet more stones until it was deemed sufficiently secure. When finished, they stood back and laughed. One of them, saluting his forehead, bent forward, shouting:

"Hail! King of the Jews!"

Then, they left Joshua hanging to die.

The two murdering thieves were likewise raised, one on each side of Joshua. Their hands and feet were still bleeding profusely from the cruel nails.

After a while, the tribune rode up to Joshua's cross. He was close enough to quietly speak to the condemned man.

"Forgive me, Joshua," he said in Aramaic. "You may not remember me, but I have never forgotten you."

Joshua squinted at him through blood and tear stained eyes. He hadn't the will to smile as he continued to wrestle with the incredible pain—wounds, muscles, thongs, and now, his chest. In a feeble voice, he called on God to forgive the Romans.

"Father," he said, "forgive them, for they don't know what they are doing."

Later, some of the High Priest's spies also made their way from the crowd to Joshua's cross. They were curious to know what inscription the Romans had nailed above their prisoner. *Is that Saul again?* Joshua wondered. He thought so. Yes, he was sure. *It is.* When they read Linus' words in Aramaic, they challenged the tribune, who remained close by, feeling a deep remorse for his unfortunate part in this execution.

"Why has it been written, 'Joshua, King of the Jews'?" Saul said. "Would it not have been better to have written, 'Joshua, who said that he was King of the Jews?'"

The tribune chastised them.

"Go back and leave this man to die in peace," he shouted down to them. "What I have written, I have written."

Saul and his companion, fearing the power of Rome, retreated.

Linus looked across at Joshua.

Joshua thought he saw tears in the tribune's eyes He warmed to him as the dreadful pain bore to a numb consistency. For a long time, they stared at each other.

Finally, Linus spoke:

"Today, you will be with your God," he said with heart-rending sincerity.

Then, he turned his horse slowly and left Joshua to endure his final suffering.

* * *

Maria observed Linus from her vantage point. *Why doesn't he come over here?* she thought. *Perhaps he feels the guilt of his betrayal. He was so full of noble intentions, but when it came to the test, he abandoned me. Funnily enough, I never really held it against him. There is only so far that Romans can go. Antonias abandoned me, too.* Her train of thought was broken, however, by Joseph of Arimathea.

"I have a sepulchre," he said, addressing Maria and Miriam. "It was recently hewn from rock in the garden of tombs close to the North Gate. I don't believe that I'll need it now. I have faith that Joshua healed me and I would like to make it over to you for Joshua's burial. Joshua the Miracle Worker must not be thrown down into the common pit. He deserves better."

Miriam looked at their new friend, astounded by his generosity. Neither she, nor Maria, had given any thought as to how they would bury Joshua should he die, and now, he was assuredly going to die. Joseph's comment brought the reality closer. But, burial to them meant a shallow grave off the roadway covered with loose stones. Not even Joachim, Miriam's father in Nazareth, had been buried in a sepulchre.

"No, sir, how can we pay you?" she pleaded.

"Don't think of it," Joseph replied. "I will arrange to collect his body. I have influence in the right area."

Joseph then looked at Jonah.

"Take care of the women," he said. "Stay here until I come back. No harm will come to you or the boy if you stay over here. I'll be back as soon as possible. In his state, I doubt that Joshua will survive on that cross for long."

Joseph left.

The puffy clouds had thickened and increased, diminishing much of the earlier blue sky.

Miriam held Maria, as the reality of Joshua's coming death became obvious. As they pressed against each other in common comfort, they could feel each other's hearts throb with anxious fear.

Marcus stared at the three sombre crosses on the Golgotha hillock.

"How have they fixed them to those crosses?" he asked Jonah.

"They impale them with nails," Jonah answered, as he recalled the mass crucifixions that had followed the 'Great Rebellion'. "They tie them to the beams with leather thongs to take their weight and then drive spiked nails through their feet and hands."

Marcus winced:

"That must hurt a lot," the boy continued, fearfully fascinated by the whole procedure.

"I'm sure it does," Jonah answered. "The agony lasts so long."

At that, the boy became more somber and said no more.

* * *

Joseph of Arimathea had no trouble in persuading the Temple authorities that he wanted to bury the body of Joshua the Miracle Worker in his own tomb. Caiaphas and Annas were only too pleased at this point to know that their mission had been accomplished and that the potential trouble that the Galilean might have caused them had been successfully thwarted. They accepted a generous donation from the Sanhedrin councilor and gave their consent. Caiaphas asked Saul of Tarsus to write out a scroll stating their approval of Joseph's request that could be presented to the Roman tribune in charge at Golgotha. As Caiaphas dictated his message, Saul questioned the wisdom of the High Priest's decision.

"Do you think it really wise to bury this phony 'King of the Jews' in a rich man's tomb?" he queried. "Surely, this will only draw attention to our expediency in having this man condemned. Many in the mob admire him, if not his claims. The tomb may become a gathering point for this unruly crowd! If so, the Romans will be even more agitated and worse could follow."

"Saul," Caiaphas intervened. "Joseph supports our coffers well. We should not upset him. He believes he was cured of his malady by this Galilean. Perhaps he was."

"Yes, my lord. That is precisely why his judgment is clouded."

Momentarilly, Caiaphas consulted with Annas.

"No," he said at length. "I will not revoke my decision. Write as we have commanded so that the Romans can release the body to Joseph. The mob will not expect him to be buried in a rich man's tomb."

It was well into the afternoon by the time that Joseph returned to the crucifixions. The sky was now quite menacing. He had to fight his way through the gawking crowd until he reached the Roman guards.

"Who is your commander?" Joseph asked in Greek.

"Gaius Cassius," one of the soldiers answered.

"Where is he?"

The soldier pointed to the man with the horse.

"Next to Tribune Flavian, the prefect's aide," he stated.

"Can I speak with him?" Joseph requested.

"Wait here," the man replied.

The soldier crossed the stony ground forbidden to common onlookers. Gaius and Linus looked in Joseph's direction. After some discussion, all three came over to where Joseph stood.

"Do you have something to say?" Linus asked.

"Yes, sir," Joseph replied.

"What is it then?"

Joseph handed over the High Priest's scroll.

"I have permission here to take the body of the crucified man, Joshua, the 'King of the Jews,'" Joseph said.

Linus looked at the three crosses.

"The man in the middle?"

"Yes. I have a tomb prepared for him in the garden cemetery outside the North Gate."

Linus Flavian read the scroll. It seemed in order and Joseph certainly looked like a respectable man—a wealthy merchant perhaps, who spoke excellent classic Greek.

"Very good," Linus agreed. "As soon as we pronounce him dead you will be able to proceed. I doubt he will last much longer, so I suggest you stay where you are."

"Can I not cross over to the far side and wait with my friends?" Joseph pleaded.

"Where?"

"Over there," Joseph said, pointing to Miriam, Maria, Jonah, and Marcus.

Linus had not paid attention to them up to this point, concentrating on the potential problems of the rabble that always gathered below the city wall like a crowd at the gladiatorial arena.

"Why are they there?" Linus asked. "They shouldn't be there. You stay where you are. I'll send them back here to you."

Gaius Cassius issued orders in Latin.

* * *

Linus rode over to the area below Golgotha where the lone spectators were standing.

When Linus reached them, he instantly recognized Maria. *It was her at the Praetorium gate,* he realised. The natual beauty in her face and those sensuous sultry eyes had not changed in the passing decade. He knew she was the Hebrew girl of his misspent youth, and immediately he saw by his face that the boy looked more Roman than Jew. *My son... Maria must be very close to the miracle worker,* he thought. He did not know whether to smile or pretend he didn't care, but he could not deny a pang of jealousy. Maria, however, made the decision for him.

"Linus!" was all she said.

"Maria from Magdala!" Linus responded.

Jonah and Miriam stood there amazed.

"You know this man," Joshua's mother asked.

Maria could not conceal the truth.

Marcus stared at Linus' great feathered helmet and shining cuirass. Linus smiled at him. He remembered how he, too, had stood as a boy in awe of his father when Flavius Septimus had worn his uniform.

"Is this your son?" Linus asked, his heart almost missing a beat.

Maria choked and nodded.

"Well, I must ask you to move," Linus said, regaining composure. "There's a man waiting for you over on the other side. That's where you're supposed to be. You can join him there if you'll follow me."

"It must be Joseph," Miriam said.

Obediently, they followed Linus, who walked his horse very slowly over the stony ground. They passed quite close to Joshua's cross. There was a soldier at its base. Maria and Miriam stopped for a moment to watch Joshua in his agony. Joshua didn't respond, but eagerly took a drink from a soaked sponge that the soldier was offering up to him. Joshua spat the liquid out. The soldier laughed.

Linus called back to Miriam and Maria:

"Don't stop. Follow me."

With one last, longing gaze at her son, Miriam turned to obey.

Maria lingered just a little longer.

"I love you!" she choked, looking up at Joshua before following the others.

Joshua gave the faintest smile.

When they reached Joseph, Linus told them:

"You'll be safe here. Your friend Joseph of Arimathea has made arrangements with the High Priest to take Joshua's body for burial. I'll see that you receive his corpse as soon as I can pronounce him dead. I know you'll want to bury him before your Sabbath begins."

Linus looked at Maria again.

"I knew him, too," was all he said before leaving them, but Maria knew that he cared.

* * *

Judas Iscariot could not keep himself away from Golgotha. News traveled fast through the streets of Jerusalem. He knew that the Master had been taken to the place of execution. Guilt gnawed at him and yet at the same time he had never thought that it would come to this—crucifixion.

Judas was surprised when eventually he came out through the Calvary Gate. There were so many people gathered at Golgotha. The city was still bathed in sunlight but moving in from the west was a bank of heavy dark clouds. They looked ominous to Judas. There was assuredly a storm coming, which he felt as much in his heart as he saw with his eyes. The crowd was orderly and it was not too difficult for Judas to edge his way through toward the front. There, before him, he saw the three crosses. Instinctively, he knew that the Master hung in the center. His personal agony was raised to such a pitch that he could not look at the cross for long. He turned away and looked to the west. A little apart from the general body of spectators, he saw Maria and Marcus with Joshua's mother and Jonah. They were with another man, but Judas didn't recognize him. *Why isn't Cephas with them?* he thought. *Where are the 'inner three'?* He looked around to see if they were about. None of the other ten 'chosen ones' appeared to be in the crowd. The pangs of deepening guilt washed over his curiosity and he melted back into the throng.

* * *

Meanwhile, Gaius Cassius and his soldiers went over to the crosses. Time was getting on and if all was to be accomplished by the evening of the Sabbath, the prisoners needed to die. He instructed the men to break their legs in order to hasten death.

The man with the mallet looked up at the first of the two robbers. The dying victim spat in his face. The insult only infuriated the brawny executioner, who swung the mallet with brutal force at the murderer's twisted legs. They cracked at the blow and spurted sinew and blood as the condemned man yelled with pain.

Momentarily, Joshua, gathered enough strength to try to look up. He saw the approaching storm clouds. Circling above Golgotha were several large black birds—the vultures of death. Then, his head fell again, jarring his body, and the ground below swam before his eyes. The greens faded into browns and the stones moved and pulsated in tones of yellow and red.

"Father," he mumbled, "You have not let me complete my task. Only Maria can now complete the work. Give her my strength and into Your hands…I give my spirit."

The ground seemed to rise up toward him. It swayed before his eyes and came closer, closer, as his head dropped completely. Joshua blacked out.

The pain had gone when he awoke.

Joshua was floating again, as when he had been flogged. As he looked down, now in the company of the black birds, he could see himself hanging helplessly on the cross. Arms outstretched like the wings of the vultures, he drifted above Golgotha. He could see the soldiers move toward his cross. When they reached it, their leader looked up at his limp body. The soldier in command stabbed his right side with a spear. His body did not resist and from above Joshua could see his own blood trickle down from the wound. The soldier in charge said something in Latin and the group, including the executioner with the mallet, moved on toward the third cross. Joshua felt at peace, gliding above the scene. He knew now, as he looked down, that Maria was there with his mother. He could see them clearly, and Jonah, too, and someone else—a wealthy looking man. Jonah had promised that he would take care of Miriam. Joshua knew he would. He saw Marcus put his arm around Maria, as they stared at his cross. Behind them, he could see the mob. It was quite a gathering. Most of them he couldn't recognize, but he thought he saw some in the crowd whom he had healed. Then, his eye caught Judas Iscariot, hiding toward the back. Joshua felt neutral. He made no judgment on Judas.

His focus shifted. Joshua left the black birds circling where they were. He rose higher, so that all Jerusalem came into view behind the city wall. He could see the Temple and Mount Zion and then, the wilderness beyond. Below him, the soldiers reached the final cross. He saw the man with the mallet swing at the other thief's legs. He heard the victim's dreadful screams. He floated backward away from the crosses and those sounds of death. It was quieting now, and as he retreated, more and more of the landscape came into view. He almost reached the storm clouds, and his vision grew sideways as it closed in from above and below. Golgotha and the city remained in the center until his field of vision became so narrow that he could make it out no more. All he saw was a horizontal streak of light. There was a pulse and he became one with the light, filled with a love and joy beyond anything he had ever experienced—Heaven.

* * *

Joshua's head dropped on the cross.

Gaius and his men returned and concluded that he was dead. Gaius reported to Tribune Linus Flavian, that 'The King of the Jews' had died.

Linus ordered them to take Joshua's body down.

The dark clouds eliminated the last of the blue. A distant rumble of thunder was heard.

Joshua's body was handed over to Joseph of Arimathea.

Joseph and Jonah tied the corpse to a plank and carried him away. Miriam, Maria, and Marcus walked with them as the light faded before the gathering storm.

Judas Iscariot had watched them from a distance. His curiosity was now stronger than his guilt and far from satisfied. He followed them around the city wall close to the North Gate where Joseph's sepulchre had been hewn. It was in a rich man's garden along with other Sadducean tombs. Judas watched from behind bushes as the women took water from the Kidron and cleaned Joshua's body. They rinsed out his loincloth until it was fresh. Damp though it was, they wrapped his body in it and then laid him in the tomb. The first heavy drops of rain splattered on the fresh face of the rock. Joseph and Jonah, heaving and straining, tried to roll the huge entrance stone across the opening.

"It's too much for us," Joseph muttered.

Jonah called over to Marcus, who was holding his mother's hand.

"Come and help us, Marcus?"

Marcus and Maria both joined the men.

"If we can just get it started," Joseph said, "it will roll itself."

Marcus and Maria lent their lighter weight to the others and ever so slowly the stone began to move. It quickened pace and rolled across the opening with a thud.

The rain increased, and lightening suddenly streaked the darkened sky, bringing a heavy clap of thunder above Jerusalem.

Judas took shelter in the rocks, waiting for a miracle to release his burden, while in sad silence the others made their way back into the soaked streets of the city presumably to return to James' house. It was very dark.

Chapter Nineteen

An Empty Tomb

Judas crouched between the rocks and felt clammy and cold as the rain soaked through his tunic. He was feverish, but he never took his eyes off the tomb in which the Master's body lay. After a while, he thought he could see an incandescent glow emanating from around the rolled stone—pulsating—or was it his head that was pulsating? In curiosity, he stood up. He felt dizzy. The light seemed to get brighter, and then, he blacked out.

* * *

Joshua emerged as soul from the heavenly white light and looked on his body. A new light danced before him illuminating the cavern of entombment in flourescent tones of pink and the palest blue. Blurred images of white, without form, but with beckoning movement, expanded and contracted within the confines, leading into cracks in the inner masonry. In his ghostly form, Joshua followed them as the cracks opened into high walls of rock, leading him toward a golden light. From the light, he could hear the beautiful high-pitched sound of...something? The melody drew him onward through swirling clouds as the golden light intensified. Ahead, he could see Maria, standing with a stranger who was dressed in the finest robes. Just momentarily, he felt the human pang of separation and perhaps a tinge of jealousy. As he drifted closer to them, their faces faded and this human sadness melted into the spiritual joy of love that had become his essence. He could see Marcus with a Roman soldier. It was the Roman who had spoken to him on the cross—the tribune. The soldier smiled and spoke to him, but Joshua could not hear his words—only, he felt kindness. Their faces also faded and the only sound he could hear came from…high-pitched music…somewhere? The music soared. Joshua looked behind him for one fleeting moment and could see his own body lying in the chasm. In the dim, pink light of the cavern, he saw his bodily flesh vaporizing under the shroud. The vision disappeared when a dazzling burst of green light excluded all other images. Joshua found himself in nothing but the brightest of light, paling to white, and ringing with…the music of God?

* * *

Caiaphas watched the rain lashing down across the inner court of the Temple. The late afternoon storm had come up with a frenzy, and it had become unusually dark. There was something sinister about this rain. He crossed the inner court to the Sanctuary, to pray before the Sabbath began. He was shocked on entering through the great bronze doors, to see in the light of the brazier that the veil that separated the outer chamber from the Holy of Holies had fallen to the ground. The cherubim and seraphim, feeble replicas of those that had once graced Solomon's Temple, lay open to the world. The light of the flickering brazier illuminated their dusty wings, catching glints of gold leaf as they curled over the old box in which Ezra's scrolls of the 'Commandments of Moses' were kept. In the eerie light, the House of God was revealed in all its musty emptiness.

"My God!" Caiaphas exclaimed.

The High Priest was afraid, not so much because he felt the central core of his faith to be shattered, but because he was ashamed. This unholy act had happened on his watch. He drew some comfort that the fallen curtain was the one that the failed High Priest, Zechariah, had hung just over thirty years before. It should have lasted, however, at least another decade, maybe longer. He didn't believe the purple wool to be so near to rotting. He also knew that the last time the Temple veil had fallen was during the invasion of Pompeius, who had brought them the Roman yoke, and before that, it had been through the horror of the Syrian, Antiochus Epiphanes. Superstition combined with his disappointment as he wondered what omen this occasion could foretell. *Today, we crucified the 'King of the Jews',* he thought. *My God, surely his claims could not have been the truth.* Shamefully, he left the Sanctuary. *How will I explain this if the Passover pilgrims ever find it out. They are so gullible.*

* * *

Cephas was back at James' house when Joseph, Jonah, Marcus, and the women returned. James was at prayer, preparing for the Sabbath.

"Did you follow him…to the end?" Cephas asked.

Maria looked at him, pitifully. Failure was written all over his face.

"Yes, Cephas. It's over. Joshua is buried," she said softly. "Cephas, you were the only one who stayed with him last night. Don't blame yourself. Remember, he said that we would fail him."

"He knew, somehow, Maria," Cephas said dolefully. Then, he looked at Jonah and Miriam. "Were you there, too?"

"Maria and Joseph came for us," Jonah answered. "Had you been back here then, they would have taken you as well. Joseph gave us a burial place for Joshua. We just got his body entombed before the storm burst."

"Joseph? You look familiar..." Cephas noted. "How did you all meet up?"

"I recognized Joshua as they brought him to the Praetorium from Herod Antipas' palace," Joseph of Arimathea answered. "I believe he cured me of my sickness when I visited him in Bethany. I knew him to be a good man. The charges against him were unfair. He has done nothing but be a force for good and a prophet of truth. For me, he was the 'Prince of Peace.'"

Miriam flinched. Joseph had used the very title that she had so often discussed with Joshua all those years ago.

"They whipped him," she said. "He was in a terrible state even before they crucified him."

She silently sobbed.

Cephas wept, too. He took Maria in his arms.

"I failed him!" he said, "Your love for Joshua gave you the greater faith!"

Maria felt pulled in two directions as her grief mingled with a new sense of the awesome responsibility that she felt Joshua had left with her. *How can I express to Cephas and the others our awareness of Divine love? So much of my understanding of Joshua's Divine spirit was revealed to me in our most intimate caresses. If I had not loved him, I could not have known him.* She hugged Cephas.

"He would have recognized your love in your present grief," she suggested. "It takes a lot for a man to cry. A man with a heart such as yours can only radiate 'his' love."

Marcus found Joanna. He described to her many of the scenes that he had seen that day, and although the colors in the feathers of the Roman tribune's helmet sounded impressive, the soldiers' cruelties moved Joanna to tears.

* * *

The rain beat down on Judas' face. His vision returned in unfamiliar shades of red and yellow, despite the darkness of night. *What did I see?* He thought. *Some strange light, no sound other than the rumbling thunder, but a great light. Was it lightening? Did it strike the tomb? Or was it something else…* He lay in the bushes. The light had gone, but he felt he had encountered the presence of God.

When the storm abated, Judas, still feeling feverish, clammy and cold, was disturbed in his vigil by the sound of voices. He saw Saul, carrying a torch, and a group of ruffians bedraggled by the rain, approaching the tomb. He watched them as he trembled with fearful curiosity. The men were carrying a plank and several ropes.

"This must be the one," Saul said as they stopped in front of the tomb. "It answers the description Joseph of Arimathea gave to the High Priest. See if you can roll the stone."

Three of the burly ruffians started rocking the circular seal. Slowly, it began to move and picking up momentum, it turned and fell away.

Saul peered in with the torch.

"Someone has already been here!" he shouted.

The others looked in.

"Perhaps he was never buried at all," one of them suggested.

"I've never trusted Joseph of Arimathea," Saul muttered. "He's a good Sadducee but a bad Jew. He bribes the Temple hierarchy with his donations, but inside, he's a rebel. He's become one of them, fooled by the man's mysterious healing powers. That's just why the Galilean was so dangerous."

"Are you sure this is the right tomb?" one of the ruffians asked. "Shall we break open some of the others?'

Saul looked around the garden of tombs. There were two open sepulchres nearby. Otherwise, all remaining hollows in the shallow rock face appeared to be well sealed.

"Open that one over there," Saul commanded, pointing to one set apart from the others. "I don't think it's the one, but let's be sure."

The burly men moved to the lone tomb. After opening it up, they saw only a dusty looking shroud partially covering the crumbling skeleton of one long since dead.

"Open these others," Saul shouted, returning to the wall of rock.

The men rolled away the stones to open two more tombs in the area. Inside, they found no evidence of recent burial, but only the decomposing corpses of the dead.

"He must have been buried in one of those open tombs," Saul said, giving up. "Someone did get here before us, either that or they still have the body. Who knows?"

Saul stared at the open tombs.

"Shall we close them up again?" one of the men asked.

"No," Saul answered. "Leave them. This desecration will turn the people against the Galilean and his followers. They will think that they came here to steal the body. Besides, we haven't time. It will soon be dawn.

Judas had watched the desecration of the tombs with horror.

When Saul and his ruffians left, in that first light of the Sabbath dawn, he looked around him to be sure that he was alone in the cemetery. Satisfied, he plucked up courage to approach the open chasm where he knew Joshua's body lay. He looked in and saw the shroud folded as it had been placed on the Master's body, but it lay flat and there was no body within. In terror, Judas pulled at the shroud and as it opened he saw a ghostly imprint of the Master's face. He screamed and threw the garment back into the tomb.

"Moses!" he cried. "This man was the Son of God! I betrayed the Lord!"

Judas ran from the tomb. He tripped and fell. He beat his head with his hands.

"Joshua!" he yelled in his agony. "Forgive me! I didn't believe…I didn't understand! I am not worthy to live!"

He picked himself up, still shaking with both fever and remorse. He ran from the awesome scene as the Sabbath dawn broke. His vision was still blurred and he saw only in dim colors of brown. Fleeing the city, he went into the barren hills. When, finally he rested, he closed his tortured eyes.

"I saw the light of God!" he exclaimed, and then broke down in sobs.

The clouds had dispersed and the Sabbath sun rose.

* * *

Early in the morning of the day after the Sabbath, Maria and Miriam gathered up precious oils and balms to take to the tomb. They had not had time to properly dress Joshua's body during the quick entombment. Cephas was anxious to come with them, and he and Jonah carried the oils and linens in a pannier. They set out at first light and arrived at the garden of rich men's tombs just as the sun was cresting the hills to the east. They were shocked when they saw the desecrated sepulchres exposing the corpses of the dead.

"What's happened?" Cephas shouted.

Miriam gasped.

"It's the end time!" she shouted, remembering how Joshua had once described how at the end time the dead would be raised from their tombs.

Maria slowly walked up to Joshua's open tomb with Jonah and Cephas. She saw the sealing stone, lying on its side. *Don't tell me they have stolen his body,* she thought, as tears began to fill her eyes. *When will they ever be satisfied?*

"The door has fallen away!" Jonah commented when he saw the circular stone. "That's impossible! It took four of us to roll that stone. It was very heavy."

While Jonah and Miriam examined the fallen stone, Maria and

Cephas looked inside the tomb. They saw the shroud in a heap thrown to one side and instantly observed that Joshua's body was gone.

Maria screamed.

The others turned.

"What is it?" Jonah asked.

"He's gone! Someone has stolen his body!" Maria shouted. "Look inside!"

Maria stood to one side with her face in her hands as Jonah joined a speechless Cephas peering into the cavernous tomb.

Miriam tried to comfort Maria:

"Who would want to steal Joshua's body?" she asked.

"Are you sure this is the right tomb?" Cephas interjected.

"I'm sure," Jonah replied, as they saw for themselves that the tomb was empty. "Someone must have stolen the body. Why? For what purpose?"

They turned back to the women.

"He's definitely not in there," Jonah confirmed.

"Who knew where we buried him?" Miriam asked.

"Nobody knew. Well...nobody unless they were friends of Joseph. Friends of Joseph might have known where he had hewn his tomb," Jonah suggested. "What about the High Priest's men? Joseph said he was well connected in the Sanhedrin."

"That sounds more like the answer," Cephas agreed. "It must be the work of the High Priest or his cohorts."

"Maybe we will find something out at the Temple," Jonah suggested. "James might find out today. Why don't we go back to the Temple? There's not much point in staying here."

"Very good," Cephas agreed. "Let's go."

"You go," Maria said to them quietly. "I'll see you later at James' house. I'd like to stay here for a while."

Miriam squeezed Maria, gently acknowledging their joint love for Joshua, her dead son.

They left.

Slowly, Maria returned to the empty tomb. She stooped and picked up Joshua's loincloth that they had used for a shroud. As she walked out of the tomb, she lovingly wound it round her arm. But in doing so, she caught a glimpse of her lover's face etched in strange markings on the material. Terrified, she screamed, dropped the cloth on the ground, and fled from the tomb filled with fear, but was stopped in her flight when she saw a stranger running toward her.

"What's the matter?" he shouted with genuine concern.

"They've stolen his body!" Maria yelled. "And…"

"Whose body?" the kind man questioned, slightly out of breath.

"My man's body!" Maria said unabashadly. "Joshua's body! They murdered him the other day. He was unjustly crucified for no reason other than his Divine love for all people."

But the stranger was now distracted from Maria as he saw the desecration of the tombs.

"What's happened!" he exclaimed. "Who has been in here sabotaging my tombs? Do you know what's been going on?"

"I don't know," Maria answered. "Whoever was here stole Joshua's body. And…" but again, she faltered.

"Explain again," the man said. "Who was Joshua? I didn't know about this burial."

"We buried him in that tomb," Maria sobbed, pointing at the sepulchre. "It was Sabbath eve. He was crucified just a day and a half ago."

"That's Joseph of Arimathea's sepulchre," the man observed. "You can't have buried him there."

Maria quaked.

"How do you know it is Joseph's tomb?"

"I am the caretaker," he answered as he advanced toward the newly hewn sepulchre.

"Don't go near it…It's…It's haunted," Maria squealed.

The man held out his hand to her.

"Don't be afraid," he said compassionately. "Tell me the whole story."

The man sat down on the heavy circular stone that had been the entrance door for Joseph's tomb. He beckoned to her.

"Sit with me."

Gingerly she joined him, not taking her eye off the crumpled shroud, now lying in the grass.

With their backs to the empty tomb, Maria recalled what she could remember of the terrible events she had witnessed; she also revealed her inner thoughts on the love that she felt for her man. The emotion became too much for her and she broke down and cried.

"I loved him," she sobbed. "I really loved him."

The caretaker put his arm gently around her.

"Maria," he said, "Joshua will always be in your heart."

Maria looked at him. There was something strangely trustworthy about his face and around him she felt that she could see that light of God of which Joshua had spoken. Comforted thus, she bravely picked up the shroud and slowly unravelled it.

"He was buried here," she affirmed. "This was his loin cloth which we used as his burial sheet."

The ghostly face of Joshua imprinted on the cloth was revealed again. It was awesome, but now, not so frightening.

"Whoever stole his body," she said, "could not take him away from me. He has left this imprint behind."

The caretaker didn't know what to say. He stared at the possible imprint of a face on the cloth—not at all clear, but so obviously real to Maria. There was something there; it was almost as if the linen had been scorched.

"It's unreal," he said. "It is as if he has been resurrected from the dead."

"Well, whoever has stolen his body did not steal his power and love," Maria said boldly.

A radiance came over her face.

"His love was the love of God and that spark of God can be kindled in all of us. Such love is everlasting and comes from our souls. We are all Divine," she said with surprising authority.

Maria's eyes sparkled in the strength of her belief. *What if I am carrying his child?* she thought. *Maybe…I hope so. What greater expression of his eternal love could he have left with me than that?*

The caretaker smiled.

"Can I take you home?" he asked. "This has all been a great shock to you."

Maria looked into the caretaker's face. It all came to her in that moment of supreme compassion. She was looking at 'His' face. It was just as 'He' had taught her. *Whenever anyone should encounter the radiance of another person's Divine love they would be encountering the love of a 'son of God.' It was just as Joshua had always tried to teach them: 'You are all sons of God.' What had Joshua said to them at their last supper together? 'Every time you eat and drink remember that just as this food and drink feeds your bodies, so does God feed you spiritually.'* In the face of this stranger, who had, for no compelling reason, shown her his compassion, Maria saw Joshua's Divine love. She felt a supreme contentment as she looked up into the caretaker's face. The empty tomb no longer seemed important. It did not matter who had stolen the body. The importance of the body had been replaced by the fullness of their hearts. She knew as she looked at this loving stranger that she was also in 'His' presence.

HEROD'S FAMILY

NOTE: This table is not complete. Herod married ten wives, by eight of whom he had issue, fourteen children in all, nine sons and five daughters. The names given here are those which come into this story. Rulers recognized by Rome as Ethnarchs, Kings or Tetrarchs are in italics. The dates below each name are those of death where known. Herod-Philip, Herod's son by Mariamme II, first husband of Herodias and father of Salome, who is mentioned (thought not by name) in the Gospels as having demanded the death of John the Baptist, is to be distinguished from Philip, Herod's son by Cleopatra of Jerusalem, who from 4 B.C. to A.D. 34 was Tetrarch of Ituraea, etc. It was their half-brother, Antipas, who was Tetrarch of Galilee in the days of Christ.

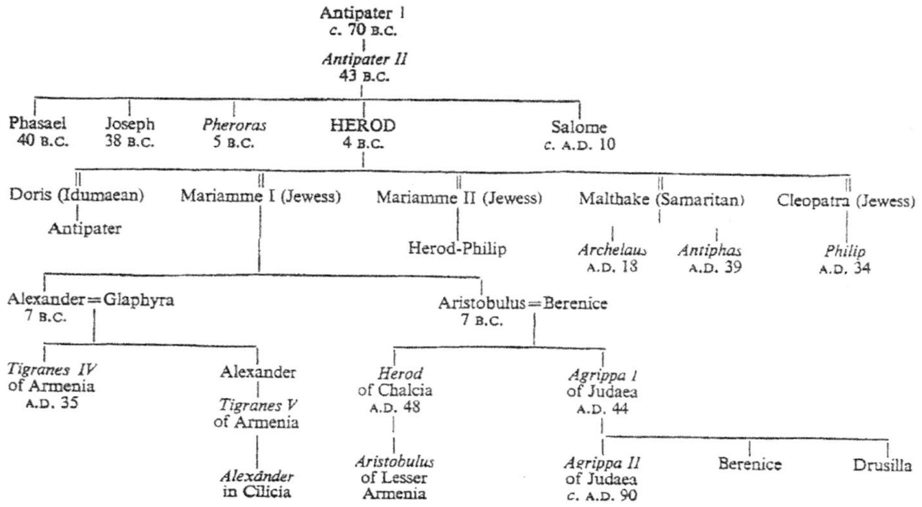

THE FAMILIES OF JOACHIM AND ZECHARIAH

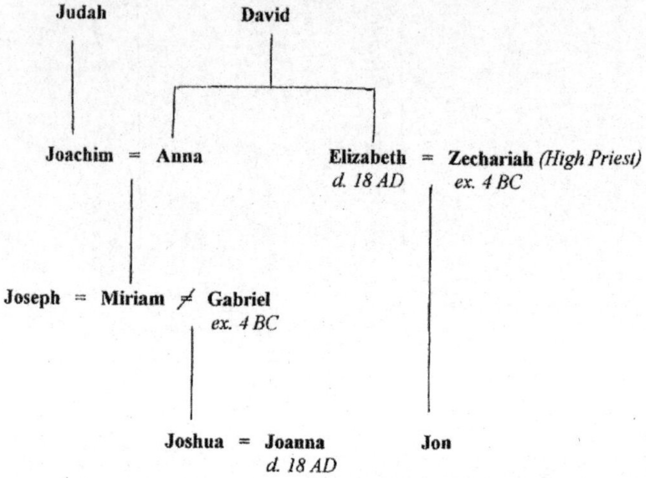

THE TARQUIN AND FLAVIAN FAMILIES

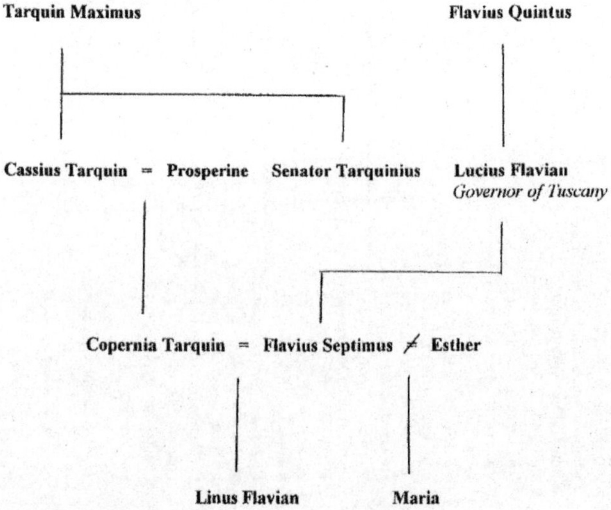

MAP OF THE PROVINCE OF SYRIA

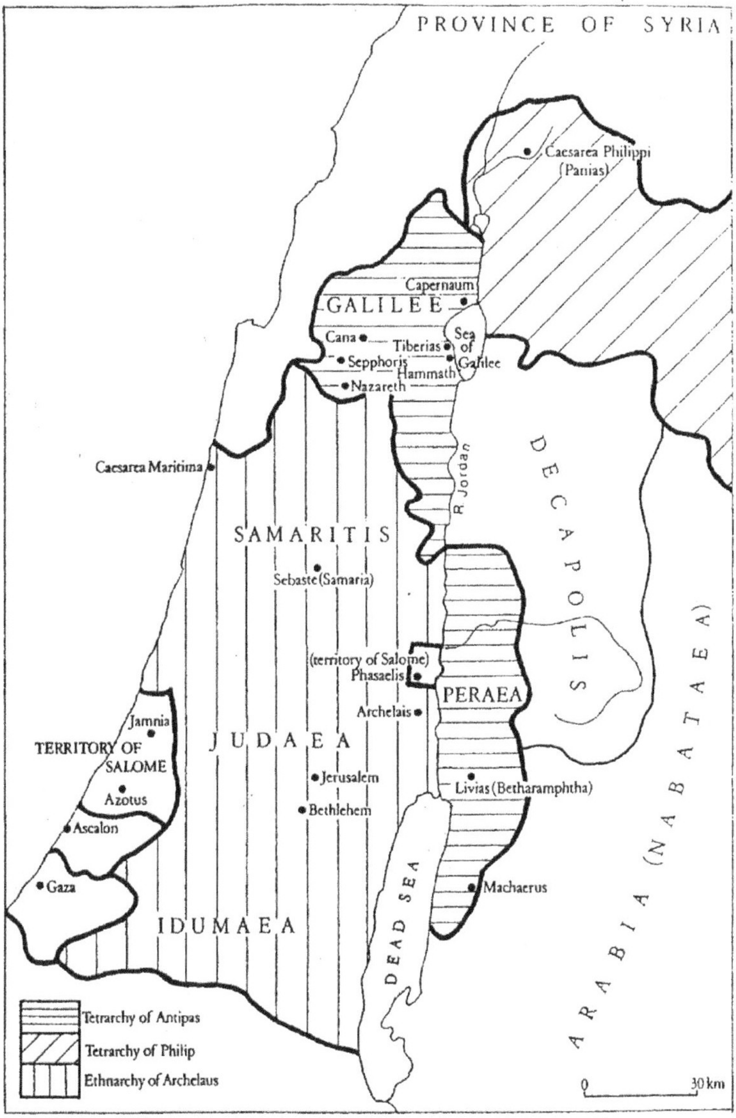

Judaea under Herod's sons

MAP OF JUDEA AND THE LEVANT IN THE FIRST CENTURY

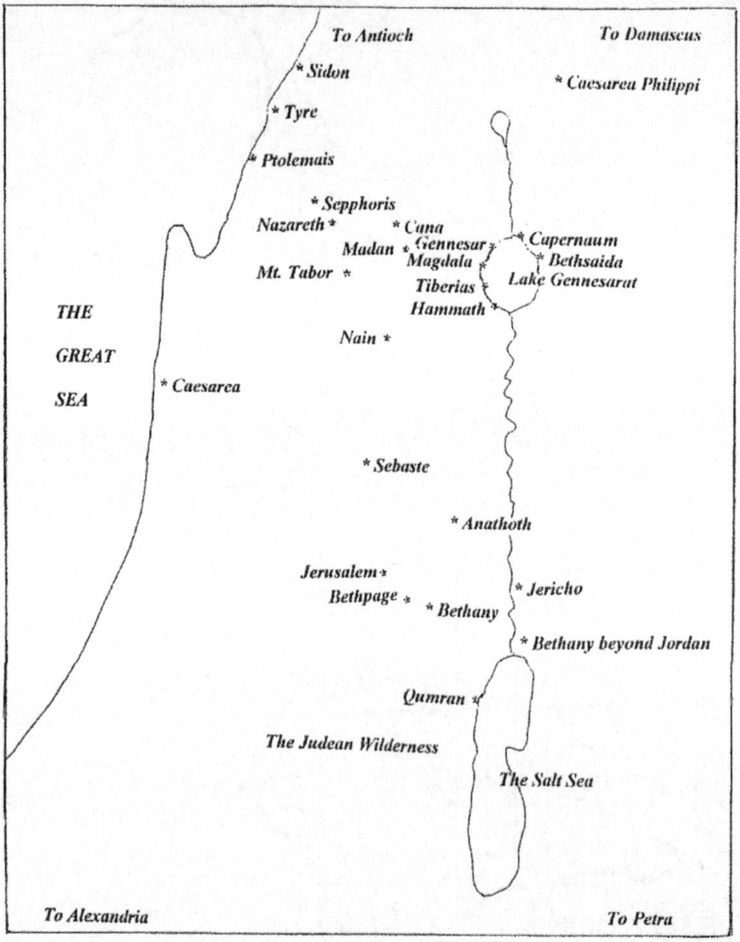

MAP OF JERUSALEM

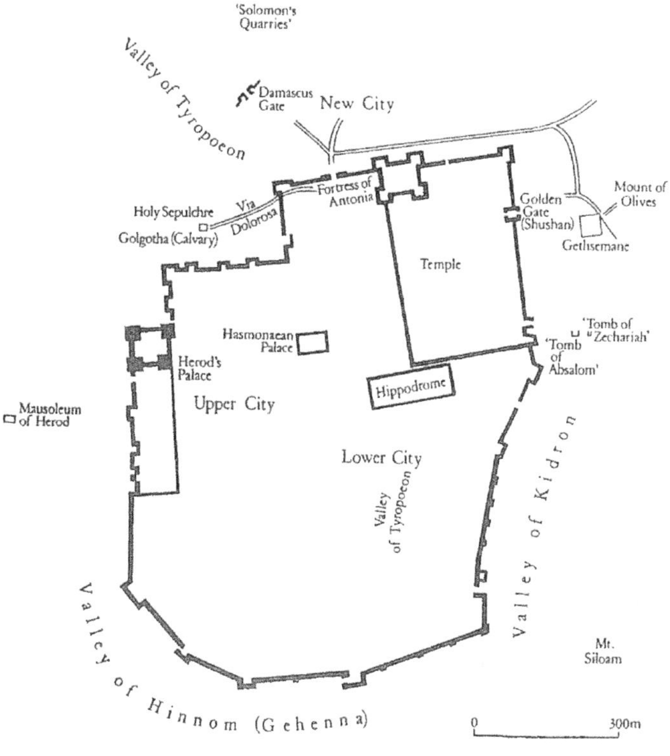
'Solomon's Quarries'
Valley of Tyropoeon
Damascus Gate
New City
Fortress of Antonia
Via Dolorosa
Holy Sepulchre
Golgotha (Calvary)
Golden Gate (Shushan)
Mount of Olives
Gethsemane
Temple
Hasmonaean Palace
'Tomb of "Zechariah'
'Tomb of Absalom'
Herod's Palace
Hippodrome
Mausoleum of Herod
Upper City
Lower City
Valley of Tyropoeon
Valley of Kidron
Valley of Hinnom (Gehenna)
Mt. Siloam
0
300m

Printed in Great Britain
by Amazon

22903741R00268